R0061758140

03/2012

Children of Wrath

ALSO BY PAUL GROSSMAN

The Sleepwalkers

Children of Wrath

Paul Grossman

ST. MARTIN'S PRESS ☙ NEW YORK

CHILDREN OF WRATH. Copyright © 2012 by Paul Grossman. All rights reserved. Printed in the United States of America. For information, address St. Martin's Press, 175 Fifth Avenue, New York, N.Y. 10010.

www.stmartins.com

Library of Congress Cataloging-in-Publication Data

Grossman, Paul.
    Children of wrath / Paul Grossman. — 1st ed.
        p. cm.
    ISBN 978-0-312-60191-1 (hardcover)
    ISBN 978-1-4299-8894-0 (e-book)
    1. Murder—Investigation—Fiction   2. Berlin (Germany)—History—
1918–1945—Fiction.   I Title.
    PS3607 .R674C47   2012
    813' .6—dc23   2011041101

First Edition: March 2012

10 9 8 7 6 5 4 3 2 1

What is weak must be hammered away.
—A. Hitler

Book One

_____

THE NEARER THE BONE

One

"I'll teach you the meaning of respect—" The schoolmarm's whip sent shivers up Willi's legs. "Drop those drawers."

Below, the knickers-clad boys trembled as their instructor approached in her shiny black boots. "Bend over." She snapped the rawhide. What choice was there but to obey, to do whatever she wanted? "This is for your own good." Her strong white arm rose. And as her wrath rained down, hilarity gripped the Admirals-Palast, for even in the mezzanine, spotlights now illuminated how the traumatized tykes were not tykes, but middle-aged men with derrieres that hung like potato sacks.

"No shame, eh? No fear of authority?" The teacher warmed them up for a real mashing. "Take that, useless weeds. And that. And that!"

The harder she beat, the more hilarious the audience grew, because these victims clearly loved getting creamed, the perversity of which tickled some deep communal funny bone. Except in a few detached souls, such as Willi. Or the Prussian baroness next to him, who observed it all as if she were cast of iron.

"So." She finally removed the cigarette holder from her mouth. "*This* is where all your precious freedom has led, Fritz." Her chin aimed cannonlike at their host. "The world hasn't seen such decadence since ancient Rome."

"Forgive me if I'm less than alarmed by your exhibition of repugnance, Baroness." A thin smirk caused Fritz's blond mustache to arch.

"What would you have me do," the baroness parried, "hide behind my sleeves?"

Caught between the two, Willi awarded her the point, because plainly she had nothing to hide behind. The ladies tonight, even the old baroness, wore only the most au courant, thin-strapped evening shifts. Not a sleeve in sight. Her victory, however, was strictly Pyrrhic, and as the spectators roiled with new hilarity, the stage screams mounting toward an unmistakable group climax, a loud sigh heaved from her jeweled bosom.

"A most ominous sign of the times." She returned the cigarette holder to her lips.

At this, one-eyed Dr. von Hessler across from her all but ejaculated, "You know, Baroness, times do change. A mere two centuries ago it would have been unthinkable for a prince to take his after-dinner shit without his guests on hand to share his royal odors."

Everyone at the table froze.

An old school chum of Fritz's, von Hessler was a scientist of some sort. Very stiff-lipped about it. Willi was never sure what he was a doctor of exactly, only that whenever they met, he'd always managed a few lines about the "groundbreaking work" he was engaged in. Pompous, and peculiar, Willi thought, though he couldn't say he knew the fellow well, despite their long mutual acquaintance with Fritz. Hessler'd been on the French front too. After the war he'd gone from wearing a standard black patch over the eye he'd lost at Verdun to a sterling-silver plate fastened on with leather straps, polished so brightly that when you spoke to him, you couldn't help noticing the strange reflection always shining back at you . . . of yourself.

"And your point with that enchanting vignette?" The baroness smiled irritably. "Are you implying the difference between virtue and vice is relative, Doctor?"

Von Hessler opened his palms in a gesture of regret.

Just then Willi spotted Vicki across the table eyeing him from beneath her brown fringe of bangs. Dear Lord, he thought. Busted in midyawn. When she cocked her head as if to inquire if he was okay, he felt a pang of guilt. Generally he told her all about his latest cases, but not this time. When it came to children, she got too upset. So he telegraphed her a reassuring wink and returned his attention to the party.

Of all those on hand to celebrate Fritz's birthday, Willi wanted to be here even less than the baroness, he was sure. Not that he didn't love Fritz. He'd do anything for his old army pal, even attend this vacuous revue on a work night. But Fritz was an aristocrat, and as glad as Willi was to know him, their friendship was a historical fluke. Willi accepted it as such. It wasn't Fritz but his choice of entertainment, this insidious mélange of sugar and excrement, that was getting under Willi's skin. And not because he was law enforcement, either. No law forbid raunchy burlesque to benefit a foundling hospital. It just rubbed him the wrong way.

After all he'd seen this morning.

A night of flooding rain had turned up a real horror show half an hour east of here, out in industrial Lichtenberg. At the bottom of a construction pit, a burlap sack was regurgitated, apparently, by a massive backup in the sewer system. By the time he'd arrived, a score of people must have been staring at the spilled contents. Truly a spectacle. Bones. Nearly two dozen of them. Not just loose, but arranged. Singled out by size and shape. Bound together into what could only be termed . . . designs. Arm and leg bones fashioned almost like bouquets of flowers. Toe and finger bones, strung with some sort of sinewy thread into what might have been . . . jewelry.

Small lumbar vertebrae bored through with little holes. Willi had never seen nor heard of anything like this. Even after a cursory exam, the pathologist, Dr. Hoffnung, had said the bones were most definitely human. And most definitely not adult. Children's bones, by size and density. Boys' bones, according to pelvic structure. Four or five different boys in all.

Willi squirmed in the seat.

As the schoolmistress and her students bowed to a storm of applause, ending a skit titled "Lesson Well Learned," his hands clapped along mechanically. Three years on the Western Front. Seven in Kripo, Berlin's diligent Kriminal Polizei. No one could say he hadn't seen his fair share of lunacy. But bone art?

"Next on hand to support the lost children of Berlin," the *Conferencier's* voice rang through the theater, "the best-looking, best-drilled ladies in town—"

Sixty-four magnificent legs tapped across the stage in perfect columns.

"Dancing in syncopated rhythm to a piece titled 'Mass Production'—"

Thirty-two lissome figures in skimpy halter tops, white short-shorts, lacy ankle socks, glittering high heels.

"The Admirals-Palast is thrilled to present, our very own . . . Tiller Girls!"

"*Ein, zwei, drei, los,*" one screamed, and all thirty-two launched into a choreographed homage to modern manufacturing, their rows devolving into rotating gears, pumping pistons, conveyor belts, even a giant typewriter. Legs lifting, heels tapping, shoulders shimmying with high-speed efficiency, every muscle worked as one. No toe out of line. The audience roared with approval. Here was a world they could be happy with, Willi thought. A world in sync. In *Ordnung*. The individual, absorbed and on the march. Long after the Tiller Girls had shuffled away as a diesel locomotive, the crowd was still cheering.

"*Phantastisch,* really," Fritz's wife, Sylvie, said, beaming with a set of glowing teeth.

"Such precision," Vicki added with near-believable sincerity. She'd prefer the symphony a hundred times over, Willi knew, but would never be so impolite as to say so.

The baroness was unconstrained by bourgeois sensibility. "An unmitigated pile of you-know-what." She stuck another cigarette in her holder. "No moral. No story. Just a big bucket of—"

"I happen to agree this time." Von Hessler adjusted his eyepiece. "The revue holds a harsh mirror to our republic. How slick on the surface, yet underneath, how badly fractured. Indeed, I am frequently struck in the streets of Berlin these days by the sensation that, in an instant, everything could just—" His hands flew apart.

Intermission had brought up the houselights. *Tout le monde,* it seemed, filled the Admirals-Palast for tonight's charity gala. The balconies were packed with lawyers and doctors and businessmen, their overdressed wives chatting excitedly. The mezzanine, where Willi sat, overflowed with industrialists and department-store owners, publishers, politicians, underworld crime bosses by the dozens, all crammed around tables. Fritz, a third-tier cousin of the deposed kaiser, and a writer for five or six newspapers, had a well-placed corner table overlooking the orchestra. Down there, by center stage, where the photojournalists could get in for close-ups, the seats brimmed with luminaries. World-renowned playwrights, architects, and artists: Brecht, Gropius, Klee, and Kandinsky. Even Albert Einstein had turned out with his wife to support the Boys and Girls Foundling Hospital. It may not have been de' Medicis' Florence, but despite all logic and against all odds, Berlin, vanquished a decade ago in the Great War, and then ravished by the Great Inflation, had emerged somehow as Europe's cultural capital.

"This country cannot survive without a rigid fist to guide it. Believe me." A sardonic grin seemed to freeze across the baroness's old, rouged cheeks.

"*Ach kvatch.*" Fritz's blue eyes danced at her. "Germany's never been better off and you know it. Democracy's rooted. The economy's flourishing. We've the highest standard of living in Europe."

"But no respectability, Fritzchen." The irony melted. "And what are we without that?" A wave of real grief washed over her face. "Just barbarians. From Monte Carlo to Moscow, Berlin's become a byword for . . . depravity."

The word hurled Willi back to Lichtenberg, factories pounding, smoke belching. At the bottom of that construction pit, besides those bizarre bone configurations, inside the burlap bag there'd been a Bible. Most of it washed away. But several passages that were still discernible had been circled in red. One stuck out. From the New Testament, Ephesians: "You were dead in the trespasses and sins in which you once walked . . . and were by nature children of wrath." Even thinking about it now, his hands got clammy.

Something dark had washed up in that bag.

As dark as he'd ever faced.

Von Hessler's eye patch glistened in the chandelier light. "The baroness is quite right, I'm afraid. At bottom we Germans have an appalling lack of self-control, which is why we crave order so terribly. Sooner or later somebody's going to have to emancipate us from all this emancipation." He gave a mad little laugh at his own joke.

A chorus of deep drums beat up from the orchestra pit. "And now . . ." The theater fell dark again. "The woman whose name has come to symbolize the Jazz Age . . . the world's most famous stage personality . . . the very sophisticated . . . terribly savage . . . absolutely one of a kind . . . Josephine Baker!"

Like a tropical storm, the legendary American Negress blew in from her usual stint at the Folies Bergère in Paris, dueling spotlights flashing across the sheen of her black hair, the giant spit curls scrawled on her cheeks, the breasts cradled in colorful sea pearls. Around her waist, the iconic banana skirt, each yellow fruit arching unmistakably upward, flapping as she leaped into her famous "jungle" dance. Unlike the Tiller Girls, every joint in Baker's body seemed possessed of a mind of its own—hips, wrists, ankles, legs, all moving in directions disassociated from the rest. Even her eyeballs appeared to orbit in her head. The most reticent in the audience had not the power to resist her, and when she finished, they rose to appease the dark goddess with reverence and awe.

"Certainly something to tell our grandchildren." Vicki slid herself under Willi's arm as they joined the glittering throng pouring from the courtyard. "The night we saw Josephine Baker at the Admirals-Palast."

On busy Friedrich Strasse, wind whipped off the river. The line for cabs stretched almost to the Weidendammer Bridge. How insane not to have taken something more substantive than a thin silk wrap, as he'd suggested before they'd left. But despite the forecast, Vicki'd refused to believe the temperature would really drop so fast. "Might I wear your dinner jacket, darling?" she had to plead.

"Forgive me." Willi practically tore it off his back. "My mind's just been so—"

. . . inside that bag, pondering the substance used to bind those bones. To him it had looked like some kind of animal gut. Hoffnung assured him the lab would determine its exact composition. But these things could take time.

Wrapped in Willi's jacket, Vicki rose in her blue silk pumps, shaking back her bangs, the beads on her dress jingling as she put her lips to his ear: "That show got me all jazzed up." A dark sparkle beckoned in her eyes. Almost ten years now, and Willi'd never stopped thanking his lucky stars for this woman.

Unfortunately, not just the Admirals-Palast, but the Wintergarten across the street, the Metropole down the block, everything was letting out, and not a free cab was in sight. After a while, she was shivering again, and he was starting to feel inadequate. He really ought to have taken the Opel.

All of a sudden an open black sports car raced up as if from out of the future. *"Alles in Ordnung?"* Dr. von Hessler's silver eye patch glistened behind the oversize wheel. "Not stuck, are you?" It was a new SSK, the most-talked-about car in Germany. According to the Sunday supplement, this 1930 model was a "Rembrandt of iron and rubber."

Only forty had rolled off the line, the last in a series for Mercedes-Benz by the brilliant Ferdinand Porsche, who'd since left to form his own company. It had a revolutionary profile some were calling *streamlined*, curved, low, sleek as a bullet, looking able to fly that fast. Along with the *Graf Zeppelin,* the Dornier flying boat, and the giant new *Bremen,* the world's swiftest ocean liner, the SSK was one of the reasons Germans were holding their heads a bit higher these days.

"Which direction?" the doctor demanded to know.

Willi waved him off as if it were Mars. "Wilmersdorf."

"Just my way." Von Hessler revved the supercharged 6.8-liter engine. "I'm in Grunewald." But sensing their hesitation, he grew impatient. "Don't tell me I'm going to have to pull rank." In his own way he seemed to be trying to let them know they weren't too inferior to travel with him. Which was thoughtful, Willi supposed, making the mistake of glancing at Vicki. Beneath those dark bangs, clutching his big white dinner jacket, she looked like one of the boys dying to try a roller coaster. Dear Lord. What the hell. Let it be one for the history books. Josephine Baker *and* an SSK in one night.

Pulling open the car door, however, a glimpse of his own reflection in von Hessler's eye patch was enough to give Willi the creeps.

It was a two-seater. Vicki had to squeeze between them. When the doctor smacked the big black gear stick, there was a tremendous rumble, and off they went, spinning into a mad U-turn, yanking back as if they were about to be sucked straight up to the overhead S-Bahn tracks. It was Friday night. Traffic jammed the Friedrich Strasse. This maniac, though, was accelerating as if he were at a grand prix final. Beyond the train station, lights from nightclubs began blending into one: *Haller-Revue... Salamander... Café Imprimator.* Advertisements spun overhead: *Aschinger am Bahnhooooo*— They flew by a yellow streetcar so fast Willi couldn't even make out the route number.

"Not afraid, are you?" The smirk on the doctor's lips seemed congenital.

Willi could see how a person might grow to dislike that expression.

Holding on to Vicki with one hand and the leather armrest with the other, he was remembering how, once, as a teenager, he'd gotten good and sick on a speedboat. Which is why he'd wound up in the infantry, sidling on his rear end under barbed wire.

"Afraid?" Vicki's symmetrical face fractured with amusement. *"Au contraire!"*

A sharp turn onto Dorothean Strasse plunged them into darkness.

"I ask only because I am a researcher of human nature," the doctor projected over the roaring 225 horsepower. "Fear is one of the subjects my studies focus most on."

"How fascinating." Vicki flung her head back, letting her bobbed hair fly. "No, we're not afraid. Are we, darling?"

The doctor could at least observe the traffic signals, Willi felt like saying.

"As a scientist of course I work under controlled observation," von Hessler shouted as they tore around the Reichstag, its glass dome all lit up, the red, black, and gold flag of the republic flapping proudly above. "But some of my most profound insights have been drawn from random surveillance." When they reached the leafy haven of the Tiergarten, Berlin's largest park, his volume diminished. You could almost see stars overhead. Which might have been romantic, Willi thought, if the doctor would just shut up.

"My experiments focus on what I call unconditioning, the breaking down of learned behavior patterns."

Von Hessler, however, apparently relished a captive audience and imagined himself now before a university lecture hall, even though Vicki had stopped pretending to listen and Willi had never even started. Concealed beneath his jacket she'd begun tickling his pant leg, sending tingles up his spine, every so often shooting him a smoldering glance.

In the busiest part of Berlin-West, around the towering Kaiser Wilhelm Church, night seemed to turn into day, everything in motion. Women in helmetlike hats walked with skirts flipping side to side. Men in double-breasted suits waved fedoras, trying to grab cabs. Advertising zipped across billboards: *Crème Mouson, for the Lady of Today; Audi, Type M: for the Gentleman in You.* In every direction, chic modernity. Stainless-steel doorways. Long, curved windows. The best boutiques. The place-to-be restaurants. The nation's premier cinemas lined up like chorus girls: the Gloria-Palast, the Capital, UFA am Zoo. Everything swank. Glittering. Frenetic.

On Kurfürstendamm, Berlin's Great White Way, the show windows reflected traffic like an avant-garde movie, full of incongruent angles and rushing rivers of light.

"So you see, this respectability the baroness was raving about is all romantic nonsense." Von Hessler honked insanely, nearly hitting a couple clutching each other for dear life as they tried to ford the mayhem. "The more we learn, the more we realize what people call *order* in this universe is actually just conditioning. What street did you say you lived on again?"

Far from crowds and flashing lights, the quiet avenues around Prussian Park ran past ornamented five-story apartment blocks with attics peaking from high-pitched roofs, plaster gargoyles and Valkyries still reigning over all. On Beckmann Strasse, in front of their solidly respectable building, Willi and Vicki practically flung themselves from von Hessler's race car, thanking him profusely. "We really ought to do this again," the doctor shouted after them, his silver eye patch fading.

"Absolutely."

Vicki waved.

Inside the lobby, with its carpeting and glass chandeliers, she threw her arms around Willi and kissed him hard, penetrating her warm, soft tongue into his mouth.

"Wow," he whispered.

Up the staircase, she slipped from her blue shoes and made him unfasten her dress hooks, all the little beads jingling wildly. What if one of the neighbors should see? he wondered. They'd never live it down. They'd have to move. He'd have to resign from the police force. But so late on a work night . . . the kids at a slumber party . . .

It really was one for the history books.

Next morning she was humming, kissing him sweetly on the lips when he came in for breakfast. While sausages sizzled, she held up bananas and started swaying her hips in a little hula dance, running her fingers through his waves of dark hair. What a holiday, not having the kids around. If only Heinz Winkelmann had more birthdays. Except for that damned party at four . . . and today half a workday . . . no escape.

Vicki dropped the bananas. "What's this?" She grabbed the newspaper out of his hands. TAINTED SAUSAGES! HUNDREDS SICKENED! Off went the flame under the *Wurst*. "Even during the war I never heard of such a thing." She squinted intensely under her dark fringe of hair. "Infected meat—here in Berlin? With all the controls we have?"

"Anything can happen in this world, sweetheart." Willi calmly took the paper back. "Even with the best controls." Another story had caught his eye, a smaller one at the bottom of the page. Apparently, the stock exchange in New York had had a bad day.

Two

They were tearing up the Alex—big-time. After two centuries of hodgepodge growth, order was being imposed on the jumble of streets that comprised the old commercial hub just east of the city center. Alexanderplatz, with all its hotels and grand department stores, famous restaurants and nightmarish traffic, was going to become an "architecturally coherent" square, with multilayers of unimpeded traffic and bright modern buildings. In the meantime, all was chaos. Jackhammers. Steam shovels. Pile drivers slamming relentlessly. Willi had to hold his ears. Pedestrians were being forced down narrow gangplanks onto convoluted courses that had them all but colliding with the convoluted courses forced on cyclists, cars, trucks. The path to paradise evidently ran through purgatory. Even on Saturday morning.

When he reached the end of Königs Strasse, the air itself shook from pounding wrecking balls. The Grand Hotel, where his grandfather had his eightieth birthday party in 1911, was on its last legs. Already felled was Haus zum Hirschen, with its dining hall boasting ninety-nine deer heads. His cousin Kurt had his wedding dinner there. A storied yesterday was being hammered to dust for a drawing-board tomorrow. Pity the Police Presidium hadn't been consigned to the hit list, Willi thought, making his way toward it through the swarms of early shoppers. Its menacing façade and sullen cupolas loomed over the whole southeast side of the Alex like a dead whale. Six floors, 605 rooms, third-largest building in Berlin after the royal palace and Reichstag, its real bloodred color barely discernible under decades of soot. As he reached the massive iron doors at Entrance Six, though, how grateful he felt to have made it here. Not many officers ever did. Even the best. Even after years of service.

Riding the brass-caged elevator up, crushed with a dozen others trying to make the eight o'clock shift, Willi acknowledged he wasn't the most likely candidate for the Berlin police. His parents, may they rest in peace, certainly never imagined it. A Jewish detective? Who ever heard of such a thing? For centuries Jews had stood on the wrong end of a billy club. But those days were gone, Willi was certain. And he truly loved his work. Believed in justice and the law. Which was very Jewish, as he understood it. Not that it made a huge difference.

He certainly wasn't ashamed of his ethnicity, but he hardly considered it the keystone of his identity. He enjoyed celebrating traditional holidays with the children: lighting candles at Hanukkah. The Passover seder, liberal as theirs were. He loved reading about the towering achievements of his people and its long trails of tears. But in everyday life in modern Berlin, being Jewish held little more significance to him than his wavy, dark hair, dark eyes, or his circumcised prick.

The Homicide Commission was on the top floor. Willi's desk was right up against a window. From his chair you could see half of the Alexanderplatz. When you stood, you could see the whole thing, the whole master plan being overlaid on it. The new subway station that would connect to the elevated station, under the new traffic island, which would distribute the flow from five major streets.

"*Guten Morgen,* Herr Sergeant-Detektiv."

Frau Garber, the unit secretary, had come around with her wooden cart. A slender, sexy grandma in her forties, she was one of the few people on the floor who didn't give him a cold shoulder. More than two years after Willi's promotion from Local 157 in Wilmersdorf, he remained the department pariah. In numerous ways, his colleagues had made it clear that was exactly how it was going to remain.

Because of the dark hair and dark eyes and the circumcised prick.

"Oh, Dr. Hoffnung called." She poured from a steaming pot, smiling. "Says he's ready whenever you are." A cup came toward him the way he liked it, black with a touch of sugar. "New beans, from Brazil."

"Your coffee's always best, Frau Garber."

"By now it's quite permissible to call me Ruta, Herr Sergeant."

Hoffnung, the pathologist, was among the most competent specialists Willi'd come across at headquarters. Smart. Straightforward. Cool as a cucumber, normally. But this morning, Willi could see, the doctor was perturbed.

"One of the more peculiar and, I'd even go so far as to say, heinous cases I've come across in twenty years." Hoffnung stuck a black pipe in his mouth. Grunting, he yanked aside a bedsheet. Willi's throat constricted. Laid out in a row on a stainless-steel counter were the burlap sack and multiple bone arrangements.

"It's no joy to report my initial assessment was correct." The doctor's pipe hung from his jaw, his eyes fixed darkly on the clean white remains. "These are boys' bones, all right. Five boys in all. Ages approximately nine to fourteen. Impossible to determine an exact time of death. But"—he slipped on a pair of cotton gloves— "one telling detail." Gently opening the ruined Bible, he used his pipe stem to point out a still-legible publication date. *Berlin. 1929.* "This 'burial,' therefore"—he shrugged theoretically—"if that's what the contents of the sack may be termed, took place within the last nine months.

"The sack, as you can see, is manufactured by a firm called Schnitzler and Son. The burlap fibers still contain bits of animal feed. Probably for cattle, maybe goats, swine; I don't know. I'm no farmer. This is what it looks like." Hoffnung used a tweezer to pick up some grain for Willi's inspection. But Willi was no farmer either.

"What about that material binding these bones?"

"Muscle, all right." Hoffnung pulled a leather pouch from his lab coat. "But . . . not animal. That, I'm guessing"—he sighed, dipping his pipe in, carefully filling the bowl with tobacco—"is the same muscle once attached to those bones. Dried out. Hand spun. Woven almost like a thread. Whoever did this is quite a craftsman."

Willi felt a shiver of dread. Human muscle, rolled into thread?

"There's more." Hoffnung anxiously rifled his pockets. "These bones, for lack of a better word"—he looked relieved to find his matches—"have been . . . cooked."

Willi's throat closed. Like during the war, when the gas shells came.

"I couldn't find so much as a microscopic shred of tissue on them." The orange flame trembled as the doctor lit his pipe. "And there's only one way bones get that clean, Herr Sergeant-Detektiv." Hoffnung's eyes blackened as he puffed. "You would have to boil them." His face disappeared behind a cloud of smoke. "For many hours."

The pile driver below knocked beams into the soggy Berlin subsoil as if into Willi's skull. From his desk, he could see to the open cut across the street where the underground station was beginning to take shape. Eventually, all the layers of traffic in Alexanderplatz would be so intricately organized that not one line would cross another on the same level. How much less complex could the mind of a person be who'd boil the flesh off children's bones?

He tilted all the way back in his chair, a dangerous habit since childhood.

Not just boil flesh, but dry the muscles, then hand-roll it into "thread." Use this thread to weave the bones together into arrangements. Place the arrangements into a burlap sack . . . with a Bible. What would drive such behavior? What kind of person would conceive it? Could it even be called a person?

Sitting back up, he fingered the black receiver. He'd just gotten off the phone with Schnitzler and Son . . . no lead there. Feed for any type of animal could be put in their sacks, they said. They had customers all over north Germany.

The buzzer startled him. "Don't forget lunch, Herr Sergeant." It was Frau Garber . . . Ruta . . . on the intercom. "Noon downstairs."

"Thanks, Ruta."

He broke apart a paper clip.

Kriminal-Kommissar Horthstaler was fond of capping off the week with a unit meeting in the basement cafeteria, one flight above the labyrinth of holding cells known as the Dungeons. Willi wished they'd meet like all the other units, in a regular room, and to hell with lunch. Not for any religious reasons or even, as Vicki suggested, the pull of the "collective unconscious"—but really because he couldn't stand the taste—he avoided eating pork, which in Germany rendered him completely outlandish. And it never failed to come up at these damned lunches.

"What, Kraus, no pig's knuckles today?" Mueller'd throw an arm around him. "I hear they're especially tender."

"Perhaps for dinner," Willi'd reply.

He'd long ago trained himself not to get hooked by these baits. In the army they'd come thick and fast. Not only about his diet, but about his nose. His hair. His "Turkish" complexion. His strangely naked prick. After the first year it pretty much wore off, once the real steel started coming down. But here, at police headquarters, the Jew stuff didn't want to quit.

The cafeteria was full. Horthstaler had reserved their *Stammtisch*, their regular table, far in the back. Everyone was in attendance. Mueller. Meyer. Hiller. Stoss. And, of course, Freksa. Dear Freksa.

Willi nodded to them all, got chicken cutlets, and paid no attention to what anyone else was eating. After a while Horthstaler belched, wiped his pudgy lips, and looked ready to begin. With Horthstaler, it was always food first. Not that he was fat. He managed to distribute it.

"So." He pulled out a folder, licking his fingers before searching inside it. "Let me start by congratulating you. Our unit once again has ranked number one in the least number of missed days. I have always maintained this is the hardest-working, most conscientious team in Homicide. And you, Detectives, continue to prove me right."

For half an hour Willi did his best to make it look as if he were paying attention to Horthstaler. But he couldn't tear his mind from the burlap bag. First thing, he figured, was try to determine what that passage from Ephesians might mean . . . *children of wrath.* Hopefully the query he'd put into the library yesterday would turn up something. If in fact it was a "burial," as Dr. Hoffnung suggested, whoever had committed it might be trying to communicate something.

The second thing would be to trace that sewer line.

"Now to the assignments," Willi vaguely heard, his mind deep underground. The overflow line that had carried that bag might well lead back to its origins. Or not, if someone had dumped it in trying to cover his tracks.

"Kraus"—he jumped. Horthstaler was looking directly at everyone but him—"did the intake the other day on that most unusual burlap bag in Lichtenberg. But the investigation will now pass into the capable hands of Hans Freksa."

Willi blinked, then looked across the table. Freksa's grin told him Willi hadn't misunderstood. They were taking away his case.

News of the burlap bag and its bizarre bone arrangements had been all over the Police Presidium before Willi'd even gotten back from Lichtenberg. Berlin had no shortage of headline-grabbing crime, but this was clearly a showstopper. And Hans Freksa, besides being a damned good detective, could never get enough of his name in the papers. *Why were police on the track so fast? One name is worth remembering—Hans Freksa.... Using advanced police methods, Freksa has scored success after success.... Hans Freksa may be Berlin's most accomplished detective....*

Berlin police were Germany's best. Eighty-five percent of the city's homicides were solved last year, as opposed to 75 percent in the rest of the nation. Freksa beat the city average, solving 90 percent of his cases; it was true. So was the fact that Willi tied him. And that several others in Homicide beat them both. But because Freksa was so personable, and Freksa looked so great in photographs, and Freksa was single, and Freksa dished himself out so shamelessly, journalists ate him up. He'd become a real celebrity. People in the street asked for Freksa's autograph. But Willi wasn't giving in to the star so easily. This was his case.

"Herr Kommissar. Naturally I accept any duty and gladly take on any new assignment you have in mind. But I'd like to request that, in addition, I be allowed to stay on the Lichtenberg find."

A moment's silence. Then Freksa's clownish mask of horror: *"Ach, nein,* Kommissar. You mustn't overwork Isidore's protégé." Freksa pretended to beg for Willi's life. "You know how frail these people are . . . from all their years of money counting."

A quick burst of violent laughter, joined in by Horthstaler himself.

Willi'd survived minefields. Machine-gun fire. Did these morons really think they could wound him? Dragging Weiss into it, though, in such an obscene manner, made him want to take his chair and clobber Freksa over the head. Good thing he had a highly developed, perhaps overfunctioning, superego, as Dr. Freud had named it.

Bernhard Weiss was not only their superior, but one of the few people in life Willi actually looked up to. Deputy president of the Berlin police, he was the first Jew since Jews had come to Germany eighteen hundred years ago to reach top-ranking law enforcement. Weiss had created the nation's first modern crime lab. Spearheaded the transformation of the Berlin police after the 1919 revolution. Fostered the spirit of democratic policing. Extremists of all stripes hated him because he was vigorously evenhanded in his defense of the republic. Omnipresent in Berlin, he was always poking about crime scenes, overseeing demonstrations, safeguarding visiting dignitaries. With his large dark eyes behind wire glasses exuding openness and confidence, he'd become the face of the modern "people's" police. And a lightning rod for all who hated what he stood for. Lately one of the city's most vicious far-right rabble-rousers had cast him as a symbol of how "Jewified" Germany had become under the republic, repeatedly demeaning Weiss with the contemptuous Yiddish name Isidore.

"Well"—Freksa shrugged—"it's no secret you people look out for each other."

Clearly Freksa read the hate-filled rants of this Dr. Joseph Goebbels.

Weiss was responsible for Willi's career, all right. But not the way Freksa imagined. Willi'd already been twenty-four, finishing his second year at Berlin University, when he met the doctor in 1920 at a dinner honoring Jewish war veterans. Willi'd met his wife at a similar event a year before. Weiss never said a word about joining the police. Never had to. Ever since Willi was a kid, since his weak-hearted father was robbed at knifepoint and taunted with anti-Semitic slurs, he'd burned to hunt evildoers. To bring them to justice. He'd just never heard of anyone Jewish actually doing it. Until Weiss, who by then was already deputy head of Kripo. But Weiss knew nothing of Willi's application to the police academy, nor did he have anything to do with Willi's acceptance into it. An Iron Cross, First Class, accomplished that. And Weiss certainly did not help Willi earn top graduate in his year.

Not until Foreign Minister Rathenau was murdered in June 1922 did Willi even met Dr. Weiss a second time. This notorious political assassination occurred in Grunewald Forest, which was in the Wilmersdorf precinct, where Willi was a first-year assistant detective. He was assigned to work on the team with Weiss, who'd come in from the Alex to head the investigation. The skill and tenacity and the energy with which this top sleuth led the pursuit was awe-inspiring. By the time the killers were cornered, Willi was a true admirer, and he and the doctor had made a connection.

Perhaps Weiss had taken a natural interest in encouraging Willi, an interest he might not have taken in say, Hans Freksa, who had whole ranks of role models. But it wasn't Weiss who'd apprehended the husband who murdered a butcher, baker, and letter carrier he thought were having affairs with his wife. Nor was it Weiss who'd solved the case of the missing pharmacist that had baffled the Wilmersdorf precinct for years. Perhaps Freksa couldn't reconcile himself to how Willi took five years to make full sergeant, while it had taken Freksa twice that. Plenty of guys here believed higher-ups were "managing" Willi's career. But no higher-up had breached the Prenzlauerberg white-slave ring. Or cracked the Neukoln tenement murders.

"Kraus." The Kommissar was insistent. "You haven't even heard yet what your new assignment is. It's a major task. A most heavy burden. Of far more consequence to millions of Berliners than whatever's in that burlap bag, I assure you."

Willi sucked in his gut. He could feel the bag and all its horrors slipping from his fingers.

"You're no doubt aware of the tainted sausages spreading terror across this city."

Willi hoped this was a joke. That it was all leading up to some hilarious punch line at his expense. But Horthstaler's expression didn't suggest wit.

"Yes, of course. It was in all the morning papers." Willi clearly recalled Vicki's reaction. "I didn't think any fatalities were involved."

"Think again, Kraus. As of noon today . . . three."

"*Oy vey*, Kommissar." It was Mueller, caricaturing the crudest Yiddish accent, cradling his cheeks, rocking his head. "Dos meat ain't kosher. Dos is pig sausages!"

The laughter this time was uncontrollable.

Fury raged through Willi's limbs as he strode the echoing hallways. At the elevators, even though it was after one and the building nearly empty for the weekend, he checked over his shoulder to make sure no one was watching. Upstairs, in the administration offices, a thousand pounds seemed to lift from his chest as soon as he saw Dr. Weiss's door still open. And when the dark eyes looked up from behind wire glasses, he practically had to keep from throwing himself on the desk and bawling, "They took away my case!"

In the two years since he'd been here at headquarters, he'd come to the doctor's office more than once, he had to confess . . . but only for moral support. It wasn't easy constantly being undermined by colleagues and superiors alike. Never once, though, had he asked the deputy president for any sort of intervention. Until now.

"Freksa wanted it because it'll be big news and he's a publicity hound. Horthstaler yanked it from me because it's his instinct to shove me aside. But I was the one called to the scene, and I filed the paperwork. So by all rights that bag of bones should be mine." Willi rested his case before his superior. "Couldn't something be done?"

Dr. Weiss's eyes narrowed as put down his pen.

"Willi. We've known each other what, eight, nine years now?" Leaning his slim, forceful torso forward, he folded his fingers on the desktop. "I know the last thing you'd do would be to use your acquaintance with me to further your career. But others might not be so certain. Think of what could happen to your reputation if—"

"My reputation?" Willi hated interrupting, but there was no point even discussing that word. "My reputation couldn't get much worse, Dr. Weiss. No matter who I am or what I do, the men in my unit only see me as one thing: a big-nosed Jew. You've never intervened on my behalf, and still you couldn't convince anyone down there, including Kommissar Horthstaler, that my whole career wasn't managed by you."

The deputy president tightened his lips, letting out a long, low sigh. "Even if I thought it appropriate, I couldn't interfere right now, Willi. I'm in a bit of a tight spot myself."

Willi stared at him, his whole throat clenching. As if whacked across the face suddenly, he understood. Under attack by virulent anti-Semites, Weiss, one of the most prominent Jews in the whole civil service, could ill afford even the smallest scandal involving Jewish patronage. Willi felt a white-hot shame rush through his face for having been so selfish. To hell with the gentile world, he raged inwardly. For putting Weiss and him in such positions.

"I know it's frustrating, Willi. More than that." The doctor's dark eyes rested on him gently, almost lovingly. "It's downright degrading. Depressing. You become a policeman because you believe in justice and at every turn meet injustice. But a passion for what's right isn't the only virtue a good police officer must possess. Patience. Wisdom. A vision of the larger picture. A sense of responsibility."

Willi could feel that bag of bones slipping farther and farther from his hands.

Why was it so important to him?

Three

"Responsibility"—Otto Winkelmann proudly puffed his pipe—"is nature's most basic survival precept. Heinz's gift will help him learn what the word really means."

Willi'd already gotten an earful about it when he'd arrived home from work earlier, Stefan and Erich all over him about how the Winkelmanns had bought their son a ten-liter aquarium for his birthday, filled with guppies. If only we could get one like that, they'd cried. Now, over dinner, Willi heard how, after the tank had been set up, Heinz had gotten quite a lesson in the birds and bees too—so to speak. In minutes, one of the guppies had gone from big-bellied to bone thin, and a dozen shiny-silver slivers were darting around the water.

"Could that really be true?" Otto's sister-in-law seemed incredulous, checking with her husband. "Don't fish lay eggs?"

"Here we go-o-o-o!" Frau Winkelmann interrupted, bursting

through the terrace door, practically invisible behind her steaming platter.

Everyone at the table sat up and oohed.

In honor of Heinzie's birthday she had bestowed the rarefied pleasure on a select few—Vicki, Willi, and her relatives the Klempers—of her deviled ribs.

Despite himself Willi felt drawn into the group trance as she placed the tray down. Not that he had much appetite after lunch at headquarters this afternoon. But some rites were too seductive to resist.

"You're the *Meister,* Irmgard." Vicki applauded as if it were opening night at the opera. "Nobody devils a rib like you."

Their host, Otto Winkelmann, struck a more commemorative note. "Remember how many times we could only dream of such meals? During the war and then the revolution and then the—"

"Oh, really, Otto," his sister-in-law erupted. "Why must you litanize such things? I can't stand even to think of them." Frau Klemper rested her plump fingers on her bosom, sniffing at the beef. "I refuse to ever think of those awful times again."

"That's idiotic, Magda." Her husband rolled his eyes as if she were really too much. "Remembering is all that keeps us from forgetting. Isn't that so, Otto?" Felix Klemper stuffed a napkin between his bulging neck and collar. A manager at some second-rate insurance firm in the Hermannplatz, he was fond of asserting superiority over his wife with such inanities, Willi recalled. The man was a certified boor.

The wife wasn't such a treat, either.

But broiled in all that hot pepper, mustard, and horseradish, those ribs looked dandy indeed. And enough to give one dyspepsia for a week. Perhaps irritation was just a natural part of life's cycle, Willi considered, noticing his gastric juices already pumping as a heaping plate passed his way. He'd never cared a bit for the Winkelmanns' pompous in-laws, for example, but found himself dining with them regularly enough.

Like most apartment buildings in middle-class Wilmersdorf, 82-

84 Beckmann Strasse was built around a central courtyard with a small patch of grass and some trees. For seven years the Krauses and Winkelmanns had lived next door to each other on the third floor. They shared a common terrace. Their boys were the same ages. And although one family was Jewish and the other Christian, their lives had grown as entwined as the vines that ran along the courtyard walls. .

Kids' birthdays were communal affairs. Luckily, it was warm enough to celebrate Heinz Winkelmann's on the terrace in only light jackets. It had been a warm autumn. Roses still blossomed on the trellis overhead. The kids, who, even on birthdays, didn't get delicacies such as deviled ribs, had already finished dumpling dinners and were audible below in the yard playing cowboys and Indians. The adults, on their third bottle of Riesling, were more than ready to feast. But just as they were about to dig in, Frau Klemper froze with her knife in midair and looked around red-faced with embarrassment. "Are you really all so convinced the ribs are safe to eat?"

The silence could have knocked down the building.

The horror in Frau Winkelmann's eyes made plain she thought her sister-in-law might just as well have stuck a knife in her throat. She'd killed the evening certainly, all her hours over a hot oven, Heinz's entire ninth birthday.

The Kommissar had been right on this one, Willi realized. The sausage scare was terrorizing Berlin.

Two more people had died this afternoon. A dozen more had gone to hospitals. The Ministry of Public Health had officially put a stop to all sausage sales until the source of contamination had been found. WURST IN BERLIN—AUS! the afternoon papers screamed in a headline size reserved for events such as the kaiser's abdication.

Casting a look as if to say she hoped she wasn't about to betray Willi, Vicki leapt in to attempt a rescue. He'd told her a few details he'd learned since being assigned to the case today, and while she'd normally never dream of bringing up such things in a social situation, this time, her glance pleaded, circumstance demanded it.

"Yes, of course, the meat's safe, Frau Klemper." Her eyes glimmered beneath their long, dark lashes. "The problem's entirely confined to sausages. Isn't that so, dear?"

The glimmer flashed on Willi.

"Oh, absolutely," he backed Vicki instinctively. "Our beef could not be safer."

He had no sure knowledge this was true, only that his word would suffice to end the discussion and rescue the Winkelmanns' party. Reason enough, he believed, to give it. For seven years the families had seen each other through births, deaths, chicken pox, broken bones, boom times, and economic chaos. A little white lie, a slight abuse of power, seemed hardly out of order. Certainly Frau Klemper took it as the next best thing to an imperial edict, all but curtsying with gratitude.

"Well, then, from a Sergeant-Detektiv in Kripo!" She nodded at Willi repeatedly, but waited for him to dig in first. He obliged, and in seconds everyone was tearing at the ribs. Which did not, however, preclude the discussion of meat contamination.

"The early edition of *Berlin am Mittag* was explicit." Otto Winkelmann picked up his knife and fork. "The bacteria have been positively identified." Chewing, he cast his wife a deferential gaze. "My dear, you truly have outdone yourself this time."

"You mean the E. coli?" Frau Klemper's eyes fluttered in agreement. "He's absolutely right, Irmgard. Your sauce ought to be declared a national treasure. Still, I'm quite certain a late edition retracted that declaration."

"The *People's Observer* affirmed it's definitely not E. coli." Herr Klemper already had Irmgard's national treasure all over the napkin on his chest. "It is salmonella. Are there no more potatoes? Are we back to war rationing?"

Willi knew it was neither E. coli nor salmonella.

"But why does it take so long to determine?" Frau Klemper opened her chubby fingers, unable to believe such a process could take more than an hour, at most.

"Shocking. Shocking." Irmgard Winkelmann came around, plunking more potatoes onto her brother's plate. "That it could happen in Berlin."

That nothing could penetrate the ring of defenses protecting the city's meat supply was not a notion entirely without merit, Willi now understood. In the short time he'd spent at the Ministry of Public Health today, he'd learned that the regime of controls established by them decades ago was formidable indeed, and, given the size of the industry, rarely breached. Even during the war, as Vicki had recalled, when four years of Allied blockade had left a million Berliners on the edge of starvation, there'd been no serious contamination of the meat supplies. In fact, there hadn't been a really major contamination in Berlin since hundreds died in the trichinosis outbreak ninety years ago, which had prompted those public health measures to begin with.

Until now. With all the controls.

As usual, the city's myriad newspapers had only gotten part of the story right. In this case, the number of victims, their ages, etc. But as far as pathogenic culprits, in their endeavors to outscoop the competition, the headlines all had it wrong. For once, though, it wasn't their fault. The Ministry of Public Health, Willi'd learned, was intentionally song-and-dancing the public.

Arriving at their big granite headquarters near the Wilhelmplatz shortly after his talk with Dr. Weiss, he'd sensed a real war fever in the air. Technicians flying down corridors. Typewriters banging. No one going home this weekend. His liaison there, head of the medical crisis team, Frau Doktor Riegler, all but pushed him in front of a microscope.

"Big trouble." She focused the viewfinder for him. "E. coli and salmonella are pussycats compared to this."

Willi's vision had filled with jerking rod-shaped figures.

"*Listeria monocytogenes,*" she whispered as if it were too terrible to say loudly. "Ten times deadlier than most food-borne pathogens. Those nasty little bugs thrive in the most outrageous heat and cold. Long after you think they're gone . . . they're back. You must keep cleaning. Testing. Cleaning. Testing."

Willi thought they looked harmless enough, though more than one killer he'd tracked had. The incessant flagellation fixated him.

"What happens when they infect humans?"

"Nausea. Vomiting. Diarrhea. In serious cases—high fever. In the worst, convulsions. We've seen it all the last ten days."

"Ten?" He looked away from the lens. The Frau Doktor offered him a tilted little smile. "How could that be? The first reports came out only yesterday."

"We don't report what we don't know for certain." Her smile sank away. "Otherwise there'd be mass hysteria. You see what's happening now as it is, Sergeant." Her voice swelled with authority. "Like many bacteria, *Listeria*'s ubiquitous. The main route of infection's through food. But that could be anything from vegetables to meat, poultry, fish, dairy. It took us ten days to get a fix on the sausages." She clutched her clipboard. "We couldn't have the whole city too terrified to eat."

True enough, Willi agreed. And from someone who'd beaten the odds to get where she had, given the number of women doctors in Berlin. Smart, accomplished. Why then the nervous tic? "Because of the fatalities," she was saying, and just beneath her left eye the muscle was jerking, Willi noticed, like one of those little bugs under the microscope, "the question of criminal intent must be considered."

She was under great strain obviously, the whole city depending on her, and now having the criminal police to deal with. But back in university, in a course titled Physiology and Psychology, he'd learned that involuntary muscle contractions sometimes confessed what the mouth refused to. He couldn't help wondering what the Frau Doktor's might be trying to say.

Why was Winkelmann grinning like that?

"Because now that Kripo's in on the act"—he was raising a glass at Willi—"you may be certain the tainted-sausage case will proceed to a rapid conclusion."

"Here, here." Everyone on the balcony toasted. "To the Kriminal Polizei!"

Willi raised a glass too, hoping his neighbor was right.

Winkelmann of course was Willi's biggest fan. He loved to boast he'd watched Willi advance from a wet-behind-the-ears cadet to a seasoned detective down at the Alex. All in seven years. Willi always felt obliged to remind him that during the same period Winkelmann had risen from stock clerk to owning his own stationery store. But Willi's career seemed a real adventure novel by comparison, and re-telling chapters was hardly unpleasant with such an enraptured audience. Winkelmann's eyes would bulge, his feet would twitch, as Willi recounted how he'd had to climb the water tower in Prenz-lauerberg to capture the slave-ring conspirators. Or hide in a dumb-waiter to spy on the Neukoln tenement killer. Even Willi's boys didn't listen with such intensity. Vicki certainly never wanted to hear his stories. She was proud enough of his profession, but the physical aspect terrified her. Sometimes Willi thought she pretended he was a sales manager at the Tietz department store or something. What had Freud called that—?

"Elsie, I'll break every goddamn bone in your—"

Along with dusk, the children had crept into the apartment, and the Klemper girl, twelve, was clearly visible from the terrace doing cartwheels across the parlor, flying past the breakfront filled with Irmgard Winklemann's Meissen figurines. Klemper's admonition sent the child scurrying animal-like back into the dark.

"See how they listen?" The insurance man adjusted the napkin around his neck. "Because they know . . . Papa's boss. And how do they know?"

"Because they've been trained," his wife and his sister blurted simul-taneously. Looking at each other, they broke into embarrassed giggles.

"Don't make fun." Klemper wagged a finger at them, flushing. Clearly he hated being laughed at and yanked the napkin off his collar. "Had I pulled a stunt like that, my father would have grilled me good. Until my butt smoked." His eyes flared accusatorily. "And don't think I'm not the man I am today because of it."

Alarmed by the unrelieved heat in his voice, Frau Klemper moved to lower the temperature. "You are absolutely right, Felix." She looked around, enjoining the others to pour a little cold water on.

But it was too late. Klemper was boiling over.

"Just the other afternoon"—his eyeballs rolled—"in the number 41 streetcar—a child was eating one of those disgusting jelly rolls next to me." His whitened lips began to quiver. "Dripping, dropping, squirting all over my trouser leg. And what did the mother do? Not offer to pay any cleaning bills, I can assure you." He slapped the table. "I had to refrain from grabbing each of them"—he demonstrated unconsciously on his napkin—"and ringing their necks."

Willi looked away. He'd heard it all before . . . every time Klemper was here. How a child needed to be filled with shame. Terrified of authority. All independence crushed. For their own good. Martin Luther had famously declared he'd rather have a dead son than a disobedient one. In this respect, Willi thought, perhaps Jewish Germans did differ from many of their Protestant neighbors.

Once, when he was nine or ten, he recalled, he'd run away to see the Eiffel Tower. Saved his allowance. Bought a train ticket. Almost made it to the French border too, when a railroad officer nabbed him and dragged him back to Berlin. "Are you going to catch it when you get home," he'd warned all the way. "I ran off when I was a kid and I can still feel it." At the zoo station, though, Willi's parents had smothered him with so many kisses the officer just stood there, mortified.

A more current recollection stiffened Willi's spine.

That library memo about the circled Bible passage.

How ironic. Before he'd left work today he'd received a response to the inquiry he'd submitted. *Children of wrath,* it explained, was a term associated with a marginal theological doctrine known as Total Depravity. In his letter to the Ephesians, the Apostle Paul described the unsaved as being "by nature children of wrath." Hard-liners in several Protestant denominations cited this phrase as proof of original sin: that all men are born inherently evil, unable to attain salvation except through God's grace. These same hard-liners, according to the library, believed the passage underscored the bitter truth that, because babies were born "totally depraved," infants who died unsaved were lost for all eternity. The Bible, however, the report concluded, never addressed any such idea, Total Depravity being a strictly human dogma. Which was a good thing, Willi supposed.

Not that it mattered anymore. He slumped in the chair.

The case was no longer his.

"*Mutter*—" An earsplitting shriek reached the terrace. "The babies!"

Everyone rushed inside.

As they huddled around the fish tank, the guppy babies, it was plain to see, seemed to have disappeared. They were not at the top of the tank. Not at the bottom. Not swimming around the ceramic castle on the Rhine with its mounted knights on a drawbridge.

"What are you looking for?" Elsie the acrobat emerged from the shadows suddenly with a strange glint in her eyes. "Those babies are gone." She seemed to derive pleasure from the news. "You didn't take proper care of them. Newborn guppies need a place to hide or to be removed to another tank. Otherwise"—she shrugged—"the mother just"—a small smile drew across her lips—"eats them."

Her father slapped the side of her head. "Liar!"

Her mother seized her arm. "Is this how we raised you, to say such things?"

"It's not a lie," the girl cried. "After she gives birth, the mother's starving and eats her babies. Every last one."

"Preposterous." Herr Klemper's eyes bulged. "Against all laws of nature."

"Then how come it's in my biology book," Elsie sneered.

Willi's instinct was to shield his boys. But the older one at least, Erich, had a protective grip around the shoulder of his younger brother, Stefan. And neither, Willi noticed, was much concerned with the Klemper girl. Their eyes were fixed on Heinz Winkelmann, whose skin had turned as white as the sand in his new aquarium.

"Is it true?" he demanded to know. "Did the mother eat her babies?"

No one seemed willing to deny it. After a protracted moment, the pudgy-faced boy, nine years old today, held his stomach as if he'd been bitten and let out a bloodcurdling shriek.

Too shocked even to move, his parents simply stared at him.

The brother-in-law, Klemper, after some moments, felt compelled to divert onus off his own child and offer a word to the wise. "If you permit the boy to carry on so, Otto, you'll ruin him for life: both for yourself and the fatherland."

Heinz shrieked even louder.

"Otto doesn't have your disciplinary skills, dear," Frau Klemper explained about her brother-in-law.

"But he'll turn the boy into a fairy."

Willi watched Winkelmann hold his own a moment, then surrender to the superiority of his brother-in-law's logic, his whole face turning to a block of stone.

"This stops right now." He demanded of his son, "What makes you think you can carry on so? We Germans don't cry. We face truth as it is." His usually gentle blue eyes were cold as steel as Heinzie sought refuge behind his mother's legs.

"Perhaps you're being too harsh on the boy," Willi said, trying to apply some brakes on his neighbor's rage.

Otto flashed him a hate-filled glare. "No. A boy's got to learn that life is a struggle—that only the fittest survive. If those babies didn't live, it was because they weren't strong enough."

"But look . . . look." Vicki was pointing. "One's still there, Otto. See, way up top, in the castle tower."

"Rescue it, Papa," Heinz wailed. "Before she finds him."

One glance at his brother-in-law and Winkelmann's glare hardened. "Absolutely not. If that baby lives, it will because of its own strength, not because we intervened and—"

Like an arrow, the mother shot up and rendered the whole point moot.

Four

"You know what they say: everything has an end," Herr Strohmeyer proclaimed as they entered the long, cold mixing rooms. "Except"—he cocked his head to make certain Willi understood a punch line was coming—"sausages. They have two!"

Willi did his best to smile. But this guided tour, he was thinking between dull pangs in his brain, seemed to prove some things had no end at all.

Tall, bald Strohmeyer, scion of Berlin's premier *Wurst* dynasty since 1892, had been walking Willi through the family plant for what seemed hours now, prattling away in little more than advertising slogans. "A good manufacturer is as discriminating about what goes into his sausage as a winemaker." Not that Willi's headache was entirely due to the Sausage King's self-promotion. Or his rancid jokes. It had been an exasperating week altogether.

A dozen deaths had now been attributed to *Listeria monocytogenes*.

Nearly a thousand people across Berlin sickened from infected sausages, some quite severely. Still, the Ministry of Public Health was nowhere near containing the menace. Across the city dozens of companies and thousands of butchers were involved in the wholesale production, distribution, and sale of this staple German food. Tracing the origin of the contamination through retailer, wholesaler, parts suppliers, stockyards . . . it was a nightmare.

"And of course, the variety. Endless . . ."

Plus, Willi'd practically had to apprentice in sausage making to assess the possibility of criminal intention.

"You have your fresh sausage." Strohmeyer was counting on his fingers. "Your smoked sausage, your dry sausage, your semidry."

It was about as much as a Kripo officer could swallow.

"Not to mention your various casings: your hog, your sheep, your beef."

The side-winding necessary only added to his frustration at having been assigned to this investigation in the first place. Criminal negligence, maybe. But intention? Willi could hardly help feeling he'd been yanked off a major multiple homicide, which by all rights should have been his, and handed a real tub of lard.

"But you mustn't underestimate what goes into it." Strohmeyer was smiling at Willi gravely. "Sausage making is an ancient art, Herr Sergeant-Detektiv. After you cut and grind and mix, you've first got to add the . . ."

Willi's thoughts escaped back to that burlap sack. What track was Freksa taking on the investigation? Was he following up on the sewer line? What about that library memo he'd passed on to him about Total Depravity? Freksa hadn't replied. His feelings toward Willi were no secret. But he wouldn't go so far as to let prejudice get in the way of an investigation, would he?

"Of course any filler must be of the highest quality and possess the proper lean-to-fat ratio. And absolutely fresh. If not"—Strohmeyer lowered his voice as if afraid to curse things further—"the kiss of death."

An ironic phrase, Willi thought, considering how many had received exactly that from his family's sausages. Not that the man's lament was difficult to understand. The Strohmeyer plant, across Landsberger Allee from the vast Central Stockyards, employed nearly a hundred workers, many of whom now stood about, observing their boss showing another official around. The giant grinders, the commercial mixers, the slicers, the mincers, the huge stuffing machines . . . all silent. Wages frozen. The meat industry and its associated trade unions on the same side for once, struggling even now to have the city-wide sausage ban annulled in court. It was easy to sympathize with their plight. But Willi couldn't stop picturing the mother of the six-year-old he'd interviewed earlier this week . . .

"We thought she just had a stomach flu." The mother kept folding and unfolding a little sweater in her lap, rubbing it across her palm. "We even sent her to school." Her voice was so hoarse it was barely audible, like when Vicki had laryngitis. "But that night the diarrhea was so terrible." Willi'd shuddered to imagine something like that happening to one of his boys. "Filled with blood. And then the fever . . . and those convulsions. We ran her to the hospital, but—" She clutched the sweater to her neck.

Over the years he'd conducted more than one interview with a grieving parent. But he'd never, as he did this time, had to wipe tears from his eyes on the ride home.

Since the first victims came from lower-class neighborhoods, investigators initially guessed the sausages might be made of *Freibank*, meat cut from the carcasses of diseased animals, sterilized by boiling, then sold via city markets to the very poor. It soon became apparent, however, that the victims came from not only the poorest but also the richest neighborhoods in Berlin, and a number of middle-class ones too. *Listeria* had turned up in half a dozen kinds of sausages, traced to at least a dozen butcher shops, all of which purchased their products from the giant wholesale market near Alexanderplatz. Willi'd grown up in Berlin, lived here all his life, seen the huge Central Market halls on Neue Friedrich Strasse countless times, just a block from the Police Presidium. But he'd never stepped inside.

Until three days ago.

A vast arcade of brick and iron several stories tall greeted him with daylight pouring through giant windows on either end. A cacophony of noise from the sea of wholesalers' stalls, many hundreds supplying a city of 4 million with meat, fish, fruit, vegetables, all under one roof. Retail greengrocers, butchers, fishmongers, thronging every square meter in search of a deal.

Willi was met by one of the top administrators, who'd dutifully shown off the refrigeration chambers beneath the great halls, connected directly to the city railroad, and the hydraulic systems that unloaded products from train cars with unparalleled rapidity. He was informed of the elaborate regulations regarding the handling of foodstuffs: meat allowed inside only at certain hours and only through specified entryways, produce through other entries at other times. He was assured that all dealerships were required to unpack their stock at least once every seven days and destroy all unsound articles. A team of inspectors was attached to each sales hall, as well as a medical station with a skilled nurse. No, the problem of *Listeria* had certainly not originated at the Central Market.

Not that anyone said it had.

The immense hall housing the sausage wholesalers was easily recognizable by its lack of customers. Day three of the sausage ban and the stalls had been empty except for the scores of salesmen wringing their hands and the piles of Bierwurst, Blutwurst, Bockwurst, Bratwurst, Landjager, Leberkase, Knackwurst, Gelbwurst. Nearly two hundred kinds of sausages awaiting reprieve. The Ministry of Public Health had focused on two dealerships: Klingel Brothers, supplier for nine of thirteen butcher shops known to be connected with the contamination, and Zuckerhof, across the aisle, supplier of seven. Both had procured their merchandise directly from local producers, largely, though not exclusively, Strohmeyer Wurst A.G. Neither, however, believed *Listeria* could have originated there.

In separate interviews both Klingel and Zuckerhof were almost vehement with Willi on this point. Strohmeyer'd been in business too long, they insisted, and was far too reputable a manufacturer. The contamination had to have begun with one of his suppliers.

And not one of the big ones at the *Viehof,* either. No, the Central Stockyards were too strictly regulated. It had to have been a peddler. Those unscrupulous bastards sold on the cheap in alleys adjacent to the markets, free from rentals and regulatory demands. They were a real menace; Willi just had to look for himself. Legitimate dealers had been complaining about them for years, and what had it gotten them? A catastrophe. Who was going to compensate them for all these goods? If the sausage ban went on much longer, the honest brokers would be dragged under and all that'd be left'd be the cockroach peddlers.

The pounding in Willi's head had started around this time, growing worse by the day.

This endless tour of the sausage factory only added to it.

"Of course we follow only the strictest safety guidelines published by the Ministry of Public Health itself." Strohmeyer had turned strident by the time they reached the casing rooms. "No one understands better than we how bacteria can spread through a workplace. We keep our facility spick-and-span, as you can see. Any surface that comes in contact with meat receives generous applications of chlorine bleach. Our employees wash their hands before entering the workplace, or after they do anything that could contaminate them—such as sneezing."

Willi stared at the rows of big hoppers with their long funnels and adjustable nozzle heads. He could almost see the fatty red mixture pressing through, filling the intestinal casings, casing after casing stuffed, twisted, links spewing forth, carefully wound around each other. A quick glance at Strohmeyer convinced him the Wurst King genuinely believed his own words. But Willi'd spent enough time poring over the records by now to know the rhetoric did not precisely conform to the facts.

A sausage, he'd been enlightened this week, was more than it appeared. In a single casing, a company such as Strohmeyer might combine not only different grades of meat, but meat from different kinds of animals and even from different slaughterhouses. They also used what were known as trimmings—fatty edges sliced from better cuts—as well as other hard-to-use animal parts, such as stomachs, throats, blood, in combination with higher-grade meat to compose their sausage innards. A fifty-fifty meat-to-filler ratio, according to the industry trade journal *Meat and Meat By-Products*, saved a company as much as 25 percent. What neither the journal nor Strohmeyer mentioned, but a 1927 Ministry of Public Health report had, was that these low-grade fillers came from animal parts more likely than others to have contact with bacteria's main source: shit.

After long, crowded train journeys across Europe, pigs, sheep, goats, cattle, arrived in Berlin smeared with feces. The giant central stock and slaughter yards, the *Central-Viehof,* required all slaughterers to thoroughly hose down carcasses before sending them to cutting floors. But this, Willi'd learned, was hardly foolproof. Feces got through. And sometimes, inadvertently, workers spread it from the hide onto the meat itself, especially trimmings sliced from outer surfaces, such as Strohmeyer used. Trimmers removed whatever feces they spotted, but, according to a report by the Amalgamated Meat Workers' Union, with a half carcass rolling down the hook lines every five seconds, oversights occurred. The tripe rooms, where intestines were gutted, were also rife with contamination.

Strohmeyer purchased fillers—trimmings, fat, blood—as well as casing intestines large and small from at least a dozen suppliers at the *Viehof.* He relied on them to test their products for bacteria and did his own testing only after the ingredients were ground together. Technically this conformed to a turn-of-the-century Ministry of Public Health guideline suggesting but not ordering sausage processors to test ingredients *before* grinding. "Optimally, every production lot should be sampled and tested before leaving the supplier and again before use at the receiver," the guideline urged. But the problem, Willi'd learned, was that many slaughterers would not sell to grinders who insisted on such strict testing, and so the grinders let things slide. According to its own safety program, in 1910 Strohmeyer had obligated itself to obtain certificates from all suppliers showing no bacteria had been found in any purchased lots. But Strohmeyer did not follow its own policy. It obtained no safety certificates whatsoever for the entire decade of the 1920s. Willi'd checked. Every single file in the company records. Not a single certificate since 1919.

"Are we perfect?" Strohmeyer asked. "No. But what we have done is to show continual improvement."

Criminal negligence, more likely, Willi thought.

"Nor will we stand still. As soon as we get back to production, Strohmeyer A.G. will take only the most aggressive measures to ensure our products' safety. But, as I have urged the Ministry of Public Health, all efforts must be redoubled to track this pestilence back to the slaughterhouses. *They* are the source."

Everyone loved to point a finger.

True, Willi thought, no signs of *Listeria* had shown up here at Strohmeyer. Not that the company's own testing was anything other than random. Plenty of batches got through untested. But government inspectors had pounced all over this plant the minute *Listeria* had been traced to sausages, and their findings were also negative. Willi now understood, though, why these things took time—because *Listeria* was so damned resilient. Some scientists postulated that under high-stress conditions these bacteria could actually reduce themselves to a dormant state. Test results could only be conclusive over time. "You must keep testing, testing, testing," Frau Doktor Riegler had said the first time they'd met. According to her, the *Listeria* would almost certainly show up here because it had almost certainly passed through. In nine out of ten cases—the doctor's cheek twitched as she told him—the tainted sausages could be traced directly to Strohmeyer Wurst A.G. Which did not, however, mean the infection began there.

The route these things traveled was up to scientists to determine. Willi was simply on the trail of gut feelings. After listening to the *Wurst* King these many hours, his had pretty much congealed: Strohmeyer was as willing to add filler to the truth as he was to his sausages.

Time had come to poke at the marrow.

"To trim costs"—he gave the man only the slightest glance—"might your company ever go outside the market and purchase from, say—an unlicensed peddler?"

One of Strohmeyer's eyebrows dropped, his voice darkening from the enormity of his dismay. "Herr Sergeant-Detektive. This is a family business. Since 1892."

"Yes, of course." Willi held up a hand. "I ask only out of duty."

Outside it had turned overcast, as if it was going to rain. Or snow. Willi buttoned his coat and looked across the street. Motor trucks and horse-drawn wagons crowded in front of the block-long sheds comprising halls Two and Three of the wholesale meat markets, where Strohmeyer and his competitors purchased their better cuts. To the right, farther south, connected by a tunnel under busy Landsberger Allee, a skyline of smokestacks rose across the horizon. A vast city within a city, kilometers in every direction. Berlin's great Central Stockyards, the *Viehof*, with its countless acres of rail yards, feedlots, sales halls, and slaughterhouses. Soon enough he'd have to take his investigation in there. But not today. Today he was going home and helping the boys with their schoolwork, maybe read to them awhile, take a bath.

Make love to his wife.

Inhaling, he pulled up the collar around his neck. Beyond the *Viehof*, barely half a kilometer to the south, was the construction pit where the burlap sack had washed up. Freksa'd better hurry up and find the bastard who'd filled that bag, he thought, recalling the library report on Total Depravity. Anyone who'd kill five kids would sure as hell kill more.

He turned into the November wind. Reaching the avenue, truck after truck roared passed. A news vendor cried out, "Court upholds sausage ban—two more die!" Unconsciously he quickened his pace. Halfway to the elevated station, though, the hair practically leapt from his neck. What a stink. Its source, clearly, to his left, a long, dark sunken lane between warehouses, packed with people and pushcarts. So there it was . . . a peddlers' market. He checked his watch. Not even certain what he was looking for, he entered the stench-filled alley.

In all his years in Berlin he'd been in few more unsavory places than this putrid passage. A visible miasma hung in the air, a dark, steamy mist rising from scores of tubs and barrels brimming with God knew what. Nothing indicated what the reeking contents of these containers were; Willi could only surmise. Those slimy mounds, long and rubbery, some kind of intestines. The barrels brimming with purple liquid . . . blood. Those crates, overflowing with hairy pink things, ears. And what looked like a pile of glass marbles next to it, eyeballs; whose, he had no idea. Everything was of dubious freshness at best, gotten for a steal, sometimes literally, across the road at the *Viehof*. As doubtful as the products were, the people looked even worse. Instinctively he reached in his pocket and touched his wallet. The shifty-looking customers were uniformly ill clad, ill smelling. The vendors appeared on the edge of total decrepitude: missing teeth, fingers, arms, legs.

So many children too.

A boy behind an open vat made Willi's throat dry up. He wasn't much older than Erich, ten at most. Why wasn't he at school? Willi'd never considered his own childhood idyllic, his father having died when Willi was nine. But compared to this . . . my God, how lucky he'd been. Erich and Stefan too. He longed to hold them suddenly. This child, dressed in filthy rags, looked around with dark eyes, hoping for a stroke of luck, it seemed, to sell out his stock so he could escape this miserable damp. But one glance at Willi and he slammed the vat closed, assuming a blank expression, as if he were deaf and blind. How out of place I must look, it occurred to Willi, in this gray serge suit and overcoat Vicki got last year in London. Then too, his peripheral vision took in the waves of interest spreading around him— none of these vendors was legal.

A sudden tightening seized his gut. Right behind the boy . . . that burlap sack. Clearly stamped across its side: SCHNITZLER AND SON.

He tried smiling. "You don't want to tell me what you've got there, son?"

The kid pretended not to hear him.

"But how can I buy if I don't know what you're selling?" Willi acted as if his feelings were hurt.

The answer from the gaunt, little face was too perceptive for comfort: "If you was here to buy, you wouldn't have to ask, sir."

Willi swallowed. He considered breaking out his badge and forcing the issue, but a harsh voice suddenly rose behind him, much too close.

"What're you harassing the kid for?"

Slowly he turned to find himself nose to nose with a massive creature several dimensions larger than himself, and a long, sharp knife flashing at his gut. A cold sweat broke under Willi's suit. It would not have been impossible to disarm the beast, perhaps. During the war he'd been in one of the most elite forward units, behind enemy lines, received the best training in martial arts, and had to use it. But from the corner of his well-trained eye Willi noticed other flashing blades in the crowd. Naturally it was his own fault—for having entered a place like this alone. On the other hand, if he had an assistant, as regulations called for . . . but they never seemed to find anyone willing to work with him, they claimed.

"Me, harassing? Not at all. I'm a visitor from Hamburg." He mustered every atom of affability he could. "A businessman." He tipped his hat twice. Last thing he wanted was for Stefan and Erich to grow up as he had: fatherless. "Have you ever been to Hamburg?" He smiled, picturing himself all sliced up in one of these barrels. "Wonderful market we have there. Not so great as Berlin's, of course. Here everything is so much bigger. I certainly didn't mean to disturb anyone." He flicked a five-mark piece in the air, which the boy instantly caught. "Buy a nice warm soup for yourself and your friend."

Backing off, relieved to still have his guts in one piece, he grabbed a look at the brute with the knife. My God. The size of an ox. And as powerful looking. Thickest set of arms Willi'd ever seen. Sometimes, he thought, reaching the street and letting out a sigh of relief, it really did pay to just pay.

Five

'Round and 'round the glass doors spun—but still no Fritz. Not that he ever arrived on time. But for a man who couldn't live without trying to pay you back for what you'd done in the past—such as saving his life three or four times—you'd think he'd try. Willi checked his watch. What the hell. What's the rush? He took a deep breath and looked around the glittering Café Josty. The only thing on the schedule today was . . . nothing.

It'd been nearly a month since his visit to the sausage factory, and inspectors were still scouring suppliers over at the *Viehof*. Testing, testing—but so far, *nichts*. At Willi's urging they'd raided the peddlers' market on Landsberger Allee, tested everything, then shut the place down. No signs of *Listeria* anywhere. But no new deaths, either. And the number of cases, dwindling. Perhaps the whole thing was just going to peter out.

He thanked the waiter as his second pot of coffee arrived. At least he'd spoken up to Horthstaler. Told him about the close shave with the peddlers, that it might have been averted if he'd had backup—as he was supposed to. "I didn't know you felt so strongly about it, Kraus; I'll make an extra effort to find someone." The Kommissar had smiled warmly. A small twist of his pudgy lips, though, suggested Willi not hold his breath.

He was tired of waiting. Tired of bacteria, and Dr. Riegler, and how her little kitty cat at home missed her favorite sausages. Sick of the whole damn case. He glanced at the pressed-tin ceiling. Half the time he found his mind wandering back to that bag of bones. Sometimes late at night he lay awake wondering, what would motivate someone to make those designs? A pagan rite? An occult sacrament? There was no shortage of bizarre fixations in Berlin. But then again, that Bible. He'd gone so far as to consult his cousin at the Institute for Psychoanalysis.

"The organized manner of these designs," Kurt said, fascinated, "suggests a highly compulsive personality, driven toward perfection. This kind of compulsion to arrange, to make order, is often fueled by the need to ward off a terrifying inner chaos. I'd say you had one very disturbed individual on your hands, in case you hadn't realized."

The problem, of course, was that it wasn't on Willi's hands.

Though he couldn't seem to wash himself of it, either.

Deep-black coffee spewed from the silver spout as he poured another cup.

Absurdly overpriced, but every so often, he glanced around the legendary café, this place was worth it—if only for the spectacle. As he sipped the brew, its bitter sweetness lingered on his lips. Josty on Potsdamer Platz was *the* spot to meet in the wildly beating heart of this metropolis. Being a true Berliner he found it hard not to feel a little sinful pride at being so at home here.

In summer, the place to be was the terrace. Ensconced in a gentle birch grove, you had a bird's-eye view of Europe's busiest intersection. Now that the first winter chills had set in, the upstairs provided an even more feathered perch. This afternoon, the gold leaf–walled room was packed with people nestled in newspapers or chatting over many-layered *Baumkuchen,* the king of cakes. How swank Vicki would say everyone looked, Willi thought, noting the stylishness, the plumage everywhere: men with wide lapels, colorful neckties, and jeweled studs, oiled hair parted sharply to the side. Women with long strings of pearls, boyish hairdos, and short dresses with sheer stockings showing off their legs.

He could recall a day women wouldn't dare show so much as an ankle here. He could recall being here with his parents to celebrate the turn of the century when he was five years old . . . his mother coming up those very steps, holding her skirt off the floor, the ostrich feathers in her hat practically dusting the ceiling. His father with white gloves, gray spats, and a jaunty bowler tilted over one eye. What a different Berlin it had been back then. The Kaiser Reich. Everything so much more proscribed and rigid . . . yet safer feeling somehow too. If only falsely.

Now Berlin spun like a mad carousel ride. Potsdamer Platz was still the center, and Café Josty still the center of the center. But it all ran at such an accelerating tempo, the city sometimes felt ready to fly right off its axis.

Willi's eyes roamed out the window. Through the double panes of glass you could take in the whole famous intersection below, in all its turbulent postwar frenzy—and not have to hear a thing. Like a silent movie. A futuristic epic. Amid flashing neon and giant billboards, all the major routes binding Berlin-Center to its western districts converged right here, forming a virtual vortex, sucking in vehicles, throngs of people, tangling them up and then shooting them out again. In the center, a five-sided iron tower bearing Europe's first electric traffic signals—like a sentinel over the mayhem—streams of cyclists and long, yellow streetcars rushing around it, double-decker buses plastered with advertisements. People pouring in and out of Potsdamer station, one of Berlin's busiest. Or through the doors of one of the grand hotels: the Esplanade, the Palast, the Furstenhof. Around the corner, the giant Wertheim department store, with its glass-roofed atrium and eighty-three elevators. And down the block, a stunning new office tower rising in glass and steel, curved to follow the shape of the street. Potsdamer Platz was leaping toward tomorrow.

According to the traffic bureau, twenty thousand autos squeezed through this intersection daily, almost all of them German-made: Audis, Opels, BMWs, Horchs, Hansas, Daimler-Benzes, Mercedes. The heart of Berlin pounded perpetually. Not many places on this earth churned with the tempo, the drive, of this one.

Willi's neck stiffened slightly. A long black sports car like a rocket ship was careening through the traffic below, cutting off cars and trucks alike. Perhaps it should have come as no surprise. As big as this city was, in some respects it was still a small town, and not many Mercedes SSKs were on its streets. Still, he couldn't help but get a jolt at the unmistakable reflection of Dr. von Hessler's silver eye patch behind the wheel.

"Looks like you've seen the devil."

Willi jumped.

It was Fritz, finally sitting down across from him in a three-piece suit, with a trilby hat, and walking stick, his thin blond mustache tilted to one side.

"Perhaps I have. You're forty minutes late, *Mensch*."

"Grisly traffic."

"Your dear old friend managed to barrel his way through. What'd he do, drive a tank in the war?"

"Which dear old friend?" Fritz slumped in the chair and began pulling off his gloves, one finger at a time. "I have so many."

"Von Hessler."

"Oh, him. Mad as a hatter. Always has been. Last time I saw him, he was convinced he was on the road to altering the course of human history. I do kind of hope he's onto something, actually." Fritz tossed his gloves on the table. "We might need it."

"What's that supposed to mean? Hey... before I forget, I'm instructed to remind you: Vicki really is sorry about New Year's Eve. We always take the kids out to her parents that night, and, well—"

Fritz smiled regretfully. "Sylvie's crushed, but she'll get over it. After all, it's no ordinary New Year's Eve." The corners of his lips twisted. "It'll be a whole new decade. And from what I gather"—his mustache shifted precipitously—"very likely the last happy days for a while."

"What's with all the thunderbolts of doom, Jeremiah?"

"Sorry. Just came from a big press conference at the Ministry of Commerce. It's pretty damned serious. A number of key foreign loans have been canceled."

Willi waited for more, but that was all.

He didn't get it.

It wasn't simply that he was no genius regarding the mechanisms of economics, but 1929 had been a year of such spectacular growth, such euphoric prosperity almost, it seemed impossible to grasp that something as arcane as foreign loans could cause that look in Fritz's eyes. After the truly terrible years of the war and the revolution and the Great Inflation, this past half decade was a godsend. The economy booming. Wages skyrocketing. Unemployment down to nothing. What they'd read about the stock market in New York of course was terrible. The days of crazy speculation obviously at an end. But it was hard to believe a few foreign loans . . .

"You're quite wrong." Fritz's gloom was implacable. "Germany's as dependant on foreign capital as a junkie, Willi. American capital to be precise. Far more than most Germans have the least inkling. You simply can't imagine the kind of money that's been wiped out. This was no garden-variety collapse. The bottom's given way. Which means no more investments. No more loans. No more orders for goods. Brace yourself, friend. It's going to be a real downslide."

Willi hung on to the pole as the streetcar swayed along busy Leipziger Strasse. Twilight had fallen and the holiday lights cast a golden haze on Berlin's main shopping drag. Judging from the crowds overflowing the sidewalks, jostling in and out of the shops and department stores, the spectacular show windows brimming with fur coats, fine jewelry, watches, leather goods, the most advanced cameras, the best toys, it seemed hard to believe Fritz hadn't fallen prey to a bit of ministerial propaganda. There had been real angst in his voice.

Or perhaps he and Sylvie were at it again.

When the streetcar rattled across the river, a near full moon hanging high over the city, the glinting domes of the Police Presidium in the distance brought back the more compelling mystery of those bones. Their grim images seemed to reflect in the rippling water below: femurs tied up like long-stemmed roses. Finger and toe bones, one after the next, linked almost like . . . sausages. How could he not have heard anything more about it? He didn't expect to be taken into Freksa's confidence—but total silence at unit meetings? And what about the newspapers? This was exactly the sort of thing the Berlin press went haywire over. *Bone arrangements! Human thread!* Five weeks, though, and not a word. Since when did Freksa shy away from headlines? Perhaps he hadn't gotten anywhere on the case. Or perhaps he had something up his—

The whole train of thought screeched to a halt.

On the far side of the Spree his attention was derailed by a small sign out front of a church . . . LECTURE TODAY, FIVE P.M. . . . THE REVEREND H. P. BRAUNSCHWEIG. The topic sent a tremor through him. He checked his watch: just past five now. He shouldn't, he knew. The case being Freksa's. But perhaps, as his grandmother used to say, it was *beschert*—meant to be. Yanking a bell for the tram to stop, he jumped off. What else could he do? Total Depravity.

The Spandauer Strasse Evangelical Church was not much larger than a chapel. A dozen or so people filled its wooden pews, all focused on the tall, gray figure at the pulpit, who watched Willi enter.

"It should not be mistaken"—the reverend's gray eyes followed as Willi removed his hat and took a seat in the back row—"that Total Depravity, or Total Corruption, or even, as some call it, Total Inability, means that people are completely evil. Oh, no. That would be looking at the issue quite backwards. Total Depravity is not an accusation. On the contrary: it is an affirmation. A spiritual underlining of God's glory."

It's hot as hell in here, Willi thought, unbuttoning his coat.

"In Ephesians two, one to three, the Bible tells us, 'And you were dead in the trespasses in which you once walked . . . carrying out the desires of the body and the mind, and were by nature children of wrath.'"

That phrase again. It shot through Willi's body. The gray gaze seemed to fix on him, as if the reverend knew precisely why Willi had entered those doors.

"What this passage means is not that people are evil, but that people are not capable of loving God as God wants to be loved. People's fundamental instincts lead them to be selfish, to ignore God. But without God, even the good a person tries to do is corrupt. Only God can overcome man's inability, his total depravity. It is through divine grace that children of glory can be fashioned from children of wrath."

Willi's cheeks burned.

He waited until the last parishioners had exited, then walked up to the pulpit. The reverend was gathering papers. When he saw Willi, he cocked his gray head, squinting curiously. "You're new here." He seemed to be trying to peer into Willi's soul. "Have you been drawn to us? Did something I say touch you?"

Normally Willi preferred being ethical with people. But when solving crime was the name of the game, deception was often a valuable tactic. Rather than unveil his badge, he sensed he might get further with this chap by stroking the ego a bit.

"Very perceptive of you, Reverend. Yes. I've come face-to-face with a truly horrifying evil. When I spotted your billboard, I was drawn to see if you could help me understand. It's incomprehensible to me that human beings, with so much love and kindness and desire to do good, can be, as you put it, so . . . depraved."

"What's your name, dear fellow?"

"Willi."

"Willi. Come to my study, won't you? Join me in a glass. I always need a little sustenance after my lectures. They take so much out of me."

Slapping Willi's shoulder, he led him into a sparse apartment behind the chapel. "People aren't as depraved as they could be." He motioned Willi to sit. "Everyone has a little good in him." He poured them each some peppermint schnapps. "You can't deny that." He clinked Willi's glass and smiled before downing his in a single gulp.

Willi partook in a little sip, as long as he had nothing particular to do at the office.

"But even though they're not entirely corrupt"—the reverend coughed, knitting his gray brows—"what corruption they have extends to every part of them, and everything they do. Consider this." He pointed at the bottle.

"Most delicious by the way." Willi was grateful for the minty warmth flowing through his chest suddenly. Quite a wallop. He took a longer sip.

"Just my point. Add a single drop of cyanide, though—and we'd both be dead." The reverend smiled sadly. "Because even though the bottle isn't filled with it, that single corruption spreads to every part. Catch the analogy? People may not be *completely* evil, but the original evil they're born with extends to everything they do. That's what's meant by Total Depravity."

That Willi declined a second drink didn't stop the reverend from pouring himself one. "Might it not be possible, though"—Willi watched him dump it down his throat again in one long gulp—"that some people have no goodness at all. That they really are *totally* depraved?"

The reverend pounded his chest several times and blinked at him. "I don't get what you're driving at."

Willi was suddenly feeling the schnapps too, surprised by how strongly it was blanketing his brain.

"For instance, those who commit violent crimes."

"You mean, like Cain and Abel—"

"I mean, Reverend Braunschweig, today, right here in Berlin—someone's murdering little boys." He hadn't exactly planned to blurt that out, but liquor always made him loose-tongued. "Boiling their bones and using their dried muscle to bind them together into bizarre—"

He halted, seeing he'd pushed too far, too fast. The reverend was losing color. All that warmth in Willi's heart transformed into trepidation. He was out of bounds here, he realized. If word ever reached headquarters he was trespassing on Freksa's case, it wouldn't be pretty. But screw it, he thought. The schnapps may have started it, but he'd be damned if he was going to stop now.

Besides, Freksa'd never follow this lead.

"Reverend, is there anyone you can think of, in your congregation, or at your lectures, or who showed any interest at all in the topic of Total Depravity who might be capable of such a—"

The reverend went white with confusion. Willi realized he'd left out the part about the Bible in the burlap bag, the circled passage from Ephesians: *children of wrath*. But it was too late. Braunschweig suddenly looked as if he feared the murderous maniac might be Willi himself.

"Reverend, I'm Sergeant-Detektiv Kraus, Berlin Kriminal Polizei." He belatedly revealed his badge.

"A cop?" Braunschweig reeled as if he'd been hit by brimstone. "How dare you deceive me like that? Pretend you were here for spiritual guidance! And not even a Christian." Color returned, bolting through his cheeks. "The moment you walked in, I thought, what's this Jew doing here? Now I see. A most underhanded way of approaching an investigation, I must say." His gray brows knit with indignation. "Perhaps that's all one can expect from you people."

"I might remind you it's illegal to withhold information from the criminal police. Except, of course, in the case of the clergy. So I can't order you to talk. Nor will I attempt to amend your beliefs about what to expect from me or 'my people.' But I do assure you little boys are being murdered in this city, Reverend. And that a very sick individual is on the—"

"Get out." Braunschweig all but spit.

Willi picked up his hat. "Okay then." He shrugged. "Thanks for the schnapps."

As he reached the door, though, Braunschweig suddenly changed tunes.

"Oh, for Christ's sake . . . I really didn't mean that, Detektiv."
Willi paused.

"You caught me off guard is all. You oughtn't surprise a guy like that. Stay for another drink, Sergeant. Sit."

The man, Willi saw, had something on his tongue.

The reverend quickly downed another schnapps, then another.

"I sure as hell don't know anyone who'd fit the bill of horrors you just presented, but I can tell you this." He looked at Willi, coughing, bleary-eyed but definitely aching to spill something. "Every congregation has its nuts. Over the years I've seen my fair share, believe me." He took a moment to glance outside as if they were all there again, lined up outside his window. "Normally I pay no attention once they're gone, but in this case . . ." He turned to Willi. "Several have joined what sounds like something straight out of a tawdry novel, only it's not. It's all too real." His bushy eyebrows arched dramatically. "A satanic love cult. Yes, it's true!" He leaned forward. "And the things that go on there, I've been told." He had to steady himself on the table. "With children too." His speech was slurring.

Braunschweig tried to aim his bloodshot gaze at Willi, but had a hard time fixing it there. "Their leader's terribly charismatic, a *very* depraved figure . . . a former member here, a rather important one I'm ashamed to admit."

With an uncertain mixture of gratitude and horror, Willi stuck a hand in his coat pocket. Was all this just a drunken rant? It sure sounded like it. But then again . . . He pulled out a notebook. "Go on, Reverend. You have no idea how much I appreciate this. What's his name?"

"It's not a him, Kraus. It's my former wife, Helga Braunschweig."

Six

Vicki stuck her head in the bathroom. "Ban's been lifted."

Under the shower spray, Willi wasn't certain he'd actually heard right. "Huh?"

"Sausages . . . back on sale."

His eyes widened so far shampoo dripped in. "Ow." He hurriedly rinsed them. "You positive?"

"Just on the radio. They found the bacteria. Save some hot water for me, will you, darling?"

It would have been nice had someone informed him. Willi shut off the shower.

Over toast at breakfast, Erich looked at him with great, brown eyes.

"*Vati,* I've made a decision."

"Have you."

"Yes. I know what I'd like for Hanukkah."

"And what might that be? Mind your crumbs."

"A model Fokker triplane, like the Red Baron flew in the war."

At least he was over the aquarium, Willi thought. "Well, I think that's very wise, Erich. There's a whole department for model planes at KDW. Surely they'll have the Red Baron's. We can go Saturday when I'm finished with work."

"Can I come too?" the little one wanted to know.

"Of course, Stefan," Willi assured him, though he realized Saturday was the day he'd hoped to poke around that preposterous "love cult" the reverend had told him about. Could it possibly be true? It seemed too outlandish. Even for Berlin. He couldn't stop thinking about what Braunschweig had said, though: "With children too." What exactly could that mean? He was almost too afraid to imagine. Clearly the line between fact and fiction got blurred under all that booze. But he'd given Willi an address card. A completely insane-looking thing with all sorts of pentagrams and Egyptian symbols on it: DIVINE RADIANCE MISSION, 143 BLEIBTREU STRASSE. CHARLOT-TENBURG. A swank enough neighborhood. Still, the kids came first. Question was, which kids? His, or the ones whose bones had been boiled by a lunatic still on the loose? What he really ought to do was turn the whole thing over to Freksa.

The phone made him jump. So early in the morning?

It was Frau Doktor Riegler.

"Sorry I didn't inform you, Sergeant." She sounded a little sheepish. "We only confirmed it yesterday. And then, let's just say politics was involved."

Willi didn't even want to know what she meant by that. Only where they'd found the bacteria. "Was it a peddler?"

"There'll be a news conference at ten. Ninety-two Thaer Strasse. *Central-Viehof.* You'll want to be there."

From the platform of the S-Bahn station Willi could see into the otherworldly landscape of the *Viehof* across a wide river of tracks. Entirely encircled by high brick walls to obscure its more unsavory aspects, the acres of glass-roofed market halls, immaculate stock-yards, high ramps, tunnels, and ultra-efficient slaughterhouses were among the engineering marvels of Berlin. This was Willi's second trip here. How vividly he recalled the first a few weeks ago, a real grand tour. Just two days after visiting Strohmeyer's *Wurst* works, it had completed his picture of the city's meat industry, animal to sausage.

Viehof director Gruber himself had met him at the station in a shiny Daimler, confessing his admiration for the criminal police and a hopeless addiction to detective novels. It was a usual enough tactic to try to sweet-talk Kripo agents who were poking around your back-yard, Willi knew. But Gruber had laid it on thick. "You boys at the Alex are the best." He'd pumped Willi's hand as if he were meeting a movie star. "And we at the *Viehof*—not so very different, if I may sing our own praises. Healthy meat's no more a luxury these days than law and order, don't you agree? We all labor for the public good."

An elephantine man with a thin mustache, he oozed professional pride.

"Before 1882," he proclaimed as they were chauffeured down El-denaer Strasse toward the *Viehof* entrance, "anyone could butcher animals wherever they wanted to in Berlin. Quite a mess, actually. Then everything was brought here, into one municipally run facil-ity. Today we have nearly eleven hundred operators, large and small, leasing space under our rules and supervision. A most propitious arrangement."

Past the main gates, the avenues, filled with trucks and carts and horse-drawn wagons, were lined with handsome buildings in tradi-tional North German brickwork, from deep reds to honey golds. Gruber pointed out the administrative center, the telegraph offices, the archives, the commodities exchange, the veterinary labs. There were cafeteria-style restaurants, coffeehouses, beer halls. Stores sell-ing every sort of supply from cleavers and hooks to hip boots and aprons. Even a kiosk of Loeser & Wolff, Berlin's best-known tobac-conists, if Willi cared for a cigar.

"We have fifty-seven buildings on a hundred and twenty acres. Fifteen miles of paved streets. Five thousand people who earn their daily bread here. The *Viehof* itself employs veterinarians, meat inspectors, sample takers, even our own fire department."

On the east side were the stockyards and sales halls. On the west, the slaughterhouses and by-product installations. Joining the two, a series of tunnels enabling livestock to be herded from one to the other. It was Wednesday, market day, so Gruber suggested they stop by and see how it all worked.

The glass-roofed cattle market was so enormous Willi had barely been able to see the other end, and so loud he couldn't hear himself think. Endless rows of corrals were filled with countless varieties of steer, and an equal number of men in hats and overcoats screaming offers and counteroffers. Gruber'd pointed out how the butchers' agents examined the gaze, the mouths, even the breaths of the livestock they were interested in. A healthy cow had bright eyes, a moist nose, easy breathing. A sick one had crusty nostrils, heavy eyes, a hanging tongue. The moment a sick beast was detected, it was sent to a special quarantine ward. Executed. Sterilized. Sold to the poor as *Freibank*. But few sick ones ever made it this far, Gruber assiduously assured.

Like everyone on this case, the *Viehof* Direktor had been trying to convince Willi the *Listeria* outbreak could not possibly have originated here—an entirely understandable impulse.

"Our animals arrive from all over Europe. Veterinary and meat inspections are an integral aspect of our work. Before any livestock ever reaches the stables, much less the trading floors, every animal is inspected at the ramp. Come, I'll show you."

He'd taken Willi to the *Entladenbahnhof*, the enormous rail station inside the *Viehof* linked directly to the *Ringbahn*, the system of rails encircling Berlin. Here, arriving tracks branched into multiple ramps, each capable of unloading a twenty-wagon freight train. A separate disinfection ramp contained a facility capable of cleaning empty train cars at a rate of fifty per hour. When it functioned as designed, the process went like clockwork, Gruber boasted.

The shrill shriek of a steam whistle turned their heads in unison. A giant black locomotive was pulling in with its load.

"I wish I could say I arranged it for you, Herr Sergeant. But these transports arrive with frequent regularity. Now you can see the whole show."

The train of twenty wooden freight cars rumbled up, originating, Willi saw, from a town in Poland. The journey, Gruber told him, had taken eleven hours. An ear-piercing screech of brakes brought the whole thing to halt. Jumping from the locomotive, the conductor looked down the length of the train, and when teams of attendants were ready by each wagon, he blew a whistle. Simultaneously all twenty sealed doors were flung open, and like a dam burst, a flood of pink pigs poured from each car, squealing, snorting, screaming, grunting, driven by men with sticks. Channeled down ramps into single files, they were met by teams of veterinary police in long canvas smocks. Before they were allowed into a holding pen, each creature had to pass muster. Most made it inside, awaiting further herding to the stockyards and market day. The few who did not were driven down a ramp directly to oblivion. In either case their fate was sealed. Once they arrived, Gruber had chuckled, the only way an animal ever left the *Viehof* was in quarters, hinds, or cutlets.

They'd driven through a gate to the western zone, down avenues lined with giant redbrick structures, each several football fields long with towering smokestacks at the end. They might have been factories, machine shops, or tool sheds. But these, Gruber explained, were the slaughterhouses. Seven of them, processing eight thousand animals per day. Nearly 3 million per year. The shiny black Daimler halted.

Blocking the road in front of them, a herd of sheep had emerged from a tunnel fresh from the market halls. Baying and bleating by the hundreds, they were driven by men with sticks up numbered ramps—26, 27, 28—into the nearest brick building and forced one by one through swinging doors.

"Care to see how it's done?" Gruber'd asked.

Willi looked at the fleecy, white bodies pushing up against each other as they pressed inside. A man wearing hip boots and a long, white apron was standing at the door smoking. His apron, Willi saw, was splattered with blood. He shook his head no thanks. He didn't need to see. But for a guy who'd killed his fair share of humans, it was kind of embarrassing.

Gruber just smiled. "Most visitors don't want to. I understand. I assure you, though, it's as humane as we can make it. Basically, the animals never know what hits them. They're isolated by sliding grates. Immobilized, stunned, suspended, bled from the throat. Then they're flayed, scraped, gutted, hacked. Conveyed by overhead carriers to the cold chambers. Once there, each carcass is inspected for parasites and other signs of disease. Then they're divided into meat and nonmeat parts. That's one of the cold-chamber buildings there." Gruber pointed to a massive windowless structure down the road.

"The temperature never rises above thirty-five degrees. Butchers rent separate areas and draw on supplies as business requires. After leaving the *Viehof,* the better meats go to the wholesale market across Landsberger Allee, where they're purchased by dealers who ship them to the Central Market at Alexanderplatz or directly to retail shops. Beef, generally, is sold by the side. Pigs, sheep, calves, usually are transported as whole carcasses to be made into sausages, hams, or cold cuts in private shops."

"What's that?" Willi'd asked of the hexagonal tower rising seven or eight stories like a medieval castle.

"The old water tower. No longer in use. Kind of creepy, huh?" Gruber'd laughed. "Maybe we should rent it out for one of those vampire movies. The modern one's over there, above the engine house. Five forty-eight-horsepower engines feed the whole hydraulic system. Naturally, we're stricter than the army about cleanliness. All our facilities, slaughter, storage, stockyards, are equipped not only with excellent ventilation and light, but plentiful water at maximum pressure. Everything has to be constantly hosed down. Even the floors here have gutters so that drainage can be discharged."

"Drainage?" Willi felt a strange tingle. "Where does it go, all that runoff?"

Gruber seemed to find the question off point. "The sewer lines, naturally." He fingered his mustache. "Come let me show you one of our most interesting sectors: the by-product zone."

Around a bend in the road, in the southernmost part of the *Viehof*, were dozens of businesses specializing in making things out of nonmeat animal parts. Everything but the excrement, Gruber had assured, was collected and utilized. Stomachs, lungs, spleens, kidneys, livers, brains, fatty tissue, hooves, hides, bristles, glands . . .

"Here we have a whole street of firms that specialize in laundering tripe for sausage casing—so necessary to the process, as you no doubt already saw at your visit to Strohmeyer's. Over there, a whole block filled with nothing but little shops that melt fats into tallow, for candles and wax."

The stench was remarkable. The heavy, oily fumes pouring out of some of these places were among the most offensive Willi'd ever encountered. Even on the battlefield.

"That street there is full of tanneries, where hides are worked into leather. And the little alley there has companies that sterilize bristles, for the brush-making industry. That particularly piquant aroma you've no doubt noticed is from way down there, the glue factories. And a bit further, the blood works. And further still, the bone boilers."

Bone boilers? The word sent another strange tingle through Willi.

"Come now, Sergeant, don't act so surprised. The use of bone grease is as old as civilization. Poor man's butter. Be thankful if you've never had to use it. Plenty in this city do. And marrow, well, I don't have to tell you . . . delicious with shallots and wild mushrooms, or grilled with herbs and spread on toast."

Now, on his second visit, no one came to greet him.

Willi had to walk the long bridge across the tracks from the S-Bahn station into the frigid wind alone, the gray sky ahead smudged with sludge from the slaughterhouse smokestacks. At least, he thought, the source of bacteria had been found. Fifteen dead. Fifteen hundred sickened. Heads were sure to roll.

Passing the main gates and into the *Viehof*, though, it wasn't *Listeria* but drainpipes and bone boilers floating through his brain. Could there be a link between this place and that burlap sack? The construction site where it'd turned up was less than a mile away.

The news conference was in the Commodities Exchange building, upstairs in the dining room, a giant feudal-styled "great hall" with Gothic arches and flying buttresses, packed now with hundreds of reporters. Willi recognized several who'd interviewed him back in the days when he was actually working murder cases—Lauterbach from the *Morgenpost,* Woerner from *Abend Zeitung.* On a dais up front the *Viehof*'s ten-man board of directors sat facing the crowd, the elephantine figure of Herr Direktor Gruber unmistakable among them. Eventually he leaned to the microphone, speaking with all the flourish he'd shown to Willi that day in the Daimler.

"*Guten Morgen,* all of you. Thank you for coming out. It's a most auspicious occasion. At last we can announce with confidence that this difficult time—this citywide nightmare—is over. Our meat supply is safe. Let us offer a prayer of thanks." He bowed his large head, then lifted it after several seconds, stroking his waxed mustache. "Following the news conference, the board of directors will celebrate with a meal of fresh sausage and beer. We'd like all of you to join us."

No apologies? Willi wondered. No admission of guilt?

"First off, let me introduce the head of the investigation on the part of the Ministry of Public Health." Gruber stepped aside.

As Frau Doktor Riegler took her place in front of the microphones, she looked pale, Willi thought. Not happy as she ought to be.

"The presence of *Listeria*—" The loudspeakers screeched as she spoke too near the microphone, causing everyone to cringe. "Sorry. Pardon me." She cleared her throat. Her cheek, Willi noticed, was twitching again. "The presence of *Listeria monocytogenes* was confirmed yesterday in a section of Slaughterhouse Seven under long-term lease by the firm Kleist-Rosenthaler, a major supplier of trimmings to the factories where tainted sausages were produced. Prior testing failed to show positive results because of the strenuous disinfection efforts undertaken by the firm after the *Listeria* infection was first announced, in compliance with directives by the *Central-Viehof.* Our investigations show no prior knowledge on the part of any Kleist-Rosenthaler employees, no breach of regulations. No efforts at a cover-up. Simply a random and thankfully very rare occurrence."

Riegler's face, Willi saw, was twitching like a firecracker.

"Lady Doktor's certainly basking in her glory."

Willi turned to see Heilbutt next to him, an investigator for the Ministry of Public Health, who headed up their lab work. He'd encountered the crusty old goat a number of times in the field. A real relic from the Kaiser Reich, nearing retirement, he was a stickler for protocol and meticulousness, completely contemptuous of his boss, whom he referred to only in a mock Russian accent as Lady Doktor, as if female physicians were synonymous with Bolshevism. When her speech turned to thanking the *Viehof* directors for their limitless cooperation, he shot Willi a real fish-eye.

"Smell that stink?"

Willi smiled, figuring the old geezer was simply casting aspersions on Lady Doktor's diplomatic niceties, which was understandable. A lot of people had died. Where was the finger of blame here? A glint in Heilbutt's gaze, though, struck him far more darkly. What might he be suggesting? Willi wondered. Had pressure to end the crisis brought about too rapid a conclusion? A cover-up? Was that what Riegler'd meant before about "politics"?

"I'm surprised the *Listeria* turned up here at the *Viehof,*" Willi probed quietly. "I'd have put my money on a peddler."

Heilbutt's gaze narrowed. "They may not be so different, Detektiv," he grumbled from the side of his mouth. "A few years back, during the inflation, you wouldn't guess what kept popping up in sausages. Bow wow-wow. That's right. You never heard about it because no one got sick, so the powers that be kept a lid on it. But that's just what it was. Dog meat. And plenty of it. We never identified the source, but it sure as heck was right here in the *Viehof.* Ask Lady Doktor about that sometime."

Seven

"Go on, ask the saleslady," Willi urged, feeling Erich was old enough to learn the proper way to address a clerk.

"Excuse me, madam," Erich said.

Willi quickly saw there was nothing to worry about.

"Have you got a model Fokker Dr.1 triplane, in red, please, like Baron von Richthofen flew?"

The boy had his mother's savoir faire. Or at least, her skill in department stores.

Unfortunately, the saleswoman didn't display a comparable level of social aplomb. "There we go." She found the box and placed it on the counter. "A most beautiful craft. And so complex. Three wings. 'For boys twelve and up,'" she read.

"I'm not quite nine but I want to try."

"Really?" She shot Willi a glance. "And St. Nick lets you pick your own toy?"

"We don't believe in St. Nicholas, ma'am. We celebrate Hanukkah."

Her eyes narrowed. "Imagine that . . . a Jewish boy wanting the Red Baron's plane." She felt no compunction in declaring, "And your people against Germany in the war."

Erich frowned as if she were absurd. Willi was stunned not merely by her misinformation but by her utter gall.

"Go grab Stefan before he wanders off," he told his oldest boy, then turned to the saleswoman, flashing his veteran's badge. "Listen, lady. I happen to be a holder of the Iron Cross First Class. So unless you want to find yourself in hot water with the Veterans' Association, I'd suggest you can the commentary and wrap the kid's plane, huh?"

As she obeyed, red with embarrassment, he stood there fuming. How dare she? Jews had been in this country since Roman times, thriving in highly advanced communities along the Rhine—Worms, Mainz, Cologne—for a thousand years, until the hordes of the First Crusade swept in and burned the synagogues of Worms, Mainz, and Cologne—with all the congregants inside. After that, German Jews were forced to live in filthy ghettos, locked behind walls each night. For seven hundred years they were persecuted, tormented, expelled en masse by princely whim. Only during the Age of Enlightenment did the ghetto walls begin to crumble, slowly.

Not until 1871, when Germany finally united as a nation-state, were all restrictions on Jews' civil and political rights lifted. But legal emancipation did not end discrimination. Even today, in 1929, if not brick walls, then certainly glass ones separated most Germans from their Jewish neighbors. In plenty of areas, Jews dared not tread. Such as law enforcement. Out of several thousand employees at the Police Presidium, only a handful were Jewish. Even if one was Dr. Weiss, the deputy president. And though mob violence and government pogroms obviously were a thing of the past, there'd been flare-ups of nasty political anti-Semitism in Germany in Willi's lifetime.

"Thank you for shopping at Kaufhaus des Westens." The saleswoman passed them the gift-wrapped box without so much as a smile.

Willi nudged Erich to thank her, and they headed down the escalator.

After the defeat of 1918, a number of far-right parties had propagated the idea that an international conspiracy of Jews had "stabbed the fatherland in the back." The Centralverein, the main union of German Jews, fought back with a vigorous counteroffensive, making it known that one hundred thousand soldiers of the Jewish faith had served in the kaiser's armies, and that nearly twelve thousand had fallen—startling percentages considering less than half a million Jews even lived in the country. Willi was enlisted as a sort of poster boy, presented at gatherings in uniform and medal, his story put out in national publications. He hadn't particularly cared for the attention. But after all, how else had he won Vicki's hand? When wooing a beautiful woman of means, having your nation's highest medal of honor doesn't hurt. A full decade on, though, he'd hoped such myths as Jewish antipatriotism would have faded away. The saleswoman in KDW made it clear they hadn't. Not that it destroyed his faith in a slow but steady march of progress. He was still quite confident that tomorrow's Germany would be better for his sons than the one he'd grown up in.

Outside, big flakes of snow were tumbling onto busy Wittenbergplatz. By the time they boarded the tram home, it was coming down heavily. The kids, oblivious to their recent encounter with anti-Semitism, were thrilled at the unexpected development. "Let's make a snowman in the courtyard with Heinzie!" Erich clutched his gift box. Stefan wiggled excitedly on Willi's lap. As they rattled around the Kaiser Wilhelm Church, little by little the sidewalks turned white.

On a newspaper across from him, Willi noticed that the firm of Kleist-Rosenthaler had announced it was closing. Hardly surprising. No criminal charges had been filed yet. His report wasn't even due until after the holidays, and he still had questions, especially after Heilbutt's insinuations. Then the Homicide Commission still had to make a recommendation. And ultimately, it was up to the district attorney's office. But with so many dead and sickened, no one in his right mind would do business with that company. Stroh-meyer A.G., Fine *Wurst* Since 1892, would likely be next. Mean-while, the criminal process would go on for God knew how long, tying him up for the duration.

Willi sighed. Far down the Ku'damm he caught sight of the giant radio tower over Wilmersdorf, casting a lonely light through the snow. He hadn't felt this bored, this frustrated at work, for a long time, he realized. Since joining the force. Perhaps that's why he was doing what he was . . . trespassing again on Freksa's case. Tonight. After dinner. Just a little reconnaissance. He'd noticed this afternoon that Freksa hadn't displayed his usual braggadocio at the unit lunch meeting. Too quiet, withdrawn almost. Clearly the star wasn't getting far with the Lichtenberg bone investigation. He was starting to get nervous about it. Willi could tell. But the Kommissar, observing his keen interest in the case, pulled him aside afterward.

"Don't even dream about getting back in on this, Kraus. Freksa's doing just fine."

At home on Beckmann Strasse after dinner, when the courtyard was covered enough for the boys to go out and build their snowman, Willi and Vicki enjoyed a quiet coffee in the dining room. In her short dress, short hair, and dangling earrings, the matching bracelets clinking as she lifted the cup to her lips, Vicki was so graceful. Willi thought she ought to be on a billboard in Potsdamer Platz advertising silk stockings or some glamorous getaway. That she was so natural in her elegance only enhanced it in his eyes.

"I know, I know"—she was trying to preempt him—"you crossed no-man's-land half a dozen times, Willi. Spent weeks behind enemy lines. But honestly, a spiritualist mission?"

She swept the dark bangs from her brow, scowling as she often did when confronted with the more frontline aspects of his job, as if to say, *Maybe it would have been better had you gone into my fa-ther's business.*

Which they both knew was nonsense. She'd never have married him.

"I'm not joining it, darling." He'd softened up Braunschweig's description, naturally. He wasn't going to tell her it was a "satanic love cult." Leaning across the table he inserted his tongue between her lips a bit. "Just snooping around."

But he knew she wouldn't like it one little bit if she ever found out what he was really up to. More than once she'd made abundantly clear she could close her eyes to the dangers of his career as long as he never put the children in harm's way. Now suddenly, he was poking about after a child killer.

It was still snowing when he climbed from the U-Bahn station at Uhland Strasse an hour later, sanitation workers in brown uniforms sweeping the sidewalks with huge brooms. On the Ku'damm crowds jostled under umbrellas, the store lights and cinema marquees flashing hypnotic rhythms against the falling flakes.

Bleibtreu Strasse 143 proved to be a Jugendstil mansion, with marble steps leading to a portico held aloft by naked nymphs. Over their heads a shiny brass sign read DIVINE RADIANCE MISSION. It was dark as hell inside. Not a light on. How disappointing. His imagination had been on overdrive since Braunschweig first described this place. Now what?

He took the steps two at a time.

On either side of the front door were small opera windows with half-open curtains. No hours posted. No phone number. Checking over his shoulder, he reached into his pocket and pulled out a flashlight.

Through the window, a handsome foyer decorated with exotic-looking urns, candelabra, a shelf full of crystals. Like a fancy palm reader's. On one wall, a large, framed oil painting in a shimmering-gold art nouveau style: boys and girls dancing in a circle—naked. LET US BE REBORN INTO A STATE OF PARADISIACAL INNOCENCE written across the top. Willi stared, then switched off the flashlight. Given the penchant for mysticism in Berlin these days, it seemed rather tame. Respectable even. Short of breaking in, there really wasn't much he could do.

Thwarted, angry, he turned to leave.

On the far side of the street, though, a small red light twinkling through the snowflakes lured his attention. Squinting, he made out a sign above a shop window: DIVINE RADIANCE BOUTIQUE.

His mood lifted.

The smell of incense nearly knocked him out when he entered. The small shop was crowded with candles, pendants, charms, potions, all, Willi rapidly ascertained, for the casting of spells. A Victrola behind the counter was pounding a tango. Next to it, a pale young woman with an angular face and even more angular haircut dyed a preposterous red ignored Willi as he perused the merchandise. Stimulation Spray . . . Potency Powder . . . Fall in Love Flakes . . . Fall out of Love Flakes . . . Revenge Dust. Two other customers, a husband and wife from the looks of it—she in a stylish fox coat—were on their way out.

"*Wiedersehen*, Brigitta. See you at Saturnalia." They squeezed past Willi, bundling up against the storm. Once they were gone, this Brigitta stuck a monocle in her eye and examined him as if he were an odd little insect that'd blown in.

"*Ja?*" She squinted through the lens.

In a man's suit—trousers, vest, a bow tie—she exuded such a sour demeanor Willi wondered if she'd ever smiled since childhood.

"Might I inquire if you have anything to make your wife trust you?" He tried to lighten the mood.

It didn't work.

"We have potency powder, if that's what you're referring to." She frowned, attacking the counter with a feather duster.

"No need for that. Something more tranquilizing, maybe. Like bubble bath." He smiled. She didn't smile back. "Say, this shop wouldn't be connected to that handsome little church across street, would it?" He decided not to toy with this one.

Her harsh expression turned almost sadistic.

"I wouldn't call it a church. But, *ja.*" She scowled. "We're connected, you could say. One and the same."

"I was just curious about the mission. Been on a sort of spiritual quest myself, you see, and—"

"What exactly is it you wish to know, *mein Herr*?" The chapped lips twitched as she adjusted her monocle, pausing to examine him.

Willi saw he needed to play orthodontist here, really pull some teeth.

"For instance, when is it open?"

"Why do you wish to know that?"

"I'm curious to learn more about it."

"About what exactly, as I already inquired."

"Well, for instance . . . the philosophy. What exactly *is* Divine Radiance?"

"Ach so." She rolled her eyes, as if the very idea of having to communicate such ideas was exhausting. But, considering it some celestial duty apparently, with great effort she removed the monocle and let it dangle from a chain on her vest.

"Well . . ." She dug into a wooden box, returning with a cigar. Lighting it on a candle, she blew smoke at Willi. "Sexual desire, you probably don't realize"—she scrutinized his reaction—"is linked with electromagnetic radiation emanating from the sun. *Ja*. When properly aligned through devotional prayer, the gratification of such desire can become . . . sacred. For us, sex is not merely a pleasurable pursuit but a ritual sacrament through which we achieve union with the All."

She waited for his response.

"Well . . . er . . . great." Willi nodded. "Who wouldn't be for that?"

He'd read recently in a magazine that nearly a quarter of Berliners were involved in a mystery sect of one sort or another—a media exaggeration, no doubt. But despite eleven hundred years of Christianity, occult and pagan roots went deep in this country, he knew. To this day grandmas in villages still placed dried animal penises under grandsons' beds to ensure fertility. Walpurgis Night was still celebrated with dancing around bonfires and straw effigies. All the big cities still had covens of sorcerers and sibyls and God knew how many "mystical" cults with mass followings. Nudists. Naturalists. Sex magicians. Devil worshippers. Even among Christians, millions of Germans belonged to nonconformist sects, many of which had their own insignia, rites, uniforms, cuisines.

"I'd love to learn more. Might I attend one of your ceremonies?"

"Not unless you're invited by a member. Interviewed by us first."

"I see. Well, can you tell me . . . who is your leader?"

Brigitta spit tobacco from her lips. "What about her?"

"Oh," he mumbled. "Is it a her?"

She put down her cigar, planted her palms on the counter, and leaned right up to Willi's face, scrutinizing it again through the monocle.

"You wouldn't happen to be a private eye, would you?"

Willi leaned back. "Why ask such a thing?"

"I'll tell you why. Because that sick bastard Braunschweig sends every dick he can grab by the balls over here to try and sniff up Helga's ass. So if you are, mister, then listen close." She crushed out her cigar. "Helga left that crazy drunk years ago. During the war, that's how long. Got that? And now she's spoken for. You got that? So keep your grubby dick paws off."

Eight

The holidays arrived. Willi's grandmother's menorah, made in Frankfurt in 1694, cast its merry glow across the living room. The family sang the traditional songs, spun the dreidel. Stefan, miraculously, won all the chocolate money. The saleswoman at KDW may have been an anti-Semite, but she was right about assembling Erich's model plane: the Fokker *Dreidecker* was no child's play. Three cantilevered wings supported by struts, a silk skin stretched across a webbed aluminum frame, brass, leather, and wood parts all requiring delicate finger work. Willi wasn't sure how much patience he'd have. Perhaps he shouldn't have let Erich choose it.

No less vexing those last days of the year were the hurdles at work.

Helga Braunschweig and her Divine Radiance Mission remained out of reach. Neither the center nor its boutique had listed telephone numbers, and the two times Willi managed to get up to Bleibtreu Strasse, both were closed.

Christmas week government offices closed, then reopened for a day and a half on Monday, December 30, when, first thing, Willi paid the Ministry of Public Health a visit. The long mazes of halls there were all but empty. Everyone still on holidays. Well deserved, it would seem, given the hard-won victory over *Listeria*. Frau Doktor Riegler was nowhere to be found. But Heilbutt was. When Willi approached him in the lab, though, the old codger turned off faster than a Bunsen burner. Pretended not to remember a thing he'd said at the *Viehof* press conference.

"One of us must have been drunk, Detektiv." He kept his eyes fixed to a microscope, refusing to even look at Willi.

Clearly someone had put the clamps on him, Willi saw. Not that he blamed the fellow. No one wanted a wrecked career.

But it got him angry.

"You told me to ask Riegler about dog meat in sausages, Heilbutt. Well, let me assure you, as soon as I see her, I'm going to do just that."

Heilbutt cast him a fast glance. "I'll be fascinated to hear Lady Doktor's reply, Sergeant."

The last day of the 1920s you could practically feel craziness in the air.

Firecrackers began going off at dawn, exploding even in the streetcar during the morning commute. By the time he reached Alexanderplatz, Willi felt as if his brain were detonating. Then who pops out from beneath the awning of Aschinger's Restaurant but Braunschweig.

"Kraus!" He grabbed Willi's collar. "God must have put you in my path." The reverend's gray eyebrows knit with frenetic hope. "Did you follow up on Helga?" When he learned Willi'd paid a visit to Bleibtreu Strasse, he refused to let him go. "Then it is providence! Come, we'll talk over coffee."

"Coffee," of course, meant schnapps at a nearby *Kneipe*.

"Oh, that dyke," Braunschweig sneered when Willi described the encounter with Brigitta. "No depths to which Helga hasn't sunk since Satan got her." The reverend downed his glass with a flick of the wrist. "I don't suppose you found out about the top-hat funding the whole sick operation?"

"The top what?" Willi had real coffee.

"Some rich pimp." The reverend wiped his mouth with the back of his hand. "Who do you think set her up in that mansion? You don't think she earned it banging a tambourine?" He stared bitterly, allowing the full tragedy of his implication to sink in. "I don't know anything more about the serpent. She was smart enough to keep it all from me."

And from Brigitta, apparently, Willi was thinking.

"I don't suppose the dyke mentioned her predecessor, either, that other crazy redheaded bitch? Waiter—another schnapps here. The Shepherdess or whatever they called her. Used to bring them goats and God knew what, for rituals. Oh, yes, Kraus, animal sacrifice. And I'm not just talking one or two. From what I hear, it's a regular slaughterhouse over there."

Braunschweig was on his third "coffee" by the time he got around to the Saturnalia Willi'd heard mentioned that night.

"Naturally it's all secondhand." The reverend checked over his shoulder. "But it's basically a Roman orgy mixed"—his voice plummeted to barely a whisper—"with the most heinous satanic ritual. Oh, yes. Their wine is made of urine spiked with hallucinogenic drugs. Their wafer—feces, menstrual blood, and sperm. That's their Eucharist. Instead of Holy Communion they kiss Lucifer's ass."

Willi leaned away, trying to look horrified. He didn't know who was crazier: Braunschweig or Brigitta.

"But don't you worry, I'll find a way to get you in." The reverend nodded with a fiendish grin. "If you're serious, Kraus."

The man was totally sloshed at 9:00 a.m. Spewing insanity. But in this game, Willi understood, you played whatever cards you were dealt.

"Oh, I'm definitely serious, Reverend. Get me in."

Minutes later, riding the rickety elevator up at the Police Presidium, Willi heard whispers that really made his neck crawl. Bones in a city park. Somewhere in Lichtenberg. His face went instantly hot. My God. He knew there'd be more.

Freksa was addressing reporters at ten.

Willi made sure to be there.

The pressroom was packed. From behind a dozen tripods, photographers were setting off a tempest of flashbulbs. On a canvas tarp below the speaker's podium were neatly sorted piles of femurs, fibulae, tibiae, clavicles, ribs—not fashioned into designs like the first batch, just stacked, like cords of wood. From the burlap bags laid out beside them, though, Willi hadn't a doubt: Schnitzler and Son. Plus they were small bones. Clean. White. Boiled.

A lot of them.

When Freksa stepped up, the storm of flashbulbs was aimed at him. Even at murder sites, Kripo's tall, blond star never hesitated to smile for cameras. Not today. As he stood before the microphones, back straight, chest out, anyone who knew him knew that Hans Freksa sounded grim.

"Three burlap sacks"—his voice was without the élan it usually exuded to the press—"were found in storm drains out near the Frankfurter Allee S-Bahn station. We believe they're from the same source as a similar find last autumn at a nearby construction site. Pathologists have confirmed the remains inside are all children's bones. Boys." He paused and looked around the room, skipping over Willi. "A total of twenty-three."

An audible gasp filled the air, Willi joining.

"Unfortunately, we have no leads regarding a perpetrator. So we're asking for the public's help. Anyone with any information must step forward." Freksa's blue eyes stared unblinking into the flashing lights. "Gentlemen of the press—there's just no way to sweeten it up. One of the most fantastic mass murderers in German history is on the loose in Berlin. And we don't know a thing about him."

Which wasn't true, Willi thought. We know several things.

We know he's able to turn human muscle into thread—hardly a common skill. We also know he feels some relation to the biblical phrase *children of wrath,* associated with an obscure doctrine called Total Depravity. Based on the fastidious manner in which the first bones were bound, we can safely speculate he's driven to remedy some kind of psychological chaos through compulsive organizing.

Willi swallowed.

Did Freksa not realize these things? Or was he using a game plan Willi couldn't comprehend? The man had just laid his career on the line, saying he had nothing to rely on other than the public. A seemingly humble, maybe even admirable gesture. But why then omit key details the public needed if it was truly supposed to help? Such as that the bones had all been boiled. Twenty-three boys, for God's sake.

Somebody must have smelled it.

Even before the news conference ended, Willi was out the door.

It was a cold, sunny day, people already walking around in funny hats, blowing party horns. He didn't wait for the streetcar but took a taxi directly to Berlin Municipal Waterworks, where his Kripo badge gained him access to the map room.

He gave himself a quick tutorial. Berlin was divided into twelve drainage areas laid out on a radial system. Sewage was pumped through concrete pipes into treatment plants before being released into one of the rivers, shipping channels, or lakes that surrounded the city. Rainwater was collected in a vast system of brick tunnels called canals and drained into the same waterways. Tracing his finger south along the storm canal that ran under the S-Bahn station at Frankfurter Allee, where these new bones had been found— *Sturmwasser Kanal Fünf*—he could see it emptied into the Rummelsburger See and from there into the Spree River. Tracing it north, his heart rate quickened. It ran directly under the construction site where the first bag of bones had washed up. The farther north his finger ran, the faster his heart beat. Until he broke into a cold sweat.

Sturmwasser Kanal Fünf, he realized, originated under the *Central-Viehof.*

He grabbed a taxi back to the Police Presidium and hurried up to Freksa's office.

The door was open but he paused outside.

Someone was in there with Freksa.

"All our units will be alerted. If we can't find him, nobody can. The important thing, Freksa, is that one way or another we've got to parlay this into an ideological victory. Remember that."

"Yes, sir," Willi heard Freksa reply. And then Willi thought he heard him call the man Herr Region-Leader.

Out the door came a dwarfish figure lost under a fedora and trench coat. Despite a badly deformed foot, he limped past Willi briskly with a quick sideswipe of his fierce black eyes. Willi was confused. Who was this guy? Was Freksa taking orders from him?

Knocking, he entered his collegeaue's office, addressing him formally although they were the same rank. "Pardon me, Herr Sergeant-Detektiv."

Freksa looked genuinely shocked. Darting his blue eyes out the door, he appeared to fear the little trench coat might return and find Willi there. "Are you insane?"

"I have a lead. An important one."

"Oh, yeah, Bible stories. Thanks but no thanks."

"I thought you needed leads, Freksa. Have you traced the storm canal? The two sites are connected. And the line originates up at the—"

"Listen, Kraus, when I need your help, I'll ask for it."

Willi noticed a small pin emblazoned with a twisted black cross on Freksa's lapel. Since when was it permissible for officers to wear such emblems, spiritual, political, whatever, at work?

"No, you listen to me, Freksa," Willi fired back before retreating. "Follow that canal—all the way to the *Viehof. Sturmwasser Kanal Fünf.*"

By midafternoon, the news was on the lips of every Berliner:

Homicidal maniac on the loose. Mass killer. Child murderer!

By late afternoon, the papers were competing to outdo each other with new details, hideous and almost entirely fictitious, about how the bones had been chewed, roasted, burned, charbroiled. So that with the last light of 1929 the Child Murderer was put to sleep. And to haunt Berliners into the new decade, when the first evening editions appeared, an even more ominous bogeyman was born:

Der Kinderfresser. The Child-Eater.

Naturally he turned up at the Gottmans' New Year's Eve party.

"We know you can't reveal secrets, but is it really all the papers are saying?" Vicki's sister, Ava, a twenty-two-year-old university student, pressed. With her high cheekbones and long neck, her sparkly chestnut-colored eyes, she was almost as pretty as Vicki and every bit as sharp.

"Maybe not *all*," Willi teased.

Despite the newspapers' "inside" scoops, he knew from off-the-record talks with Dr. Hoffnung, for instance, that while the bones had been boiled, no direct indication existed of actual cannibalism. Still, questions completely outnumbered answers at this point, and Willi could only hope Freksa'd follow through on that damned storm canal. It might not tell them who or why but at least, perhaps, where.

"One can't help but wonder who these children *are*." Bette Gottman, Vicki's mother, toyed with her colored beads. She was especially stylish tonight, in a shiny black dress edged with fringe. "Where are their parents? Why hasn't anyone come forth to claim their remains?"

"There are so many homeless kids in Berlin, Mother," Ava said.

She was highly stylish too tonight, her freshly bobbed hair short in the back and hanging over one eye. The Gottman women were seamlessly fashionable. Willi had a sister every bit as pretty, he thought, but far more concerned with politics than clothes. Perhaps it wasn't surprising Greta'd joined a Zionist youth movement and emigrated to work on a dairy farm in Palestine. Four years ago now.

"I see these poor kids every day on my way to classes." Ava pushed the hair from her eye. "They wander over from the Alex or God knows where, sit around Unter den Linden under the trees smoking cigarettes, some no more than Erich's age. It's heartbreaking."

Bette wrung her hands dramatically, turning to Vicki. "Maybe Stefan and Erich ought to stay with us until they catch this madman." Bette had been an actress in her youth and, in Willi's opinion, never entirely abandoned the stage.

"Mother," Vicki said. "Don't be silly. They have school."

Not that the kids would mind being out here, Willi mused. Vicki's parents lived in a beautiful house in suburban Dahlem, with a huge garden out back, a veritable forest all around, and two golden retrievers the boys could never get enough of—Mitzi and Fritzi. Max Gottman had made a great deal of money in the lingerie business. If Vicki had married the kind of man her mother preferred— one of the scions of Berlin's Jewish dynasties, a department store heir such as Wertheim or Tietz, or a publishing magnate, Ulstein or Mosse—she could have lived a lot better than in a two-bedroom apartment on Prussian Park. But Vicki had wanted Willi. And Bette Gottman could not complain that her eldest daughter was unhappy.

"Well, thank goodness your husband isn't assigned to the case." Bette readjusted her beads. "How awful. A child killer."

"Willi has nothing to do with it." Vicki looked at her mother as if she was becoming annoying, then shot Willi a weary eye roll as if exhausted by the melodramatics.

Willi, with a handful of peanuts in his mouth, sank back in his chair slightly, glad he didn't have to respond. He'd never told Vicki about that day Freksa stole the case from him because he didn't like complaining about the indignities he suffered on his job, even though he could have used her comfort. Now he wasn't exactly sorry he'd kept it a secret.

"Besides," Vicki went on, explaining to her mother, "the police assign these things very carefully. Detektiv Freksa's a bachelor. Nobody has to worry about him, and he doesn't have to worry about anyone else." She took a rather long sip of champagne.

"He still has a mother, doesn't he?" Bette Gottman sighed. "Anyway," she said, making a conspicuous effort to change subjects, "have you seen the Paris previews?" She yanked a magazine off the coffee table and showed it to her daughters. "Hemlines are dropping lower than stocks."

Beneath her dark bangs, Vicki's eyes winced as she scanned the illustrations. "I can't believe it."

"Three inches below the knee." Her sister scowled. "Maybe there'll be a big revolt and no one will wear them."

"I wouldn't count on it," her mother advised. "They're calling it the New Femininity."

"New? It's like they're turning back the hands of time."

"They'll succeed too. Mark my words—the days of the knee are *finis*, my dears."

"The days of a lot of things are *finis*," Max added gloomily. "It's the end of an era."

"You really think so?" Vicki squeezed his shoulder.

"I wish I could say it wasn't." He patted her hand. "But I've never seen anything like what's going on now."

The lingerie magnate's eyes skipped out the window to the horizon, it seemed, and over a precipice no one else could quite fathom.

"Maybe because things were so damned good these last few years," he said as one of the retrievers nudged him for affection. "Like we'd reached a plateau—stability, progress." Gottman absently scratched Mitzi's neck. "Now, the loss of confidence is so total." The dog panted happily. "Everyone's panicking. Hoarding. Too afraid to spend a dime. Prices are collapsing. Bankruptcies snowballing. It's really . . . calamitous."

They all sat still, not sure what to say.

"Really, Max, I've never heard you so glum." Bette straightened on the couch, fidgeting with her beads. "After all we've been through. Whatever lies ahead, we'll weather it as we always have, as a family, heads held high."

"Everybody," Erich called from the radio. "Chancellor's on."

"Chancellor! Chancellor!" Stefan jumped up and down.

They gathered around.

"My fellow Germans—"

Hermann Müller was giving his New Year's Eve address from the Reichs Chancellory. A Social Democrat, he headed the Grand Coalition of liberal and centrist parties that had seen the republic through its years of greatest growth and stability. October, however, had rained duel blows on his government. Foreign Minister Stresemann, winner of the 1926 Nobel Peace Prize for steering Germany into the League of Nations, had dropped dead at age fifty-one, leaving a major vacuum. And then the Wall Street crash. Müller was hardly an inspirational speaker, as Stresemann had been. But everyone leaned toward his voice.

"In his address from the White House tonight, American President Herbert Hoover has assured his people that the worst of the economic predicament is now behind us. That industrial output and world trade are positioned for a healthy rebound. I wish to assure our people likewise: Germany is poised for recovery."

Willi could see that Max wasn't buying it. But Bette paid him no attention.

"You see?" She opened her hands. "I say we have a toast! Willi, break out the champagne."

Willi obliged with a little bow and poured them all a round. Then he took the lead in raising his glass to a happy and healthy 1930.

Nine

The new decade did not bear good tidings.

On January 2, on an icy shore of the Spree near Treptow, a trio of children's leg bones washed up, bound together with an unnamed substance. Two days later, on the banks of Museum Island, right next to the National Gallery, a group of nuns stumbled upon a child's skull.

Berlin reeled in collective shock.

If tainted sausages had caused fear, *Der Kinderfresser* unleashed horror. From one end of the city to the other—the swankest neighborhoods off the Tiergarten to the poorest in Neukoln—parents put children on tethers. Schools ordered doors and windows bolted, guards at all entrances. Children could travel only in groups. Since Willi regularly walked his boys to school and Vicki walked them home again, they soon found themselves escorting a convoy that included not only Heinzie Winkelmann but half a dozen other kids from the block whose parents couldn't thank them enough.

The tension and stress were matched only by the wild speculation about who the bloodthirsty fiend could be. Neighbor looked upon neighbor askance, nobody above suspicion. With so few clues it could be anyone. And what about the boys? Why had no one reported them missing? Willi was sure his sister-in-law, Ava, had gotten it right: nobody reported them missing because nobody missed them. They had to be street kids, of which Berlin had no shortage. With the financial crisis, there were sure to be more. Whether Freksa was pursuing this angle, Willi had no way of knowing. And little time to find out, since he was still all tied up with *Listeria*. Kommissar Horthstaler, though, had gotten wind of the advice to Freksa about the storm canal and didn't like it one bit.

"I warned you to keep your big nose out of this, Kraus. I'm not warning you again."

Although Willi had begun to prepare his report, the case would be difficult to complete without Dr. Riegler, and Willi couldn't seem to find her. Hourly he phoned but got no answer. Heilbutt also didn't pick up. Several times he went to the ministry and had no luck there, either. After days of this, he lost his temper and stormed into the office of Riegler's superior, Dr. Knapp, insisting to know where Riegler and Heilbutt had vanished. The news was rather shocking: Riegler had been hospitalized, he was told. Werner had no idea where or why, only that he had received a phone call from her several days ago. She sounded quite ill and he didn't want to press her. He hadn't heard from her since. As for Herr Heilbutt, on December 31 he had retired. Was there anything else he, Dr. Knapp, could help the Sergeant-Detektiv with?

Willi was too perplexed to respond.

Outside, he put on his hat and looked down Wilhelm Strasse. All the granite ministry buildings were lined up as if on parade. The Foreign Ministry. The Finance Ministry. The Chancellory. The Presidential Palace. It didn't make sense. Werner didn't know which hospital she was in, or why.

Something really was fishy.

Part of him wanted to forget it, just do the best he could on the damn report and wash his hands of it. He never wanted to be on this case to begin with. Riegler's report had recommended no criminal charges be made. He should just follow her lead. Only he couldn't. He needed to find the Frau Doktor.

The dead demanded it.

Back at his office he called every medical center in Berlin. Riegler was not at any of them. Heilbutt was right, Willi realized, tilting backward in his chair. Something definitely stank here. And his suspicions about Riegler's cheek had been justified. That twitch was trying to tell him something. Only what?

First thing next morning he went back to the ministry, upstairs to the lab, and requested copies of the reports showing the presence of *Listeria* in Slaughterhouse Seven. The clerk came back half an hour later and said they weren't there.

"That's ridiculous." Willi had to contain himself. "They were only filed two weeks ago. This is a major criminal investigation."

He invited Willi to look for himself, which Willi did.

The lab reports had vanished.

Rushing downstairs to demand the truth from Knapp, he learned the senior administrator hadn't come to work today. His secretary refused to divulge information such as Dr. Riegler's home address even under pain of arrest. Willi was just in the mood to haul her down to the Alex too, when he flashed on a conversation he'd had with Riegler during the sausage ban—about how her cat missed her favorite bratwurst from Schlesinger's on Kant Strasse, around the corner from where she lived.

He dropped the secretary and hurried there.

The waiters knew exactly whom he was referring to, and the precise address—since the nice lady doctor often ordered food delivered up. It was a prestigious building with a doorman and concierge.

No, no, he was told, the Frau Doktor had not been seen for at least three days. Although someone thought she might have left her garbage out because there was a real—

Willi demanded to be taken up immediately.

The concierge fumbled to unlock her door. *"Mein Gott.* Such a nice lady. I hope she's all right."

When they stepped inside, though, the stench hit like a sledgehammer. Frau Doktor Riegler was about as all right as a three-day-old corpse could be. Stiff as a board. Purple-faced. Bloated. But peaceful in bed. Clutching a small glass vial stamped with a skull and crossbones. No note. Nothing. Just a hungry brown cat meowing on the windowsill. Willi stood there, overwhelmed with pity and then, gradually, anger. Surely it didn't have to happen this way.

Only one person, he figured, knew why it had.

Heilbutt's address was in the phone book, but he lived all the way out in God-knew-where. From the U-Bahn station Willi had to walk through a gale hunting for Heilbutt's street. The ferocious wind brought him back for a second to that desperate winter of 1917, in the trenches. It was worse then, naturally. He was younger, true, but he didn't know whether he'd be alive ten minutes later. Whereas now, he was pretty sure he'd find who he was looking for, get to the bottom of this, and survive.

Pounding on the buzzer marked HEILBUTT, though, nobody answered. The tips of his fingers were frozen numb. He hustled down the block to a tobacco shop. At least it was warm inside, but the guy had never heard of Heilbutt. And Willi had no photo. Not wanting to face the cold, he lingered, perusing the afternoon headlines: Hansa Auto laying off a third of its workforce . . . unemployment expected to spike . . . children reported missing across Berlin mostly turning up by the end of the day. He gulped down some heated air and forced himself back through the door.

Persistence, luckily, didn't take long to reward this time. Just across the street at Schmidt's Tonsorial Parlor, both the barber and his assistant claimed to know Heilbutt many years. They broke into an argument about where he'd said he was going.

"Bremen."

"Bremer*haven*."

"Perhaps Bremer*haven*, but on the *Bremen*."

"The *Bremen*?" Willi was trying to grasp this. "You mean, the ocean liner?"

"What other *Bremen* is there?" The barber looked at him. "Herr Heilbutt said it was costing him a fortune, but it was a once-in-a-lifetime thing, to visit his sister in America. So he'd cashed out on his pension and was happy to spend it."

"This was when?"

"The day before yesterday."

"No, it was Tuesday."

"That *was* the day before yesterday!"

Willi checked his watch: a quarter past four. It would take a miracle, he realized, but yanking his collar he hurried back out into the pelting wind, breathless by the time he made it back to the U-Bahn station. A train was just pulling in, and even with two transfers he managed to arrive at the passenger service desk of the Norddeutscher Lloyd Line on Unter den Linden with ten minutes to spare, where he got a bit of good news. If Heilbutt was leaving Germany on the *Bremen*, the man was still in the country, he was informed, because the ship wasn't sailing until tomorrow night. Unfortunately, they didn't have the passenger lists here. But they could call Bremerhaven.

"If you'd be so kind."

Willi waited.

"Are you positive? . . . H-e-i-l-b-u-t-t. . . . Okay, thank you. . . . Sorry, sir. No, it doesn't appear any Herr Heilbutt will be sailing with us tomorrow."

The man was scared, Willi realized. Whatever had driven Dr. Riegler to kill herself was causing Heilbutt to flee. He might easily be waiting to purchase a last-minute ticket so he couldn't be traced. Or even traveling under an assumed name, with false papers. It was a long shot. But in seven years Willi'd learned one thing: if anyone got the story straight from the horse's mouth, it was usually the barber.

Next morning he was out of Berlin on the eight o'clock train. The going proved painfully slow. Track work. Delays. Not until two did the giant Becks brewery pass outside the window, then another hour through redbrick suburbs to the mouth of the Weser River and one of Germany's great ports. Even as they pulled into the station, he could see the huge black-and-white superstructure towering over the berth across the road and the famed twin orange funnels of the SS *Bremen*.

Flagship of the Norddeutscher Lloyd Line, *Bremen* had ushered in a whole new era in ocean travel last year. Her sleek profile and slender smokestacks exemplified "streamlined" every bit as much as the Mercedes SSK. Her revolutionary bow, bulbing just below the waterline to reduce drag and increase speed, had proven a stunning success. On her maiden voyage in July she deposed the Cunard's famed *Mauretania*, crown-holder for twenty years, beating the old Brit by half a day to become the world's fastest ocean liner. On her return from New York, she broke the record again by another three hours, thrilling the whole of Germany.

At the pier, noisy crowds already bunched around the boarding ramps, the elegant ship scheduled to depart in less than three hours. There were mountains of luggage. Stevedores shouting. Children jumping. Willi wondered how he was going to find somebody in all this. Looking up at the graceful white bridge, he realized there was only one possibility: help from above.

His Kripo badge gained him access. From the first-class gangway he was taken directly to the chief purser, whom he soon enough learned was a big fan of the Berlin Kriminal Polizei. "The whole country applauds the victories of our capital's famed detectives," he informed Willi while thumbing through the passenger lists. "For instance, that fellow who chopped up his wife and shipped her to the department store where she owed all that money. Was that you who brought him in?"

"No," Willi answered. "My colleague Hans Freksa."

"*Ach ja,* Freksa! A real sleuthhound. The name *Heilbutt,* however, is not on my register, I'm afraid, Herr Sergeant-Detektiv."

Since Willi had no photo of him, the case was taken directly to the highest levels.

"Descriptions of the man will be sent to all officers at all ramps," the captain assured, even though the ship had of course been boarding for several hours now. Perhaps, Willi suggested, the best thing would be to observe things from right here. "Yes, with our new high-powered binoculars, the bridge will be the just the place for you to keep an eye on things."

It proved a spectacular perch. The whole ship, a quarter of a mile long, came into view. And all around, the great dockworks, steel cranes, and brick warehouses of Bremerhaven. The wide, green Weser estuary all the way to the sea. The sky so vast. So promising. The air so sweet. The whole panorama, it seemed, beckoning.

Willi was amazed by how powerful the binoculars were, far stronger than anything the Zeiss company had made during the war. And far lighter. He could see distinct expressions on couples strolling halfway down the ship on the forward promenade. The hand signals of sailors on the boat deck. What he wouldn't have given for these behind French lines. At the first-class gangway he spied the irritated scowl of a woman toting two Pekinese dogs and her husband. Further down in tourist—a well-scrubbed family excited to leave on holidays, the children hardly able to contain themselves. For an instant he fantasized about taking his family on a trip to America. How the kids would love it. How wonderful it would be sailing into New York harbor on a grand ship like this, past that lady lifting her lamp, Vicki on his arm.

They would do it someday. Soon.

He aimed at the third-class boarding desk. Several young people in worker's caps and kerchiefs were lugging heavy canvas bags, clutching tickets to what they no doubt hoped was a better tomorrow. For seventy-five years Bremerhaven had been one of the main ports of emigration to America, not only from Germany but all across Central Europe. Many millions of people had set off for the New World from here.

Heilbutt apparently intent on joining them.

Which class might he be traveling in? For a man of his rank, tourist would be logical. But the barber had specifically said Heilbutt mentioned it was costing a fortune, so maybe he'd splurged on a better ticket.

There was nothing to do but watch.

For the next two hours Willi stood on deck, scanning, scanning.

Evening fell. All along the hulk of the ship portholes illuminated, turning the water below shimmering silver. The cargo ramps were drawn in. A series of bells announced an hour left until departure. He grew uneasy. He couldn't stay on the bridge forever. It would be pure luck to spot Heilbutt at this point anyway, so he decided just to wander around and let fate take its course.

The ocean liner was huge. Magnificent. He passed luxurious dining rooms, card rooms, smoking lounges, and indoor pools, boutiques, and theaters. The long hallways were crowded with people coming in and out of staterooms, saying farewell to those not sailing. Everybody in the world seemed on board but Heilbutt. Finally uniformed stewards began walking about hitting three-tone xylophones announcing only twenty minutes until departure. All guests needed to head toward the exit ramps.

Which is when Willi spotted him.

Halfway down the hallway. There was no mistaking that ill-tempered face. Or the intense fear on it when he recognized Willi. He may have been over sixty, but with all the agililty of a mountain goat Heilbutt pivoted and disappeared down the third-class staircase.

He had a good head start. People trying to get off the ship obstructed Willi's progress. He had to make his way down narrow corridors filled with hippolike *hausfraus* and beer-bellied *burghers*, feeling more than one blow against his back as he pushed past. In the third-class reading room, he thought he caught sight of Heilbutt leaping from the rear door, but hall after hall, room after room, he couldn't find him again.

Finally, furious, he exited onto the third-class promenade deck and found himself staring at the tricolors of the republic on the stern flagpole, flapping in the wind. He'd reached the end of the ship. It was freezing out here. He could hear stewards calling the fifteen-minute warning. What to do? Go to the captain? Delay departure? Have everyone in third class paraded past him? Or let the old man flee in peace? Let whomever cover up whatever they were covering, and just go home to his wife and—

There he was.

Left of the flagpole. Willi'd cornered him. There was no way to get by and nowhere to go, except overboard. When Heilbutt realized this, he peered from the guardrail, then turned around ashen-faced, panting.

"Okay, so you got me. Proud, Kraus? A man twice your age. What are you gonna do now, toss me in?"

After the run the old fellow had given him from Berlin, Willi kind of felt like it.

It was a clear, cold night. Stars studded the sky. Somewhere up near the bow of the *Bremen,* bells were clanging.

"You know she took poison," Willi said furiously.

Heilbutt's head dropped.

"Three days before I found her. Not a word of explanation. Now, you are going to tell me why."

The older man clenched his eyes as if to make himself invisible—which Willi wanted him to understand was not possible. No more vanishing acts.

"Let's see your passport."

The eyes popped wide. "But I—"

"Passport! Passport!" Willi demanded.

The eyes darted as if Heilbutt was thinking maybe it was worth going over the side after all. So Willi yanked him away from the rail, stuck an arm in his coat, and just pulled the passport from his pocket.

A forgery.

"Joachim Baumeister. How interesting. I'd say you're in a pretty precarious situation here." Only feet away people were throwing streamers over the edge of the ship. "Fleeing the country under an assumed identity . . . evading an officer of the criminal police. My guess is you're looking at least, well, let's be honest, at your age, the rest of your life."

Heilbutt went white. "Can we go inside?" His voice was a whisper. "I'm rather chilled."

From high overhead an earsplitting blast of steam broke the night.

Willi got right up to Heilbutt's face. "The only place you're going is back to Berlin, straight to the Dungeons at the Alex if you don't tell me what I came to find out. Now!"

Heilbutt searched the sky a moment, then looked back at Willi. "If I tell you, will you let me go?"

There was another furious blast of steam, and a sudden rain of confetti.

Willi had no time to waste. He needed the truth, fast. He didn't want to deal with dragging the man off the ship, unless absolutely necessary.

"In principle I have nothing against you visiting New York. Unless—"

"Unless you need me to testify?" Heilbutt's ill-humored expression filled with a gleam of hope. "Listen, Kraus, if it ever got that far, believe me, I'd—"

"Get on with it, then. And don't leave anything out."

Heilbutt wiped his forehead, lowering his eyes. "She didn't have to do that." His wrinkled cheeks trembled. "She could have left, like me. Or kept her mouth shut." He swallowed as if the words burned on the way out. "God knows, she managed to all those years—"

"Get to the meat, Heilbutt. Start with the bow-wow stuff."

The ill-tempered face nodded obediently. "You remember the inflation, what it was like. People carting their life savings to the butcher in a wheelbarrow. Everyone trying to cut costs to the bone, so to speak."

As if Willi could forget. A loaf of bread shot up from five marks to 5 million in a week. A week later it was 10 million. A month after that half a billion. They kept printing higher denominations—a 10 million mark note, a 100 million—but the money wasn't worth the paper it was printed on. Germany's hyperinflation of 1923 was the worst in history.

"Get to the meat, Heilbutt."

"The first few months of '23 we kept receiving reports about funny tastes in sausages. Nothing unusual. People always complaining about this or that. Sure enough, though, random tests start turning up samples with ten, maybe twelve percent filler of what we figure out in the lab is unmistakably *Canis lupus familiaris*. Dog. No bacteria. Nobody's getting sick. Just . . . dog. We're all disgusted, naturally. But the higher-ups insist we keep it hush-hush. Times are insane enough without making people afraid to eat, so we investigate quietly. Make progress too. I'd say halfway there when suddenly all the samples are turning up clean. No more dog. Whoever's doing it must have caught wind we're closing in because it never turned up again. Plus, by then we'd had the currency reform, inflation's over. In no uncertain terms we're told: case closed."

"You got halfway to where?"

Heilbutt's eyes flared. "We found it being sold at a peddlers' market off Landsberger Allee, labeled mutton. The vendor was twelve years old. Can you believe it? Didn't even know his boss's name. Clearly the stuff was coming from the *Viehof*. Our guess was the south side, by-product zone. I wanted to keep going on the sly. But Henrietta—that was Dr. Riegler's name, you know—was terrified of losing her job. She told me she'd worked too hard to throw it all away on some antisocial miscreants. As long as no one got sick."

Heilbutt's worn-out eyes filled with sudden tenderness. "What can I say? She came from a modest family. Had a real struggle to get into medical school. Can you imagine"—he smiled dimly—"the only girl in her class. Completely devoted to her career. Never married. Being my boss, of course, it couldn't have worked, but I might have asked her myself, Kraus. I pretended not to, but—"

There were three short blasts of steam. The loudspeaker blared with finality, "All ashore that's going—"

"Tell me, this time . . . what's the cover-up?"

Heilbutt's lips clenched.

Another loud, shrieking whistle of steam, and the very deck began to rumble. The anchor, Willi realized, was being drawn in.

He grabbed Heilbutt's lapels. "Tell me!"

The older man shook his head. "They swore they'd break my legs."

"They'll never find out."

"These are powerful men."

Willi stared at him, making it clear he had no choice but to answer.

Heilbutt inhaled. "There was never any *Listeria* found at Slaughterhouse Seven. No *Listeria* found anywhere at the *Viehof*. The reports were total forgeries."

"What?" Willi pictured Dr. Riegler's cheek twitching like mad little bacteria under a microscope. "But why?"

"There hadn't been a new case in weeks. The industry and trades unions were frothing for us to lift the ban. Word finally came from above we had to do it. We couldn't just tell the public, 'Okay, back to normal. We don't know what happened—we never found a trace of the bacteria we've been hunting across Berlin for the past six weeks, but now it's fine to eat sausage.' It doesn't work that way. Somebody's got to take blame. They paid Kleist-Rosenthaler a hell of a lot to be the ones. Even the workers got a nice shake. All Henrietta and I got were midnight calls from an anonymous 'friend' who suggested we might be happier if we left the country awhile."

"Who was this friend?"

"Who? What difference? *They.* Thugs. Union thugs. Management thugs. Everyone wanted it hushed up."

Whoever *they* were obviously also made sure the phony lab reports disappeared.

Willi could hear banging against the hull. The mooring lines were being unbound. A rising tide of excitement swept the deck.

Something struck him: as outrageous as what Heilbutt had just confessed, it still didn't explain why Riegler's cheek had been twitching from the very first time he'd met her.

Another earsplitting blast of steam.

Bells clanging. Corks popping.

The whole deck gave a mighty shudder.

The motors were on.

"Separate from *Listeria,* though . . . having nothing to do with it," he guessed, knowing he had about ninety seconds to turn and leave if he didn't want to sail to New York, "there was something else you found in sausages, wasn't there, Heilbutt? Just like the dog meat."

Heilbutt's face went as gray as the smoke curling from the great stacks.

Suddenly Willi wasn't sure he really wanted to hear this.

Heilbutt seemed unable to spit it out. Tears rose in his eyes. "It wasn't even in the same sausages making people sick." He shrugged at the irony. "We found it incidentally. Riegler and I were the only two who knew. But we found it, all right." He nodded, squinting, wincing, seeming to see it again.

Willi stepped backward, stumbling slightly, thinking he understood.

"Take this." Heilbutt thrust a card at him. "How to reach me in New York."

Willi's limbs wouldn't cooperate. "How"—he forced out the words—"did you know?"

"Under a microscope," Heilbutt whispered tensely, shooing him away, "there's no mistaking it. Human fat, Kraus. And bits of human flesh. Now go, for Christ's sake!"

Book Two

THE SWEETER THE MEAT

Ten

**BERLIN
APRIL 1930**

The bell clanged. The streetcar doors flung open. Willi stepped into the sunshine. It had been a long, hard winter. Like everyone else in Berlin he was grateful it was over. But as he wandered back to work after lunch, despite a warm breeze blowing across Alexanderplatz, he couldn't shake the chill from his bones.

Passing the rubble field that used to be the Grand Hotel, he recalled his amazement the other morning at the sight of a real *Zigeuner* encampment that had appeared there overnight, a dozen Gypsies with house wagons and horses, cooking breakfast over open fires. By lunch they'd rather brutally been expelled by police, and now a colorful billboard replaced them, he saw—depicting two gleaming structures soon to be the cornerstones of the New Alex. When complete in 1932, the Alexander and Berolina houses would have second-story glass galleries overhanging a ground level of shops and restaurants, their own entrances to the U-Bahn station, floors full of sunlit offices. If only things materialized as portrayed in artists' renditions, he thought, admiring the modernist designs. The future'd be so rosy. But how little seemed to turn out as advertised.

This bright new decade, for instance. So far it stank.

The Big Slump, as they were now calling it, was dragging down the whole world, nowhere faster than in Germany. In Berlin companies were failing left and right, production shifting into low gear. Every week thousands were getting thrown out of work. Willi could see a long line even now—not just laborers and factory workers but salesmen, accountants, business owners, executives, all queuing across the street for unemployment insurance, which was about to get cut off by the new government, the Grand Coalition of center and liberal parties having collapsed a few days ago—another victim of the Slump. The new chancellor, Brünning, a hard-line conservative, was the first head of government not from a majority party but installed directly by the president of Germany, a decidedly antidemocratic development according to Fritz, from whom Willi'd just gotten an earful.

"I interviewed Brüning the other day at his new office in the chancellory." Fritz shrugged as he bit into a forkful of shrimp cocktail at the Excelsior. "An absolute authoritarian. Told me he planned to ram through his austerity program with or without the Reichstag."

"I thought we had a constitution."

"Yes, but under dire conditions Article Forty-eight allows the president to take 'emergency measures' *without* parliament."

"Hindenburg'd back him?"

"They're in it together, kid. Plum reactionaries. At best they want a rewritten constitution limiting parliamentary rights. At worst, an end to democracy. What they'd seriously like is my third cousin back in his goddamn palace."

Willi'd stared at Fritz as if he were telling a fairy tale. It seemed impossible history could take such a backward leap. The kaiser again?

But a year ago, who'd have imagined the Big Slump?

And when he was a kid, who'd have imagined anything that lay ahead?

If you'd told them in July 1914 that they were on the precipice of the greatest conflict in human history, it would have seemed as ridiculous as the discovery of leprechauns. And defeat? Revolution? A liberal republic?

An organ-grinder's melody drew Willi's attention back to the sidewalk: "Yes! We Have No Bananas." A crowd applauded the monkey on a leash dancing in a grass skirt. Willi could barely make his way through all the hawkers out here, one after the next.

There'd always been vendors on the Alex, selling inexpensive neckties, underwear, bras, offering shoeshines or your weight from a scale. On weekends there were jugglers, mimes. Men on stilts. But since the crash the salesmen had trebled and their offerings degenerated. Now every step you took another hand was shaking a cup of pencils at you, or rubber bands, or shoelaces. The saucy sarcasm that once prevailed—*Come on, fella, face reality. See how much you weigh!*—had completely given way to despair: *Just a penny a pencil, sir. What's that to you? Surely you could use a—*

Willi held his head low.

Every time he passed beneath the fluttering awning of Aschinger's, one of the city's most popular eateries, a sickening feeling crept through his gut. For all he knew, hanging in that window, in those long, luscious-looking salamis . . .

But how could he do any more than he already was?

Naturally, as soon as he'd gotten back from Bremerhaven he'd gone straight to the Kommissar.

"Human flesh, in sausages?" Horthstaler seemed too preoccupied with a long list of figures on his desk to look up. "Quite an assertion. You have evidence, Kraus?"

The problem was, Willi didn't.

The lab reports, Heilbutt had shouted to him in those last seconds before the ship sailed, had disappeared along with the rest of the *Listeria* files. Willi tried to explain this, but his superior grew unwilling to devote even a pretense of interest.

Two years ago Willi had been placed under the Kommissar's command without the least input on Horthstaler's part, and the Kommissar had never taken pains to hide his antipathy. Generally this took the form of strict indifference, as in this interview when he never for a second stopped scribbling, erasing, or licking at his pencil. At other times it was outright hostility, such as when he joined in on the humiliating jokes at the weekly lunch meetings. Still, he could hardly help acknowledging Willi's skill or his series of victories.

"Well, at least you're keeping your big nose where it belongs, for once. Oh . . . for Christ's sake, do whatever you think is necessary, Kraus. Just keep me posted."

On one hand Willi'd learned to appreciate Horthstaler's disdain. Being a pariah held certain advantages. Horthstaler never wanted to waste time on him or involve the rest of the unit in Willi's cases, as he did with the others. So Willi was able to operate in the margins, without anyone hanging over his shoulder. He worked well that way. He'd had to more than once behind enemy lines. On the other hand, going solo made things that much more difficult. In this case, the legwork alone was overwhelming. Plus, it always helped to have backup.

"By the way, regarding an assistant . . . ?"

"Still working on it, Kraus. Still working. I've had half a dozen men in for interviews. Unfortunately once they find out you're a Jew . . ."

"Perhaps the Kommissar needn't mention it?"

Now Horthstaler'd looked up. Human meat in sausages didn't get to him, but this had.

He tossed down his pencil and stared at Willi with a look of real disappointment. "You can't be serious. What an awful thing to do to someone, Kraus."

A door down from Aschinger's, in the window of the World Wide Fur Salon, a saleswoman was lovingly draping a fox stole around a mannequin's shoulders. Willi's tenth anniversary was coming up, he remembered. What to get Vicki? The beady eyes of the fox seemed to stare back at him as he looked in the window, trying to imagine various furs on her. Black mink? Russian sable?

He knew very well he should have reported Heilbutt's confession to the Ministry of Public Health. But he hadn't. If the government became involved, the meat industry would get wind of it, and he didn't want any midnight calls from any "friends" advising him to leave Germany, thank you. It'd be far more expedient, he'd decided, to handle this on his own.

Lynx? Chinchilla? Nothing seemed right for Vicki.

He trusted his own judgment, generally.

Even after all these weeks he wasn't sorry he'd abstained from recommending homicide charges in the *Listeria* case. Dr. Riegler may have succumbed to a guilty conscience, but his didn't trouble him. Theoretically Strohmeyer Wurst might have been charged for its failure to test purchased products, but they had broken no laws— only their own security policy. Anyway, the company, as he had foreseen, had folded; the Wurst King and his family had fled to Paraguay.

Giving up on furs, he took advantage of World Wide's window to straighten out his tie. During the war it had been hammered home that one had to pick one's battles wisely or risk being spread too thin. He tilted his hat slightly and continued walking. Fighting the meat industry, no matter which way he'd cut it, hadn't seemed worth it. Yes, they'd pressured the ministry to fabricate a story to deceive the public that sausages were safe. But by the time they had, the sausages *were* safe. So what the hell?

Up ahead he saw the Zwilling J. A. Henckel sign. WORLD'S FINEST KNIVES.

On the other hand, that fiend peddling human flesh needed to be stopped.

More than ever Willi was convinced it had to be the same person who'd made the bone art. In other words, *Der Kinderfresser.*

The two cases were one.

Absently he stared at the glistening displays slowly rotating in Henckel's window, going over for the thousandth time how everything pointed to the *Viehof.* The boiled bones. The storm canal. Heilbutt's claims about the sausages. Unfortunately, with so many companies and so many thousands of employees, it required pains-taking effort. The logical place to start, he'd figured, was not at the *Viehof,* but where the dog meat had shown up. And where he was sure the *Listeria* had originated from.

The peddlers' market.

It hadn't taken long for the main one off Landsberger Allee to reopen after the raid last November. He could hardly forget the grimy knife he'd faced in there. Since he had no intention of repeat-ing that folly, after cautious reconnaissance he'd utilized an old warehouse along the market perimeter with a back staircase nobody seemed to know about, fixed himself a camouflaged perch on the roof, then gone out and gotten top-of-the-line binoculars. Now he could see people's tonsils down there.

Once in a while, such as today, he showed his face at the office so they wouldn't forget him. But basically for two months now he'd been crouching up there. The hardest part was the cold and the snow. And the rain. Bit by bit, though, he'd pieced together a picture of how the place worked. Who the operators were. How the prod-ucts were delivered. By tracing the license-plate numbers on the trucks, he realized that even after the *Listeria* nightmare, all the big sausage producers continued purchasing cheap fillers from these vendors. There were dozens of stalls on the most crowded day, hun-dreds of customers, and no way of telling which slime-filled barrel might contain bits of children. But the man who seemed to pull the weight, Willi saw, was the same one who'd pulled the knife on him. A massive, bald ox with arms the size of beef shanks. Drove a small, enclosed truck with no plates at all. Obviously Willi was going to have to trail him. But he'd like to get to know half a dozen other creeps as well.

Around and around the displays of cutlery rotated in Henckel's window.

Vicki loved cooking, all right, but he needed to get her something . . . wonderful. Not just because he was feeling guilty even thinking about *Der Kinderfresser*—which he knew would upset her. But my God. Ten years.

It was something seriously to celebrate.

At the corner of Dirksen Strasse he waited patiently with the crowds for the policeman's signal. The investigation was time-consuming, of course, as most good detective work was. And meanwhile *Der Kinderfresser* remained at large. But Freksa for all his resources hadn't had any success. A score of men following hundreds of leads turned up nothing all winter. A huge humiliation for the whole Berlin police force. COPS BAFFLED! the headlines screamed. WHAT'S HAPPENED TO OUR KRIPO? And the whole time bones kept washing up on the banks of the Spree as far away as Spandau.

Halfway across Dirksen Willi got caught on the traffic island and had to wait while a streetcar rattled past, car after bright yellow car with advertisements: KAFFEE HAAG . . . JOSETTI CIGARETTEN . . . NIVEA CRÈME FOR A SOFTER YOU—

Freksa claimed the new bones were not new but all from the same batch. That one of the burlap bags had torn and sent individual pieces downstream. A clavicle here. A tibia there. No additional children had been victimized, he insisted, according to the newspapers. Yet each new bone triggered hysterical headlines, restoking public terror. And when February became March and no break came, even the press began turning on him—TIME FOR FRESH BLOOD IN THE KINDERFRESSER CASE?

Crossing the last stretch of street, Willi almost felt sorry for the guy. Golden Boy was under a real rain cloud. A few days ago the same clubfooted dwarf he'd seen once in Freksa's office was in there again, berating him hysterically behind the closed door.

"You must do something, or I warn you, Freksa, the consequences will be dire. We backed you all the way on this, and now you're making us look weak, just when the time is ripe for us to grow."

What had Freksa gotten himself into?

Reaching police headquarters, Willi's eyes scanned the corner news kiosk, expecting the usual headlines about the slump. But this time his heart nearly leapt into his throat. KINDERFRESSER CAPTURED!!

He couldn't believe it.

Upstairs he found out nothing more than what the papers said: that Freksa allegedly had the monster in custody. That a news conference had been called to disclose the details—but that only select press would attend. For reasons of obvious security, the location would be kept a secret except to those invited. So secret even Willi couldn't find out. And he definitely wasn't invited. Everyone he asked pretended not to know. He had to call Fritz, who had to call his contacts to get the address.

It turned out to be an old factory complex surrounded by a tall iron fence. In Lichtenberg, just a few blocks north of where the three bags of bones had been found. Freksa was out front to meet the press, some two dozen including photographers, plus Willi, whom he clearly was not thrilled to see. The whole unit was on hand: Mueller, Meyer, Hiller, Stoss. Even Kommissar Horthstaler stood behind Freksa, glaring coldly at Willi. But Willi was too dismayed to care. How had all this happened so quickly?

Against a cyclone of phosphorescent flashes Freksa announced he had the so-called *Kinderfresser* just inside that gate right in the factory courtyard, and that it was not a man at all. It was a band of men. A band of *Zigeuner*. Gypsies!

Gypsies?

Six renegade Roma men kidnapping boys and using their bones in heinous secret rituals.

Willi was dumbfounded.

At Freksa's urging they were led inside to the courtyard where awaiting them like a set from Bizet's *Carmen* was a real Gypsy encampment: three gaily painted house wagons—the same ones evicted not long ago from the rubble field on Alexanderplatz—drawn up now on the cobblestoned yard in a semicircle. In the center, six black-haired men restrained by handcuffs, heads hung low.

Far on the other side, locked behind the fence, their wives, children, and extended family members emitted a long, low, collective wail. This plaintive cry, however, was all but drowned out by men in uniform, perhaps a dozen, all wearing brown caps, brown shirts, brown pants, and black boots, standing just opposite the press. "Race shame! Race shame!" they barked with terrible anger, banging snare drums. "Germany, awaken!" Who they were or what they were doing here when the location was supposedly such a secret, Willi had no idea. Only that they added a chilling menace to the scene. He couldn't help noticing their bright red armbands bore the same black insignia he'd seen on Freksa's lapel pin. Had Freksa joined some radical party?

With a shrill whistle the men ceased chanting as Freksa stepped before the reporters. Slowly, dramatically, the hero encircled the villains.

"Denounced by members of their own clan"—Freksa raised his arm and seemed to decapitate them all with a mighty blow—"each of these so-called men has confessed to the murder of the twenty-three boys. Irrefutable evidence—the burlap sacks, the cleavers of death, the means of disposal—have all been found right here in this abandoned factory, the nest where these vermin scurry about in their nefarious existence.

"At my feet"—Freksa held out his hand, and Willi noticed for the first time the open manhole cover—"is a sewer that leads directly to Storm Canal Five. It flows below the park near the S-Bahn station where the bags of bones turned up."

So he *had* listened to me. Willi shivered, astonished.

Could Freksa possibly have gotten this right?

Eleven

"Not in a million years."

"You think?"

"With that right hook? Trust me: he'll pulverize him."

The elevator was packed with shirtsleeved detectives going home, speculating about whether Germany's new heavyweight boxing champion, Max Schmeling, had a chance at the world title coming up in New York. But Willi, pressed behind Freksa's big, square shoulders, was too damned angry to care. Every time he thought about those Gypsies, it was this moron he wanted to see pulverized.

A week after that nightmarish news conference he was still ashamed to admit he'd considered the possibility—if only for minutes—that Freksa'd actually solved the case. That the Gypsies had done it. Then halfway home it had hit like a left jab: Freksa's theory might have held for the burlap sacks found near the Frankfurter Allee S-Bahn station, south of the Gypsies' factory. But the construction site Willi'd gone to, where the first sack had washed up, was nearly ten blocks *north*, almost at the *Viehof.*

Storm Canal Five flowed south.

That first bag, his bag, had not floated upstream.

Now, the recollection of those tear-stained Gypsy faces, the wailing wives and shrieking children, refused to let go. In all his years on the force he'd never imagined, much less witnessed, such an abuse of power. Clearly Freksa'd been pressured, just as Dr. Riegler had, to bring the case to a rapid conclusion. And again the most expedient means had been employed—a scapegoat.

Only these poor Gypsies weren't getting paid for taking the rap.

It was horrifying to watch how enthusiastically the press, and subsequently the public, had embraced the Gypsies' guilt, relieved apparently not only that the monsters had been caught, but that they weren't German, the headlines screaming things like: GYPSY TERROR PLAGUE!

Zigeuner, Gypsies, had a long, painful history in Germany. Romanticized as colorful figures in caravans, playing music, dancing with tambourines, or stigmatized as congenital criminals unwilling to do a day's work, they were in either case shunned and persecuted. Even today, in 1930, although everyone supposedly enjoyed equal rights under the law, Gypsies were subject to special laws: prohibited from roaming in bands, required to provide proof of employment whenever authorities demanded or face forced labor, compelled always to register with the police, to get photographed and fingerprinted, even children, babies. As if the whole race were guilty at birth. It was shameful, Willi thought.

Freksa no doubt had found the police *Zigeuner* files more than helpful in piecing together his cynical ploy. What a desperate tactic, though, Willi considered as the elevator reached the ground floor. It might placate the public for now, but what would happen if more bones showed up?

He let the others go ahead, then followed out to the lobby.

Maybe they wouldn't. Maybe that was all the bones there were.

Maybe whoever the real killer was, he mused, would be glad some-one took the blame and quit while he was ahead.

Maybe. But not likely.

He put on his jacket and exited the building. Outside, the five o'clock sun was just kissing the big glass globe atop the Tietz department store, sending orange rays across Alexanderplatz. Breathing in, he watched Freksa up ahead standing on the corner waiting for the light to change. What might he be planning next? To trump up a whole trial against those six poor men? Find them all guilty . . . have them executed?

Willi couldn't let things get that far.

But how to expose the awful fraud? he wondered, heading toward the same corner. The media would eat it up, and he had enough connections to get it out there. But Freksa and Horthstaler were sure to know who'd leaked the story. And he couldn't afford that. Yet. He needed more ammo. All he had so far were theories. If the real *Kinderfresser* thought he was off the hook, he might get sloppy. Make a mistake. So for the time being the poor Gypsys were just going to have to . . .

He stopped. Freksa was still standing there, being accosted, it seemed, by the strangest-looking half boy, half man . . . half girl. Weirdly dressed in a poncho and bush hat, he had a gold ring dangling from one ear and more makeup on than a street whore.

"Please, Herr Detektiv," he was practically begging. "Even now it hasn't stopped."

Freksa looked completely repelled, as if the kid had leprosy. "So help me, if I see you out here again," he called over his shoulder as the light changed and he stormed across Dirksen Strasse, "I'll book you for vagrancy!"

The boy just stood there.

Willi'd seen him before, he realized, not on this corner but over by Tietz's. That kerchief . . . the feathered cap. Wasn't he the "girl-friend" of the Red Apache chief?

You couldn't traverse Alexanderplatz long without getting acquainted with the gangs of Wild Boys, homeless teens who worked the different blocks—steering customers to illicit institutions, running shell games, picking pockets, dancing for their supper—so to speak. Among them, the Red Apaches were probably the most visible. They hung around the base of Berolina, the big copper statue on the Tietz department store side of the square, dressed in outlandish outfits, annoying passersby with antics and girly shrieks. It was all but impossible not to notice the handsome "chief" or his lanky mate, who were always the loudest. But what could the kid want so desperately to talk to Freksa about?

Willi decided to find out. As he approached, though, the kid, uncertain who he was, took one look at him and bolted.

"Hey, wait," Willi cried. But it was too late. In a fraction of a second the boy was halfway down the block. Willi had to decide what to do. He hadn't gotten where he had in detective work by ignoring his hunches. So he took off after him.

It was rush hour and the sidewalks were dense with people leaving stores and offices. It was almost impossible not to knock into someone. The kid glanced over his shoulder, and when he saw Willi had followed, he really started to run. Willi had to practically machete his way through. People cursed after him. Someone hit his back with a rolled newspaper. But gradually he was gaining, almost in reach of the wool poncho, when the kid darted straight into traffic and grabbed a passing streetcar, leaping and landing between cars, making a getaway. Willi, panting, prayed this was worth it, then, waiting for the last car, leaped too, grabbing the rear door handle and hanging like a fireman en route to a four-alarmer.

The wind nearly blew off his hat as they made a sharp bend onto Kaiser Wilhelm Strasse, and he came close more than once to getting his head knocked off by a tree branch. But the kid didn't seem to notice he'd been followed. When the tram rattled across the river, slowing by the main entrance to the cathedral, Willi jumped off and followed the boy into the Pleasure Garden, the manicured heart of the old city, a giant square filled with statues and fountains, surrounded by the most monumental buildings in Berlin.

"Hey, hold on." He finally caught up with him, landing a firm hand on his shoulder. "I just want to talk. I'm from the same unit as Sergeant Freksa."

The kid froze, then turned around. His eyes, Willi saw, close enough for the first time, were lined with black mascara and purple shadow. His lips glossy pink. The fingernails, dirty green. Something fragile in the blue gaze, though, made Willi see through the costume—and recognize a frightened child, desperate enough to repeatedly approach a threatening figure from the criminal police. But Willi clearly hadn't won his trust, even after showing him his badge. The kid just stood there staring, his gold earring dangling, chest rising and falling.

"I didn't do anything," he finally mumbled.

"I didn't say you did. I just want to know what you wanted to talk to Sergeant Freksa about. It seemed important."

The kid's pink lips tightened.

"Listen," Willi tried, getting frustrated. "I can only imagine how tough it must be living on the street at your age and everything." He was in fact nearly physically revolted by the clownish spectacle this boy made of himself, indulging in thoughts of taking him home, scrubbing him up, and getting him something decent to wear. He wouldn't be a bad-looking kid. "But I can tell you this in all sincerity, son, I understand what it feels like to be an outsider. Really understand. To be mocked and feared and—"

"It's the missing boys." The kid's mascaraed eyes fluttered shut. When they opened, it was evident he'd decided to give this a chance.

Willi's chest expanded. His hunch had been right.

"That stuff about the Gypsies." The kid drew his plucked blond eyebrows together, inhaling deeply. "It's all bullshit. They didn't do it."

Now Willi's heart leaped into a back flip. "Why don't you sit down and tell me all about it. No rush. Nobody has to know. In fact, let's have an understanding to keep this strictly *entrez nous,* okay? Between us. What's your name anyway?"

"Kai."

"Kai, pleased to meet you. Detektiv Kraus here. Willi Kraus."

Taking a bench near the Altes Museum, fronted by its eighteen Doric columns, Willi found himself having to ignore the many stares that came their way and his own desire to wipe the lipstick off this boy's face. He quickly learned that Kai was from a rural village originally and had lived on his own since he was seven. Never been to school a day since. But that didn't mean he was stupid. Or uneducated. Pals taught him all he needed, reading, writing, arithmetic.

Willi never ceased to be amazed how these children survived.

Nowhere in Europe was it tougher to be a kid than in Germany. In the countryside especially, obedience to *Mutter und Vater* was absolute. Kids were expected to meet the needs of adults and not vice versa, to earn their daily bread through hard work and plenty of it. When times got rough, more than a few were just dumped as excess baggage, pawned off to a friend or relative or a traveling salesman. Sooner or later most made their way to the City You Haven't Lived Until You've Seen. More were on the streets of Berlin every day. In train stations. Hotels. Parks. You felt horrible for them, but what could you do? The government had to take more comprehensive action.

Willi looked around. Overhead, white flowers danced in the linden trees. To their left, the gargantuan dome of the cathedral, with its five generations of Hohenzollerns interred in the crypt, took up half the sky. Straight ahead, the great gilt halls of the Imperial Palace loomed dark and unoccupied. Since the abdication eleven years ago, no one had any idea what to do with it, whether to make it a museum or just blow it up. Willi shuddered, remembering what Fritz had said—that after just this short time with democracy, plenty of Germans wanted nothing more than for the kaiser to move back in.

"All right now, Kai, please tell me . . . what's this all about?"

The boy's mascaraed eyes tightened, then flared up with an explosive light. "For nearly a year now all over Berlin—in Wedding, Pankow, Friedrichshain, Kruezberg—Wild Boys have been disappearing. A pair here, a pair there. Week after week. Month after month. A few days ago gang leaders from all over Berlin finally got together. When they calculated the losses, it came to over forty."

Willi's throat clenched so tight it hurt.

"None older than fourteen. Most around eight or nine."

My God. Erich's age.

"We've gone to the cops till we're blue in the face." Kai's pink lips pursed bitterly. "That Freksa guy especially. But he says the sight of us makes him sick. That Gypsy thing he came up with is pure crap."

"How do you know?"

"Because"—Kai's eyes flamed—"since he captured the so-called murderers, four more kids have disappeared."

Willi's stomach soured. "Can you give me their names?" he asked, pulling out his notebook. An awful lot of people had begun to mill around the park, he noticed.

Kai shook his head no.

"How about where they disappeared from?"

The kid had no knowledge.

"No one's seen or heard anything, in all this time?"

Kai shrugged helplessly. "Not that I'm aware of. Only that it's happened to kids both when they're alone and in pairs. They take off somewhere and never come back."

By now it had grown impossible to ignore a rising tide of noise behind them. Thousands of people were suddenly pouring into the Lustgarten, breaking out in song: "Arise, ye workers from your slumbers! Arise, ye prisoners of want!"

Waving red flags, bearing banners—DOWN WITH THE BRÜNING DICTATORSHIP—rank after rank of Communists marched in, clenching fists high. Germany had the largest Marxist movement outside Russia, and like the homeless, their numbers were swelling each month of the economic downfall. Vicki's father ranted about the day they ever came to power, saying the country would be destroyed and the Jews would suffer more than anyone else. But plenty of people, sometimes even Fritz, were convinced it was almost inevitable the red flag would someday fly over the Reichstag.

To avoid being swallowed by this revolutionary mob, Willi and Kai had no choice but to abandon their bench and back off toward the cathedral, where they paused in the afternoon shadows.

"There's really not much more to say." The boy shrugged. "I'm just glad someone on the police force finally knows the truth."

This kid had an affable personality, Willi thought. A good head on his shoulders, under all the makeup. But what sort of future could possibly be in store for him?

"Well, I'm not assigned to the case, as I told you." Willi handed him a card. "But if you ever get any information at all . . ."

"Thanks, Detektiv. You know where to find me, I expect."

Kai's pink lips broke into a smile as he gave an ironic shrug, causing his earring to dance. "Anyway, I'm going in to have a few words with The Man Upstairs, if they don't bar me at the door. I really do appreciate your talking to me." He took a step away, then turned. "Oh, by the way, I doubt this'll help, but I have heard talk, Sergeant. Sounds kind of crazy, but some kids don't think a man's doing it. They say it's a woman. At the leaders' meeting I heard stuff about a red-haired lady kids in Neukoln were calling the Shepherdess."

Willi's head nearly exploded. Where had he heard that name?

After Kai disappeared, Willi just stood there. Nearly forty? It seemed inconceivable. How could one man could kill so many children?

Or one woman.

Despite the shouts of a thousand Communists he felt very much alone suddenly. As if he needed someone to talk to. A bit of support. He hated disturbing him, but even though it was after six, the deputy president, Willi knew, would probably still be at his desk.

At the Police Presidium he took the main elevator up to the administrative offices. The secretary was gone but he could hear a voice in the doctor's office. Willi popped his head in and saw Weiss alone, on the phone. Disappointed, he was about to leave when the doctor looked up and emphatically motioned Willi to come in and sit.

"Yes, of course I realize it's only propaganda." Weiss's eyes rolled as he put his hand over the receiver and mouthed to Willi, *My lawyer.* "But I can't let it go on, Freytag. I've got to fight back."

On Weiss's desk, Willi noticed a newspaper with stiff, angry letters slashed across the masthead: DER ANGRIFF!

The Attack.

Beneath it, filling half the front page, a cartoon of a donkey on an ice pond, its four legs comically splayed. The face on the beast had an unmistakable and grotesque likeness to Dr. Weiss's. An article following was titled "Isidore on Thin Ice." By Joseph Goebbels.

Willi looked up and saw the anger and hurt glistening behind the doctor's spectacles, so prominently featured on the beaklike nose of the cartoon. This Goebbels was clearly getting to him, Willi could see. And it made him furious because he worshipped Weiss.

"Twice a week, issue after issue, he uses me for target practice." Weiss flipped open the paper as if showing it to his lawyer. "He's called me Isidore so many times people think it's my real name."

On the page now open Willi spied a photograph of a man at a podium he was sure he recognized. That scrawny frame leaning into the microphone, those fierce black eyes. It was the same guy in Freksa's office, the lame one who liked to scream. And that twisted insignia on his armband. The same he'd seen on those brown troops shouting at the Gypsies. The same on Freksa's lapel.

He tilted his head to read the caption: *Dr. Goebbels addresses a rally of the National Socialist Workers Party.*

So this was Goebbels.

And these were the infamous Nazis, who lived to start street fights with the Communists and blamed all Germany's troubles on the Jews. It all came together. No wonder they were picking on Weiss, one of the most prominent Jews in Berlin.

"I know the man's no fool." The doctor was clearly getting irritated with his lawyer. "He's got a Ph.D. in philosophy. The philosophy of hell! But I don't care if I do lose." He broke a pencil in two. "This time I'm taking the son of a bitch to court."

Willi squirmed. Obviously this was not the moment to come seeking support.

"Stay, stay," Weiss said, motioning him.

But Willi whispered he'd just dropped by to say hello and would come again another time, when Herr Deputy President was less engaged.

On the street Willi realized how depressing this was. Not only had Freksa framed six innocent men, but he was part of a racist, reactionary movement scheming to undermine the Berlin police and destroy the republic.

Evening had fallen. Darkness lay ahead. Willi wasn't sure what to do. Only that it had to be something. He breathed out a sigh of despair, feeling suddenly as if the weight of all Germany, all Europe, had fallen on his shoulders, when in a flash the streetlights blinked on, casting the whole Alex in an incandescent glow. And like lightning in his own brain he remembered where he'd heard that name: the Shepherdess.

Braunschweig.

Unable to penetrate the mystery of the "love cult" and thwarted by the good reverend himself—who never got him into Saturnalia as promised and was drunker every time Willi spoke to him—he'd basically dropped that trail and focused on the peddlers' market instead. Now he grabbed a cab and told the driver to step on it.

The little chapel on Spandauer Strasse was dark, but a light was on in the rear apartment. When Willi knocked on the door he heard groaning. "Reverend?"

More groaning.

Stepping on a ledge and peering through a grimy window, he saw Braunschweig on the floor, face up with his arms over his head, pants halfway down to his knees. My God. He was drunker than ever, if that was possible. Willi called his name again, and this time Braunschweig pulled up his pants, then collapsed, motionless. After much concerted knocking and calling, he jumped again, crouched to his knees, but couldn't get his legs firm enough to stand up.

Willi felt like kicking in the door. Somehow he had to get to this guy. He was thinking seriously about breaking the window when miraculously Braunschweig rose, walked over, and opened up the door, inviting Willi in as if nothing were wrong. "Hello there, Detective!" he said merrily, arching his bushy gray eyebrows before falling sideways, right back to the floor.

His limbs were rubber. He couldn't sit. Even his fingers were too limp to clasp anything. Each time Willi helped him to a chair, Braunschweig slid right back to the floor. Finally Willi just crouched next to him.

"Listen to me, Reverend. What do you know about the Shepherdess?"

"The who?"

"Brigitta's predecessor. You called her the Shepherdess."

"Stay and have a drink with me."

"You told me she brought animals, for rituals."

"For who?"

"That it was a slaughterhouse over there. This is urgent, Braunschweig. Lives depend on it, for God's sake."

"Don't lecture *me* about God. I'm the one who lectures around here. Our topic today will be, aw . . . don't get all insulted, Kraus. Stay, have a drink." The reverend was holding out his arms from the floor. "Tell me, how come she doesn't she love me anymore?"

"The Shepherdess, Braunschweig. The Shepherdess."

But the reverend had passed out. Willi looked around desperately. Filthy dishes. Open tins of food. Bottles, glasses everywhere. Total Depravity. He couldn't take it.

"Damn it, Reverend—at least tell me how I can find your ex-wife!" he cried at the scarily bloated, red face.

It must have been the magic word because from the depths of his stupor Braunschweig replied, "Dawn, Kraus. Maybe I forgot to say. That's why you never found her. Go before sunrise, Tuesdays. Fridays. Tell them at the door . . ."

The reverend teetered on the edge of blackness again, then somehow managed to spit out the strangest words Willi'd ever heard: "*Yasna Haptanghaiti.*"

And that was it. Braunschweig was out.

Yasna Haptanghaiti?

Twelve

"Yasna Haptanghaiti," he said at the door, praying he'd gotten it right.

"Mazdaznan." The mustached man in a red turban held out his hand.

Finally. Willi was in.

That he could remember the tongue-twister was miracle enough. That the Reverend Braunschweig had gotten all this right seemed divine intervention. Four thirty in the morning, pitch-dark, the air crisp and chilly, and people were hurrying up the steps of the art nouveau mansion on Bleibtreu Strasse uttering the same crazy words and darting into the Divine Radiance Mission. Who could have imagined such a witching hour, in the heart of swank Charlottenburg.

Only a handful of candles lit the lobby, emitting a scent that made Willi vaguely nauseous. He gave his eyes a second to adjust.

The shelves of crystals and mystical figurines looked familiar. But the last time he'd spied in the window he'd obviously missed that larger-than-life oil portrait on his left. Good grief. There was the High Priestess in all her glory, flying in a chariot along the banks of what was presumably the Nile, based on the Sphinx over her shoulder—a bosomy Teuton with Kewpie-doll lips and platinum hair oiled in marcel waves. The caption over her head blazed HELGA— SENTINEL OF ANTIQUITY! She made the Wurst King look modest. And in the corner, mounted on a marble pillar, an enormous bust straight out of a Norse myth: a woman warrior in winged helmet, long braids. A Valkyrie—with Helga's face.

From what Willi could make out in the dim candlelight, the membership appeared affluent enough in tailored suits and smart leather accessories, middle-aged mainly, though some looked not much older than students. Some artist types. Definitely no children, though he couldn't exactly stare. Oddly, he noticed, no one was paying much attention to anyone else. Silence reigned as the women headed through one door and the men another.

He took a deep breath and followed.

Inside, he was surprised to find himself in a dark chamber among a small throng of men in various stages of undress. Apparently, one was supposed to trade one's street clothes—all of them, from the bare asses he saw—for a black robe hanging on one of the hooks. These floor-length things, Willi could see from those already in them, had hoods that nearly concealed the face.

Did he really have to do this?

He could flash his badge of course, demand to be taken to Helga. But then he would never find out what was happening here. To beguile the time, look like the time, he thought. Off came the shoes, the tie and jacket. The trousers. At the last second, though, instead of butt naked, he slipped the robe atop his underwear, breathing a sigh of relief when it went unnoticed. He had no intention of walking around without even shorts on. But no one seemed the least concerned about him. They were all too busy preparing to ascend a circular staircase at the far end of the room.

Feeling completely aberrant in this hooded outfit—a Jew in monk's robes—he joined the pilgrimage, climbing around and around until halfway up it struck like lightning: his Kripo badge. He'd left it in his jacket pocket. He turned, determined to retrieve it, but saw the narrow staircase full of men behind. If he didn't want to cause a scene, he was going to have to keep going.

Dear Lord. He really felt naked now.

Four full flights led to what had to be a rooftop penthouse, a dark auditorium drenched in mauve light. No chairs, only pillows on a carpeted floor, which was quickly filling with seated figures. Entering from an opposite staircase was another procession in hooded robes, only in white—the women. At the front, several steps led to what appeared to be an altar draped in blue satin curtains. Atop it a winged lion painted glittery gold looked vaguely Babylonian. Two of the walls had murals depicting sunrises over the Seven Wonders of the Ancient World. Corny, and plenty costly. The dues around here were probably astronomical, he surmised.

A few minutes before the clock struck five a tom-tom started beating. Then a flute, floating through the air. Softly at first, then louder, the congregation began chanting: *"Mazdaznan . . . Mazdaznan . . ."*

Were these the same Berliners he'd seen minutes earlier—hurrying down Bleibtreu Strasse in their tailored outfits? Perhaps it wasn't surprising, Willi thought—with all the amazing advances in wireless communication, brain chemistry, atomic physics—that urban sophisticates might be drawn to the primitive and mystical, the metaphysical, especially now when the rug was being pulled out from under them, everything solid liquefying. But this group really seemed over the edge. It brought him back for a second to that crazy car ride home from the Admirals-Palast after they'd seen Josephine Baker. What had Dr. von Hessler meant, he was studying human fear?

At five exactly, like magic, the blue curtains drew away from the altar. Helga the High Priestess appeared—sitting on a bed enclosed in some strange polyhedron-shaped cage. *"Mazdaznan . . . Mazdaznan . . . Yasna Haptanghaiti . . ."* The beating tom-tom seemed to waken her and gradually she rose, standing with her back to the congregation, slowly lifting both milky arms. "Aurora," she cried. "Goddess of the Dawn—open your gates. Let Shamesh arise!"

Willi had to keep from snickering. This was tackier than a Friedrich Strasse revue. Even with her back to them he could see Helga was no kid, but a mature woman in her forties, her ripe figure draped in a metallic-gold gown that left her shoulders and most of her back bare. She radiated power. Her voice. Her posture.

At last she turned and faced her congregation, a siren from the wrong side of the tracks, her sultry smirk seeming to declare, *What you see is what I made. And if you don't like it—kiss my rear.*

Behind her, a sour-faced redhead Willi recognized as Brigitta drew back another set of curtains, unveiling a panorama of Berlin-West all the way to the Tiergarten, across which the first pink rays of dawn were just now falling. Raising some sort of scepter with one arm, Helga faced the city like a figure in a stained-glass window.

"Torch of Heaven, Bride of the Gods. From you planets are born. From you life is nurtured. In the name of Titan, Helios, and Ra, we welcome you with *Mazdaznan!*"

"*Yasna Haptanghaiti!*" the congregation returned.

What an insane goulash of thirty dead religions, Willi thought. Though Helga dished it out with real panache.

"The ancients"—she held her white arms out, seeming to offer succor—"believed that to enable the Divine Energy to ascend all thirty-three chambers of the spinal medulla and bring about absolute bliss, years of practice were required."

She smiled, cocking her head, implying how little those ancients knew. Then her gaze, scanning lovingly, affixed like two magnetic beams—on Willi. For a moment, the strangest quiver shot up his spine.

"Today of course we have the Space Crystal, which enables us in a very short while to achieve what the ancients even with so much hard work had no guarantee of reaching—spiritual ecstasy. Yes. Inside the aura field of our polyhedron, our twenty-nine sacred movements galvanize the soul directly into contact with the Fourth Dimension."

Leading her flock through a series of stretches and toe touching, Helga shouted, "Flux and Flow! Feel the Light!" as the drumbeat intensified, the movements quickening. "Remember: space does not exist!" Finally, as rising sunlight fell on the red silk bed, she announced, "Now is the time to fuel the unfurling cosmos."

It didn't take long before Willi got the picture of what exactly in the cosmos was about to unfurl.

On opposite walls the white and black robes began forming separate lines, the subliminal tension mounting to overt anticipation.

"Ego's death and arousal of Astral Body climaxes in the Angelic State!"

Helga nodded to the first man and woman on each line. They dropped their robes and slowly, ceremoniously, stepped toward the Space Crystal. As they reached the red silk divan and climbed in together naked, everyone started chanting, *"Yasna Haptanghaiti . . . Yasna Haptanghaiti . . ."*

Weird. And disturbing. But not criminal, as far as Willi could tell. Consenting men and women were free to do as they wanted in this country. Clearly the child abuse accusation was unjustified, since there wasn't a kid in the place. And not a drop of animal blood. In ten years of marriage, though, he'd never cheated on Vicki, and he had no intention of starting now. But what an inspired racket, he thought. A celestial sex club. People paid to screw anonymously and feel they were getting enlightened.

High Priestess Helga, he noticed, whispered something to Brigitta, then ducked out a side door. Thank you, God, he thought. My exit visa. He counted to ten, then, yanking his robe so he wouldn't trip, slipped through the door after her. Tiptoeing down a long flight of steps, he felt ridiculous in his getup but more determined than ever to corner this babe. He'd been on her trail for months already.

At the bottom of a long, carpeted staircase, down a dark hall, he spotted a glint of her gold gown disappear through a doorway. Hugging the wall he inched forward, almost too late noticing the chair across from her room with a big mustached man in it. The same red turban who'd let them in downstairs. A bodyguard, naturally. He pressed into an alcove.

Now what?

The ceiling all but trembled with groaning couples copulating evidently right overhead. Willi broke into a sweat. He remembered Vicki's expression when he told her he was scouting out this place. If she ever saw him now . . . Wiping his forehead, he realized he could make out the guard's image in a brass vase across the hall. The mustached fellow was just sitting there, tapping his foot. A fine spot. He couldn't exactly go back upstairs. And how long could he stand here without being seen? Fate, however, or perhaps human nature, finally took a hand. The turbaned man found the sexual goings-on upstairs too stimulating to ignore apparently and began underneath his tunic working to relieve himself. Willi closed his eyes. Moans were coming from all sides now, testing his endurance. Luckily, it wasn't long before he heard a muffled yelp and some panting, then, opening his eyes, he saw the turban waddle down the hall and disappear into what presumably was a bathroom.

Flying, he could only pray the High Priestess's door was unlocked. Please, knob, turn! Abracadabra. It did.

Helga's private quarters dispensed with the spiritual, everything chrome and mirrors. A white couch. White carpet. Big bouquets of flowers. Seated at a dressing table, Helga was changed into a white silk robe, smoking a cigarette.

Soon enough she spotted him in the mirror.

"Couldn't you even wait until—" She spun around, her eyes doubling in size. "What the—?"

Her whole torso shivered, and for a second Willi saw she was really afraid, as if something from her past had finally caught up to her. And what a past it must have been. From up close, Helga looked as if she'd been around the block. Plenty.

Willi pulled off his hood. "Sergeant-Detektiv Willi Kraus, Berlin Kriminal Polizei," he said to calm her. "Just here to ask a few questions."

She breathed again. But not happily.

"You've got some nerve busting in like that." She reached for the cigarette and took a long drag, disappearing behind a veil of smoke. "Aren't you supposed to identify yourself with a badge or something? And why are you wearing one of our robes?"

"It was the only way I could get in to speak to you. Sorry. My badge is in the changing room. With my clothes. "

"I see." A light rose in her eyes as she turned back to her mirror and began tugging at her face here and there. "What's so urgent you had to sneak in here like a fox, Sergeant? How'd you get past Zoltan, anyway?"

Just then the door swung open and Brigitta entered. "Helga, I—" Instantly she recognized Willi. "You." She snorted.

"You know him?" Helga turned, intrigued.

"Sure. A private dick. Came around a couple of months ago . . . sniffing after your ass. Braunschweig sent him."

Now both of Helga's eyebrows arched with real amusement. She took another long draw on her cigarette and shot smoke through her nose.

"He's not a private dick, Brigitta *Liebchen*. This is Sergeant Kraus. Of the Berlin Kriminal Polizei. Don't worry. I can handle him. Leave us a while."

"But, Helga—"

"I said go."

Brigitta's bony face crumbled before she slammed the door behind her.

"Jealous cunt." Helga crushed out her cigarette, then smiled at Willi, loosening her robe slightly, showing more cleavage. "So. My ex-husband sent you. How fascinating. He's never been able to forget me. How is the dear?"

"Stone drunk."

"You're kidding. I'm shocked."

"Look, it's imperative I speak to you about someone named the Shepherdess."

The High Priestess lost a shade of color.

Slowly she opened a silver case and pulled out another cigarette, knocking it hard against the metal before sticking it in her mouth. "What do you want to know about her?"

Despite the coolness, Willi could see her hand trembled slightly as she lit a match.

"I need to find her."

"Why?"

"If you don't mind, I'm asking the questions."

She shrugged, rolling her eyes slightly. "I have no idea where she is. It's been a long time."

"How long?"

She smiled coyly, pursing her Kewpie-doll lips. "I believe it was Einstein, Sergeant, who said time was relative. That in some cases—"

"Look, if you prefer to continue this downtown—"

"Well. You needn't persecute me. I told you I have no idea where the bitch is. I haven't seen her in years."

"How many years?"

"I don't know. Two. At least two years, if not more."

"But you do know who I'm referring to?"

"Yes of course I do."

"What was her real name?"

"Ilse."

"Ilse what?"

"I've no idea. She never told me and I never asked."

"You must know someone who can find her. Think."

Helga stared at the smoke curling from her cigarette. "No. Not a one."

"Where did you and Ilse meet?"

"Tell me, Sergeant, are you always so brusque? Why don't you sit and have some tea. You don't mind if I put on a little face cream while we chat? I know I'm not supposed to, but I put a premium on staying young."

"I asked how you met Ilse."

"It just so happens I'm an idealist." She began rubbing cream on, making circles with her fingers. "I tend to paint the world in pastel colors, see only the best in everyone. As a result I befriend all sorts of people, some of whom I shouldn't."

"Is there a reason you're evading my question?"

"You're so perceptive. I feel naked in front of you. I guess I'm embarrassed because I met her at church. There, I said it. My husband's church. Funny, huh, looking back? Ilse was a congregant. When I left, she came with me."

"What was the nature of your relationship?"

Helga shrugged. "Close, for a while. Until I moved on. She got jealous. It's the Hydra I'm always up against. My desire for harmony's such that I generally avoid confrontation. But this girl, well, I finally had to lay down the law. She had a mean streak."

"How mean?"

"Ugly mean."

"Why was she called the Shepherdess?"

"Because, Sergeant, she used to bring us animals. For rituals. Although we *don't* do that anymore." She seemed anxious for Willi to understand this.

"Did she have connections at the *Viehof*?"

"The *Viehof*?" Helga stopped rubbing and stared at Willi in the mirror, her face a ghostly mask. "What an odd question. Why do you ask?"

"Because that's where you'd get live animals from in Berlin."

"Oh, I see. Yes, how clever. Could you turn on that light for me, darling?"

He switched on a nearby lamp, noticing the little red Indian stamped on the shade.

"Now that you mention it"—she ran her hand along her side—"I do sort of recall a family business involving the *Viehof*." She stopped at the waist, pinching herself. "But don't bother asking me what. You don't suppose I'm getting fat, do you, Sergeant?"

She grabbed Willi's hand and placed it on her.

He pulled away. "I'm happily married."

"Oh?"

"What about Ilse was so violent and ugly?" he pressed.

Helga's eyes darkened, her expression growing faint. "I just don't think she had a very happy childhood, that's all. God forbid you made her feel unwanted. She practically ran amok."

"Amok? Explain."

"Explain?"

"Yeah. An example, Helga. A specific time you made her feel unwanted and she practically ran amok."

Helga gave him an almost gut-wrenching look, then shrank in her chair as if really afraid of something.

"A specific time. Well, let's see. For instance, there was the day I told her I'd reached a new plateau of spiritual understanding."

"Yes."

"That I wouldn't be needing live animals for rituals anymore."

"I see. And what did she do?"

"What did she do?"

Helga's eyes began fluttering, her fingers twitching in her lap. "You want to know what she did?"

She jumped up and spun around, staring at Willi, her face still half-covered in cream.

"I'll tell you what she did." Her voice careened up what seemed a full octave as it flooded with hysteria. "She threatened to skin me alive. Can you believe it? Skin me alive! I hardly think you can blame me, Sergeant, for deciding the time had come to terminate our friendship."

Thirteen

For the dozenth time Willi looked at his watch. Sweat dripped down his forehead. Afternoon sun baked his car. If he ever made Inspektor, he'd be entitled to use a department vehicle. In the meantime the family Opel would have to do. One way or another he was determined to find the home base of the fellow he'd officially dubbed the Ox. The big, bald steer who'd pulled a knife on him last autumn seemed best friends with just about everyone in the market. If anybody, he'd know who was chopping up kids.

Two men trudged by lugging a crate of slop. Willi hunched in his seat and lowered his hat. It would have been nice to find a more secluded spot—in the shade. But this was where he needed to be right now: across from the market entrance, the Ox's black van square in his rearview mirror. Three hours he'd been sitting here. He could use a trip to the toilet about now. Except that yesterday when he'd gone, he'd missed the son of the bitch. Times like these he sorely lacked backup. Only the image of those six Gypsies languishing in prison made him feel less sorry for himself.

At least, though, finally, he was on the trail of *Der Kinderfresser.* He was sure of it. Who'd have imagined—a woman. It seemed impossible. But the instant Helga'd described that threat to skin her alive, he was certain it had to be her—this Ilse, the Shepherdess—he was after.

Just her, though? Could it possibly be? One woman kidnapping, killing, boiling the bones, and making designs of so many children? Selling their flesh? It'd be hard enough for one man. A woman'd have to have accomplices, wouldn't she? Even if they weren't aware of what they were doing. Unless he was really selling this one short. As High Priestess Helga warned against.

"I'll do what I can to help, Sergeant. But trust me," Helga'd insisted, "whatever the crime, don't think this bitch isn't capable of it."

What sort of crazed being was he up against?

The next morning, first thing, he hurried across Alexanderplatz in pursuit of the other lead he had on the Shepherdess.

"Kai!" He found the boy at his haunt near the base of Berolina, the giant female warrior looming near the Tietz department store. The dozen or so members of his gang, all wearing eye makeup and painted fingernails, whistled as he walked toward Willi in his Mexican poncho and bush hat.

"Never mind them." Kai's earring sparkled as they moved to the busy area near the store so no one could hear them. "Fine to see you again, Sarge."

"You told me kids in Neukoln were talking about a lady."

The boy's mascaraed eyes widened. "You mean she's real—the Shepherdess?"

"I need to speak to those kids. Can you arrange it?"

"I could take you right away."

The Black Knights, largest of the Wild Boys groups in working-class Neukoln, had a permanent residence in a basement off Hermannplatz, right across from the giant new Karstadt store. Unlike Kai's group, who stuck together for survival, this gang was a tough lot of pickpockets and shoplifters, boys who liked girls and grew into men who made a career of crime, a sort of school for the adult *Ringverein,* which regularly recruited from them. Yet a score of these gangsters-in-training managed to overcome their aversion to law enforcement when they heard a Kripo detective had come to hear about the Shepherdess.

It was standing room only in the smoke-filled basement. The few females on hand looked tougher than the guys. The leader, a pimply-faced veteran of seventeen who called himself Friedrich the Great, sat in the center of a busted-up Biedermeier couch, a big-bosomed girl under each arm. He started things off with a real tirade about how the cops didn't care if they lived or died.

"Eight of our boys, all under fourteen, have vanished around here since the beginning of the year. Two more just last week, after the supposed criminals were in jail. No matter how many times we try to talk to you guys, nobody listens. It's like we don't exist."

"Yeah!" the other kids started shouting. "No wonder we turn to crime!"

"I'm here," Willi'd assured them, "to find out everything."

He might as well have tossed a grenade, so raw was the explosion of anger and fear, everybody talking at once.

"She lures with money!"

"She's got a knife!"

"She works with a man!"

"She works alone!"

"Has anybody actually seen her?" Willi tried to bring some order to it.

"She's tall with short red hair."

"Short, with long red hair."

Everyone was certain it was a red-haired woman—yet not a soul had seen her. The boys vanished either alone or in pairs. Yet where she took them, how she got them there, or even how anyone came to call her the Shepherdess, no one had a clue.

Whoever she was, Willi realized, this lady had talent.

"From now on," he instructed, "travel only in groups of three and four. Spread the word. And keep your eyes open. If anyone actually sees this Shepherdess, I want to be told. Immediately."

He was taking a huge risk here, he realized. If word got back to the Kommissar he was involving himself in Freksa's case after all, he didn't want to imagine. Nor did he want to imagine if Vicki found out. At least, though, Wild Boys across Berlin would be organizing for protection. And on the lookout for the Shepherdess. So was the High Priestess and her entourage, Brigitta, the bodyguard. Eventually someone would spot her. He prayed.

In the meantime he continued his reconnaissance at the peddlers' market, sitting in his little black Opel, waiting. If the missing boys were ending up as sausage filler, he figured, it might be possible to work the trail backward, trace his way to where the cutting and grinding were done. Had to be some god-awful place.

On the overhead tracks the electrified S-Bahn slid into the Landsberger Allee station. Part of the ring of railroads responsible for so much of Berlin's industrial might, these commuter trains shared the lines that split off and ran into the *Viehof* a quarter mile farther. The very same rails that shuttled people by the hundreds of thousands brought livestock from across Europe to feed them. The sound echoing off nearby buildings, he could hear the conductor warn, *"Zuruck bleiben!"* and see people trampling down to the street. When the train slid out, he glanced at his rearview mirror.

There he was. The Ox's massive arms were hustling along two lanky boys who looked exhausted but relieved to be out of the hellish market. Throwing in some empty crates first, they climbed in the back of the van, which the Ox then slammed shut before lumbering up front.

The man really was the size of a small steer. His limbs twice the width of Willi's, solid muscle. Amazing he could even fit behind the wheel, Willi thought, taking a deep breath and waiting for him to pass before turning on his own motor. And how'd he get away with having no license plates? In this town they pulled you over for a dirty windshield. Keeping a car's distance behind he was glad he didn't have to give chase. The Opel didn't do more than 50 mph. Fine for taking the kids to Grandpa's. But it'd be nice to get a faster car one of these days. Of course, given this traffic, speed was the last thing he needed to worry about.

Inching along Thaer Strasse onto Eldenaer, he saw the Ox make a left finally through the main gates into the *Central-Viehof.* Allowing an empty truck to pull between them, he turned in behind. The graveled streets were a tangle of cars and trucks and horse-drawn wagons. The handsome buildings in red and gold brick glowed in the late-day sun. Fifty-seven structures on 120 acres, he remembered Herr Direktor Gruber boasting. Eleven hundred individual firms. Five thousand people who earned their daily bread here.

And at least one mass murderer.

Making sure to maintain a vehicle between himself and the van, he followed past the huge, glass-roofed cattle market, then the sheep and swine halls, the acres of outdoor corrals, on through the tunnel that led to the south side of the complex. If they continued beyond the slaughterhouses, he told himself, feeling perhaps there might be a little payoff for all his patience, he'd be heading just as Riegler and Heilbutt had postulated, straight into the by-products zone—which might narrow things down considerably.

One by one the brick slaughterhouses passed, each with its towering chimney at the far end belching smoke. He rolled up the window but it made no difference. The odor of fresh blood and burning fat seeped in like poison gas. Willi'd hardly believe people could work in such stench, if he hadn't spent three years on the Western Front.

The truck in front decided to stop suddenly and wouldn't move. He gritted his teeth. This whole area was a warren of little streets the Ox could vanish down in an instant. He honked, receiving an angry gesture from the driver, then stuck his head out praying there was room to pass. To his dismay he saw the road ahead blocked by a herd of cattle trudging by the hundreds onto the slaughterhouse ramps. He couldn't believe it. After all his patient waiting! He jumped out and climbed on the running board, straining to see if he could spot the black van through the dust, but it was useless. All he could make out were brown-and-white figures clomping toward the butcher's mallet.

Tired but not dispirited, he headed home. He'd been at the game long enough to know that a fish who slipped away one day wound up a fine fillet the next. In the meantime, hopefully, no more disappearing kids.

It was dark by the time he reached Wilmersdorf. He parked in front of his apartment building and pulled the brake tight, wondering if his choice for Vicki's anniversary present was really the wisest. She'd love it, of course. So would he. He was entitled to the days, he reminded himself, getting out and breathing in the neighborhood air. But could he afford it? It'd be one thing if lives didn't depend on it. On the other hand, he considered, entering the carpeted lobby and starting up the stairs, he didn't want to end up like so many cops obsessed with their work. Divorced.

Ten years. My God. He and Vicki deserved a second honeymoon.

Upstairs, he found the boys playing with the new doctor's kits their grandmother had given them, pretending to operate on Heinzie Winkelmann, who was sprawled out on their bedroom rug.

"*Vati!*"

Hugging them, he couldn't help but notice that damned model airplane still half-finished on the desk. Not that it seemed to bother Erich.

"Don't worry, *Vati*. We'll get it done."

"*Guten Abend*, Herr Sergeant-Detektiv." Heinz looked up from the operating table.

"*Guten Abend*, Heinz. How is everything at home?"

"Not very good." The boy was too young to be embarrassed to announce. "Because of the slump my dad lost his store. Now we don't have any money at all."

Willi's throat closed. How awful—like a terrible plague he'd been hearing about had appeared across the hall. Poor Otto. He'd worked so hard for that store. Now what would he do?

Vicki already knew from Irmgard.

"Oh, Willi, I wish there was somehow we could help them."

"So do I."

They were both so upset Willi didn't even bother telling her about their second honeymoon, until later, when they were in bed. Holding her from behind, he cuddled near and whispered in her ear, watching her eyes gradually light.

"Just like ten years ago? A whole week in Venice? Oh, Willi—" She flipped around, bursting into tears. "You couldn't have chosen a better present!" A moment later, though, she took his face in her hands. "But, darling, let's not tell the Winkelmanns, okay? It seems kind of rude. We'll say we're going to visit my great-aunt Hedda instead."

Then, pressing her lips against his in a grateful kiss, she slid atop him, running her fingers through his chest hair.

At breakfast, though, when he saw the morning paper, Venice seemed a fool's paradise: KINDERFRESSER TRIAL SET! GYPSIES FACE GAL-LOWS.

Willi completely lost his appetite.

It was Saturday. Half a workday. At eight o'clock as he approached the Police Presidium, he could think of nothing else but stopping Freksa. The prospect of that unit lunch meeting later made him slightly ill. Entering the elevator, though, his stomach really clenched. He couldn't believe it. The only other person in there was the big, blond, smug-as-hell Nazi himself. Half of him wanted to step out and wait for the next car, the other to charge full steam ahead and just tackle the guy. But he gritted his teeth and simply stood there until the doors closed. Freksa gave him a quick glance, then broke out a newspaper, turning to the second page.

As they lifted off, Willi's head felt as if it were going to explode. Each floor only made it worse. Two long years he'd borne the guy's insolence. His arrogance. His insults. His treachery. Those six Gypsies could be dead by the time the real *Kinderfresser* got caught. Maybe there was a reason they wound up alone like this.

An imaginary whistle shrieked in his ears, the signal to attack.

"About those Gypsies." His throat clenched as he pointed to the front page of Freksa's paper, a photo showing the six accused lined up in prison stripes. "You'd better figure out a way to get the charges dropped, Freksa. Because I have no intention of letting you get away with it."

Relieved to actually have done it, Willi nevertheless felt sweat pour down his back. This—as they called it in the war when you climbed from the trenches to storm the enemy—was going over the top. From now on everything Freksa had in his arsenal would come flying at him. But it was time to face the fire. And he couldn't help thinking it was worth it too, just to see the expression on that big, square face—as if the organ-grinder's monkey had stood up and sung "Das Lied von der Erde."

Feigning a smile, Freksa offered an exaggerated could-a-guy-like-me-ever-do-something-wrong? look, the way he probably did with girls whose panties he was trying to get into—still, at the age of forty.

"I have no idea what you're talking about, Kraus. Get away with what?"

"Let's put it this way." Willi feigned a similar look back. "Try to bring those Gypsies to trial, Freksa—just try. And you'll find out."

Perhaps it was stupid. Perhaps he should have gone to the Kommissar and told him everything first. As if that would have helped. Either way, Willi realized, war with Freksa was inevitable. At least now it had been declared.

At lunch, everybody acted as if nothing were wrong. But Willi couldn't escape feeling like a condemned man eating his final meal. Horthstaler had warned him—warned him repeatedly—to keep away from the *Kinderfresser* case. Even so he'd barreled in anyway, all guns blazing. It was only a question of how severely the Kommissar would come down on him.

After they finished eating, Horthstaler wiped his pudgy lips and let the napkin drop. "I'm sorry to announce we must begin our weekly meeting with a most unpleasant matter. Apparently, one member of this unit seems to have come to the conclusion it's permissible not merely to trespass on his colleague's case, but to slander and threaten that colleague as well."

Even though he knew it was coming, the bile surged in Willi's throat. Four years in the army. Seven with the Berlin police. Never once had he been dressed down this way.

"Obviously"—Horthstaler's eyes fixed on him with an expression of repulsion, as if Willi were an ant on the table—"a most serious breach of regulation."

And never once had he spoken back to a superior. But—

"You're not acquainted with the facts, Herr Kommissar," he said with all the dignity he could muster. "Freksa's case against the Gypsies is—"

"Slander!" Lieutenant Mueller jumped to his feet, balling his hands into fists.

Everyone in the unit rose with him.

"Sit down, for Christ's sake. I'll handle it," Horthstaler barked at them furiously, then turned on Willi. "Kraus, your behavior is outrageous. I could not have been more explicit about keeping your big nose out of this. But you have lived up to the creed of your race, so infamous for its meddlesome audacity."

Willi had to battle like a gladiator not to be lured into this. "Kommissar, please hear me out. Children are still disappearing. Someone's operating from inside the *Vie*—"

"Halt!" Horthstaler's meaty fists balled as if he was ready to take a swing now too.

Willi could bring the Kommissar down in half a second, he knew, if it came to it; probably take them all. But he fought, fought to keep himself calm.

"As of now you have nothing more to say on this matter, Kraus, because you are on official disciplinary suspension."

The phrase slammed like an iron ball into Willi's brain.

What?

He grasped the table for support.

He knew it was going to be bad, but never this. Short of dismissal, no more severe punishment could be meted out to a German civil servant, a ball and chain that could never be removed. No more promotions. No more raises. Pension capped. Through a blur of nausea he could just make out Freksa's vengeful face across the table. *You're lucky you're not getting worse*, the blue eyes seemed to spit at him. *But watch your back, Kraus. You're on the list.*

"Because your record's unblemished until now"—Horthstaler's thick lips opened and closed—"I'm only giving you two weeks' suspension. But my leniency is predicated on you. If you manage to control yourself, you may return to work on the thirteenth. However, should I hear that these egregious slanders have in any way persisted . . ."

Fourteen

Only once before, when his father had died, had Willi seethed with such indignity. Then he was nine, and it felt as if his world had collapsed. Now he was thirty-four and his sense of self felt almost as badly assaulted. All his years of hard work had been indelibly tainted. And why? Because he'd opened his mouth.

At first he'd wanted to run to Dr. Weiss, protest his maltreatment, and reveal all about Freksa's shameful conspiracy. But Weiss had already made himself understood on the matter of intervening on Willi's behalf. Besides, this time Willi'd disobeyed his superior. There was no crying for help.

What he needed to have done, he thought, painfully chastising himself in the days that followed, was opted for stealth in the first place. Planted stories in the media the way he'd considered and carefully camouflaged the source. The risk may have seemed too high, complete destruction of his career if discovered. But what had a reckless frontal assault accomplished? Freksa was proceeding anyway, more determined than ever to invent enough evidence to convict the Gypsies. The innocent remained accused. The guilty hailed. The republic undermined.

And *Der Kinderfresser* still out there.

Plus, the humiliation was terrible. He was so embarrassed to have received the most severe of all disciplinary punishments, he felt like a kid who'd peed in his pants. He certainly didn't dare tell Vicki. She might be sympathetic to his plight, but she'd be livid too, that he'd gone out of his way to involve himself in a case she viewed as potentially harmful to the family. Each morning he had to leave the apartment pouring all his energy into convincing a woman who noticed everything that nothing was wrong. Maybe in Venice next week, he kept reminding himself, things would look different.

He went to work every day. Not to the Police Presidium but to his perch above the peddlers' market. Staring down through his binoculars at the unkempt men and barrels of putrid slop, however, he kept feeling fresh shock waves at the realization of what had happened. Disciplinary suspension! As long he remained in law enforcement, no matter how long his list of accomplishments, his record would bear this blackest of marks. He might as well have been branded.

Focusing his lenses on the kids in the market, he felt new sympathy for them. How listlessly they stood behind their slime-filled barrels, not even talking to one another, doing their work with mechanical dullness, dishing out whatever they were hawking, weighing, counting. Between customers they relaxed a little, sitting on crates, closing their eyes. But when the Ox came, they jumped, obviously terrified of him. Who wouldn't be? For a kid he'd be like a bull elephant.

Willi was going to have to trail the beast again.

He wasn't giving up.

Horthstaler couldn't have given a clearer demonstration of how the reins of power got pulled in their department. But as badly bruised as Willi felt, he had every intention of charging on.

Right after his second honeymoon.

A week into his shameful punishment he and Vicki packed their bags for the previously planned trip. At the massive Anhalter Bahnhof, Berlin's gateway to the south, with its great glass roof arching over the many bustling platforms, the kids were on hand to see them off with Aunt Ava, who was minding them for the week. How smart she looked in a soft-brimmed hat and new long skirt she'd vowed not to wear. The boys brought a big bouquet of daffodils in honor of their parents' anniversary and sang the traditional "Hoch Sollen Sie Leben." It was so sweet he and Vicki each had to use a handkerchief. When he hugged them good-bye, Willi couldn't help thinking of all those kids who not only lived on the streets but were dying on them too now. The Shepherdess. The Gypsies. Everything had to be left behind for a week. He had no intention of letting conspirators, serial killers, or his own bad conscience ruin this trip for Vicki.

Ensconsed in a private compartment with soft, frosted lighting and leather banquettes, a blessed relief gradually crept over him, deepening the farther the train sped from Berlin. Especially once they ordered champagne. After several glasses he and Vicki slouched in each other's arms, snug under a blanket of nostalgia, reviewing, as if photos, those wondrous days a decade ago, their wedding on the blossom-filled shores of the Schlachtensee, that first night at the Adlon, their week in Venice. All the hopes they'd had. The dreams and plans. As they stared out the window at the star-filled sky, everything, they agreed, had turned out even better than they could have imagined.

Two lucky people.

Venice the next day was glistening in sun-drenched color, and, despite the slump, every bit as packed with tourists as it had been in 1920. They checked into the Vittoria, the same hotel as on their honeymoon, a former monastery for barefoot friars, so happy to be back they practically danced up the staircase. Without bothering to unpack, they dove into the same king-size bed they'd begun their marriage in, falling into each other's arms again with the vigor of newlyweds.

In some ways it was even better than their first honeymoon, a decade having rendered them imperceptibly calmer, more appreciative people, not only of each other but the world around them. The art. The architecture. Food. Everything seemed more wonderful the second time around. Heavenly as each day was, though, Willi found it almost impossible to keep his thoughts from making the unpleasant journey home. Even on a boat ride out to Burano one beautiful afternoon, as they sped across the green lagoon, he found himself pondering how exactly he was going to keep afloat in the shark-filled currents of Alexanderplatz, especially when his sole intention was going to be to shoot Freksa out of the water.

It'd require a real balancing act.

Later, as he and Vicki strolled the lido, she turned to him with glowing eyes.

"This is the best anniversary present you could have given me, Willi, honestly. The most thoughtful. The sweetest. Definitely the most romantic."

"You're not sorry you didn't marry a Wertheim or a Tietz?" he asked her stupidly.

She pulled him near and kissed him deeply, right in front of the Hotel des Bains. But even lost in her wet lips, he flashed on how furious she'd be if she ever knew he'd involved himself in the *Kinderfresser* hunt. In ten years he'd never hidden anything of consequence from her, no affairs, no dalliances. Vicki, though, would consider this a breach of trust. What was it, then, that kept driving him to risk not only his career but his marriage on this goddamn case?

At the end of the week they felt bereft when they had to leave, as if they'd never see Venice again. In the train, they sat for hours staring out the window in silence. After they'd crossed the Austrian frontier, though, Vicki brushed aside her bangs and took his hand.

"All right now, Willi. Go on. Tell me."

One glance and he knew the jig was up. All this time he thought he'd been fooling her, she'd been fooling him. A cold sweat broke out down his back. He had an urge to bolt out the window and hide in the distant forest, but she was scrutinizing him relentlessly, offering not even a chance of escape. So he coughed several times to clear his throat, checking one last time for any sign of reprieve, then submitted to confession.

As the train sped across precipitous valleys and into dark Alpine tunnels, he told her everything. About the boys and the bones and the Gypsies and Freksa. About his disciplinary suspension. And by the time they were approaching Munich, he could have offered testimony for Freud's talking cure, he felt so much lighter. Vicki, though, as he'd feared, was furious. He didn't think he'd ever seen her that angry.

"I can't believe you did this." Her whole upper lip was twitching. "I feel like I don't even know you. How could you go behind my back like that and put the boys in danger?"

"They've never been in danger."

"Oh, easy to say! Maybe even to convince yourself, Willi. But not me. Whoever this *Kinderfresser* is, he's obviously a very sick individual. How the hell do you know he wouldn't come after the person who's coming after him? Or worse, after his kids? Or me?"

"Vicki . . ."

All the way to Nuremberg she refused to say another word, to even look at him. Finally, though, they had to have lunch, and in the dining car, gradually, her anger eased.

"I don't know what drove you to do it, Willi. Really I don't. But okay, it's done. You received your punishment; I don't want to make it worse. You've got to promise, though, keep away from that case. And that first thing tomorrow you'll go directly to Dr. Weiss and tell him everything you told me, verbatim."

"I can't do that, Vicki."

"You've *got* to."

"I'd be finished in the department forever."

Her dark eyes flared with more fury than a sirocco. "Then tell me, Willi, how do you plan to live with yourself if those Gypsies hang?"

Fifteen

Rain swept Alexanderplatz, coming down in silvery sheets, rushing over the Belgian cobblestones and webs of iron streetcar tracks, turning the new subway trenches into muddy canals. It pelted the beautiful art nouveau façade of the Tietz department store and shook the awning of Aschinger's Restaurant, drenching everyone underneath, gripping the whole Alex, it seemed, in Sturm und Drang.

Willi turned from the window on the sixth floor of the Police Presidium and fell into his chair. Since his return to work several days ago, everyone had basically ignored him: business as usual. Except for the unit secretary, Frau Garber—Ruta. She had made a concerted effort to ask how his travels had gone.

"Imagine . . . a second honeymoon," she'd sighed, pouring him coffee from her cart. "To Venice."

Didn't she know he'd been on disciplinary suspension too?

"You have real heart, Herr Sergeant. That's what makes you stand out around here."

Of course she knew. She was showing support. He was so touched he remembered he'd brought her a souvenir. "Oh, by the way," he'd said, handing her a little canvas bag filled with beans. "For you."

"Italian roast! Herr Sergeant . . . you're an angel."

Leaning back in his chair now, though, listening to the fury of the storm, Willi didn't exactly feel like one. Unless angels could be gripped by uncertainty.

This whole week had thundered Sturm und Drang.

First day back he'd had to force his legs to take him over to Administration, each footstep down the long granite hallways seeming to echo an accusation. He'd never turned in a fellow officer before. But he'd reconciled himself to Vicki's argument: what *did* honor and reputation matter when innocent lives were at risk?

Dr. Weiss looked glad as always to see him, although slightly worn-out too. The personal attacks against him in the Nazi press were relentless, Willi knew, causing real distress for the deputy police president. It wasn't the greatest time for one of the few Jewish officers in the building to come schnorring for a favor. Nevertheless.

"That's quite a story." Weiss's sharp eyes flashed behind his wire glasses when Willi'd finished. Examining the drain maps and other evidence before him, Weiss rubbed his temples. "My God, these people take wickedness to new dimensions, Willi. I knew they've been trying to infiltrate Kripo, but I'd no idea they'd gotten this far. *Verdammt!*" He slammed the desktop. "Goebbels, in this building."

Weiss picked up a pencil. "Thing is, what to do about it now?" He drummed the desk. "Not such a simple matter. Politics, politics." He started doodling. "Give me a few days. I'll get back to you." Willi saw he was making a swastika. "This time you did the right thing, coming to me." Weiss circled it and dropped the pencil. "Oh, and Willi." Weiss stopped him from leaving. "Don't worry about the suspension. I'll make sure it comes off your record, sons of bitches."

Walking the same long halls back to Homicide, Willi's whole body had pulsed with a mixture of satisfaction and misgiving.

Mostly satisfaction.

Weiss moved faster than expected.

Late the next morning Freksa had appeared in Willi's office doorway, lurching like an attack dog. "You really think you fixed things, don't you?" His thin lips snarled. "A real Jew conspiracy."

Willi took a deep breath as satisfaction spread through his chest. "Funny word out of your mouth, Freksa. A man with no qualms about framing six men and letting a mass murderer go free."

Freksa's square jaw trembled with rage. "I do as I'm told, Jew boy. Just like I've got to now that your hook-nosed friend's threatened to throw the book at me. But I'm warning you, the day of reckoning's near."

Willi'd said nothing.

In truth, though, Freksa'd gotten off easy. Too easy, Willi thought—although he understood the logic as Dr. Weiss described it. Given the state of things, the deputy president had explained by phone, public exposure of such terrible deeds on the part of Germany's most famous detective would be far too destructive. Along with the army, the police were one of the few stable cornerstones of the republic these days, and it couldn't afford such a devastating blow. Freksa merely had to clean up the mess he'd made and suffer the humiliation of having been caught. Willi got scant pleasure at his comeuppance—until the next day, when headlines screamed EVIDENCE FOUND INCONCLUSIVE—ALL SIX GYPSIES FREED!

Vicki was so proud she gave Willi one of her special foot massages that night.

"There now, don't you feel better? You did the right thing, darling. Let's put the whole thing behind us."

Willi wasn't fool enough to imagine his troubles with Freksa were over, but the next day's drama had nothing to do with the Nazi. Stepping out for the bottle of milk left each morning at their door, he'd heard strange sounds on the landing above. Tiptoeing up, he'd found his neighbor Winkelmann sitting there on the steps, bawling like a baby.

"Otto." He'd sat next to him. "My goodness. There, there."

"I've lost it all," Winkelmann bleated, gasping for air. "Everything."

"Now, *Mensch*. A terrible thing's happened; it's true. But you'll weather it. Just like we've weathered so much already. Vicki and I will do whatever we can to—"

The crying stopped and Otto's eyes flared with sudden rage. "You don't understand, Kraus. You've got it made. I thought I had a chance in life. That store was my baby." His voice broke. Tears streamed down his face. "I did everything I could to nurture it."

Willi put an arm around his shoulder. "Of course you did. You can't blame yourself. It's wretched all around. This slump's becoming a real depression, they say."

"We have a bit stashed aside, but then what? You see all the families getting evicted, standing on the sidewalk with everything they own? I can't let that happen, Willi. I'm so ashamed."

Willi's throat closed with pity. He didn't know what else to say.

The tempest seemed to pick up by the minute, rain pounding the windowpane like a constant drumroll. Willi was glad at least not to be on the rooftop above the peddlers' market, where he'd spent most of the week. With the first real heat of the season, the stench, even five floors up, had practically asphyxiated him. He'd no desire to be around there in July. Unfortunately, all his efforts to find the Ox's base of operation remained unrewarded. He'd only managed to trail the guy once—to a beer garden in Kreuzberg. After that, he'd totally vanished, which was odd because the Ox was always at the market.

More than once Willi's thoughts grasped at other possibilities— Helga, the High Priestess Helga, or Kai, the street boy, for instance— wondering what he would do if they should pop up with sudden news about the Shepherdess. He wasn't certain, considering the promise he'd made to his wife. Yet on his way to work yesterday, out of the blue it struck him: it wasn't just Helga who knew the Shepherdess but her ex-husband, the Reverend Braunschweig—that Bible passage from Ephesians. Of course. Overcome at the prospect of even a morsel of new information, he'd jumped off the tram at Spandauer Strasse and hurried down the block without compunction, only realizing as he reached the chapel that he was breaking his word to Vicki after not even a week.

Perhaps the news the church cleaning lady offered was all for the best, then, he tried to console himself. "Three months at a dry-out clinic in Baden-Baden." She shook her head sadly. "Church made him go. It's his only hope now, I'm afraid."

Willi'd taken it with mixed emotions, but what else could one do except wish the poor fellow luck?

Then to top things off, this morning, amid all the wild wind and rain—the note. Hand-delivered with coffee.

"Everyone's addicted to Italian roast now." Ruta'd winked as she poured him a cup. "You'll have to return to Venice soon, for more."

Wouldn't that be nice.

"And"—she'd reached into her apron, pulling out an envelope—"Herr Freksa wishes me to give you this. An invitation of some sort, to a very fine restaurant, I suppose."

Willi looked at her, astonished both at the envelope and to realize the unit secretary knew everything about what had happened between him and Freksa. Had she just taken sides? Backing from his office with her cart, he saw her give him the slyest grin.

His heart raced when he'd torn open the envelope. The note did not ask him out to a fine restaurant. But it was an invitation, all right. One of the odder ones he'd ever received: *Can you meet me in the center span of the Oberbaum Bridge, please, at noon?*

Now, staring at the envelope on his desk, listening to the howling wind and rain beating on the glass, Willi felt pelted by uncertainty. Should he go? Should he not? If only he had backup. The very sight of Freksa's handwriting made his shoulders stiff. Like when he had had to pick his way through a minefield, he felt his every move had to be calibrated. Tilting the chair back on its hind legs he cast his eyes skyward trying to think, when all at once he realized.

He'd tilted too far back.

When he was a kid, his mother always warned him: "Four chair legs on the ground, Willi!" And though he'd slipped once in a while, he'd never had a real problem. Until now.

Now he knew he was flipping backward. He saw his whole family—Vicki, Erich, Stefan, even his sister—staring in horror as he hit the floor. Neck broken. Paralyzed for— He jumped against gravity, grabbing the desk, managing to gain a hold of the edge and balance on his feet as the chair crashed behind with a bang.

Standing there dazed, he took a deep breath, then picked up the chair. *I should have listened to you, Mom.* He sighed, sitting again, four chair legs on the ground. Now think, for God's sake. Think, think! Why would Freksa want to meet on the river? He massaged his temples, staring at the sheets of rain waving across Alexanderplatz. Might a gang of brownshirts be lying in wait to avenge Freksa's humiliation? It didn't make sense. The Oberbaum was one of the busiest bridges in Berlin. Even the U-Bahn crossed it. It would hardly be the place for an ambush. Although the railings weren't high. Freksa's note, though, was so damn polite. Pleading almost.

Willi looked at his watch.

Not its most beautiful but certainly the most famous of the city's Spree River crossings, the Oberbaum Bridge almost succeeded in appearing medieval—although it was barely thirty years old. Its Gothic brickwork studded with knightly crests and two tall, fortresslike towers made it a favorite with locals and tourists alike, as did the splendid views it offered of the heart of the German capital. Coming off the steps from the Stralauer Tor U-Bahn station, Willi yanked his hat against the storm and set out. A poor day to hike the bridge. Even under the covered walkway that ran along one side of the span, windswept rain sprayed his face. Cars and trucks splashed from the road.

The U-Bahn roared overhead. And with each new step uncertainty mounted about what the hell he was heading toward. Obviously Freksa had something to tell him and didn't want anyone knowing it. But couldn't they have met in a museum or something?

Intentionally, he arrived several minutes late. At center span, though, no Freksa. He pulled his collar tight and looked around. The normal panorama, the whole center of Berlin from Treptow to Tiergarten, domes and spires and the great gray river snaking through it, was completely obliterated by clouds. He felt hemmed in, uneasy suddenly. Had Freksa backed out? Was all this some kind of sophomoric hoax? What were those heavy boots approaching from behind? He snapped around just in time to see a detachment of Italian tourists marching by, bundled against the storm.

Through sheets of silvery rain he spotted a figure on the open-aired walkway across the road, leaned against a banister. He was tall and thin like Freksa, wearing the same style trench coat and fedora. But why was he standing there in the rain? After some time Willi realized it was Freksa and shouted at him. But even though Freksa saw him, he just stood there. Getting good and angry now, Willi waited for a break in the traffic, dodging oncoming trucks, not even bothering to say anything once he got to Freksa because the minute he saw him he knew the man was in some kind of altered state.

"Hello," Freksa muttered drily, as if they'd run into each other on a corner.

Willi felt shocked by his demeanor. Normally, Freksa was a relatively handsome guy who projected such Olympian certainty it lent him a godlike aura. Now, though, he looked like a toppled statue with its patina cracked off, the marble underneath cold and dead, the thin, pale lips pulled apart. "Good you came." Empty eyes seemed to look right through Willi. "You're a better man than I. Although, I never had the advantages you people have."

Willi stepped back. Freksa may have been down, but not enough to keep from taking potshots. Just what advantages did he suppose Willi'd had? His father'd dropped dead when Willi was nine. His mother had to work selling underwear at Wertheim's. They never starved, but they sure as hell never summered in Deauville.

And was it really necessary to stand in the rain when shelter was right across the road? Freksa's disconnection, though, was so extreme any reaction other than pity seemed beside the point.

"I was on my own when I was twelve," he was mumbling like an automaton with half its wires blown. Gaze too wide. Voice, monotone.

It took a second, then Willi began to recognize it. He'd seen this before, many times, in the trenches after the dust of a bombardment settled, nervous systems short-circuited or completely melted down. Shell-shock. Not the most severe kind that left a man twitching like a broken toy the rest of his life. But the type that flung men into a dissociated dream-daze for hours or days or even months, then faded, leaving them seemingly normal . . . with a ticking bomb beneath the surface. It didn't take much to imagine what had set off Freksa's. His fall from grace had been swift and hard. Plus, what must Dr. Goebbels have said when he found out the Gypsies had to be freed?

"I was one of the lucky ones." Freksa was laughing now, seeming to see his youthful fortune sauntering toward him. "Landed a real fine job at the Kaiserhof. Stripes up the trousers. Rows of brass buttons. *Bellboy First-Class Freksa at your service!*" He saluted with two fingers. The salute dropped. "Christ, what they did in the back room if those buttons didn't shine."

Rain was coming down in buckets. Willi couldn't take much more.

"Is that why you dragged me out in the middle of a typhoon, Freksa, to tell me about your bellboy outfit?" Willi tried to snap him out of it. "We've got a monster on the loose!"

The anger seemed to penetrate at least one defensive perimeter because Freksa's foggy eyes turned toward him and appeared for a moment to focus through their haze. "How come you never told me you were *rückwärtige,* Kraus?"

Willi blinked. Freksa'd never addressed him so personally. It took him by surprise. He'd never mentioned he'd been *rückwärtige*—

behind enemy lines—because in the two years since they'd been in the same unit, when might he have brought up such a topic? Freksa'd never shown him anything but malice. Willi wasn't even sure how Freksa'd found out about his war record, unless, of course—Dr. Weiss.

"Those were the only guys we had any respect for." Freksa's eyes seemed actually to take Willi in for an instant. "Not even the fliers got our admiration like the ones who went behind."

Willi didn't know what to say. He longed to get Freksa out of the rain, which was pouring over the brims of their hats like waterfalls, but he sensed he oughtn't disturb the guy, the way you're not supposed to wake a sleepwalker. "So, then, you were there" was all he could think of.

Freksa's reply would have seemed insane to most. Up and down, from the side of his mouth, he emitted a sharp wailing-siren sound, coupled with a fast-clicking tongue. But anyone who'd fought in the front lines knew exactly what it was. And it sent a chill right through Willi.

Of all the great horrors in the World War—flamethrowers, tanks, rapid-fire machine guns—the ones that epitomized the heights to which the twentieth century had elevated man's inhumanity to man were chemical weapons. Over a million soldiers had suffered the very best modern science could produce: chlorine, bromine, phosgene, chloropicrin. Really suffered.

Freksa was sounding the alarm for incoming gas.

Right there in the pouring rain, he tore open his coat and unbuttoned his shirt, revealing his whole upper chest. The skin looked like a big plate of whipped cream. A grotesque meringue of pink and white scars that could only have been caused by one thing: the most widely used chemical of the war. A vicious blistering agent named for its tangy smell. Mustard gas.

"These are *my* medals, Kraus."

Willi inhaled. It was a gruesome honor, to say the least. And maybe why Freksa was still a bachelor at forty.

"Perhaps we understand each other more than we realize, Hans,"

Willi said, hardly noticing he'd used Freksa's first name. "Please, though, cover up if you don't want to catch pneumonia."

Freksa started buttoning his shirt absentmindedly. "Ironic, huh? I became a cop because the uniforms reminded me of bellboys. But I never even wore a police uniform." He was getting the buttons seriously mixed up. "Because I became a detective, I don't have to tell you. Tops in the field. Till I messed up in politics."

"Here, let me help." Willi reached.

Freksa let him redo the buttons.

"I felt important being one of them," he mumbled in a half whisper, like an adolescent before a judge. "Part of a historic movement. But I was a detective long before I was a Nazi. And when they forced me to trump up a case—"

He grabbed Willi's hand, stopping him.

"Can you imagine the shame when I had to put on that show for the press?" Freksa seemed to be asking for Willi's sympathy. "After all those years of honest detective work? Not that I cared about those goddamn Gyspy scum."

He lost whatever he might have gotten. Willi pulled away.

Freksa yanked the coat around himself. "But *Der Kinderfresser* was still out there, and those sons of bitches didn't care. I asked that little freak Goebbels—what do I do if there are more killings? He says—lie again! Bigger and better next time. The bigger the lie, the more they believe."

Freksa shook his head. "Christ, I hated you for stopping me. But as much as I did"—his whole torso jerked with a sudden dam break of emotion—"I was so goddamn happy too. Because now I knew we'd catch that motherfucker."

Gradually, Willi got the implication. "We?"

Freksa leaned in with a fractured smile, his eyes aglow now with flickering blue lights. "Come on, Kraus. Don't tell me you never thought of it. You and me . . . a team? There'd be no stopping us!"

Sixteen

Willi wasn't so deluded as to believe in miracles. But Freksa's idea of partnership was Mephistophelian.

"We'd have to keep it incognito, of course. I couldn't be seen with you. Or share credit in any way. I'd still have to act as though I thought you were a pig. But you'd be the brains, Kraus, really." Freksa let himself be led across the road. "The thinking will be all yours; I'll just do what you tell me. I've already begun."

Reaching the sheltered walk on the far side they finally got out of the rain.

"What do you mean, Hans?" Willi shook himself off. It'd be a miracle if they didn't both catch pneumonia. "You've already begun?"

As they trudged back across the bridge toward the U-Bahn, Freksa explained with mounting pride how Dr. Weiss had mentioned

Willi's theories about the peddlers' market. So the other day, at that stinking rat lair off Landsberger Allee, Freksa'd gone around passing out his card, letting it be known he was offering fifty marks to anyone who had information regarding the big, bald fellow who—

Willi stopped short.

Now he was the one in shock. He couldn't believe Freksa'd done that. In a single morning he'd compromised everything. From countless hours behind binoculars Willi knew damned well everyone in the market was terrified of the Ox. Now Freksa'd not only tipped the brute off, but sent him stampeding for cover. No wonder the Ox had vanished.

Freksa was convinced, though, his offer had paid off. Someone'd called in already claiming to have information worth far more than fifty marks, he boasted.

"We're meeting tonight, just the two of us. And you'll never guess where." Freksa tilted up his chin, his long, pale face still wet with rain, a slight smile on his lips. "You were right, Kraus. The *Central-Viehof.* Slaughterhouse Seven. Eleven p.m. The section once used by Kleist-Rosenthaler."

Willi's whole back tensed. "You can't be serious. Don't do it, for God's sake. The slaughterhouse? Alone at night?"

"Awww." Freksa stretched his neck and brayed. "How touching, Kraus. You're worried about me?" He patted his trench-coat pocket. "I never travel alone."

The rain had eased but lightning still cracked the sky as Willi made it home to Beckmann Strasse, shaking out his hat before entering the lobby. On the staircase up, he ran into Otto Winkelmann coming down.

"Hey, *Mensch.* How are you doing?" Willi hadn't seen him since that morning on the landing.

"Yes, yes. Much better. You remember my brother-in-law, Klemper? He's gotten me in at his firm."

"Well, congratulations!"

"Naturally it's not what I'd prefer." Otto's head shook severely. "A clerk in the mailroom. Plus, I had to make certain other involuntary adjustments, I can assure you. But at least I'll be able to pay my bills, yes?" He seemed both immensely relieved and in a hurry. "So bye-bye, Willi." He waved as though he wasn't sure when they'd see each other again. "Felix is taking me to fill out some paperwork."

Probably making him join a union, Willi figured. A mailroom clerk. How sad.

Vicki was in the kitchen making salad.

"Thank heavens." Her eyes glistened when she saw him. "I was afraid you might have gotten washed away."

She shook her bangs back and lifted her face, waiting for his kiss.

He came around from behind instead, nibbling her neck.

"Daddy's biting Mommy!" Stefan shouted from the hallway.

"Because I'm Nosferatu." Willi made his fingers into claws and started chasing him. Erich joined and the three of them had a screaming rumble before Vicki put a stop to it.

That night, when the kids were in bed and he and Vicki were listening to Furtwängler conducting Brahms's Seventh, she caught him staring into space.

"Kathe asked about Passover," she said softly, as if not to disturb anyone. "I told her I had to check with— Willi?"

"What? You needn't check, Vic. Of course we'll have them."

"I mean now . . . what's wrong? Is it that awful Freksa again?"

Not the way she thought.

Nothing he'd said had been able to dissuade Freksa from going to the *Viehof* tonight. And the more Willi'd considered it, the less he liked it. The guy wasn't in his right mind. What harm could there be in a little covert backup? But what was he supposed to say to Vicki, lie to her straight-faced? He picked up a newspaper and tried to read, only the words wouldn't form in his head.

"Sweetheart." He finally threw the paper aside, figuring a half-truth was better than none. "I'm really concerned about a colleague. I know you hate when I go out at night—"

"Oh, Willi."

"Sometimes I put myself in your shoes and I think, God, if anything ever happened to her . . ."

But the idea of Freksa out there alone unnerved him.

Graveyard shift. In another few hours, waves of workers would begin pouring into the *Viehof* to prepare for the busy day ahead. But now, only lonely horse-drawn wagons clomped here and there, hauling trash. Willi drove past the empty administration buildings and vast glass market halls, which he could hear being hosed down inside. Even the acres of corrals filled with cows and sheep and pigs were quiet. All deep in one final sleep.

The storm had ended. The clouds, when they broke, allowed beams of moonlight to tumble down. At the end of the tunnel when he emerged at Slaughterhouse Row, all the long buildings and chimneys were cast in a silver pall. It was nearly eleven. Why would an informant want to meet in such a place? he kept asking himself. None of the answers came up reassuring.

At Slaughterhouse Five he pulled into the shadows and turned off the motor. His time behind enemy lines made stealth second nature. He navigated the rest of the way by foot without making so much as a crunch on the gravel. The night was dank, chilly. But the storm had chased away the stench, and for the time being the air was almost sweet. He halted at the sight of Slaughterhouse Seven. A lone Horch was parked out front. Next to it, the building entrance, he saw, was ever so slightly ajar. He went up to it and peeked through. It was dark as hell in there. Absolutely silent. He slipped inside.

Barely breathing, he stood a moment and let his eyes adjust. A shock of ammonia pinched his nose. It had to be twenty degrees colder in here, the two-story arcade and stone floors designed to keep temperatures down, he remembered Gruber telling him. For sanitary purposes.

The clouds opened, sending moonlight pouring through the grime-covered skylights, illuminating the interior like a photo from the kaiser's time, filtered in rusty sepia. The place was huge. Blocks long. Subdivided into semi-enclosed zones for different types of animals. Some were leased long-term by companies whose names hung from signs: R. J. Hessen, Jinks-Escher. Since partitioning walls were only partial, everything was pretty much visible.

To Willi's right he saw Plussgart & Son had dozens of thick chopping tables with sharp hatchets resting on each, and enough stray feathers missed by the cleaning crews to indicate it was a chicken abattoir. To his left, a far larger section leased by Goertner Brothers was filled with ramps and swinging gates through which obviously small quadrupeds were herded. Awaiting them were rows of wooden "cradles" that immobilized them for a swift blow to the head. A lineup of spikes and iron mallets stood against the wall. Running the length of the ceiling, long steel tracks contained numerous hooks, onto which the stunned creatures were evidently bound and yanked up by the legs, then sent down the line for a quick coup de grâce. All the throat-slitting scalpels hung in shiny rows. The slate floors were lined with graded gutters. Farther down, the skin- and fat-stripping areas had enormous vats on tracks, which allowed for easy disposal.

It was quite the assembly line.

Willi paused, listening. What was that? Had something just crashed in the distance? Or was it only the creaking of those hooks in the wind? He heard it again. Way at the other end of the building, a definite banging, like thunder. Could that be all it was, the storm returning? He picked up his pace, careful not to make a sound, then clouds blocked the moon and forced him to feel his way through darkness. No doubt, though, something was making a major commotion up there. It was growing in intensity as he neared, until all at once it exploded into the most hideous, bloodcurdling scream he'd heard since the battlefield.

My God.

He stopped, senses thrust to full throttle, ears poised like radio receivers, picking up nothing for what seemed eternity, then . . . running. A door slamming. A motor starting outside. A truck? It revved, then grew louder until it passed on the road outside and disappeared around the block.

His heart pounded wildly as he hurried ahead, not caring anymore about noise. At the far end of the building his shoulders were so tense it felt as if he'd taken a bullet. The area, he saw with a strange chill, continued to display the name Kleist-Rosenthaler.

He smelled it first. Sharp. Pungent. Then, scanning desperately, he spotted it: an enormous, almost machetelike cleaver dripping with still-steaming blood. At his feet, a gutter along the edge of the slate floor flowed red. His eyes followed until they froze in disbelief. A pair of hands, fingers downward, swung an inch off the floor.

He looked up.

Suspended upside down from two hooks, blond hair dangling in a pool of blood, eyes wide, tongue out, Freksa was strung up like a side of beef, practically split in two.

Book Three

WASTE NOT

Seventeen

BERLIN
JULY 1930

Distant screams filled the air.

Swept up by the excited crowds, Willi could barely keep a grip on the boys. It was peak summer. He'd been working relentlessly for months, and it was great taking a day off. But one couldn't be too careful right now. Especially about kids.

Past the main gates they descended the terrace staircase, and he recalled coming down these same steps when he was a kid. Luna Park was a Berlin tradition. In the plaza below, the fountain still shot five stories high, beyond which cable cars sailed above the shimmering Halensee and its peddling swan boats. Ferris wheels. Waterslides. Roller coasters and sideshows. There couldn't have been a starker contrast to the world they'd just stepped out of.

It had been a terrible summer. And only half over. The economy wouldn't quit coming apart. Everywhere, revenues were plummeting. Businesses folding. Tent cities popping up. The Reichstag had rejected all the chancellor's harsh austerity measures, so the chancellor had dissolved the Reichstag and called for new elections in September. The campaign had turned violent. Radical parties of left and right supplemented sloganeering with brass knuckles and truncheons. Brown-shirted Nazis and Red Front Communists clobbered it out in the streets and parks and on the U-Bahn. Schupo, the security police, were unable to put a lid on their turf war, which only added to the public perception that Berlin was spinning out of control.

That *Der Kinderfresser* couldn't be caught only escalated the vertigo.

Around the central plaza the scent of roasting peanuts hovered in the air. Flags waved. Clowns juggled. People surged in a dozen directions. "Roller coaster! Roller coaster!" The kids, if no one else, presented a united front.

Willi loathed roller coasters. He didn't mind speed as long as it was horizontal. But he sure as hell wasn't letting them go alone. As they waited to buy tickets, he saw how happy Erich and Stefan were to have Heinzie Winkelmann along; they always got on better when their plump, good-natured chum joined in, although Willi wondered about Heinz's father. Otto had no time to chat anymore, passing in the hall with a curt nod, never once asking about the *Kinderfresser* case—which was very unlike him. Willi assumed he still was depressed about losing his store and having to accept such menial labor in a mailroom, and embarrassed, perhaps, because Willi'd caught him crying that morning. After all, he'd made such a fuss at Heinz in front of them about how Germans didn't do such things. Yet Vicki said she'd noticed a slight detachment on the part of Irmgard too.

Between the boys, at least, all was laughter. On the roller-coaster dock Willi got in with Stefan while Erich and Heinz jumped in ahead. As the cars yanked off on the long climb to the first precipice, Willi's stomach began to knot. He'd rather slither through no-man's-land than endure the twists and turns of this thing. But as they reached the peak and swept over, the kids cried with such delight that Willi just clenched his eyes and prayed they didn't notice him. How would that look: one of Berlin's top cops more frightened than his children.

With Freksa's death the spotlight had suddenly fallen on him.

His reputation had been redeemed.

Because he'd already pointed a finger at the *Viehof* and because it had been his to begin with, the Kommissar had finally awarded him command of the *Kinderfresser* case. "You wanted it, Kraus? It's yours. Don't fuck up!" The whole of Berlin was familiar with his name now, and he was treated with a modicum of respect—even by his unit. But the ups and downs of the bloody ordeal remained every bit as nauseating as this ride. As were the complications set in motion with Vicki.

Whoever'd killed Freksa had gotten away with it. For now. The cleaver used to hack him in half held no fingerprints, nor were any discernible tire tracks found on the road outside. The more Willi recalled the noise of the motor, however, the more he was convinced he'd heard a small truck drive by that night. Maybe the Ox's. The man had vanished entirely. Multiple raids on the peddlers' market with their mass interrogations had yielded little and only metastasized the problem. The big market had dwindled but smaller ones sprang up in half a dozen other locations, making it impossible to monitor them all.

As the roller coaster swung down a steep bend and back up for another precipitous drop, Willi couldn't help but clutch the seat. Ahead, Erich and Heinz were waving their arms crazily. Up, up, then over— Willi's stomach bounced into his heart. He really did hate this thing.

Minutes later he was happier on the Auto Scooter track, which traversed a weird expressionistic landscape of tilted buildings, trees, and mountains designed to induce double vision. Willi, who very much liked fast driving as long as he was the one doing it, tried his best to help Stefan catch Heinz and Erich, but they couldn't quite make it. Like the Shepherdess, he thought—always just out of reach.

Everywhere. Nowhere. For weeks he'd gotten reported sightings of this red-haired abductress, but not a single hard fact. Even High Priestess Helga claimed she'd seen her. And where? In a dream.

"My sheets were drenched with sweat when I awoke," she'd told him over the phone. "Positively horrifying. But I can't remember a thing about it, Sergeant."

Great. Even the dreams were vague.

Sometimes he'd wondered if this Ilse really existed or was just some phantom of the collective unconscious.

When they got to the fun house, the boys went wild in the hall of mirrors, trying to find each other in the maze of reflections. Even Willi began to get confused about what was real and what only seemed it.

Like everyone else in Berlin, he'd adopted the term *Kinderfresser* to describe the perpetrator of a whole set of kidnappings and murders. Whether this Ilse, the Shepherdess, was doing more than grabbing boys off the street, he didn't know. But this was no one-woman operation, Willi was certain. In the last two months another six boys had gone missing. Even with the whole city on guard.

And Ilse had certainly not cleaved Freksa in two.

At lunch the boys ate schnitzel and kraut while Willi stuck to coffee, his mind drifting back to the lengthy conversation he'd had with his cousin at Passover. After seder, he and Kurt retreated to Willi's little study while the boys went to Erich's room to work on the Red Baron's plane. Amazingly, they came running out an hour later to show it off, completely finished. It had only taken a little diligence, and a thing of singular beauty took flight, some odd three-winged bird. Kurt's theorizing, meanwhile, suggested a criminal even more bizzare, and without the accompanying beauty.

"Just as the compulsion for order may defend against inner chaos"—he'd taken off his glasses grimly—"this selling the flesh, making designs of the bones, utilizing them, could very well serve to bolster an illusion of usefulness." He stared at Willi without blinking. "More than likely to compensate for some equally deep-seated belief in his or her own useless*ness*."

Poverty might play a role.

Certainly there had to be some experience in leather making.

Luna Park's famous lane of sideshows contained small cabanas, each offering lurid peeks at circus-style oddities. Sword swallowers. Fire-eaters. The boys begged to see the bearded lady, but Willi put his foot down. He had no intention of letting them gawk at some unfortunate woman.

Since the peddlers' markets had dispersed, he'd switched tactics and focused surveillance on the *Viehof* directly, the by-products zone specifically—where leather makers and bone boilers abounded.

He'd had a rather strange encounter there.

After a week of poring over maps and registration papers, he'd gained all sorts of insight into a world he barely knew existed. Dressed in the long white jacket of a *Viehof* inspector, he was able to poke around for days, speaking to people and getting to know how their operations worked. A web of interlocking streets contained dozens of varying businesses, the largest of which, the tanneries, occupied whole blocks. He'd gotten to inspect the workings of some of these massive facilities, which employed scores of laborers. Truck after truck of freshly skinned cowhides arrived each day from the slaughterhouses. Soaked in huge vats, scraped by hand, tumbled inside drums, and strung out to dry, they were eventually slid between giant rollers, pressed, folded, and shipped to make everything from watchbands to upholstery.

Not as large but far smellier were the plants for rendering fat into tallow. Barrels full of the stinking stuff arrived after each big slaughter, processed for use in candles and soap, shaving cream, lipstick. The gelatin works were of a similar vein, skin, tendons, ligaments, and hooves boiled down to make liquids used as ingredients in everything from marshmallows to shampoo. Horns. Feathers. Quills. Bristles. Nothing was neglected. Plants even rendered oils from the placentas of cow uteruses for use in cosmetics. Several gut-works spun intestines into thin, tough string for such things as musical instruments, tennis rackets, surgical thread. These interested Willi in particular. As did an entire street full of bone boilers and bone crushers, processing marrow and grinding powder for fertilizers and vitamins.

The other day, on an especially stench-filled lane shared by a number of small gelatin and bone works, surrounded in a haze of dust and oily smoke, he did a double take at the vision of a man in a white, blood-splattered smock. The fellow, shaded by a black worker's cap, was spread-kneed on a stool, smoking. For a second Willi was sure it was the Ox. He was almost as big, and practically as fearsome, but the closer Willi looked, the more he felt certain it wasn't the Ox. In fact, the more he felt certain it wasn't even a he. Inadvertently their eyes met, and Willi saw a swift black shadow race across the meaty face before it turned away.

"Blistering hot, eh?" he said to strike up a conversation.

Barely a grunt came in reply, but the voice was coarse and masculine. The facial features too. Even the hands, permanently stained, it seemed, with several sanguine coats, were thick and strong as a man's. Only there wasn't a strand of hair on the forearms. And on the neck, no Adam's apple.

"Must be tough to work here," he said. "For a woman. You're the first I've seen at the *Viehof.*"

A look of terror flashed across her face. After darting her gaze back and forth to see if anyone was near, she cast a quick glance at him. "I don't mean no harm."

She definitely wasn't from Berlin, her accent so thick it was hard to even understand her, somewhere from the sticks. But Willi could hardly miss the fear still burning in her eyes. Clearly she wasn't the Shepherdess. Helga the High Priestess had described her former devotee as slender and attractive. This woman was hideous. A thick, red, bulbous nose. Blubbery cheeks webbed with veins. God only knew what she ate to get that size. Truly a freak of nature, Willi thought. Both repellent and deserving of pity.

"I've been here since the war." Round, glassy eyes fastened on him in a furious gambit for sympathy. "When the men were at the front."

Willi knew in those days women practically ran Berlin. Factories. Streetcars. The *Viehof* too. Must have done a good job because nobody starved in the city, which certainly wasn't the case in the countryside.

"Didn't want to lose my job when the war ended so I pretended to be a man. Please, Herr Inspektor, I'm alone in the world . . . a little sister to support. Don't report me." The beefy hands clasped between fat knees in what looked like prayer.

Willi felt bad for her. Why shouldn't a woman be allowed to do the same job as a man, if capable? He took down her name, where she worked, and her employee number just to make himself look official, but told her not to worry. As long as she was properly registered, he assured, her secret would be safe. The next day, though, when he glanced over the employment files for Reiniger Gelatins where she claimed to work, he couldn't find the name she'd given him, and the employee number was false.

On the giant Swaying Staircase, which you had to descend while being tossed as if in an earthquake, the kids were laughing so hard they could barely stand. It felt like Willi's own life these past few months. Every step at a new angle.

All of Berlin had been horrified at Freksa's death and turned to his replacement to fill the top sleuth's shoes. Overnight Willi'd become a minor celebrity. The press hounded him. The mayor of Berlin had paid a visit. He'd never before faced such a level of attention and expectation. But access also to certain basics. Such as support, finally.

A few days after his appointment to the *Kinderfresser* case, Kommissar Horthstaler had pranced in with his new assistant, Gunther—a giraffe of a kid, six feet four inches, who soon enough was following Willi about like a duckling. A country boy who'd never been to Berlin until Police Academy, he was almost impossible to dislike, but sometimes rather absurd. Such as when they walked outside and his ridiculously long neck turned ten directions simultaneously, the buildings, traffic, everything transfixing him. Especially the girls. He tripped over his huge feet looking at them all.

On the job he was smart and eager. His enthusiasm knew no bounds. Willi practically had to ask him to stop smiling. Which was why, halfway through his first week, it was impossible not to notice the sullen grimace etched acrosss his rectangular face one day after lunch. When Willi asked about it, the kid at least was honest enough, his bony Adam's apple plunging like a bucket down a well.

"Is it true, sir, you're a . . . Jew?"

Even in 1930, Germany's rural population was for the most part barely literate peasants. Gunther, not surprisingly, had never been in the same room, much less acquainted, with a Jew. He certainly knew enough about them, though. Jews had not only killed the Son of God but were too arrogant to accept faith in Him after all these centuries. They were shiftless, unscrupulous, swindlers, thieves, perverts. They'd caused the Russian revolution *and* the depression. And, during the war, turned against the fatherland, conspiring with their international brethren to defeat and humiliate Germany.

Willi didn't have the energy to combat two millennia of hate. But he didn't want to lose the kid, either. He'd waited too long for a good assistant. So he invited Gunther over for dinner, to Beckmann Strasse. The kid wasn't sure what to make of it, but was tempted enough by the prospect of a home-cooked meal to consent. By the end of the evening he was so infatuated with Vicki and the kids he didn't seem to want to leave. He was especially amazed when the boys showed off Willi's Iron Cross for bravery in combat. Then Vicki came out with a blue silk scarf she'd bought in Paris but Willi never wore.

"Here, Gunther, a present for you."

She was trying hard, Willi could see, to reconcile herself to a situation she was anything but pleased with. His assignment to the *Kinderfresser* case had made everyone happy but her.

"Come. I bet you look divine in it."

"You're giving this to me?" Gunther couldn't believe it.

"Well, my husband won't wear it." She feigned a look of despair, though Willi was only too well aware of the real thing lurking just below the surface. "He thinks anything lighter than dark gray's too bright."

"But I'd always heard Jews were so cheap."

She just stood there slack-jawed as Gunther took the scarf.

The kid didn't even realize he'd said anything wrong. "Thanks so much, Frau Kraus." He wrapped the silk around his neck, touching it like a golden fleece. "I've never had such a beautiful garment."

On the walk back to the U-Bahn Willi felt the need to put his cards on the table.

"Look, Gunther, we could find ourselves in some tight spots ahead, you and me. Trust might mean the difference between life and death. If you're to be my backup, I need to know: can you say with one hundred percent certainty you're behind me?"

Gunther was obviously caught by surprise at such forthrightness.

"Well . . ." He opened his palms, seeming to weigh the situation. "I was taught to judge a man by what I see, not by what I hear. You and your family"—he held out one of the huge, bony hands—"are all right." He clasped Willi's hand tightly. "I can say I'm behind you, yes, sir. One hundred percent."

Left. Right. Left. Right. The carnival staircase shifted whichever way you stepped on it, until at the bottom, a huge blast of air shot from the floor, blowing up the ladies' skirts, and sending the kids into further spasms of hilarity.

By now, everyone was dying for a swim. For ten pfennig each they got suits, towels, and admittance to the famous Sea-Pool, with its ever-so-much-fun-to-jump artificially generated waves. In the locker room, chubby little Heinz had to sit on the toilet forever from all the excitement. Then his zipper got stuck and Erich and Stefan got cranky having to hang around, so while Willi, hot and tired himself, helped Heinz, he told his sons to wait outside by the changing-hall door. Under no circumstances should they venture farther, especially not down to the pool. A poor choice. Moments later when he and Heinz came out, Erich and Stefan weren't there.

Willi's eyes darted back and forth. Swarms of people surged in and out of the changing hall, overflowing the paths to the pool. Keep calm, he told himself. They couldn't have gone far. But if his stomach had gone into his heart on the roller coaster, now it burst through his throat. That the boys were together, normally reassuring, didn't help at all.

Illusory though she seemed, Willi knew the Shepherdess was definitely real. And definitely still out there doing her dirty work. At least he could take pride in one small accomplishment—since word had gone out among street kids to travel only in groups of three or more, not a single one had gone missing. Unfortunately, now kids had started disappearing from orphanages.

The progressive government of the German Republic prided itself on its social-welfare programs, from modern health care and penal reform to homes for unwed mothers. None was more touted than the progress made under the Youth Welfare Law. Although countless kids remained on the streets, half a dozen first-rate facilities had opened around Berlin for orphans lucky enough to get in. Now, though, three of these had reported missing boys.

Kopenick Haus was typical. A bright, sunny facility with grassy gardens, game rooms, dormitories filled with cots and fresh linen, all under the watchful gaze of women in white uniforms. But the place was packed to the rafters. Kids in the gardens. Kids in the dorms. Kids in the playpens and cribs. Row after row, room after room, of them.

Nurse Wolff summed it up: "The facility's superb. It's just that we're bursting at the seams. With the economic crisis, not merely infants but school-age children are turning up practically by the busload. We do our best, but it's impossible to keep an eye on them all. At night of course we lock up, but during the day anyone can walk in."

Two boys, seven and eight, had vanished yesterday. The janitor claimed to have seen a woman walking out with them but hadn't thought anything about it because she was wearing nurse's whites. Willi spoke to him.

"Is there anything you can remember about how she looked or spoke or acted? You must try to recall even the smallest detail. It could be terribly important."

"Just that she was kind of ugly for such a young gal."

"Ugly? How? And how young would you say?"

"My daughter's age, maybe. Twenty-four, -five. Slim as a broomstick, but spongy face, pockmarked. Was the eyes made her ugly, though. Ice-cold. Gave me a real bright smile as she passed. Acted charming, but underneath . . ." He shook his head. "Oh, and one of them little red-and-black twisted-cross buttons on her uniform lapel."

"Interesting. Did you happen to notice her hair color?"

"Hair? She had a nurse's cap, like I said. But underneath, why I believe it was—red."

So there it was. The first real sighting of the Shepherdess.

And that's how she got her kids. One way, anyway. A nurse. Turned on the charm when she wanted. Nazi to boot.

The information was a huge step forward.

But cold comfort now that he couldn't find the boys.

As he scanned the crowds heading to and from the pool, there wasn't so much as a sight of them. It was Vicki's eyes he saw staring back at him, dark with accusation.

"Why? Why?" She'd cried the night he'd been given the *Kinderfresser* case. They'd already climbed into bed when he told her. "What is driving you to do this? Isn't the danger you usually face enough? Do you have to take on extra? Are you trying to prove something? Is it because you're Jewish?"

"Someone's out there, Vic, abducting little kids. Doing terrible things to them."

"You have children too!"

She'd no idea he'd never lived up to his promise to stay away from the case all this time. But Freksa's murder sure didn't help her warm up any to the idea of his taking over now.

"I can't say no, honey. And besides, honestly, I want to. So help me. I'm sorry."

"Sorry? Crazy is what you are."

She threw her feet from the bed and jammed them into slippers. "You want the case, fine. I'm leaving. Taking the boys and going to my parents. I don't care if they do have school. Their lives are more important. I'll register them out there. You want to get killed, I can't prevent you. But I sure as hell am not letting you—"

"Listen." He'd stopped her, making her face him. "I understand your fear, Vic. Honest. And I think you've every right to it; whoever's committing these crimes is crazy. And dangerous. But remember the old saying: 'Fear makes the wolf look bigger.' The boys will be safe as long as they're watched. From now on, we'll make sure they are. Every minute. Every day. No more walking to or from school without adult accompaniment. No more unsupervised play—not in the park or even the courtyard. The Winkelmanns will pitch in, and when I take them to school in the morning, I'll go to the headmaster and make sure he understands. Until this case is solved, Erich and Stefan are never to be out of adult sight. Ever. But you can't run away with them, honey. The whole city's looking to me for reassurance. If I send my wife and children packing . . ."

She wouldn't turn around. But she didn't reach for her robe, either.

"I know it's a lot to ask. I really need you, though. Please don't pull back."

But she had. She didn't leave. But she had pulled back. He could feel it in a dozen ways. And if anything ever happened to Erich and Stefan . . .

Like any nine-year-old, Erich could get mischievous, especially under the sway of a long day at the amusement park. Though explicitly warned not to, Willi found it hard to believe he could have taken his younger brother anywhere but the pool. Grabbing Heinz by the hand, he hurried down the path to look for them. Unfortunately, Luna Park's famously gigantic pool was crammed on this broiling summer day with what looked to be hundreds of people. "Keep an eye out for them would ya, Heinzie?" Willi said as they headed toward the shallow end.

For a moment, he allowed his darkest fears to bubble up. But a tide of such black grief swept him, only the next-door neighbor boy's chubby little hand kept him from going under. He had to force himself not to start running around, shouting Erich's name. Surely they had a loudspeaker system here. Erich and Stefan could not be the first lost boys in Luna Park. But as he scrutinized the pool, looking at the countless heads in the artificially generated waves, and all the moving figures on the walkways, he found himself sinking in desperation—searching not only for his son, but any glimpse of a redheaded nurse. Might he have been, as Vicki feared, specifically targeted? How would anyone even know they were here?

Frantically scanning face after face, he couldn't keep out the recollection of his recent meeting with Dr. Hoffnung.

After all these months the pathologist had finally determined a cause of death in the burlap-sack victims. Highly advanced techniques in spectrophotometry, he'd explained, which used wavelengths of infrared light to identify substances otherwise invisible to the naked eye, had uncovered tiny specks on the evidence. Seven, to be exact: five on bones, two on the burlap. All turned out to be blood. Further testing through something called chromatography, which heated tiny fragments of these samples into a gaseous state and measured their composition, had revealed that all the blood contained massive amounts of HbCO, or carboxyhemoglobin, unambiguously proving the cause of death to be hypoxia, a pathological condition that starved the body of oxygen.

Willi'd worked with Hoffnung a number of times and never known him to soft-shoe around. Now, though, he was clearly so uncomfortable with what he was trying to say he couldn't even look at Willi.

"Plain German please, Doctor. I'm sorry. I'm just not following."

"How exactly it might have been executed, or why"—Hoffnung's voice cracked as he averted his eyes, clenching his pipe—"I simply cannot ascertain, of course." He struggled with a little burp. "But before their flesh got chopped up and used, as you tell me, for sausage filler, and before their bones got boiled"—he managed a fast, unhappy glance at Willi—"these boys were murdered by carbon monoxide poisoning, Sergeant. In other words, gassed."

Willi thought it couldn't get worse, but Hoffnung looked away again.

"Plus the spectrophotometry revealed multiple tiny grooves caused by human incisors. Whoever did this may have chopped up the flesh, but they also gnawed directly on the bones. There's no doubt about it, Kraus. We're dealing with a cannibal here. *Kinderfresser*'s no misnomer."

The recollection made Willi feel faint. In desperation he turned from the pool back up toward the changing-hall entrance, squinting through a sheen of tears, needing to blink. Exactly where they were supposed to be, Erich and Stefan had suddenly rematerialized. His heart pounded wildly as he dragged Heinz over. They'd just gone around the corner to the drinking fountain, they cheerfully explained when Willi got there, having no idea he'd even missed them. He could have strangled them both.

Eighteen

Thundering drums shook the Sportpalast. Trumpets and fifes and jolly glockenspiels blared a pounding march. Tides of red and black swastikas swept the aisles. *"Heil, heil, heil!"* Thousands greeted the arriving youth brigades. Caps and boots, straps and epaulettes— they made their Communist counterparts look like rabble. Hardly your run-of-the-mill campaign rally, Willi thought.

And sure as hell nothing to snicker about.

"What a circus," Fritz had proclaimed yesterday over lunch when five or six open trucks had roared past Café Kranzler filled with these Hitlerites tossing leaflets: TOMORROW: THE FÜHRER SPEAKS! The Ku' damm was ankle-deep in paper. Someone was bankrolling the circus, big-time.

"You remember my old school chum, von Hessler?" Fritz glanced at a leaflet, grimacing. "He's conducting some kind of scientific experiment at this thing, measuring brain energy, he claims. Needed a ton of equipment so I wrangled him a press box, best in the house. He was so grateful he begged me to join. Promised a once-in-a-lifetime show. Why not come too, Willi?"

Sounded like a fun night out. Willi knew precious little about Nazis—other than that they believed Germany's greatest misfortune was Jews. How entertaining. But the fact that the Shepherdess kidnapped orphans while brazenly wearing their swastika pin made him take Fritz up on it. Knowledge was power, and he needed all he could get on this case. Three more boys had just gone missing. This time right out of grade schools.

The Bismarck School in working-class Schöneberg was in the middle of summer session. The principal couldn't grasp it. "No one saw a thing. The kids lined up after recess and our count showed two missing. I take full responsibility. But how did it happen, Detektiv? We're all in shock." It was similar at the Lessing Academy miles away in Friedrichshain, the teacher beyond consolation. A missing boy, barely seven, waiting out front for his mother to fetch him after school, and that was it. Last anyone saw of him. The Shepherdess was clearly roaming ever farther afield, seizing targets of opportunity. And ever-younger boys.

How the hell did she get away with it?

"Heil, heil, heil, heil!"

Nazis were the tiniest of the Reichstag parties, Fritz explained as they awaited its leader. In the last election they'd managed to eke out twelve seats—one held by their talented propagandist, Joseph Goebbels.

Goebbels, Willi thought. Small world. Dr. Weiss had won his libel case against that man. But it barely even slowed the pit bull down. When kicked, Goebbels only chomped harder, ratcheting up the viciousness of his attacks. Weiss was having to take the son of a bitch to court all over again.

Extremists of all stripes were feeding off this economic crisis like sharks, Fritz observed. The Nazis dreamed of tripling their strength in the September election. It didn't seem implausible to Willi, considering how every day another factory shut, another store went bust. In Berlin, everywhere you looked, the *Arbeitslos*, the unemployed, milled about aimlessly, filling park benches, standing in line for charity. Men whose clothes still bore testament to last year's prosperity, fine suits and leather shoes, tattered now and covered with dust, faces registering a grim metamorphosis from disbelief to resignation. It was appalling to witness the rate at which the misery was compounding.

From 1914 to 1924 Germany'd endured such terrible years. War. Starvation. Revolution. Hyperinflation. A great boom followed, but now the bottom was falling out again, and people were panicked, desperate for leadership. Willi certainly shared that desire, but what he was seeing here wasn't politics. This was a new religion. And hardly a joke. A quick glance at Fritz revealed, indeed, the smirk had disappeared.

On the stage below, awash in swastikas, the band conductor led ranks of musicians with a murderous conviction, thrusting his baton as if a dagger into someone's heart. He couldn't have been more than sixteen. Hundreds of women marched up the aisles in long black skirts halfway to their ankles, white shirts, black scarves.

Might the Shepherdess be among them? Willi searched for red hair.

Hanging thirty feet in the air, parallel to the podium, the press box offered an unrivaled view. "I told you they put on a real show," von Hessler said without the least interest in it. He'd made perfectly clear he'd come not to see Hitler, but to pursue his own scientific work, and had a curtain drawn over the box door to create a small, private laboratory, where he was busy now fussing over an ordinary-looking woman seated up there with them—the subject of his experiment. The doctor's silver eye patch glistened as he covered Frau Klopstock with a barber smock and began hooking her to a bizarre-looking piece of machinery it had taken two workers to haul up. Filled with rows of buttons and switches and sprouting dozens of wires, von Hessler claimed it measured "brain waves."

"If we could see into the cranium, we might view how a person thinks," he lectured to no one in particular, focusing on attaching wires from the machine to Frau Klopstock's skull, as she stoically smiled. "Until experiments on live humans are permitted, I'm afraid, though, this is the next-best thing. It's called an electroencephalogram—EEG. My colleague Hans Berger invented it last year." Using gel and cotton pads the doctor went on adhering wire after wire to poor Frau Klopstock's head until she looked like a deep-sea fish. "It detects electrical activity on the scalp produced by neurons firing within the brain. Berger has so far deduced two kinds—alpha and beta waves, each of which gets recorded in separate lines on this machine here, a double-coil recording galvanometer made by Siemens. Frau Klopstock, I believe, has always cast her ballot for the Catholic Center Party. Am I right, Frau Klopstock?"

"Yes, quite, Herr Doktor." The woman managed a brave face despite her ungainly tiara.

"Given the current situation, she's become uncertain who will get her vote this September. In recording her brain waves I am attempting to measure her psychic response to this rally. She could, for instance, deny that she is in any way excited by Herr Hitler, but her brain waves might show differently."

Indeed, as he turned on the machine with half a dozen switches, zigzag waves began appearing on a rolling piece of paper. They moved each time the band below burst into another military march and new uniformed detachments arrived. But sank into inactivity during the long waits between. Von Hessler repeatedly told Frau Klopstock she was doing "just excellently."

Unfortunately the featured speaker, this Führer, never seemed to arrive. The lines on the double-coil galvanometer were drooping. Willi was envisioning calling it a day, sneaking off to the comfort of home, when suddenly a spectacular explosion of shouting shook the building from outside. With the force of a tidal wave it burst through the doors, filling the arena and instantly sending fourteen thousand people to their feet screaming, *"Heil! Heil!"* Even Frau Klopstock, who had no particular feelings about Hitler, she'd claimed, had to be warned not to pull out the wiring von Hessler'd so arduously placed. Willi had no such constraints. The energy was so intense he jumped to his feet with everyone else to witness this arrival.

"Heil! Heil! Heil! Heil!"

Surrounded by a small entourage, a uniformed figure strutted up the center aisle holding up a palm. The roar grew deafening. Willi'd never heard anything like it. Even the most exciting football match didn't produce such a din. People were screaming, crying, pressing forward, thrusting out their arms. They were hailing not a politician, he saw, but a savior.

"My God," Fritz stammered into Willi's ear. "Europe hasn't seen anything like this since the messianic cults of the Middle Ages."

After what seemed like an hour the screaming finally stilled as the head of the Nazi Party reached the podium, the hall silencing in tense anticipation. Willi could clearly see the man's face. Besides the rectangular "toothbrush" mustache popular among the lower-middle classes, little about it was distinctive. He could have been a grocer or a clerk at the post office. Except for the eyes. Even from thirty feet above Willi could feel their fire.

In his tan uniform and high black boots, thick leather strap across his chest, the Leader stood before his yearning masses and said . . . nothing. For what felt like eternity he gazed about the auditorium, holding his right arm with left hand, then switching, then folding both arms across his chest. The audience grew guiltily silent, as if it was their fault he couldn't begin. Then the Führer appeared to remember something and pulled the podium nearer, scanning his notes as if for some essential point—although from Willi's vantage point it was obvious he wasn't even reading. From Willi's vantage point, every movement Hitler made was obviously not merely rehearsed but thoroughly calculated for effect. The longer he refused to begin, as graphically illustrated by Frau Klopstock's brain chart, the more urgently the audience craved his words.

"Extraordinary, isn't it?" Von Hessler's eye patch seemed to radiate enthusiasm, not for the speaker but for the galvanometer. "You may not realize it, gentlemen, but what you're seeing is a perfect illustration of an internal condition. On that roll of paper is a precise portrait of nervous excitation. Frau Klopstock may be sitting still, but all her peripheral nerve endings are frantically transforming energy, ushering it into the central nervous system. From the motion of that stylus I can safely speculate that she is far more excited by Herr Hitler that she might have expected. Am I right?"

"Oh, quite." Frau Klopstock could barely tear her eyes from the podium.

Hitler looked around, coughing into his fist. With the same hand he smoothed the flap of hair across his forehead, then coughed a little more. Finally, almost inaudibly, he croaked out, "People of Berlin—"

And the whole arena sprang to its feet. *"Heil, heil, heil, heil!"*

It took a few minutes to settle down again so the Führer could commence. When he did, his voice was so quiet the audience had to lean forward.

"Success," he all but whispered, "is the sole judge of right and wrong. We have only to look at the streets of our capital." His pitch, almost imperceptibly, began to rise. "At the millions without jobs. Without dignity. Without hope." Steadily, each vowel seemed to grow in volume. "To understand the hell this republic has brought to us."

Until at last his words began to thunder from the loudspeakers.

"Not private gain, but common good must be foremost on the minds of those who lead Germany. The day of individual happiness is over. The doom of this nation can be averted only by a storm of passion. By those who are passionate themselves and can arouse passion in others."

Willi's throat had gone dry. He found himself strangely moved by the words, conscious of their appeal, even agreeing to some extent. It was no exaggeration to assert that the republic was fraying at the seams, the government paralyzed, the economic crisis apparently bottomless. Perhaps someone with Bismarckian charisma was needed to hold it all together and push the nation back toward prosperity and self-respect. But Hitler's voice had grown so shrill, so harsh, so aggressive, it began to grate at Willi's eardrums.

"There must be no more ranks or classes." He stabbed the air violently. "All Germans are one! And it's not enough to affirm your agreement. The time has come to fight!"

He turned to the uniformed rows at his feet.

"To my beloved youth—remember always: it's not by the principles of humanity man lives, but only by the most brutal struggle. You must steel yourselves. What is weak must be hammered away. You are the flesh of our flesh and the blood of our blood. And those who do not want to fight in this world do not deserve to live."

He was pounding his chest, clutching his throat.

"National Socialism is Germany's future. Around us marches Germany! In us marches Germany! Behind us marches Germany!"

The whole audience was back on its feet again shouting. *"Heil! Heil! Heil! Heil!"*

Hitler, Willi saw, had blasted straight to the central nervous system von Hessler was trying to read, stimulating passions his listeners probably didn't even know they still had. Bent old women, one-armed veterans, hausfraus, burghers—all staring like teary-eyed lovers on honeymoon. Like toddlers at their stalwart papa. The Leader would pick them up. He would lift them and make them strong. He would make them good again.

"Our enemies think we're mud to be trampled on." Hitler reached with both hands, seeming to strangle someone in front of him. "But we are the greatest people on earth! And we will have our place in the sun." His fingers turned to his own chest, clutching at it as if to tear apart the rib cage and display his naked heart.

"I will lead you there. I swear by God!"

His eyes were rolling, spit drooling down the sides of his mouth.

Willi leaned back, horrified. There was no denying Hitler's magnetism; his ideas even contained certain truths. But the man was certifiably insane. And this was no political rally but mass hysteria. Even Frau Klopstock in her crown of wires had tears rushing down her cheeks, her EEG readings flying off the paper.

"Fantastic, isn't it," von Hessler cried, not just of his test results this time but of the Nazi leader. "Completely validates the theory of energy liberation: the unleashing of heat and force in accordance with laws of physics. The process that enables cells to renew, like a nation must to regenerate!"

Willi wanted nothing more but to get out of this madness.

At least now, though, he grasped the appeal this movement had for a troubled soul such as the Shepherdess. Order. Purpose. A place to lose herself. An idol to worship.

Somewhere in the screaming mobs he could practically feel her out there.

And once he found her, he would find *Der Kinderfresser*.

Nineteen

"How 'bout it, Kraus?" the crowd of reporters shouted as he stepped from the Police Presidium. It was nearly six but heat still beat down on the Alex, the glass globe atop the Tietz department store shimmering like a mirage. The reporters' faces, Willi noticed, were slick with sweat and tension. How he longed for the day he'd be able to stand out here and tell them—the whole city—what they were waiting to hear.

"Nothing today, fellas. You know I'll give it to you as soon as I have."

"But we thought the orphanages were secured," Woerner of the *Abend Zeitung* shouted as Willi turned away. "How many more kids have to die, Kraus?"

Willi ignored him, walking off. But it felt as if a bullet had hit his gut. As if he didn't ask himself that every hour. Each disappearance was another torture to him. Even now he could see headlines up at the corner kiosk: TWO MORE MISSING FROM TREPTOW HAUS. It was nauseating. He might have been closer than Freksa'd ever gotten. At least he knew what he was looking for. But in this business, close was shit.

"Sorry"—Woerner ran by, jumping onto a passing streetcar—"nothing personal, Willi, you know that. You're the best Homicide's got. But a job's a job."

"Yeah, sure." Willi supposed he ought to manage a smile.

Traffic was heavy, the sidewalks packed. Instead of posters for toothpaste and movies, the advertising columns were plastered now with campaign placards, hammer and sickles and pictures of Hitler. It reminded him of that mad throng at the Sportpalast last night, sending a small shudder through him.

Upstairs earlier, he'd overhead Mueller and Stoss in the hallway chiding young Gunther about working for a Jew.

"Ever check your wallet before you go home at night, kid? He might be picking your pocket."

Gunther hadn't laughed along, but he hadn't defended Willi, either.

"Detektiv Kraus," he heard now, surprised to see Kai emerge from the darkness near World Wide Fur. The place was empty. Out of business.

"You've got to come, please." Even beneath the lipstick and makeup he could tell the kid's face was white.

At the corner of Leipziger and Charlotten Strassen, in the heart of Berlin's shopping district, they entered an upscale leather store. Willi'd actually been here once with Vicki, looking for a briefcase. Bei Schröder. He immediately spotted other boys of Kai's gang bunched around a display case. Although silent, their flamboyant feathers and earrings couldn't have screamed louder in the understated décor.

"So you're the detective." A short-haired woman approached in a sleek black dress and pearls, dropping her head as if ready to gore him. "Get these *things* out of my store! Have you any idea how many customers have left becau—"

"Okay, ma'am." Willi held out a hand to her. "This'll just take a minute. Kai, which ones?"

The kid pointed to a display case of small, tan evening bags with what looked like ivory clasps. Expensive, Willi saw. Seventy-five marks. Even Vicki's mother'd probably never paid that. Each little bag, not big enough to carry three or four items, was clearly custom-made, though, its own unique insignia dyed into the leather. One had a black knight. Another a leaping lion. A third— His breath stuck when he saw it.

Exactly as Kai described . . . a small red Indian head, like the one in the front window that first caught the kids' attention. The boys yanked up their sleeves and showed Willi their shoulders. They all had the same.

To be a Red Apache you had to get one.

Each gang had its own. The Black Knights. The Leaping Lions.

"It's d-d-definitely Manfred's tattoo," a boy with a broken tooth stuttered. "I k-k-know 'cause I inked him." He hiccuped and choked back tears. "S-s-slipped on the last feather and made a t-t-tiny extra line. L-l-look, Detektiv."

Bending nearer, Willi focused on the last feather. Sure enough . . .

"Manfred disappeared last year." Kai's pink lips quivered. "That's him, Detektiv."

"Preposterous." The woman, who proved to be Madam Schröder herself, was redder than the Indian.

"Madam," Willi finally stammered, "I'm afraid I'm going to have to ask you to close your shop doors."

Within the hour Dr. Hoffnung arrived with the mobile crime lab. The boys of the Red Apaches had to wait outside. After summoning Gunther to get here at once, Willi interrogated Madam Schröder in the back office.

"From one of your own, Detektiv." Her anxiety sought refuge in a scapegoat. "Of course I know who. I have the receipt right here. What kind of business do you think I run?"

She flung open a file cabinet and began hunting.

"'A rare opportunity. Only bunch of its kind,' he told me. 'All handmade. The highest quality.' That, I could see for myself. I happen to have an extremely discerning eye. Since he offered it exclusively, I grabbed the whole lot—two dozen and one. Sold four in the past two months, which isn't bad, considering. People find them alluring. One has to compete on a street like this, with so many fine shops and all the big Jewish depar— Here it is. 'Grenedier Strasse 139. Schmuel Markoweitsch. Dealer in Fine Leather.'"

A soft rap interrupted them. It was Hoffnung at the door. He had a sickly look.

All he had to do was nod and Willi understood.

The bags were human skin, all right.

And the clasps weren't ivory, but bone.

Just a stone's throw north of Alexanderplatz, a small, crowded district called the Scheunen Viertel was home to Berlin's *Ost Juden,* eastern Jews who'd fled fighting and pogroms in places such as Russia and Ukraine and taken refuge in Germany, many illegally. At the heart the untidy, colorful, bustling little slum ran Grenedier Strasse. The minute you stepped on it you felt as if you'd entered Bialystok or Minsk, the sidewalks crowded with bearded men in long black coats, store signs in Hebrew lettering, sweet oniony scents wafting from tea shops. Sticking like glue to Willi's side, tall, blond Gunther looked as if he'd landed on another planet.

It was twilight, businesses already closed. Barefoot kids were playing in the street, adults hunched on stoops and windowsills, clustered on the sidewalks. No one answered at number 139, Markoweitsch Fine Leather. A woman finally stuck her head out an upstairs window: *"Vus?"*

Willi knew bits of the language of the *Ost Juden,* Yiddish, because his father's parents had spoken it. But he hadn't even a chance to respond when the kerchiefed head seemed to intuit he was not someone Markoweitsch wanted to see.

"*Gevalt!*" She slammed the window shut.

"You wait here, Gunther. Don't let anyone in or out. I'm going around back."

"Yes, sir! But, sir?"

"What?"

"What if someone tries to sell me something?"

Despite the seriousness of the situation, seeing the childish fear in Gunther's face, Willi couldn't help it. He burst out laughing. "Unless you're one hundred percent sure it isn't cheaper around the corner"—he shook a finger at the kid—"don't buy."

Almost every building in Berlin was built around a courtyard. Some had courtyards within courtyards. Some even had courtyards within courtyards within courtyards; 139 Grenedier was one of the latter. As Willi penetrated deeper into the maze of brick alleys that opened onto brick yards, he was following his gut until his ears took over. From the upstairs apartments a symphony of clattering dishes and fighting family members was soon superseded by what he was certain was singing. Not just singing, but prayer. A service. He even recognized the song. "Adon Olam." Master of the Universe. It was coming from the deepest courtyard in the building, inside a doorway over which was painted a small sign in Hebrew letters. Like most Jewish boys, Willi'd done his Bar Mitzvah at age thirteen, and he wracked his memory now to try to translate the sign. *M-A-R—*

All of a sudden, with a loud "*Ah-main,*" the song ended and the door was flung open, a pale, bearded face just inches away staring at Willi from under a white shawl. More pale faces under white shawls filled the room inside. Clearly they knew he was coming.

"Which one's Markoweitsch?" He strained the extent of his Yiddish, breaking out his badge.

He might as well have been a specter from the other world judging by the way their jaws dropped. A cop who spoke Yiddish? A bearish fellow in his forties pulled off his shawl and stepped forward, half astonished, half terrified.

"Papers I've got, sir."

"Not my concern," Willi switched to German. "My interest is strictly your merchandise."

Markoweitsch was now really astonished. "You're here to shop?"

Half an hour later they were in his apartment upstairs, Gunther accepting second helpings of honey cake from the kerchiefed wife.

"Never," Markoweitsch insisted over a glass of hot tea. "And believe me I would have noticed. Right here on Grenedier he stops me next to his truck. Such bags he shows. Stolen, I was sure. But, no. On the holy book he swears his sister made them, right in Berlin. Two years' hard labor, that's how he put it. How could I resist? These were grade-A goods. I went to the shop, got cash, and paid him on the spot, two hundred reichsmarks for twenty-five. Minute he was gone I shlepped them direct to Schröder. I know my customers. She went after them like a *chazzer* to stuffed mackerel—you understand me? Because they're unique. Bags like these you don't see around, Sergeant. Paid me five hundred. And she'll make a nice profit, if business picks up."

"You never asked him what they were made of?"

"Made? What, they're not calfskin?"

"I don't suppose you got a receipt?"

"Receipt?"

"No card, any way to reach him?"

"A corner transaction, Sergeant. Hardly uncommon in this neighborhood, you should know."

"A bald man, you say? Extremely big?"

"Like a golem. A giant. Tell me—he did something wrong?"

Not unless you think kidnapping kids, gassing them, selling their flesh, and using their skin and bones to make handbags is wrong, Willi thought, without saying anything. At least he was zeroing in. Truck without license plates. Big as a giant.

Arms so strong they could stun a man with a single blow and, in seconds, lift him upside down, hang him on meat hooks, and split him in two.

The moment he'd seen the red Indian tattoo he'd known he'd seen it before—or something almost just like it. At Helga's. From Markoweitsch's, he and Gunther hurried directly there. The mansion on Bleibtreu Strasse was dark, but they could hear odd noises inside. It took minutes of pounding before the red turban answered the door. When Willi flashed his badge, Zoltan smiled as if they were dear cousins.

"But Sergeant-Detektiv, she's meditating. You wouldn't want to disturb her communion with—"

"I sure would." Willi brushed past, Gunther covering his back.

There was noise, all right. Coming from downstairs. Like, screaming.

"Oh, no, Herr Sergeant, you—"

Yanking an appropriate-looking door, Willi found himself atop a long, dark staircase, the screaming immediately amplified. There was more than one voice, he could tell. Oddly muffled. A small sign overhead proclaimed STRAFZIMMER. Punishment Room. He took the steps two at a time, Gunther tagging along. Flickering light from what proved to be flaming torches revealed the outlines of chains. Cages. Whipping posts.

Gunther'd seen a lot today. Boys in makeup. Jews in caftans. He'd taken it all in admirably. But this time he let out an audible *"Mein Gott."*

Three women in schoolgirl uniforms were tied next to each other on a bed, bare buttocks in the air, some kind of plug stuffed into each mouth covering the shrieks as one by one they received blows from a leather paddle that left their rumps swollen and red. Doing the paddling, Willi saw, a "headmistress" in thick, black glasses and tweed suit, was Brigitta.

"You!" she cried when she spotted him. "What the fuck do you think you're—"

"Shut up." Helga rose from a pile of pillows, where she'd obviously been enjoying the show, snacking on cherries. Wiping her fingers, she walked toward them in silver heels and a tight gown with no back. When she reached Brigitta, she cracked her across the face. "How many times must I tell you—authority is to be respected. Always. Now out of here. All of you."

Grumbling with disappointment, the women untied themselves, pulled out their mouth plugs, and trudged upstairs. Brigitta threw her schoolmarm glasses on the bed and shot an enraged glare at Willi before storming off with them. In the flickering torchlight Willi could see Helga was amused.

"We were just warming up, Sergeant. You ought to have come an hour from now." She lit a cigarette, raising an eyebrow at him. "You're welcome to join sometime. Yes, why not? Bring the little woman." She blew smoke at Gunther. "Who's your boy? Lanky—"

"Never mind," Willi interrupted, seeing Gunther's face go redder than those slapped behinds. "Upstairs with you now too."

In the chrome-filled room where they'd first met, Helga sat at her dressing table, rolling her eyes but making the best of things by grabbing her silver comb and touching up her coif in the three-sided mirror.

Gunther, sweating, broke out a pad and pencil.

"Describe Ilse for me, physically," Willi instructed.

"Scrawny. Ugly." Helga sighed, smoothing out the platinum waves, then seeming to recant. "No, not really." She squinted, thinking back. "The features were decent. She had a certain charm, actually. But that skin." She dropped the comb and spun around to Willi. "I always thought it must have been terrible acne when she was a kid, but you never got a true word out of Ilse. I finally taught her how to use a good base to cover it. Guerlain, nothing else. With the right lipstick, a little mascara . . . for heaven's sake, what are you staring at, Sergeant?"

"That desk lamp."

Willi saw the color fade from Helga's cheeks. "Why?" She crushed out a cigarette and lit another. "Is it so fascinating?"

From touring the tanneries he knew how many different types of leather it was possible to produce. A single cowhide could be rendered strong and inflexible for something such as shoe soles, or soft and pliant for jackets and gloves, turned any color, or cut so thin as to be nearly translucent. The difference all lay in the chemical treatments and dyes.

"That little red Indian head. How unusual. What's the shade made of?"

"How the hell should I know?" Smoke shot through her nostrils as she deigned to glance at it. "Casts a nice diffuse light, that's all I care. Gives me a healthy—"

"It's human skin, Helga."

The cigarette dropped from her mouth to the floor. "What?"

"Where did you get it?"

"From her!" Helga reached, blindly searching with her hand. "Four or five years ago. A Christmas present."

As Willi watched her grovel, the carpet starting to smolder, he realized pieces were falling into place.

The Ox and the Shepherdess were in this together.

Twenty

Vienna may have given birth to it, but Berlin quickly adopted Freudian analysis as its own, and in the decade following the Great War the Berliner Psychoanalytisches Institut had grown into the movement's undisputed international home. Staffed by such luminaries as Karen Horney, Theodor Reik, Wilhelm Reich, and Melanie Klein, the Institut not only furthered exploration of the unconscious but was the first to begin training new generations of analysts. It even provided cost-free clinical treatment to those who couldn't afford it. Willi could think of more than one anguished soul he wished to God would partake.

Arriving at their building on Wichmann Strasse, he hurtled up the stairs two at a time. His cousin Kurt, bony-faced and ebullient, was one of the rising stars here. In his sun-filled office as Willi brought him up-to-date on the latest horrific twists in the case, his cousin leaned back in a leather armchair, slowly removing his eyeglasses.

"It seems to me, Willi"—Kurt sighed, pulling out a handkerchief—"that by taking these children apart and sewing them back together"—he wiped his lenses diligently—"the *Kinderfresser*'s probably seeking to bind up his own fractured psyche. You see, a real schizoid has no unified core personality. They chronically teeter on the edge of fragmentation. Even the minutest rejection can completely tear them to pieces."

God forbid you made her feel unwanted. Willi heard the High Priestess again, describing Ilse. *She practically ran amok.*

"To ward off such a devastating attack, for example, as an accusation of worthlessness"—Kurt returned the frames to his bony face—"a schizoid might strive to construct a personality of unsurpassed utility. In this case, going so far as to compulsively convert his victims' body parts into something of value—food, clothing. In all likelihood, it's a ritualizing reenactment of the tortures he himself once endured. I suspect that as a child, our murderer must have felt as if he were being virtually dismembered. Eaten alive. Although"—he rubbed his chin, concerned—"the fact that more than one person's involved might undermine my thesis."

Not necessarily, Willi was thinking. If the people were, for example, siblings.

The Ox had said those bags had been made by his sister.

Two years' hard labor.

"But these aren't straitjacket cases, Kurt. They're out there running some kind of business. Operating under everyone's noses—for years now. I have a feeling they might even be related: brother and sister."

"Fantastic." Kurt's leather chair squeaked. "But certainly not outside the realm of possibility. And there are plenty of schizoids who present engaging, interactive personalities, Willi. That's just it. They appear interested. Make normal eye contact. But internally, they're so cut off"—Kurt leaned forward, squinting behind his clean, clear lenses—"outer reality's not just frightening to them, Willi. It's genuinely life-threatening. Their social behavior's pure survival instinct. Animal camouflage."

"Hermann Braunschweig?" Vicki said, putting down the *Tage Blatt*. "Isn't that the poor pastor you told me about?" She handed him the page, pointing to a black-bordered announcement. Willi looked. Baden-Baden had evidently failed the reverend. His funeral was Thursday. How sad. He felt oddly obligated to go.

Up in Pankow at the Evangelische Friedhof that day, just as he was getting out of his rickety Opel, a long, white Daimler pulled up. Zoltan's red turban was visible at the wheel. From the back, High Priestess Helga emerged in a black dress fringed with beads. Even behind dark glasses she seemed relieved to see him, her glossy lips tilting in a smile.

"Kraus, I didn't expect you." She let him accompany her down the ivy-laced path through the headstones.

"I might say the same about you, High Priestess."

"Yes, well." She cast him a glance, carefully negotiating the vines in her high heels. "Death transcends even divorce." Her confidential tone implied Willi'd become a dear old friend by now. "I was married to Braunschweig eleven years." She inhaled with what seemed disbelief. "Six, actually. The rest I was married to a bottle of schnapps." She stopped, turning to Willi, her rows of beads shimmying. "Listen, Sergeant, I've got to say—that lampshade business the other night." She held her hand over her heart, swallowing. "It was too much. Even for me."

She took off the dark glasses, and for the first time Willi saw something like authenticity in her eyes. "I don't feel safe here anymore. Everywhere I turn, I think she's lurking. So I'm closing up shop. Taking the show on the road, so to speak. Getting as far away from Ilse and Germany as I can—southern California. See if I can't give that Sister Aimee a run for her money."

Willi couldn't say he blamed her.

They walked together down the lane of headstones. Halfway she took his arm.

"Gee"—she shrugged, throwing him a girlish smile—"you're the nicest cop I ever met; too bad you're so happily married."

At Braunschweig's grave they joined the small crowd, Helga's dress dancing with the dry summer breeze.

As for man, his days are like grass . . .
the wind blows over it and it is gone.

When they lowered the coffin, she leaned on Willi for support. He gave her his handkerchief to wipe her face. Each threw a rose into the pit, then they returned together along the viny path. But when a little gray rabbit jumped ahead of them, Helga suddenly gasped and froze solid, as if it were a wolf.

"Dear God." She held her chest, breathing deeply. Willi kept waiting for a word of explanation, but she seemed unable. Finally she shook her head. "All of a sudden I remember something. And I've no idea why." She turned to Willi. "That town Ilse said she came from." Her voice lowered. "She went on about it like there was no worse place on earth. Practically foamed at the mouth when she told us about it. Wanted to *rid* the world of the slime who lived there, she said. That's how she put it too—*rid the world*. Makes me shiver now. But back then—we thought she was just an unhappy kid. Wasn't eighteen when she joined our congregation. Hermann and I practically adopted her. Didn't have parents. Only siblings."

Siblings? Willi felt his heart quicken.

"What were they, Helga? Brothers, sisters?"

"I don't know."

"Think. It could be crucial."

"I have no idea."

"Then tell me exactly, when did she first come to you?"

"When?"

"The day, the month. Anything."

"Oh, why do you torture me?" Helga clutched her throat. "I can barely remember what year we're in now." She balled her fists, sighing, then popped her eyes wide. "Wait a minute, the end of the inflation. What year was that, '24, right? That must have been it. I'm sure now. They'd just introduced the reichsmark—and Ilse brought us steaks to celebrate. We'd never seen such juicy cuts. "

Memory was indeed inscrutable. Willi scribbled in his book. Everything was down there, somewhere. Called up by the most random things sometimes. Or were they even random?

"Okay, now tell me—what was the name of the town?"

Helga held her stomach, her glossy lips twisting as if her appendix had burst. "I never knew where it was exactly, somewhere in the provinces. Saxony, I guessed from the accent. But whenever she mentioned it she used that same creepy windup doll's voice—like she was casting a curse . . . *Niedersedlitz* . . . *Niedersedlitz*. The devil himself, she told me once, had moved there straight from hell."

Clenching her bosom, Helga reeled, stumbling into Willi with a muffled yelp, as if she saw Ilse right there in the cemetery, wielding a bloody knife. "Keep her away!"

Willi had to help her back to the limousine, Zoltan holding the door. Before she climbed in, she grabbed one of Willi's lapels. "God, Kraus." Her voice was hoarse with fear. "If that crazy bitch ever found out I talked to you— You've got to get her!"

There was indeed a town in Saxony named Niedersedlitz—just south of Germany's beautiful city of art and music on the Elbe River, Dresden, and Willi and Gunther set off there by train first thing next morning. Vicki'd hardly been thrilled to hear he was leaving her with the children, even though she wouldn't be alone because her sister was coming. When he'd gone to kiss her, she'd turned a cheek. He got angry and asked if she preferred he arrange for armed protection. She didn't reply, and he left. She had a melodramatic streak, he knew. Like her mother. She was overacting, but he felt lousy anyway, getting her upset. Not enough to make him stay, though.

Entering Saxony, fertile farmland rolled past the dining-car window.

"Needle in a haystack," Gunther mumbled, dropping bits of a roll from his mouth. "Worse. We don't even know it's a needle we're after."

"Well, the bone doesn't come to the dog, Gunther. And better one-eyed than blind." Willi appreciated his assistant's enthusiasm, if not his table manners. "In terms of hard facts, it's true we don't have much. But a good detective must try to fit together even the loosest pieces. And if you think about it, we're not doing badly. Nieder-sedlitz, the 'haystack' as you call, isn't terribly large. And we know that by the time she was eighteen, Ilse had a violent hatred toward it. So much so that she told Helga she wanted to 'rid the world' of its inhabitants. That 'the devil himself had moved there straight from hell'—a rather extreme posture in regards to your hometown, wouldn't you agree?"

Gunther nodded wide-eyed, chewing. "I only hated how ugly the girls were."

"Clearly the place was connected with some prolonged trauma, child battering probably—which nobody rescued her from. If the Ox really is her brother, then it's not a needle we're seeking at all—but a pair of very sick siblings. And if in fact they did grow up in town, somebody in Niedersedlitz will remember them."

"You know, boss"—Gunther swallowed hard—"I learn more from you in an hour than all my textbooks put together."

Dresden, Germany's Florence on the Elbe, was a storybook city of chocolate and porcelain, Wagner and Strauss. Towering baroque cathedrals and palaces. The long glass *Hauptbahnhof* from 1892 was among Europe's finest. But when they arrived, the main hall over-flowed with dusty, slump-shouldered figures, the unemployed. In front of the station, dueling phalanxes of uniformed Nazis and Communists were forcing campaign literature on everyone passing by. Willi and Gunther had to run a raucous gauntlet to reach the #6 tram.

Forty minutes later they were on a little green streetcar rattling through Niedersedlitz, a picturesque mix of pastures and heavy in-dustry, wide fields golden with rye framed by mile-long factories. Off they got at the town center and headed straight for the *Rathaus*, a mélange of Gothic, Renaissance, and art nouveau. First stop—the Hall of Records.

A sallow-faced clerk manning the front desk didn't even look up when Willi asked how they could find any tanneries or leather works, and if there were documents pertaining to battered children from twenty years ago.

"Room 2D, Commerce and Industry. Legal's down in—" He stopped, checking to see who would ask such a question, a swastika pin all but blazing from his lapel. "No Jews allowed." He looked back at his paperwork.

Gunther's eyes widened. "What'd you say?"

"You heard me: no Jews."

"You stupid ass." Willi was shocked to see Gunther reach over and threaten to grab the clerk by the collar, his whole face flashing red. "You're addressing a Sergeant-Detektiv of the Berlin Kriminal Polizei here, working on a case of national importance. So unless you feel like having your ass raked over hot coals . . ."

The guy admitted them, but muttered loud enough to hear, "Just what stinks in this republic, Jew detectives."

"Never mind." Willi restrained Gunther, delighted by his assistant's show of support, but concealing it. Once again he found himself appreciating Gunther's fervor more than his finesse. Saxony was known for its illiberality. Plus they only had twenty-four hours here. Barely enough time to get into fisticuffs with the local Nazis. "You go downstairs; I'll go up."

The mustached clerk in room 2D, by contrast, Herr Eisenlohr, all but shined Willi's shoes when he learned he was a Kripo agent from Berlin.

"Oh, yes, sir, Herr Sergeant-Detektiv. Here we are." He bowed like a waiter bringing the house specialty as he handed Willi a leatherbound volume: *Major Industry in Niedersedlitz—1900 to Present.*

Willi'd barely gotten the huge book open, though, when Gunther was back over his shoulder.

"Fräulein down in Legal says she needs special keys to unlock police files. Thing is, fellow who authorizes them's all the way down in—"

"Gunther," Willi cut him off, "I don't have time for this. Figure it out." He thumbed down the list of key industries. "We've got to see those files."

Gunther just stood there.

Willi glanced up. "Remember the Kripo manual? In addition to *Zuverlässigkeit* and *Unbestechlichkeit,* an ideal Kripo agent possesses *Findigkeit.* Ingenuity. In other words, kid, use your brain."

Gunther smiled sheepishly, lumbering off.

Poring through the massive volume, Willi saw that Niedersedlitz had manufacturers of refrigerators, locomotives, world-class cameras, and macaroni, but no tanneries or leather works. Anymore. There had been a sizable firm here for decades. But Amalgamated Leather burned in 1916, during the terrible "Turnip Winter" at the height of the war. An asterisk on the matter caught his eye. The plant foreman had, apparently, been convicted of setting the blaze and sentenced to twenty-five years hard labor. Willi inhaled, closing the volume, deciding to find out more downstairs and see how Gunther was making out.

Not badly, apparently.

In the basement corridor a tall, gawky young woman who could have been Gunther's twin rushed past him, smoothing her hair and then ducking into the ladies' room. When Willi walked into Legal, Gunther looked up, restraining a grin.

"Mission accomplished." He dangled a set of keys, oblivious to the lipstick on his mouth. The kid obviously felt he'd found his forte. Willi didn't have the heart to lecture him about discretion too.

Gunther's use of ingenuity unfortunately yielded few results— even with the help of his newfound darling, Ingeborg. They uncovered plenty of files on children hit by cars, drowned in wells, murdered by itinerant foreigners. But in all the reams of police files for the past quarter century, none reported a parent hurting his own child. Not that it was all that surprising, Willi bore in mind. Only recently had they begun reporting such cases in Berlin. Still, he had to ask himself, might someone other than a family member have been the "devil" the Shepherdess hated? Nothing they came across in the files suggested that, either. Perhaps the origins of her trauma had been purely psychotic.

Going through birth records based on the High Priestess's memory, Ingeborg produced a list of seven girls given the name *Ilse* from 1905 to 1907. They weren't sure the Shepherdess was even born in Niedersedlitz, and with no last name it didn't much matter. But Willi read and reread the list hoping something might click. Finally, though, sighing, he shoved it aside. Any one of these could be the Shepherdess—or all this could be a big waste of time. It was pure luck.

An hour's search, though, and not a single file on the Amalgamated Leather factory fire had nothing to do with luck, he knew. Someone had clearly tampered with the records. A trial had to have documents. Ingeborg called in Herr Eisenlohr, but the man could only yank out his hairs at not being able to further assist.

"If I had a *shred* of information, so help me, Herr Sergeant, I'd hand it to you on a golden platter. All I can tell you is this: during the war, if anything even hinted at civilian sabotage, it was removed by military authorities. Those files could be buried somewhere with the kaiser's love letters."

"We could try the jail." Gunther calculated on his fingers. "There'd still be another . . . twelve years on his sentence."

"Problem is, which jail?" Willi wondered. "In a city the size of Dresden there's got to be half a dozen. We don't even have a name to ask about. But maybe—" He straightened up. "The local paper. They must have covered the story. I'll bet they keep archives."

"Superb reasoning." Eisenlohr applauded. "Better hurry, though; everything here closes *pünktlich* at five."

The offices of the *Niedersedlitzer Beobachter*, however, were several blocks from the city hall, and by the time they got there, it was one minute past five. A bald man with a long mustache was just on the other side of the door but refused to let them in, even when Willi flashed his badge. They saw him grab his hat, slip out the back, and hurry down the block. Willi had a mind to run after and book the son of a bitch for obstructing justice, but reason held sway. He led Gunther around back instead and, using the metal pick on his army knife, unlocked the door.

Gunther looked at him as if he'd gone mad.

"Come now." Willi shrugged, guiltlessly probing for the bolting mechanism. "You know the old saying: *the more laws, the less justice.* Keep an eye out for God's sake and make sure nobody's watching. Order may be half of life, but only half. And besides, many roads lead to Rome. We're on the hunt for major mass murderers here. With wolves one must howl. And sometimes, Gunther, what the lion can't manage"—the lock popped open—"the fox can."

Working with flashlights, they found an archive dating back to the 1880s, and soon enough unearthed a whole set of articles regarding the 1916 Amalgamated Leather fire. Strangely, though, disappointingly, not one exceeded three paragraphs in length. The Battle of the Somme raging in France no doubt overshadowed local arson, but clearly the story must have been censored. The company apparently manufactured boots, bags, and rucksacks. Some fifty men were employed there when it burned the night of November 5. Two days later plant foreman Bruno Köhler was arrested and charged with arson. No motive was given, but if you read between certain lines—"surly attitude" and "sloppy at work"—the implication was that he was either drunk or disgruntled or both—perhaps with the war, perhaps not. In those days any dissatisfaction was treason.

Subsequent articles summarized the arson trial in even vaguer terms: the "substantial" evidence presented by the prosecution, including more than one eyewitness account, and finally, a confession by Köhler himself, whom the *Beobachter* quoted as telling the jury, "What I did, the devil demanded."

It was the final article, though, the one on the convicted man's sentencing, that made Willi's neck hairs stand. In what they probably felt was a note of patriotism, that even a child was against sabotage, the newspaper pulled no punches conveying how Köhler's ten-year-old daughter told them that twenty-five years wasn't enough for her father. That he ought to be locked up for life.

Who would even make up such a thing for a ten-year-old to say?

"Gunther, quickly." Willi's pulse jumped. "Get out Ingeborg's list of Ilses."

Sure enough, there she was. Third to last.

Ilse Köhler. 1906.

Twenty-one

Amber light broke through a colonnade of distant smokestacks. Across the street a field of grain waved in the late-August dawn. As Willi watched from his hotel window, a hawk swooped down and grabbed a rodent, flying off with it. For some reason it reminded him of that afternoon at the *Viehof,* that huge woman dressed as a man. He'd had such difficulty understanding her. Wasn't her dialect similar to the one here?

The moment the clock struck eight, they were at the post office putting through a call to Berlin. Willi instructed Ruta to contact Direktor Gruber at the *Central-Viehof* and find out if anyone, business or employee, was registered under the name Köhler.

"And don't let them dilly-dally. It's urgent. Call me back, at the Niedersedlitz *Rathaus.*"

At the nearby Hall of Records they got to work digging. First find: a wartime registration card listing all the family members;

their religion—Protestant; and their parish—First Reformed. Ilse had not one sibling, it turned out, but two: Magda and Axel. It had to be him, then, Willi thought. The Ox. Ilse's birth cerfiticate was there, but neither of the others'.

What they did find, however, was a death certificate.

Clara Köhler, mother of all three, drew her last breath giving Ilse life.

Mandatory employee records submitted at the end of 1914 included a letter to the Dresden draft board stating that Bruno Köhler had been employed at Amalgamated since he was fourteen, had been chief foreman of the factory for the past eight years, and was considered essential to productivity. A model worker.

A widower with three dependant children.

"My God, look at this," Gunther said, handing Willi a police report, dated three years later—March 1917.

Good thing they hadn't started looking in prisons for him because Bruno Köhler, model worker and father of three, never made it into one. According to the Niedersedlitz police, following a court-granted last night at home with his kids, his body was found "cut into more than twenty pieces and strung like Christmas ornaments around a backyard pine tree—head on top." All three children vanished.

My God was right.

The phone rang. It was Ruta from Berlin. Gruber's office, she said, reported that no one named Köhler was employed or currently leasing space at the *Central-Viehof.*

Damn. Where did that leave them?

He was about to hang up when Ruta stopped him.

"Sorry, Herr Sergeant. Kommissar Horthstaler wants a word with you."

"You'd better have a good reason for prancing off to Danzig, Kraus."

"Dresden, Herr Kommissar."

"Don't correct me, damn it." The man was beside himself.

Two more boys had gone missing yesterday. Sons of very rich

industrialists this time, out riding ponys in the Tiergarten. The horses had returned but not the boys.

"Street kids and orphans are one thing—but this. The whole city's in an uproar. Mayor calling saying his wife wants to send away their sons. *Le Monde* from Paris calling saying they want a story on the Monster Child-Eater of Berlin. Who's it going to be next, Kraus?"

Willi assured him he was working as fast as humanly possible.

"Well, you'd better work faster. Call on the Lord your God for a miracle or something—because let me tell you, a lot of people are suddenly wondering why a Jew's been named protector of our children."

The Köhlers' former home, 159 Heimgarten Strasse, was a plain, little stucco cottage on a dead-end street surrounded by woods. A young couple with several kids lived there now—no idea what happened fifteen years ago.

"Mind if we look around?" Willi held up his Kripo badge.

Beyond the sparse furnishings there wasn't much to see. Just a strange indentation beneath a worn rug in the kitchen they would have missed had it not been for Willi's veteran eye. Underneath, a trapdoor.

"I hadn't a clue that was there." The young husband was astounded.

A short flight down led to a tiny, windowless root cellar full of cobwebs. When he came back up, Willi closed the door behind him and pulled the rug back over. "Might want to clean it up," he suggested. "Use it for extra storage."

He didn't mention the iron clasps he noticed bolted into the wall that looked like chain fittings.

"Sorry we couldn't help," the wife said in a thick Saxon accent, bouncing an infant. "Try the Bachmanns next door. She's not so friendly, but they've lived here for centuries."

"Okay, Gunther," Willi said as they headed to the next house.

"I'm going to need you to step up and turn on a little country charm."

Frau Bachmann was a sharp-faced woman with a pile of silvery hair knotted atop her head. "*Ja?*" She cocked her chin with stern authority.

"What a beautiful home you have, *gnädige Frau*," Gunther said with a humble bow. "So full of love and warmth. Might we come in? We're with the *Morning Observer*. Here to do a story on some local history."

The kid could think on his feet, Willi saw. He'll do all right.

"Newspapermen?" Her face brightened as she ushered them in, throwing a glance at Gunther. "Imagine that. My son, Alfred, wanted to be a newspaperman before the war. You look just about his age when he left for the front. Flanders." Her wrinkled hand touched her throat.

"My condolences." Gunther touched his heart.

"No, no." She waved him off, laughing. "I didn't lose him. Entirely." The laugh faded. "He was such a sincere young man, of course, once." Her expression slowly soured. "Yearned to serve his fatherland. But, *ach*, now . . ." A bitter grimmace overcame her. "So cynical. I don't go visit him much, even though he's just outside town, at the veterans' home." She cocked her head, squinting at Gunther as if he were a photograph. "You really do look like he did."

"We're writing a story about the people who lived next door during the war." Willi felt the need to press forward. "The Köhlers."

Clearly she'd been caught by surprise. "I don't remember any family by that name." She turned gray, shaking her head.

"Didn't you live here during the war?"

"No. Back then we lived over in—listen, gentlemen." Her face seemed to calcify. "I've been ill lately. You'll have to leave." Her spotted hand rose toward the door.

From the brittle look in her eye, Willi saw she meant it. That nothing short of torture was going to make her talk. So, reluctantly, he motioned Gunther, and they beat a frustrated retreat.

Outside, the tall green pine next door swayed from the hot gusts of wind. You could practically see those Christmas ornaments dangling from it still.

They knocked at every house on the street, spoke to shopkeepers, people out walking dogs. Spent hours trying to find someone who'd tell them about the infamous Köhlers, but oddly, no one seemed to recall even hearing of them. Picturing that bloody head propped atop that tree, though, perhaps it wasn't so odd, Willi thought. They were still out there, after all, the Köhler kids. Ilse wanting to rid the world of the "slime" who lived in Niedersedlitz.

These townsfolk probably remembered them, all right—all too well.

Trudging next to Gunther in the heat, Willi wondered what the hell that father could have done to provoke such vengeance in his children, and how he'd gotten away with it so many years. He recalled what Kurt had said, how plenty of schizoids presented normal personalities. Made eye contact. Seemed friendly. This guy must have been a doozy, Willi thought. Turning out three homicidal maniacs without anyone even—

He froze, an icy chill crackling in his skull. Could that be it? He looked at Gunther without saying anything. Were all three of these siblings working as one—kidnapping, killing, and processing children's bodies, like some demonic hydra? It seemed inconceivable. But then again, hadn't everything in this case—bags of bones, human lampshades—until he'd seen it with his own eyes?

Back in town, he found himself seeking any excuse to stay and keep hunting, but coming up empty-handed. Kommissar Horthstaler had made it amply clear he was to return at the earliest possible moment. Willi hated to admit it, but Niedersedlitz appeared a dead end. Except—the old lady, Bachmann. Not a good actress. She'd obviously lived in that house for years. If she had a son who'd served in Flanders, he calculated, the kid would probably have been around the same age as the boy next door, Axel.

A taxi to the edge of town left them at a barrackslike building with a federal flag flapping out front. Inside, they were shocked by a blast of soggy air laced with heavy ammonia, and visions of endless beds filled with shadowy figures. A white-hatted *Krankenschwester* at the front desk led them down the center aisle of a long, dim-lit ward. Halfway there, Gunther began losing color. Bed after bed was filled with grotesque travesties of human forms: some eyeless, some noseless, some gagging still from gas attacks years past. Some sat in little groups playing cards, others alone in bed convulsing. Searching the faces of these beat-up figures, Willi, shivering, tried to maintain himself against blood-soaked waves of memories.

At bed #39, though, they saw a big-chested fellow merrily enjoying a cigar, projecting a nearly comical joie de vivre considering his surroundings—and that he had only one arm and no legs and was held up by a canvas harness rigged to a swivel pole. When they introduced themselves, his big head cocked, much as his mother's had.

"Kripo!" Alfred Bachmann's well-shaved face parodied a look of alarm. "My God—here to arrest me?" He let out a bellowing laugh, balancing the cigar between his fingers. "Don't you suppose this place is prison enough?"

Willi didn't need to wonder what had happened to the poor devil. Didn't need to close his eyes to see him sprawled on Flanders's fields, blown to bits by high artillery yet clinging somehow to life. This Alfred, however, for whatever reasons, appeared to have transcended the shock and anguish, the isolation and helpless rage, and managed, after all these years, to appreciate the few slim pleasures his world could offer. A corner bed. A tree out the window. Nurse to do his bidding.

And Kripo agents all the way from Berlin.

After hearing what they'd come to talk about, though, the good humor drained like a lanced boil.

"Oh." His eyes fled out the window.

An old battle-ax in nurse's uniform growled from across the aisle, "Those guests want tea?"

Alfred Bachmann sighed wearily. "What do you think, Schmidt, they're like you, no earthly desires?"

Willi pulled up a chair, motioning Gunther to do the same.

"It's crucial you help us out here, Bachmann. Lives may be at stake."

"Lives," he snickered. "And don't call me Bachmann, huh? Reminds me of the army. Alfred'll be fine. Thanks, lover," he nodded to the nurse. "Put it there."

"I know where to put it." Schmidt dropped the tray on the counter.

Bachmann's chest expanded as he plugged the cigar back in his mouth, eyes flying out the window again. "I don't know what you think I can tell you, Sergeant. I haven't seen them in years."

"You did grow up next—"

"Door. Yeah, sure. But it won't help you find them now."

"Never know. Sometimes the smallest detail . . ."

Bachmann's lips tightened on the cigar. "Anyway, I'm kind of busy today. My schedule's all booked up. Try again tomorrow."

"You and Axel must have been pretty good buddies then, huh?"

"Buddies." The eyes flashed back on Willi with a strange derision. "From the day I could walk till the day I went into the infantry, that bastard was my best friend. And I was"—his lips trembled slightly—"his whipping boy. And his slave and confidant all in one." Bachmann's nose flared as he fingered his cigar. "I know what he's capable of. What they all are. The little one most of all. She made the rest look sweet."

"How about let's start at the beginning." Willi grabbed his notebook.

"No thanks." Bachmann shook his head.

"Alfred." Willi felt it was time to lay it on the line. "They're killing little kids. A lot of them."

Bachmann's harness twisted. "You mean *Der Kinderfresser*?"

Willi nodded ever so slightly.

Bachmann swallowed hard. "Well, then"—he shrugged, inhaling—"guess there's nothing I can't reschedule—except maybe my enema at four."

Twenty-two

Several minutes into the story Willi understood why High Priestess Helga, without apparent cause, had so suddenly recalled the name of Ilse's hometown. It wasn't without cause at all. It was that little rabbit hopping by.

"Perfect Niedersedlitzers those Köhlers were." Smoke from Bachmann's cigar rose curtainlike, seeming to draw him back. "Father had a good job. Mother on the church committee. Walked to services every Sunday together. Made quite a picture with the twins."

"Twins?" Willi and Gunther looked at each other.

"Didn't you know? For years no one could tell them apart, Magda and Axel. She always wore her hair extra-short. Talked real deep. So boyish everyone mistook her for him."

Then that must have been her in the *Viehof* that day dressed as a man. No wonder he'd mistaken her for the Ox, Willi understood.

My God, he'd almost had her. But she'd sweet-talked her way out of it.

A schizoid's social skills, Willi . . . pure animal camouflage.

"That father, though"—Bachmann contorted in his harness— "two people all in one. He used to take me and Axel fishing when we were real young. Some of the best fun I ever had. But by third or fourth grade, I'd run at the sight of that man. My pa could strap me with the best of them, but once I saw Axel's rear end, I never complained. In public he was so considerate and concerned. Everybody loved him. Axel used to tell me stories, though, made my skin crawl. Believe me, that man did things no parent ought."

Bachmann's eyes shrouded. "Below the kitchen he dug out this chamber. Used to lock them down there as punishment. No food, no water, total darkness, two, three days sometimes. When we were thirteen, Axel told me he nearly died from the stench of his own shit. Said if he cried, his father'd come down and chain him to the wall, take a knife to his throat—and threaten to skin him alive."

Gunther's jaw hung.

Willi's heart raced. He could practically hear his cousin Kurt at the Institut: *. . . a ritualizing reenactment of the tortures he himself once endured. I suspect that as a child, our murderer must have felt as if he were being virtually dismembered.*

"How come you never told anyone, Alfred?"

"Are you kidding?" The eyes snapped out of the past. "Axel made me swear on a stack of Bibles. Said his father'd really skin them alive if he ever found out."

"Bruno Köhler did this to both his twins?"

"Regularly." The corners of Bachmann's lips bunched.

"The little one too, Ilse?"

"She got it full brunt." The lips thrust forward. "Bruno blamed her for killing his wife. The twins at least went to school. Not her. My younger sister her age never even saw Ilse. I remember Axel once said she got real sick, whole face covered with pustules. Pox, he called it. Didn't kill her. Tough, she was. Got tougher too. And mean. Oh, boy, I'll never forget the time Ax and I heard such terrible screaming from their backyard. We went down and there she was, long and skinny with great big eyes, couldn't have been more than nine. Had a rabbit strung up, alive, pulling its skin off, like a mother yanking clothes off an uncooperative child. I can still hear that poor thing's screams, Sergeant. Had to club it with a rock to put it out of its misery. Ilse said her sister promised to make her a purse if she brought the hides."

With a shudder, it occurred to Willi that Ilse'd probably told this story, or others like it, to Helga, who'd pushed it as far back into her subconscious as she could, until that day at the cemetery when that little rabbit hopped by. No wonder she'd gotten hysterical. Ilse had threatened the same to her. Skin her alive.

"Did the twins have jobs at their father's leather plant?"

"All of us did. Two years almost, from when the war bogged down to when Ax and I got call-ups in '17. He never went, of course—after what happened with his pa, as I'm sure you heard. Pretty creative, huh? It always impressed me the way they left him strung up for the whole town to see, as if it was a big 'Fuck you, Niedersedlitz.' I mean, people knew. They had to. Everybody beats their kids. But that . . ."

"You remember what kind of jobs at the plant they had?"

"Yeah, sure." Bachmann didn't grasp the point of this question but had no trouble answering. "Ever see a picture of Axel? Built like a bear. Magda too. Ilse was scrawny. But Axel's arms—twice the size of mine, even before he lifted weights. Had him doing manual labor naturally, lifting bales of hides. But as the war went on, we all did whatever necessary—purchasing, ordering, delivering goods. Magda was made an apprentice craftsman." The recollection seemed to please Bachmann. "Got taught all the finest points . . . dyeing, finishing, fancy stitchwork. Could have had a real profession if only—"

Schmidt was standing over them suddenly with a short hose and rubber bag full of water. "Four o'clock."

Willi tried smiling at her. "This is kind of an important police investigation. Might it wait?"

"Sorry, Sergeant." She rolled up her sleeves. "Got a dozen more on line. They talk tough, but they're just big, helpless babies, is all. Can't even evacuate without my help. Don't let me stop you, though." She spit on her hands and gave a hard yank, shifting the harness so Bachmann's face tilted to the mattress. His hospital gown fell down, revealing his hairy rear end. "No room here for daintiness."

She nodded by all means to carry on, as she hooked her contraption up.

Bachmann's face turned on the mattress so he could keep talking. "Most guys drafted before '16 never realized how harsh things became at home." He winced as Schmidt let loose a big gob of spit, then shoved in the nozzel, working it up with sharp, staccato twists, like a sink plunger. Willi winced too, while Gunther turned almost canary yellow. But a serene gaze washed over Bachmann's eyes as she let go of the hose and began squeezing the bag. "In the army at least you got fed twice a day. Not in Niedersedlitz. You'd think with all the farms here, but every morsel was requistioned. If they found you with so much as an unauthorized grain . . ."

When the bag emptied, Schmidt plucked out the hose and hoisted Bachmann to an upright position again.

"Naturally everyone began losing weight." He went on casually, his face flushing pink. Reaching for his cigar in the ashtray he indicated to Gunther he'd appreciate a light. "The weakest started really starving: old women with sunken cheeks, kids with swollen bellies. At the factory they gave us enough to keep going. So when Magda's belly started swelling, everyone knew it wasn't starvation. Schmidt . . ."

The dour-faced *Krankenschwester* hoisted his harness and shoved a bedpan under him, while Bachmann, eyes rolling, released a noisy gusher. It came out in thick, black, heavy clumps, making Willi and Gunther both lean back as far as possible.

"She was a huge girl, of course, so no one really could tell until the last month, and then, the gossip." Bachmann went on while Schmidt wiped his rear end with a towel. "Wasn't even seventeen."

Swinging Bachmann down again, face to the bed, Schmidt began another round.

"Everyone was certain it had to be one of the Polish guest workers." Bachmann yelped at the insertion this time. "But that wasn't the case." He fell silent while Schmidt pumped the bag, then hoisted him again. "Well, there's just no nice way of putting it, Sergeant," he said, wiping sweat from his face. "Bruno Köhler fucked those kids. And I don't mean symbolically. Axel used to come to school so sore he couldn't walk. And Magda's baby wasn't any guest worker's."

Willi just sat there for a minute.

"Did she have it?" he finally managed to ask.

"Oh, yeah." Bachmann seemed to feel the liquid in his innards this time, closing his eyes and taking a deep breath. "She had it, all right. But that son of a bitch"—the eyes slowly opened, twitching slightly—"said it was a devil's spawn. Schmidt, love!" The nurse waddled over. "As soon as Magda gave birth"—a fresh pan came under him, and a loud sigh accompanied a second release, only slightly less foul smelling—"that fucker took his own newborn babe to the backyard and"—Bachmann's finger made a slitting motion straight across the base of his throat—"like a suckling pig. That's just what Axel told me—he had no reason to lie. Magda went nuts for real because she was religious, see, and the baby never got—"

"Baptized." Gunther completed the sentence for him. "So she thought it was lost for all eternity."

"Very good." Bachmann nodded.

"Total Depravity," Gunther said to Willi.

The nurse, taking a glance in the pan, gave a satisfied grunt. "Okay, majesty, one more should do it. Make it nice and clear for me, huh?"

Clear indeed, Willi was thinking. That Bible passage. *Children of wrath.* It wasn't Ilse, it was Magda who'd circled it. And Magda's sack of bones.

And Magda's purses.

Ilse was shepherding these kids to her sister. And her brother was dealing the body parts.

"Where did they go when they left Niedersedlitz?"

"Berlin."

"You're certain?"

"I saw Axel the night they left." Bachmann relished the last of his cigar. "Still had blood under his fingernails. Told me Berlin was the only place they could disappear. That Magda'd gone completely daft and Ilse was out of control. That he was going to try to find work to support them, at the *Central-Viehof* maybe. They needed forged papers. New identities. A draft deferment for him. He could afford them now, though, he said, because they had eleven hundred marks— from their father's safe."

"But how can you be certain they wound up in Berlin?" Willi had to know. "You went to Flanders, didn't you? Got injured."

"One thing I'll say about Axel." Bachmann blew a perfect smoke ring. "Loyal as a dog. Showed up here one day to visit."

"Here at this hospital?"

"In that very chair, Detektiv."

"How long ago?"

"During the inflation. I remember distinctly he told me it cost him fifty million marks to take the train. That was what, seven years ago? Just opened my eyes and there he was. Huge as a steer. Arms the size of tree trunks. Said he lifted hundreds of pounds a week at the gym. Never intended to let any bastard get the better of him again."

"What was he doing? Did he work at the *Viehof*?"

"Magda did. Posing as a man. Made me laugh so hard when I heard. Axel had a number of shady schemes going. Ran a peddlers' market of some sort. Plus the little one, Ilse, had a connection at a lab that used dogs for experiments. Paid five marks a head, so they went all over Berlin, stealing dogs. Imagine? Same lab paid them another five to remove the dead dogs, full service. Axel didn't want to tell me what they did with the carcasses, but somehow he made a profit off them too. Never lived better, he told me. Decent apartment. Plenty to eat. Joked and said if only the lab switched to human beings, he could make a real killing."

Twenty-three

"Sure it'd be nice." Vicki flipped her magazine pages. "A lot of things'd be nice, Willi. But a month in America?" She sat up in her beach chair, checking to see if he was watching the boys as closely as he ought. "All four of us? Come on." She leaned back with a sigh. "It's rare you even take a day off."

Lying on a towel at her feet, Willi took a breath, understanding but not exactly appreciating her attitude. You couldn't blame him for fantasizing a little, he thought, running sand through his fingers. The pressure he lived under was relentless; the whole of Berlin hanging on him, waiting for his big breakthrough. Plus the boys were right in plain view, not ten feet away, building a castle. Despite that nothing even vaguely untoward had disturbed their home life, Vicki persisted in fearing every second pulsed with mortal danger.

Willi gazed around the crowded lakeshore and did every so often feel a little twist of angst... not that one of the Köhlers would show up and slit their throats, but that someone would recognize him even under dark glasses, a parent of one of the murdered children, God forbid, and ask what the hell he thought he was doing at the beach when *Der Kinderfresser* was still on the loose.

If only he were a machine. He'd never have to rest. Or fantasize.

It was the first weekend of September, a cool breeze fanning the sunny bay along the Wannsee. The huge, shiny lake reflected puffs of clouds in the sky. Behind, four new pavilions in sand-colored brick—shops, restaurants, changing halls—were portraits of the new International Style being pioneered in Germany: sleek and functional. They had long, flat roofs doubling as sundecks, which nationalists complained looked "un-German." For the thousands who'd flocked here by car or S-Bahn today, it hardly seemed to matter. Framed by shady green forests on one side and countless sails skimming the glassy water on the other, the bathing beach at Wannsee was Berlin at its most sublime.

It had been a week since he'd gotten back from Niedersedlitz, and he was battling to close in on Magda Köhler—or whatever she called herself now. Based on where he'd seen her that afternoon, he'd narrowed down her workplace to six possible businesses in the *Viehof,* all on one little lane appropriately named Bone Alley. He couldn't just barge in and search the places; he knew he had to tread carefully. The lesson of Heilbutt's story on the *Bremen* that day had not been lost on him: during the Great Inflation when they were peddling dog meat for sausage filler, the Köhlers had sensed investigators closing in—and quickly disappeared. Willi had no intention of letting that happen again.

Direktor Gruber was lending support, albeit begrudgingly. He'd provided Willi with blueprints, maps, even informants. But he made it clear he thought it was all a big waste of time. Such characters as Willi described couldn't possibly be operating out of his *Viehof* because his *Viehof* was too well controlled.

In moments of weakness Willi feared the Direktor might be right.

For three days now he'd had eyes trained on every inch of Bone

Alley from rooftops, parked trucks. Even undercover agents inside. A dozen men had the block surrounded. He'd gone so far as to send out scouts to local training gyms in search of Axel. But so far no one'd seen anyone resembling either of the massive twins. And they were hardly easy to miss.

Was it too late already?

One thing was clear: the blueprints he'd gotten from Gruber were useless. The other night he and Gunther had gone in for a pre-dawn reconnaissance raid dressed as municipal water inspectors. Using *Viehof* master keys, they'd entered all six businesses on Bone Alley, beginning with Lutz Brothers Grinders. Finding their way through the gritty facility with flashlights, past big crushing vats and piles of bones, they descended a short flight of steps into a cramped, dusty basement. But no matter how hard they looked, they couldn't find a trace of the sewer lines indicated on the blue-prints. Reiniger Gelatins, Becker Glue, Hansenclever Bristle Works—it was all the same. Either the blueprints were wrong or there'd been some major reconstruction below street level.

He was going to bring it up first thing Monday with Herr Direktor.

Glancing out at white sails skimming across the lake, Willi took in a deep breath. The boys had constructed a rather impressive castle in the style of Antoni Gaudi, he thought, with a swell of fatherly pride. Perhaps they'd become architects. Letting his eyes wander back around to the new pavilions, though, he sat bolt upright.

"Vicki," he said, squinting to make sure. "Grab your things, dar-ling."

He jumped from his towel and ran to get the boys.

Even this breezy idyll wasn't immune to the political whirlwinds battering Germany's capital. The nearer the election, the more elec-trified the atmosphere had grown. Barely a day passed without bloody clashes between Nazis and Communists erupting some-where in Berlin. And Willi got the feeling the combustible mixture had converged right here. Not even a day at the beach could persuade people to put aside politics. Buttons, badges, insignia were pinned to hats and bathing suits. All the maintenance men, he'd noticed earlier, brandished bright red neckerchiefs. The customers at the restaurant pretty much all brownshirts. Several of whom were now gathered around someone on the ground—brutally kicking him.

In the seconds it took for Willi to grab the kids, a loud series of whistles brought reinforcements, both red and brown, running from every direction. An all-out riot broke loose. Chairs flying. Heads bleeding. On the staircase back up to the street Willi had to hold Vicki and the boys to the railing as a small herd of stormtroopers stampeded past, brown boots thundering. Back at Beckmann Strasse later they heard radio reports that fighting at Wannsee had lasted for four hours—and even spread to the S-Bahn heading back to the city. They'd left not a moment too soon. Dozens had been injured, including bystanders on trains who had nowhere to hide.

That night Willi dreamed he and his family were on an ocean liner, steaming somewhere far away.

Gruber's office was in the first building on the right after the main gates at Eldenaer Strasse, its paneled walls filled with citations and photos of visiting dignitaries. The elephantine *Viehof* Direktor had dropped the fawning attitude of the *Listeria* crisis, finding no reason now for sycophancy.

"That may be." The very slant of his pencil-line mustache underscored his enmity. Willi was here as a spoiler, out to sully the reputation of his beloved institution—with a gang of criminals that made Jack the Ripper look nice. "I'm afraid what I gave you, though, are the very latest we have, Herr Sergeant-Detektiv. Perhaps"—he turned to a box of bonbons—"there are other municipal authorities with higher budgets for updating their maps and blueprints."

He offered Willi the box.

Why hadn't he thought of that? Willi wondered. Municpal water.

He had to go right now. They'd know where the feeder lines to *Sturmwasser Kanal Fünf* began.

He declined a candy, then changed his mind, thanking Herr Direktor.

A sweet taste of chocolate still lingered on his lips as he got into his car. It was a fine sunny market day, a relentless stream of vehicles pouring in and out of the *Viehof.* Willi had to sit there waiting for a break in traffic to make the U-turn to leave; all at once his neck went hard. A van turning through the main gates looked familiar. Black, with no license plates. He squinted to see who was at the wheel, but the sun was in his eyes. Forming a visor with his hand, his stomach flipped. It was him, all right.

Axel.

An instant later their gazes interlocked.

Willi saw Axel wonder why he was being looked at and if the face seemed familiar. Clearly, he read the newspapers as well as any Berliner and knew the top cop heading up the *Kinderfresser* hunt. After a flash of perception his face seemed to harden into steel. In what appeared to be slow motion Willi watched his huge hands grab the steering wheel and yank it, hard. Then he saw the black van leap from its lane. Like a projectile it picked up speed—and took aim, he realized, directly at him.

My God. The guy's insane, Willi thought. Literally.

And trying to kill me.

Inches to impact, Willi saw the enraged eyes still locked onto him. Flooring the gas, the Opel lurched not a moment too soon into traffic. The black van screeched to a halt, nearly hitting a hydrant. In his rearview mirror Willi watched the van manage the turn and take off after him, only vehicles behind.

This is ridiculous, he told himself. I'm supposed to be chasing him.

At the first cross street he made a right, hoping to evade the guy, loop around, and reverse things. But Axel stayed hooked to his tail. Soon, they were both snarled in traffic coming out of the cattle market. In a face-off on foot, Will felt certain, he stood a chance—even with Axel's size. That Frenchman he'd bested outside Passchendaele had been no slouch. But he'd need a few seconds to position himself, and at the moment Axel had the momentum. Until he found a way to turn the tables, there seemed little choice but to outrun the maniac.

Conditions weren't favorable. The van was twice the size of his Opel and clearly had the greater horsepower. Even though he was going as fast as he dare in this traffic, the next time Willi looked, the Ox, he saw, was only one vehicle behind. Because of its size the Opel at least was more maneuverable, easily skirting a beer delivery truck while Axel's fender caught a wooden barrel and sent it shooting torpedolike, exploding against a wall. Willi smirked—until his gaze returned to the road and he saw a wagon piled high with feed hay . . . way too near. He leaned on the horn, swerving hard left— only a motor scooter was in the way, and a second later a landslide of hay pounded his car. He had to switch on his wipers, praying to see.

He recalled Gruber boasting the *Viehof* had its own fire department. What it didn't have apparently was its own police—because no one was trying to stop this. People were jumping this way and that—honking, screaming, shaking fists. Yet the chase went on.

Willi made a quick turn down an alley, hoping it might be too narrow for the van. Too bad Axel brought a set of wheels onto the sidewalk and kept right on following. A man trying to get across was clasping what looked like a hundred balloons but were cow intestines, Willi knew, inflated to dry for sausage casings. The poor fellow, not sure whether to run back or forward, panicked and threw everything in the air, sending all his intestines floating away like bubbles.

Axel was right behind Willi now, approaching with deranged fervor. Willi urged on the Opel but it could give only so much. His heart contracted as he could see those insanely glowing eyes again, looming nearer in the rearview mirror. Pointlessly, he swerved back and forth trying to outdance him. With a sudden jolt, though, he found himself having to lock elbows and press back just to keep his head from snapping to the windshield. That maniac had slammed him!

A few seconds later it happened again.

The only way out seemed the tunnel on his left. He spun furiously, plunging into darkness.

Dear God, he gasped when he saw what was ahead. A sea of white sheep filled the tunnel roadway. He hadn't time to stop. Cringing, he fully expected to feel the thuds of their woolly bodies and see a spray of gore on the windshield. But like the Red Sea they miraculously parted, allowing him to pass. Axel's van, twice his size, didn't get the same blessing. Hearing the bleating screams, Willi cringed at the sight in his rearview mirror of sheep being squashed left and right against the tunnel walls.

Finally, as he emerged from the blackness into daylight, his spirits soared. He only needed to reach the by-products zone just past Slaughterhouse Row. There, a dozen men under his command were positioned around Bone Alley. If he could somehow lure Axel into their midst, he might actually bag this son of a bitch. And if he did, he'd soon enough have the two darling sisters as well. Then he could stand before the Kommissar and the press and the whole damn world to announce the long nightmare was over.

Unfortunately, he hadn't made it past Slaughterhouse One when he realized that if anyone was about to get bagged—it was him.

Axel's blood-splattered van was out of the tunnel and dead on his heels again. This time, a solid wall of brown-and-white cattle trudging into Slaughterhouse Two was never going to part. In a last desperate effort Willi jammed on his brakes and swung madly left, intending to burst through a wooden gate, but never made it. Axel cornered him on the bend and rammed him at thirty miles an hour. Willi lost consciousness.

When he came to, he perceived a massive figure climbing from the van, turning toward him, eyes aflame, tree-trunk arms lifting a butcher's hatchet that had to be four feet long. It would be perhaps three more seconds, Willi calculated, before it took off his head. The first of those seconds he used to check what had happened to his car:

the van had crushed the entire rear, but the front looked clear. The next second he simply sat there, watching the odious hatchet, sharpened to what looked like a razor's edge, rise with the massive arms. The third second, just before it guillotined him, he used every ounce of energy he had to throw the door open and smash it into Axel's stomach.

The blow was strong enough to send the beast staggering, allowing Willi time to slip out of the car—though not enough to reposition himself. A quick glance over his shoulder told him his opponent had stumbled but not gone down. With a shocking dexterity Axel'd managed to regain his balance and pick up his ax, looking even more deranged.

In seven years with Kripo this was hardly the first time Willi'd found himself running for his life. Those white slavers up in Prenzlauerberg had given him quite a go. But he'd never had anyone so beside himself with fury sticking to his skin like this. Axel looked as if he didn't even need a hatchet to tear someone apart.

Willi realized he'd soon find out.

He'd reached a dead end. Brick walls on two sides. High fence on the other. The only possible refuge was within the mass of spotted bovines clomping toward their doom. To Willi they suddenly appeared like angels, and he threw himself at their mercy, diving deep into their ranks. Though shocked by their stench, he was thankful for each huge, shit-smeared body—especially when he saw that raised hatchet glistening just a beast or two behind. Something knocked hard into his foot, though, and for a second he feared his salvation might prove his doom—huge rib cages pressing from all sides, hooves crashing down. But another fear loomed when he realized his cover was actually thinning out, getting coerced into smaller files by a series of narrowing ramps.

There had to be men around. These animals weren't just walking themselves into the slaughterhouse, were they? Willi clutched his Kripo badge, ready to enlist the first human he saw. But there were only cows, mooing, bellowing, pink-nosed and brown-eyed, clattering up the ramps. Did any of them realize they were feeling the last few seconds of sunshine on their backs?

For all he knew, so was he.

That possibility seemed horribly real an instant later when he sensed danger in the nape of his neck and, turning, saw Axel a mere foot away. Bending in half and throwing himself under the belly of the nearest cow, Willi popped up on the other side and moved forward as fast as he could until he found himself alone with one particularly enormous creature rushing through a swinging gate. As soon as they were in, the gate shut automatically—and wouldn't open again despite Axel's obvious yanking—clearly calibrated to allow in only one steer at a time.

Willi sighed.

He hadn't had time to catch his breath, though, when two arms reached from the darkness, grabbed the cow by the horns, and threw a harness on its head, immobilizing it. Before Willi could say a word, an enormous mallet smashed between its horns. The cow cried horribly, then all four legs sprang horizontal as if it had learned to fly. Willi got knocked into a corner. The cow crashed to its stomach, and a second pair of arms was instantly sliding chains over its rear hooves, a mechanized pulley hoisting it upside down, the brown eyes still looking about, confused, as it went flying again—down a conveyor belt.

In one glance Willi took in the operation.

Cows were entering by the dozens, getting clubbed, hoisted, and joining their brethren on the conveyor belt. Men in hip-high leather boots made quick slashes with silver blades that opened their throats. Showered in red spray, these men barely had time to finish one slash before the next throat arrived. The floor was ankle-deep in blood. It poured like waterfalls down drainage grates, collected for things such as sausages. Relieved of their agony, the cows shuttled on to teams of men in high rubber gloves, where they were unseamed, stripped of organs, and hustled down to the skinners, who denuded them of hide and fat. Without a second's pause they were rushed into the slicing machines—the huge, relentless jaws of death—where ribs were crushed and flesh rendered into sides. The place was so noisy you couldn't hear what was happening two feet away. Things moved so quickly a worker barely had time to focus on anything but his task.

Which was why no one even noticed Willi was there.

"Slaughterhouse, beer hall, bordello, bed," Willi remembered Gruber telling him. "That's all there is for these men, Kraus."

As the cow Willi'd come in with hurtled to its destiny, the gate reopened and allowed not just another one in, but Axel too. Now it was Willi's turn to face fate. There was no point seeking help. He was going to have to take this guy down as surely as these animals were going. Axel's manic frenzy had not subsided. If anything, he looked more crazed, jumping around the cow as it received its flying head blow.

By the time it crash-landed, Axel had homed in on Willi and raised his hatchet, unconcerned whether anyone was watching. An image of Freksa sliced in two flashed through Willi's brain as he tucked his shoulder and rolled, the hatchet landing an inch from his face. His jacket and his pants, he realized, were drenched in blood. But not, thank God, his own.

Plus he'd gotten where he needed to be: behind Axel.

He stood a chance.

Backing up, facing his adversary, Willi lured him with a smirk, his eyes casting about for something to seize the advantage with. When a piercing whistle filled his ears, he could have shouted for joy. At last. Someone must have realized what was happening and sounded an alarm. But no. As he inched back farther, his shoes squeaking with blood, he realized the machinery was all turning off, the workers leaving.

That was no alarm. It was lunch.

The smirk now drew across Axel's face.

He lifted his ax and charged.

Willi grabbed two big metal hooks stationary on the overhead conveyor belt and leaped, coiling his legs and releasing them full force into Axel's chest. It knocked him back, and he slipped on the slimy floor, toppling. As Willi jumped to seize the opportunity, his own feet flew out from under him—and they both were down.

As if from the dead, Axel got up first, covered in blood and gore, slowly approaching with his hatchet. Willi looked up at his furious face, readying to make a split-second choice which way to roll. As Axel lunged, though, his feet slid again, and like one of the stunned cows, he collapsed, right atop Willi. In seconds his bloody hands were trying to seize Willi's throat.

Struggling to repel the grip, Willi managed to keep breathing, but the leviathan arms were implacable. Gradually he grew aware Axel's eyes were boring into his now—and that they were locked in a struggle with only one conclusion. In another few seconds it would come, Willi knew—unless he could think of something. Axel's grip was beginning to close Willi's windpipe.

From the depths of his being, he summoned one last hope.

"Worthless monster," he forced raspy words past Axel's fingers. "Cut off my head and put it on a tree, did you?"

What was the only thing Axel had ever feared?

"You're going to the cellar. And if you cry, I'm gonna carve the skin right off your body and eat you for—"

Axel froze, stunned to hear his long-dead father summoned—and with such precision. In a flash of confusion his grip eased long enough for Willi to get in a swift blow to Axel's throat, which sent the beast backward, gasping.

Quickly refilling his own desperate lungs, Willi glanced about furiously. Several bloodstained mallets leaned against the wall. He twisted, bolting out from under Axel, and reached with all his might, managing to grab one and push himself off the floor.

Now he and Axel faced each other again, both struggling to regain their breathing. But Willi had the advantage. He carefully wielded the heavy instrument, angling for a strategic blow. Axel warily staggered back, accidentally elbowing one of the control panels and turning the machinery on, ignoring the rise of mechanical clatter as he readied for interception. There'd be just one chance, Willi knew; it'd have to be a deathblow or his own head would end up pulp. Axel's massive hands were ready, his eyes bulging, black with hate. Axel moved a leg back to brace himself, but his foot stepped into one of the chain loops used for hoisting cows, setting it off automatically. A terrible cry arose from his throat as his massive body flipped upside down and he went hurtling down the conveyor belt, dangling by one leg.

Willi's throat was still afire. He was unable to fully keep his balance. Stumbling for the control panel, he couldn't focus on all the tiny switch signals. Which had Axel hit?

"For God's sake!" Axel reached his gigantic arms out.

He was shuttling straight for the jaws of death.

Desperately Willi searched for the main plug.

Axel wept. "No, Daddy. No!"

Willi found it, yanking with all his might.

And the giant saw ground to a halt.

But not before a hideous shriek preceeded the definitive crunching of ribs.

Twenty-four

Vibrations surged through Willi's body.

He sat up, pushing back his shoulders, trying to concentrate. But the edges of everything were hazy. Those two men across the table had strange ethereal glows, like beings from another world come to assist him. He couldn't have been more grateful if they actually had been.

Eberhard and Rollmann, both hydraulic engineers, were poring over maps of the infrastructure beneath Bone Alley, the main lines, sewer lines, holding tanks, storm canals. On the far side of the room Gunther's voice throbbed with barely subdued enthusiasm as he coordinated plans with the assistant from the *Viehof* Direktor's office, a gangly brunette named Trudi. Gerd Woerner, of the *Abend Zeitung,* was pacing back and forth taking notes, every so often glancing outside.

Willi glanced outside too.

From the third-floor office of the *Viehof* pump house, in one direction you could see the giant *Entlandungbahnhof*, the complex of disembarkation platforms and inspection ramps where from every corner of Europe livestock arrived hourly by freight car—and on the other, the acres of facilities where they got turned into meat and by-product. Thaer Strasse below was crowded with late-day traffic. Trucks jostling for parking spots. Agents rushing to conclude deals. Everything back to normal, it seemed.

Except Willi. He was still in shock, he knew.

Floating in a strange amniotic-like sac.

Just hours ago, although it felt like months . . . years . . . seconds . . . he'd been rammed by a truck, nearly strangled to death. And witnessed a man sawed in two. Plenty of people would never recover from such a day. He at least had practice. From years at the front he knew the rubbery sensations following such trauma, and how to keep going despite the drag they placed on the soul. How to keep centered on all the other feelings that made the going worth it.

What choice was there? The mission had to be accomplished.

And for that to happen he had to keep pumping as determinedly as those five huge generators below.

"This could be it, then." Eberhard, who managed the *Viehof* water system, pointed at the area map. Rollmann, a chief engineer from municipal water, seemed to agree. Woerner, the reporter, leaned over to look where Eberhard was pointing.

Willi looked too. Had they finally found the entrance to this thing?

His mind was reeling through time.

Seconds after Axel went through the jaws of death, a white light had flashed through Willi's eyes. Not divine revelation—but a camera bulb. Woerner of all people, from the *Abend Zeitung*. The one who'd shouted out in front of everyone, "How many more kids have to die, Kraus?" He'd gotten a call about a crazy chase through the *Viehof* and hurried over. Noticed a van and an Opel all smashed up outside. His eyes had grown huge as he took in Willi covered head to toe in blood, and Axel—hanging there. "God Almighty."

Willi'd had no choice but to try to enlist him. "Nothing's to stop you from running straight to press with this, Woerner. But you'd be compromising a major case. And there's more to the story. A lot more, promise. I'll give you the scoop, only—you've got to help me out first."

"Bribery aside, Willi, for you—sure."

Willi had Woerner summon Gunther, *schnell*—and bring all the men from Bone Alley. Then Willi'd had Woerner find him a place to wash and a set of fresh clothes.

"You're the only one I'd do this for, Kraus," the reporter'd said, standing guard while Willi showered in the slaughterhouse locker room. "Freksa, Horthstaler, any of them over in Homicide, I'd have been out of here so fast with those photos they wouldn't have seen me leave. You have any idea what they're worth? Death of the *Kinderfesser!*"

"I keep telling you," Willi'd gurgled from under the water, sensing it might be wise in the long run to have a journalist record whatever they found down there, "it wasn't him. Just stick with me, Gerd. This one's for the history books."

The reporter's voice darkened. "I'm almost afraid to know, Willi. Ten years on the beat in Berlin, I never saw such blood."

Willi watched it swirl down the drain as he scrubbed his hair and ears and between his toes.

Meanwhile, Gunther proved his mettle, leading up a team in getting Slaughterhouse Two sealed off for an alleged "health inspection," covering up the wrecked vehicles outside, giving a false report about the reasons for the chase through the *Viehof,* and hiding all traces of Axel's remains. Willi ordered everything possible done to keep a lid on Axel's death.

He damn well hadn't wanted it. He'd needed Axel to help him snare Magda and Ilse. Even without the brother, he had a horrible suspicion those sick sisters could keep their operation going. And who was to say others weren't involved in this mass-murder-for-money scheme? The Köhler siblings might be mere cogs in a wheel. All the more reason they had to be stopped. Fast.

Once these girls heard what happened to Axel, there'd be no finding them.

Their brother had unfortunately shielded his family even in death. Not a single piece of ID on him: no driver's license, no address. Nothing with the name he'd taken after killing his father. In his pocket just a wad of blood-drenched bills and some keys. His van, of course—no license plates. Even in a city as controlled as Berlin, somehow, for a decade and a half, these three children of wrath had survived under the floorboards.

"Like rats." Eberhard sighed, running his finger along the map, tugging Willi's brain back to the attack plans. "Of course they have more than one entrance to the lair."

Willi stared at the route Eberhard was showing, and then out the window at the *Viehof*. For the moment, there was nothing to do about Ilse, he conceded. In all this time he'd had only one real sighting of her. That tall, red-haired "nurse" with the pockmarked face was slippery as an eel. But Magda he'd seen with his own eyes. She was no eel. If cornered, she might well turn dangerous. But she wasn't slithering away anywhere fast. Tonight, one way or another, they were grabbing her. Hopefully alive.

It proved a good thing that on their reconnaissance raid the other night Willi'd had Gunther render sketches of the layouts they'd found under Bone Alley. Comparing those now to *Viehof* blueprints and matching both with the municipal water plans, they'd come up with a rough idea of what was going on beneath that little street in the by-products zone. The distinct outlines of a two-level subterranean bunker. A cold sweat broke out on his forehead when Willi understood—the Köhler children had re-created, enlarged, and enhanced the underground dungeon of their childhood.

How to penetrate it as quickly as possible without giving Magda a chance to escape was the task at hand. Besides an apparent hidden driveway, there was at least one other way in and out, they knew—a connection to the city sewer lines—because several substantial burlap sacks full of bones had washed out through them as far as two kilometers away. If they could determine precisely where those sacks had entered the system, they'd have a back door into the Köhlers' dark realm.

Berlin had nearly ten thousand kilometers of storm-water drainage, completely distinct from its waste disposal. The main storm canals were fed by subcanals, feeder lines, and thousands of individual surface shafts catching runoff from street gutters. In heavy rains, the system often backed up, Eberhard explained. Last October had been a dilly. Beginning on the twenty-fifth of that month, three days of storms had caused tree limbs, tires, and other large debris to accumulate at a bend in *Sturmwasser Kanal Fünf,* as he pointed out on the map, where the canal turned southwest to meet the Spree River. This backed up the entire line all the way from the substation under Frankfurter Allee, where the second set of bags turned up, beneath the construction site where the first bag appeared, right to the feeder lines under the *Central-Viehof.*

"If we look at this map here"—Eberhard opened up a yellowed plan of the area dating from 1852—"we can see that before the *Viehof* was even built, a small brewery occupied the site where Bone Alley is today. It's highly possible that whoever rebuilt the basements of these buildings also opened the brewery cellar, which has entry ducts twenty-seven to twenty-nine directly on Feeder Line J to *Sturmwasser Kanal Fünf.* Feeder Line J was completely backed up the night of October twenty-eighth and flushed out the following morning."

Willi could hardly forget that fateful day, seeing that burlap bag for the first time. The bones so neatly arranged. The circled phrase in the waterlogged Bible. He'd never been certain if someone had actually dumped the burlap bags into the sewers or they'd been swept in accidentally. Eberhard's description of the flood made the latter appear more likely, which is probably why the Köhlers kept right on with their dirty work, never realizing someone had found the evidence and taken up the hunt.

Now at last the pieces were falling into place.

Minute by minute, Willi was inching nearer.

Viehof Direktor Gruber himself, of all people, had just come through with an astonishing tip.

Well aware of the mayhem playing out in the streets of his beloved stockyards, Herr Direktor apparently felt it best to fully cooperate finally in hopes of ending the ordeal. He had personally phoned half an hour ago to mention a seemingly insignificant detail.

"Since you're so damn relentless about this, Kraus, something did occur to me."

He'd explained to Willi how various reports had reached his ears over the years, mostly of a casual nature, about an incongruous bit of traffic coming in and out of the Muller-Schlosser Fertilizer plant right outside the *Viehof*, on Thaer Strasse. An ice-cream truck— the kind that served children near schools and playgrounds—was seen entering and leaving on one side of the dusty factory complex, apparently disappearing into some kind of underground garage. Since it wasn't his jurisdiction and didn't seem to be causing any problems, he'd never paid much attention. Until now. And he thought, well, perhaps it might be of help, Gruber said.

Checking the maps, they'd found the address was outside the *Viehof* wall, all right, but less than thirty yards from Bone Alley. Rollmann and Eberhard both concurred a short vehicular tunnel could easily lead to the Köhlers' underground lair. A hidden driveway with a disguised entrance.

And an ice cream truck. My God. Willi'd all but gasped when he'd heard. All this time he'd wondered how the Shepherdess lured so many boys off the streets of Berlin and dragged them away without being seen. How fiendishly brilliant, he realized now. He could picture her in a clean white uniform offering a temptation impossible to resist. "Wanna see inside the truck? Right this way, boys." And bolting the door shut. The last anyone ever saw of those kids . . . until they turned up as handbags or lampshades.

Plus, no wonder these Köhlers were so difficult to find. They'd furnished their underground lair with an underground passage.

You couldn't say they weren't resourceful.

Adrenaline squirted from Willi's adrenal glands, causing his heart to shoot fire through his veins, incinerating his lethargy. They had it now, two ways in and out.

It was time to move.

A coordinated raid. Group A, including Willi, Gunther, the water engineers Rollmann and Eberhard, Woerner of the *Abend Zeitung*, and a four-man team from Schupo—the security police—were going in at 5:45 through the water tunnels. Group B, a full detatchment of security police, were surrounding the perimeter, then entering the underground drive via the fertilizer plant fifteen minutes later, preventing Magda's escape and providing backup in case of trouble. Willi wanted to make certain he was the first to penetrate the Köhlers' lair and oversee Magda's capture. He had a personal stake, he felt, in taking her unharmed.

Down the long, revolving staircase they came to the ground floor of the pump house, passed the five forty-eight-horsepower generators feeding the *Viehof* hydraulic system, giant turbines whirring, pistons pounding, maximum pressure building for hosing detritus from even the tiniest nooks and crannies.

Through a door marked AUTHORIZED PERSONNEL ONLY, the nine men of Team A descended another longer staircase, Willi modulating his breathing as the air closed in and grew heavy. At the bottom an iron gate blocked their way. While Rollmann opened it, Willi looked at his watch. It was 5:45, precisely.

Right now, he knew, 4 million people in greater Berlin were carrying on as usual. In front of the war memorial on Unter den Linden, goose-stepping soldiers were performing the final changing of the guard to hundreds of clicking cameras. Nearby at the glamorous Hotel Adlon, guests were swigging cocktails at the Grill Room. Along the Spree, coal barges were chugging past the Royal Palace. At Templehof Field, silver planes glided past the semicircular terminal. At Nightclub Resi, maids were polishing the house phones on each table so patrons could call each other and exchange a few whispers tonight. While in the tenements of working-class Wedding, organ-grinders played old chestnuts to housewives who hummed along from courtyard windows. On Koch Strasse, as on every evening, competing newspapers rushed to get out late editions, especially with elections just a week away. And as patrons sat a few blocks north for schnitzel at Lutter and Wegner, worshippers arrived across the street for evening services at the French Cathedral. Or the nearby Hedwigs church. Or the Nikolai church. Or the mosque in Wilmersdorf. Or the great synagogue on Orianienburger Strasse.

But beneath Berlin's diverse, vibrant streets lurked another, far darker world.

Twenty-five

A dim, low universe of brick.

Sky, horizon, everything, vaulting overhead like a medieval castle, but barely tall enough to stand in. Down the center, flanked by narrow sidewalks, a thin stream of water moving almost imperceptibly. Black, silent. Here and there incandescent bulbs reflecting off slick surfaces. Cold, still. A suffocating catacomb tapering into nothingness.

Sturmwasser Kanal Fünf.

Brick arch after brick arch lured the nine-man team deeper into this claustrophobic netherworld, every step echoing back. Even Willi's heart, it seemed, reverberated off the curvatures. And weren't those his fears dripping down through the drain grates? What if Magda'd been tipped off? What if she was already out of Berlin? What if he was wrong altogether about this underground dungeon?

Woerner perhaps liked him personally, but a failure such as that would be front-page news.

A large, brown rat scampered across his foot. Back in the trenches he'd learned to endure their slimy tails and harsh claws. But the newsman behind let out a yelp that wouldn't stop echoing.

A feeder line forking in from the left added more water to the slow-moving flow. It hadn't rained for a couple of weeks. The flooding last October, Eberhard pointed out with his flashlight, had completely filled this tunnel.

A thin line of mud still clung to the ceiling.

Willi's rib cage seemed to contract. If it happened again with them down here—he looked around—there'd be no escape.

His mind filled with images: burlap sacks tumbling through rapids, white bones knocking into each other. Axel crying as he hurtled upside down.

Had that really been just hours ago?

A dim nausea shuddered through his heart.

Suddenly, he felt himself pushing back walls. Ceilings. Everything closing in. He had to command his knees not to buckle. They were going rubbery, like poor Reverend Braunschweig's, may he rest in peace. An irrational fear skidding through his innards, something about to grab his ankle, drag him under. Never again to see his wife or children.

He forced his thoughts ahead. He couldn't stumble now. Magda was somewhere just up ahead. A woman raped and tortured by her father, whose baby by him he'd slaughtered like a lamb—grown into a murderous monster herself. No doubt she'd put up a fine fight with a butcher's knife. Probably skilled as hell with one, he reminded himself. The Köhler kids had been schooled by a master.

You couldn't overestimate their determination.

He concentrated on placing one foot in front of the next, ignoring the rats, the walls, the water, his nose seeking out whatever fresh air it could find. For a moment he pictured those three children, alone in the dungeon. Days on end. Dying from stench. Their own father, the man supposed to nuture and protect them, threatening to skin them alive and eat them. What worse could a father do to a child?

And Bruno Köhler, what must his father have done to him?

"In here." Eberhard pointed with his light. "Feeder Line J, right under the old brewery basement."

Willi had to suppress an urge to punch this guy in the nose. All those maps he'd shown upstairs gave no indication how tight, how airless, these tunnels were. Storm Canal Five was the Grand Canyon compared to Feeder Line J.

But he took in whatever oxygen he could and stooped.

Hunching all the way over at the waist, he felt like a caveman. After a while he realized his knuckles were scraping the floor, as if they were reverting to chimpanzees. What next? Slugs on the sewer bottom?

"Man, my camera better not get ruined," Woerner moaned.

One of the officers lost control. "I can't breathe," they could hear far at the end of the line. "Oh, God, get me out of here!"

"You're all right," another officer was trying to calm him. "Take a deep breath. We're almost there."

Willi followed the advice too.

But what happened to grates 27–29 that drained the old brewery? They were supposed to open over their shoulders somewhere right about here, easily accessible with the turn of some screws. Suddenly, though, Eberhard and Rollmann weren't so sure. Apparently the flood last October had washed away not only the burlap sacks but all the sign postings too. The layer of dry muck still coating this section of feeder line was so thick it obscured all evidence there were even drain grates here.

"Clearly your maintenance crews have been asleep." Rollmann angrily shone his flashlight about the ceiling.

"With all the layoffs," Eberhard snapped back, "it's a wonder there are crews left at all."

Let's not bicker, gentlemen, Willi was thinking, checking his watch. In three minutes the backup team would penetrate the fertilizer plant and begin descending the underground driveway. It would take approximately four minutes by foot to reach the Köhlers' hideout, where they would bust in whatever doors they found and enter. If these drain grates remained elusive, Team B was going to beat them in and possibly upset his whole game plan.

Magda may have been psychotic, but she was cagey as hell. She'd already outsmarted Willi once and, along with her siblings, managed for years to carry out some of the most heinous crimes in recent history. Willi didn't want to think what might happen if she had only security cops to deal with, and not him. But Rollmann and Eberhard couldn't agree suddenly if this was even Feeder Line J.

Willi wanted to knock their heads together.

While they argued he squeezed past them, resolutely slowing his breathing and roving his flashlight overhead. During the war he'd penetrated no-man's-land between German and French lines half a dozen times, and he'd never lost the skills he'd had to hone on those death-defying missions—parting barbed wire and slithering into fields raked with machine-gun fire, pregnant with mines. When he aroused full concentration, his vision grew almost microscopelike, able to focus in on even the tiniest objects, his brain swiftly assessing their usefulness or harm. Now, ardently tickling his fingertips along the dry mud, he stopped short at an unmistakable indent—a perfectly straight line. And several inches above it, another one. A grate, all right.

After two minutes' manipulation they coaxed it open, spraying debris into the feeder line and sending up a cloud of dust. When they squeezed through and pushed themselves up, they were able to stand fully erect on the floor of a dark brick cave.

"This is it," Eberhard whispered as if they'd entered a pharaoh's tomb. His flashlight fell on a large stack of wooden kegs still stamped with TANNHAUSER BIER. Decrepit equipment lay about: tubing, filters. The fetid air felt as if it hadn't been changed in a century. An abysmal gloom hovered over everything. Perhaps the place wasn't even connected with the Köhlers' bunker after all, Willi feared.

But then he spotted them.

At the far end of the room—burlap sacks. A lot of them. His

whole throat clenched when he shone a light and saw on each the now-familiar SCHNITZLER AND SON. There must have been scores. Aligned in straight rows. Like headstones in a cemetery. And full, all right. He walked over to one and ripped open the top, then another and another. His stomach turned. Each was stuffed with clean, white bones.

"Hey, look." Gunther's flashlight aimed at the wall above.

All the bricks had been scratched with names and dates:

Ernst Adler—6.26.28

Kristof Furth—3.16.29

Someone had taken great pains to knife everything in using elementary-school block letters. Every brick on the entire wall was incribed this way. There had to be a hundred names. The earliest, Willi saw, dated back to 1924. The year the Köhlers had gone from kidnapping dogs to children.

Checking his watch, Willi saw it was now after six. Team B had already set out. Magda was somewhere overhead. He had four minutes to find and grab her before her door burst in and set off every alarm she had. Yet there was no apparent way out of here, as if they were trapped in a well. No stairs. No doors. The ceiling had to be twenty feet high. How the hell did they get these burlap sacks down here?

It was Gunther, again, who spotted it first.

"Look, chief." He pointed out a set of tracks embedded in the wall leading all the way to a second story, where they could vaguely make out a set of wooden doors. "We had one like it in our barn. A grain elevator."

"But how does it work? There's no electricity."

Gunther began pushing aside bags until he found a rickety wooden platform attached by ropes and wheels to the tracks. "You turn this handle, which yanks these pulleys." He demonstrated.

Willi swallowed. Not a promising option. Even if the ancient-looking contraption held, only one person at a time could get on. Plus, it hadn't been oiled in God knew how long and made enough noise to wake the dead.

What choice was there, though?

He sent Gunther first, able to watch only through one eye as the kid began to rise. The two Schupo men broke into a real sweat turning the pulleys, but going slowly managed to keep the noise to a minimum. Reaching the top finally, Gunther whispered down that there was a decent-size platform, able to accommodate maybe five or six men. Which was good, Willi thought, because when they pried open those doors, he wanted to enter in force.

Willi went next. As he climbed on and jerked skyward, he had to suppress a rush of doubts. Perhaps Magda'd already heard the squeaking pulley and was fleeing through some exit they had no idea about. Perhaps she was already at the door, hatchet raised, about to swipe. He peeked down. One severed rope and his spine would snap as fast as a pretzel. But he forced his eyes upward and realized, after all this time, how near he'd gotten to his goal. Whether its origin was Bruno's father or his father's father all the way back to Adam no longer made a difference. All that mattered now was that he put an end to it, once and for all—the Köhlers' tortured legacy. Rising over the memorial of names, all the rust seeping from the iron tracks made it look as if the walls themselves were weeping blood.

The three Schupo men followed, hoisted by Rollmann and Eberhard, then Woerner came, camera ready. All the while the clock ticked. In less than two minutes Team B would break through. When everyone finally crowded on the ledge, a Schupo man began wedging a crowbar between the doors. Willi's heart pounded. From the day he first saw the bizarre contents of that burlap sack, he'd known he was up against something truly terrible. Now he didn't really want to have to see.

As the doors rolled apart, he smelled it first. A long, low chamber opened before them—no hatchet but a stench as sharp as one slicing at their noses. Willi knew at once what it was: rotting flesh. It brought him back to those hospitals at the front. Only here, an unearthly silence reigned—because staring at them, mute with shock, were eight or nine young boys.

They looked more like creatures from the depths of the ocean, heads shaven. Eyes bulging. Ears sticking out. So emaciated their collarbones seemed ready to break from their skin. But they were boys, all right, seated at low tables with lamps, each with different work in front. Their feet, Willi saw, bare and raw, were chained to the floor. Like—

Slaves.

A taller one, not as emaciated, the overseer evidently, patrolled with a small cane whip. He too stared in mute amazement at the invaders, as if those bones in the basement had reincarnated and arisen.

No one batted an eyelash, so stunning to each side was the apparition of the other.

Only the reporter held his mouth, to keep from retching.

Two large vats fired by orange flames added to the hellish atmosphere. One, Willi saw, contained bones. A batch of fibulae and tibiae on an adjacent cart were clean and white. The second, he guessed from buckets of thick, gray fat nearby, was probably boiling gelatin or soap—one of the reasons, though not all, for the violent stench. The opposite wall held long wooden racks filled with strands of bloody muscle hanging like spaghetti. Two little boys were rolling them into the leather thread that was Magda's trademark. Next to them, two more skeletal figures were boring holes with hand drills into knuckle bones, passing finished products on to a third, who shined them up with sandpaper. Another was at a sewing machine, pushing pedals with his feet, the way Willi's grandmother used to.

Only she never stiched human skins.

On the far side of the hellish workshop a wooden handcart was draped with naked corpses. One had already been dismembered, judging by the remains on a nearby butcher's table. Two still in the cart, Willi realized, looked familiar. He'd seen their photographs not long ago: the sons of industrialists who'd vanished off horses in the Tiergarten. His throat clenched when he realized each of their right arms was missing. And their skulls appeared to have been sliced open at the top.

Suddenly, atop a short staircase overlooking this chamber of horrors, a loud, twisting scream came from a set of hinges, and a door opened. Lit from behind, Magda's massive body cast a shadow over the silent children, a white apron covering her front completely drenched in red, her whole face smeared with it, her hair, her hands. For a second, she just stood there looking at Willi as if she wasn't sure who he was. Then like a little girl happy to see her daddy, she gave a great big smile and proudly held aloft the child's arm she'd been gnawing to the bone.

Book Four

TOWER OF SILENCE

Twenty-six

BERLIN
SEPTEMBER 1930

The giant radio mast over Wilmersdorf scanned the night sky with a powerful searchlight, its antenna beaming high-frequency waves across the heart of Europe—plays by Brecht, concerts by Schönberg. A towering symbol of Berlin as transmitter of modernity.

A third of the way up its truss-work spine, accessible by high-speed elevator, the four-sided Terrace Restaurant beckoned with a 360-degree panorama, enhanced by the rhythms of the finest dance orchestras. From here the whole city—the good side, anyway—seemed to throw itself at one's feet. To the north, the old Charlottenburg Palace with its sprawling baroque gardens. To the west, the flat, green expanse of Grunewald, woods and lakes and luxury villas sailing toward the horizon. Southward, handsome Wilmersdorf, with its pretty plazas and respectable apartment blocks, the festive lights of Luna Park. And east, the elegant shops, cafés, and movie palaces along the tree-lined Ku' damm, racing into the heart of the city. It was a fitting vantage point to celebrate Willi's thirty-fifth birthday.

And his triumph over *Der Kinderfresser.*

Imperfect though it might have been.

Several of Woerner's hair-raising photos, along with his heart-palpitating, if slightly inaccurate, firsthand report proclaiming the case of the Child-Eater closed, had catapulted Willi into a national hero: Catcher of the Beast. By the end of the week his face had appeared in newspapers across Germany. The chancellor had called to thank him. Sigmund Freud phoned to discuss certain details of the case. Even Kommissar Horthstaler, who wouldn't think of missing this celebration tonight, got into as many photographs with Willi as possible, insisting to whoever would listen that he'd always known he'd had a master sleuth on his team.

A hundred people must have turned out for this party, which his father-in-law had said he'd be "honored" to pay for. The orchestra was playing "It Will Never Be Like This Again," and as Willi and Vicki swayed in a gentle fox-trot, people kept coming over to have their picture taken with him, asking for an autograph.

"Go on, for goodness' sakes," Vicki kept urging.

"Thank you for giving us back our city," they all said.

The whole of Berlin was breathing easier. Schools, playgrounds, orphan homes, even the gangs of Wild Boys, could relax now that *Der Kinderfesser* was behind bars.

Which there was no doubt she was, thanks to Willi.

He gave himself credit where it was due.

But even if no one else wanted to admit it, he for one knew the final nail in this coffin had not quite been driven in.

Once they'd grabbed her, Magda'd gone easily enough, lingering in a state of severe regression while they got her into cuffs, mumbling "Ring Around the Rosie" the whole way to the Alex, even as they locked her in the Dungeons:

Ringel, Ringel, Reihe
Sind wir Kinder dreie

She certainly hadn't relinquished her secrets as easily. While medical teams from Charité Hospital worked to save the boys she'd tortured, Willi and Gunther faced her in the cell. By then she'd been made presentable, dressed in a prison gown and clean, white headscarf, all washed up. An awful stench, though, discharged from her mouth; half her teeth, Willi saw, were rotting and black. Even with a woman's scarf on, nothing about this woman was womanly. It spooked Willi how closely she resembled her brother.

Only a day ago that maniac had nearly taken off Willi's head.

At first, she seemed cooperative. Nearly rational. Offering grim excuses in her own defense.

"You think I wanted to?" Her voice was less enraged than Axel's but more deeply bitter. "He locked me down there. You think I had a choice? I was given quotas of how much I had to produce, like during the war."

Willi was relieved at least she was cognizant of reality, however much she may or may not have meshed with it.

"Who locked you up, Magda?" He could tell she knew exactly who he was and that they'd met before. "Who forced you to do all those terrible things?"

"You know who." She shot him a glance, twisting her lips in a grin. "My better half."

You could almost feel sorry for her. The woman had endured such a childhood of torture that her eyes were still shellacked with many coats of pain. But recalling how she played him that first time they'd met, he knew well that pity was what she was aiming for. And that it was only meant to distract him.

"You mean, your brother?"

She shivered, seeming to expel something from her bloodstream. Then, peeking at Willi, she snickered and broke into a storm of such hilarity she had to hold her middle with both hands. "You sure took care of him, didn't you!"

Startled, Willi couldn't help wondering—if she'd known about her brother's death, why hadn't she tried to flee? Perhaps she'd felt too secure down there in her slave-filled dungeon. Perhaps she was just ready to give up.

"When I spoke to you in the *Viehof,* I don't recall any chains around your feet, Magda, like you put on those little boys. You looked quite free to leave."

"How the fuck do you know?"

Clearly he'd taken the wrong approach.

Her massive weight shifted as if she was about to tackle him. He opened his hands to warn her off, and she fell back with a pitiful whimper, holding her arms over her head, trembling as if she were about to get clubbed.

"Oh, please don't hit. God, please. No. Please."

"No one's hitting, Magda."

It was too late.

Curled in a ball, she'd taken leave of her senses behind some invisible wall and wouldn't come out, appearing at first not to understand, then as if she didn't even hear Willi. In the blink of an eye she fell sound asleep and started snoring like a drunken sailor. Gunther and Willi looked at each other, unsure how to proceed. In just a few seconds, though, she was wide awake, stretching as if from a long night's sleep. "Jesus." She looked around. "Where are my kids?"

"They're all being taken care of," Willi assured her.

He tried to coax her into revealing what he needed to find out most: her sister's whereabouts. But the minute he mentioned Ilse, Magda went wild.

"You leave her out of this!" she screamed, and balled her fists, then tenderly pretended to cradle a baby in her arms. "My sweet little angel. Cares for everybody—but herself."

Willi had to give her his handkerchief, she started sobbing so profusely.

"Always worried about the future of the world." She mopped her rubbery cheeks. "Out there doing good. On her own, unrewarded."

Every time Magda blew her nose, her face appeared to expand. "Cleaning up neighborhoods. Getting rid of rodents." Finally her whole head looked like it were about to explode. "That's all they are, you know: vermin needing extermination." Her eyes detonated with delight. "And, boy, did they come running when Ilse yelled, 'ice cream.'" A blast of laughter tore from her heart. "'Ice cream, ice cream!' A real Pied Piper."

Magda threw up her meaty hands, then let them fall in a gesture of deflation.

"So can you tell me, Sergeant, why does she keep falling in love? It breaks my heart. First the doctor. Then the priestess. Now that mustached little schemer. She gives them everything, and what does she get?" Magda leaned back, swaying. "I like it alone. Just me and my boys." Her voice descended to a whisper. "Such sweet things, ain't they? Theirs is a Christlike suffering."

She winced, stabbed it seemed, deep in her side.

"Little shits!" she screamed again, murderously looking around. "I'll make something useful out of them."

She sighed, leaning back, taking a deep breath. "The living I'll make work, and the dead I'll make into—"

Sensing perhaps she ought not say what she was about to, she froze and, in a desperate ploy, ripped open her prison gown, unleashed one of her enormous tits, stuck it in her mouth, and started suckling.

"Mmmm, Mother, I'm so hungry."

Willi had to concede about this time she was more than he could handle.

The Terrace orchestra broke into a lively Charleston, a dance that had practically defined the last decade, but now sadly seemed too jubilant. Gunther and Vicki's sister, Ava, however, were out there making the best of it: arms, knees, heels flying in a dozen directions. Willi spotted Fritz at a table chatting with Willi's cousin Kurt.

After that insanity with Magda in the jail cell, Willi'd turned to Kurt for help. With two out of three siblings plus the underground lair down, he was confident the Köhler death ring had been knocked out. But he couldn't feel as if this thing was over until he'd gotten Ilse too. Little angel.

Hoping Kurt could wrest something out of Magda, he'd gone to see him. It was a fine day, the first hint of autumn in the air. Turn-of-the-century mansions in the Tiergarten district glistened in the sunshine. Approaching the handsome Insitut building, he'd spotted his bony-faced cousin out front talking to a man in a trench coat and gotten a real start when he realized the guy was wearing a silver eye patch.

Kurt knew von Hessler?

Nearing, Willi could hardly help but overhear the scientist's strident polemic.

"You speak as if there really is such a clear separation between sanity and madness. What if this 'psychosis' you place such stock in is simply an extreme expression of thoughts or behavior present in the entire population?"

"Willi." Kurt spotted him and looked immediately relieved. "Doktor, I'm afraid I'm going to have to bid adieu. This is my cousin Sergeant-Detektiv Kraus, of the Kriminal Polizei."

"Yes. How could I not know the Herr Sergeant-Detektiv." Von Hessler reached out a hand while adjusting his eye patch. "The sergeant's on more magazine covers than Marlene Dietrich. Besides, we've met on several occasions. Congratulations on your success, Kraus. The whole city breathes a sigh of relief."

"Thanks. Now we've got to try and untangle some of the knotted strands in a very mixed-up mind."

"A futile endeavor." The doctor guffawed as if Willi'd just said the most preposterous thing ever. "You'll never understand such a mind. Or any mind for that matter. That's what I've been trying to get across to your cousin all this while. And what my experiments once and for all will prove to the world. Exploring the past is pointless. Reformation of the human mind is possible only through reconditioning. We must discuss it further, gentlemen, but in the meantime, please enjoy this beautiful afternoon."

As they watched von Hessler leap into his sleek, black SSK and race off, Kurt said, "Sometimes I think he's the maddest one of all. How do you know him, Willi?"

"He's a childhood friend of my old war buddy Fritz. You?"

"We went to medical school together. He was studying to be a psychoanalyst—until he jumped ship. Just happened to be driving past when he saw me out here so he stopped to try and convert me to his new religion." Kunt took off his glasses and wiped them clean. "Remember that Yiddish word Nana used whenever we bothered her?"

"*Nudnik,*" Willi replied.

Kurt returned the glasses to his nose. "That's him. A Behaviorist *nudnik.*"

They'd opted for a walk through the park, so Willi could explain details of the *Kinderfresser* case left out by the newspapers, as well as his experience up close in the jail cell. He wanted Kurt to be as well armed as possible for his interview with Magda. Entering the enormous old Tiergarten, though, his cousin kept frowning and scratching his head, as if he found what he was hearing too crazy even for a psychiatrist to believe.

They'd strolled the famous Siegesallee toward the Victory Column in the Platz der Republik. This leafy walk was lined on both sides with a historical chronology of Prussian royalty—nearly one hundred towering figures in Carrara marble commissioned by Kaiser Wilhelm II in the late 1890s to celebrate his thirty-sixth birthday. A grand pedestrian boulevard; nowadays it was fashionable for Berliners to lampoon it as the Avenue of Puppets, symbol in stone of the grandiose delusions that had tripped Germany into the trenches of apocalypse. But for Willi its very monumentalism rekindled memories of something else too that had reigned before the Great War—the rock-hard optimism. How firmly in those days everyone believed humanity was on a march of progress, that tomorrow would always be better than today. Like the very solidness of the ground they stood on, no one conceived otherwise. Until 1914.

Then how hollow, how distant such faith felt.

Proceeding down this timeline of overthrown hegemony, his cousin began to speculate on the disorders of the mind.

"When I was in medical school," Kurt said as they passed the statue of Albert the Bear, who died in 1170, "they were still calling everyone *minderwertig*—mentally deficient. Now, slowly," he added as they approached the dingy white figures of Dukes Otto I and II, "we're better able to distinguish characteristics of what we call psychopathic personalities. Depressive. Fanatic. Explosive. Compassionless." Beyond the two shining-faced Johannes, they moved toward Waldemar the Great. "Some believe these pathologies are wholly environmental in origin. Others that they're hereditary. Or like myself, probably a combination of environment entwined with inborn personality."

Nearing the multiple pairs of Ludwigs, Kurt said that, even without meeting her, Magda appeared to display a schizoid personality cluster that included a number of paranoid and psychopathic types. Detachment. Alienation. Defensive episodes of suspicion. Rage. "When she feels herself breaking into fragmented pieces, she switches into a dissociated state, trying to put herself back together, so to speak."

Past all the Friedrichs and the Joachims, the Wilhelms and the Friedrich Wilhelms, they reached the sprawling Plaza of the Republic. Ahead, the giant Victory Column, celebrating Prussia's conquest over France in 1871, and ornate memorials to the men who made it possible: Bismarck and Moltke. Off to the right, the mammoth granite Reichstag, the red, black, and gold flag of the republic flapping over its great glass dome.

Kurt stopped and turned to Willi. "But Lord Almighty, Willi"—he shook his head and took off his glasses, wiping them incredulously—"all psychoanalysis aside—these girls sound like witches from a medieval fairy tale, roaming the forest in search of children to eat. Locking them in an underground lair, savoring them one at a time."

"Worse, Kurt. What they had down there was a death factory. And their victims had to do the dirty work. It was all systematized. Rationalized. Thought they were doing a big favor to the world, ridding it of useless mouths."

When the Charleston wound down, Willi saw Ava and Gunther collapse back into their chairs, panting. It reminded him of Kurt after he'd finished interviewing Magda that afternoon: stumbling into Willi's office, white with exhaustion. He'd taken off his glasses and didn't even bother putting them back on. Having spent over three hours in the cell alone with her, he said Magda seemed to confirm every theory of mental illness there was—simultaneously. Both environmental and biological schools of thought as well as the Adlerian and Freudian approaches to criminal behavior. She had every type of inferiority complex imaginable.

"I've never seen a more disjointed personality. You know what she said:

" 'It makes me feel good to hold them when they're dead. Not so alone. But I'll let you in on a little secret, mister—just 'cause you're so nice. That lady under Bone Alley's not really me. Oh, it's me, but when I was a teenager. See, I had a baby then, but I lost it for all eternity. Papa wouldn't let it get baptized before he killed it. And now I have to protect all the dear ones—inside me. 'Cause Daddy didn't just kill my baby, he cooked it for dinner and made me eat it.' "

What was truth and what was delusion, Kurt said, he had no way of knowing.

Willi didn't have to wonder. Except the idea that it wasn't her down there, the rest was probably no delusion.

"What about Ilse?" he asked Kurt anxiously.

His cousin could only shrug. Unfortunately, he said, the interview with Magda ended because she'd suffered a comprehensive break with reality. As if to avoid what she perceived as certain imminent destruction, she'd retreated into a psychotic womb and could now be found cuddled in the corner, sucking her thumb. How long it would last, Kurt said, was impossible to predict. In some cases people never came out.

Willi suppressed the urge to go down there and smack her out of it.

Magda'd given up nothing about her sweet little sister.

The ice-cream lady.

High above Berlin the band played on. As they took another round on the dance floor, Vicki pressed her cheek against Willi's.

"Forgive me, darling, for not trusting you more," she whispered in his ear. "And for giving you such a hard time. I'm terribly ashamed. And so proud of you now. We all are. The boys especially."

Deep within, Willi felt the strangest mixture of pride and guilt.

Kommissar Horthstaler was at the podium suddenly, halting the band, hushing everyone. Saying he had an announcement. It was clear he also had a few glasses under his belt.

"I realize that a lot of what's been broadcasting from the radio tower over our heads hasn't been very good news lately." He chuckled at his own cleverness, having come up with that association. "Especially for those of the Hebraic persuasion."

Silence deadened the room.

What shockingly poor taste, here of all places, to refer to the outbreak of violence the other day, the likes of which the city had never seen since . . . well, ever.

It had been a bloody season altogether on the streets of Berlin, but Thursday things had gone from bad to worse. Uniformed gangs of brownshirts descended on busy Leipziger Strasse in the middle of the day and began beating up anyone they thought looked Jewish—even women—painting swastikas and large-nosed caricatures on Jewish-owned shops, breaking windows on Jewish-owned department stores. Nearly fifty people had been injured, one of whom died. Never before had Jews been targeted in the heart of the capital, and it sent shock waves through the whole of Germany's Jewish population. Now, people could only hope that after tomorrow's election the simmering cauldron would just settle down. Even the anarchy of 1919 seemed preferable to the brutality of 1930.

"But"—Horthstaler put out his hands to quiet his listeners, although a mouse could have been heard—"tonight we have excellent news. And I am so delighted to be able to welcome the deputy president of the Berlin police to personally convey it."

Willi's throat clenched when he saw the kind, dark eyes of Dr. Weiss behind their wire glasses. The deputy president was up to his ears combating not only political mayhem but his personal nemesis. Three times he'd taken Joseph Goebbels to court for slander, and three times won against him. But nothing stopped the Nazi propogandist. He'd latched onto Weiss like a dog that wouldn't let go, continuously ratcheting up his attacks, his newspaper showing cartoons of "Isidore" stuffing his pockets with money, Isidore in cahoots with the Reds, Isidore hanging from a Nazi noose. For Weiss to have taken time out to honor Willi tonight was truly special. But the toll these last months had taken on him was evident. He looked completely haggard.

"I had the privilege of meeting Willi Kraus when he was still fresh out of Police Academy. We worked together on the Rathenau assassination case, and I thought then that he was as smart, as even-tempered, as dogged a detective as I'd ever met. Tonight, I've changed my mind. I think he's even smarter and a more dogged detective than I've ever met." A wave of laughter traveled the room. "And so, on behalf of the Department of Criminal Police, I'm proud to announce his promotion from the position of Sergeant-Detektiv to full Inspektor, with all the accompanying benefits and responsibilities. I have no doubt he will continue to make all Berlin proud."

Willi was so taken by surprise he had to fight back tears.

Vicki threw her arms around him. The boys ran up and gave him hugs. Then before he knew it, they were rolling out a giant birthday cake ringed with candles. As he stood before it staring at the swaying circles of flame, he couldn't suppress all the thoughts dancing through his brain.

He'd come a long way since he'd grown up on those streets down there. Lost his father and had to care for his little sister while their mother worked. Was Greta happy in the Holy Land, milking cows? He'd survived three years on the front lines of the largest conflict in human history. Married the most wonderful woman on earth. Had two of the greatest kids in the world. What was turning out to be a stellar career.

There was so much to be grateful for.

And he was.

Yet so many questions still nagged him about this supposedly shut case.

Why had Ilse only gone for boys? Was there something sexual about it? Nothing in the case indicated it. And what the hell was the Tower Labs they'd found reference to when they'd uncovered Axel's apartment?

Magda certainly wasn't telling.

She remained in catatonic regression, transferred to the Berlin-Buch Psychiatric Hospital, Ward 6, for the criminally insane—where even if she ever saw trial, she was likely to remain for the rest of her life. Perhaps, he told himself, he'd have to accept never knowing all the answers to his questions.

The crowd gathered near, awaiting him. He saw his wife, his children, all the faces from his past and present, staring together, eyes aglow. It had been a hard-won battle, he had to admit. One of the hardest. He deserved a pat on the back. So filling his lungs until they could take no more, he blew as hard as he could, aiming in circles at each of the thirty-five candles.

He got them all too. Almost.

One wouldn't go out.

Even as all his well-wishers crowded around shaking his hand, offering congratulations, hugs, kisses, a single question indeed burned brighter than the others.

If Ilse had captured them . . .

And Magda had turned them into product . . .

And Axel had sold them . . .

Who actually killed all those children?

Dr. Hoffnung determined the cause of death was carbon monoxide poisoning. Yet there was no means whatsoever for gassing that many children in the underground lair. They'd checked. Every goddamned inch of the place.

Twenty-seven

The next morning, Sunday, September 14, trucks with loudspeakers rumbled down Beckmann Strasse trumpeting martial music, urging people to vote. Vicki and Willi pulled themselves from bed finally, remembering it was Election Day. Time to get up and dress. When she slipped into her new tweed suit, though, not only her knees but half her calves disappeared. Willi hadn't seen her in such a long skirt since they'd gotten married.

"You hate it, don't you?" she asked ruefully.

What could he say? Women hadn't been allowed to show so much as a shinbone until after the war, when among the most ubiquitous signs of modernity was the hemlines' rise. Now dress lengths were plummeting again. It seemed not only a contradiction of progress but a damned shame, considering how much he liked legs, Vicki's especially.

"Well, er—" He took her in his arms and distracted her with a kiss. "I sure don't hate you in it."

Having already eaten, Erich and Stefan were downstairs playing with Heinz in the courtyard. Irmgard was on the terrace hanging laundry, no doubt wishing she had Vicki's electric dryer. "Yes, yes, we voted early," she said with a shade of disapproval at their tardiness. "Go on. I'll keep an eye out." She shooed them with a flicking wrist. Lately she'd been rather dour, they noted.

Stepping from the building, they crossed Beckmann Strasse hand in hand, Vicki's dark bangs bouncing in the breeze. Willi was so happy being back in her good graces he could have skipped down the block. The sun was shining, clouds sailing across a bright blue sky. A yellow streetcar clanged by, number 89. As he took a deep breath, the world felt in order. He'd grown up less than three blocks from here. His parents used to vote at the same school they were heading for now. Vicki'd grown up only a few blocks farther west. These clean, tree-lined streets were their streets. These stores, small and tidy, the ones they'd always shopped in. These streetcars, lines they'd ridden all their lives. And as uncertain as the times had become, strolling on a Sunday through this handsome neighborhood filled them with pride. Especially on Election Day.

Streams of people moved in the direction of the Goethe School, a sense of solemnity hanging in the air. Until twelve years ago there hadn't even been elections. They'd lived under iron-fisted tyranny. Now at least they had some voice in shaping their own destiny. Or had they?

Across the street Willi noticed a throng of people queued not for the polling place but a soup kitchen. Sometimes, he thought, it was hard to escape a feeling of being swept out to sea in currents no one had control over. Hard to believe just a year ago Germany, Europe, most of the world, had been thriving on an economic gusher that lifted whole populations. Now, international trade had shriveled. Production dried. It was as if the foundations of prosperity had collapsed, leaving the whole of humanity sinking.

Except, somehow, Willi. He'd managed to buck the current.

As they headed up sunny Brandenburgische Strasse he was still floating slightly off the ground. Full Inspektor at thirty-five was an honor few men achieved. It meant he'd have a whole team working under him eventually, in addition to a substantial salary increase. He couldn't help toying with the idea of helping out the economy a bit, such as by buying a new car. They needed one now that the Opel was totaled.

In front of the old school, all the major parties had contingents out, distributing literature, chanting slogans. Among them, red-neckerchiefed Communists and brown-shirted stormtroopers kept to opposite sides of the street, a sober air of business prevailing. Even the brownshirts smiled politely, offering pamphlets to Vicki and Willi.

Hitler and his Nazis had waged a campaign unlike anything Germany'd ever seen. The "savior of the nation"—that barking voice still clanging through Willi's brain—had traveled one end of the country to the other, delivering speeches, attending mass rallies, kissing babies. His chief propandist, Joseph Goebbels, had orga-nized torchlight parades and plastered Hitler's face from the Baltic to the Alps. But all the latest straw polls, as well as the near-unanimous consensus of political journalists, Fritz included, was that the Nazis and the Communists both had undermined their mass appeal through violence, and that now the center would hold. Those most versed in German politics seemed to concur that when the tallies were an-nounced tonight, the Social Democrats and their allies would receive enough votes to form a new government with a mandate to jump-start recovery.

With this hope Vicki and Willi entered the school they'd both attended as children, where their own child now went, and joined the queue to cast ballots.

Later they drove out to Fritz's for dinner and to await the election results. Vicki's father had lent them his Mercedes for the week, since he'd gone abroad on business, a Type 260 Stuttgart, the company's most solid family car. After Willi's rickety Opel it was like a magic carpet, floating them down busy avenues and out into the deep-green forests, landing them in Grunewald in record time. Fritz's three-story villa was a riot of historical styles, built during the Wilhelmian period. He'd been bitching for years about how out-of-date it was and had just weeks ago commissioned one of Germany's most avant-garde architects to build him a new one up the road.

Helping Vicki out of the car, Willi flashed on the dark, miserable hovel he'd seen a few days back, where Axel Köhler had lived, careful not to let his wife in on his thoughts. Like the rest of the world, Vicki felt relieved to think the case of *Der Kinderfresser* had been put to rest, which for expediency's sake he preferred. In fact, though, after the tidal wave of news reports following Magda's capture, people had come forth with all sorts of new information, including the superintendent of a lightless, airless basement apartment a mere two blocks from the *Viehof.*

"I knew there was something wrong with that guy," the man said when he'd taken Willi in a few days ago.

The place was sparse, depressing. A bed and several chests of drawers. A thorough search, however, revealed plenty: not only half a dozen forged identity cards bearing Axel's photo under various aliases, but also a leather account book at the bottom of a pile of dirty underwear. In meticulous pencil, starting in 1924, Axel had kept an exact record of all the boys delivered to something called Tower Labs, no address, phone number, or any other information. Only that for each child he was paid 150 reichsmarks. It was a fortune. Especially for otherwise "worthless" street urchins.

And then, for each "Pickup and Disposal," another fifty marks.

In six years the total number delivered and disposed of, according to this ledger, was 244 boys.

If correct, it would be by far the largest mass murder in German history.

"By-Product" and "Leather Goods" sales, depending on the year, had increased Axel's income handsomely. He probably took in as much as *Viehof* Direktor Gruber. But he hadn't spent it. From the layers of crap under his bed they'd exhumed a cigar box stuffed with banknotes. Twenty-five thousand RMs.

The man should have worked for the government.

Approaching the high brick wall around Fritz's property, Willi's heart raced as he pictured the name in the ledger entered over and over in thick block letters, so similar to the ones on that wall of names in the dungeon under Bone Alley. TOWER LABS.

Whatever it was, it had to be found.

As did Ilse.

Holding Vicki's arm as they entered the front gate, they saw a gray hare pop its head from the flower bed. "Don't tell me you've developed fear of rabbits?" Vicki laughed, feeling him tense. "What do they call that, leporiphobia?"

His wife read more psychology than his cousin Kurt.

"A little stitch in the side is all." He pretended to smile.

He knew he'd nearly given himself away, though.

The maid let them in and Sylvie greeted them in a shimmering, low-cut cocktail gown, clearly having had a head start on the wine. Kissing them profusely, she ushered them in, complaining they never came to see her anymore.

The only other guest was Count Oldenburg, a veritable dinner party unto himself, one of the brightest stars in Fritz's galaxy. A gap-toothed bon vivant clearly hyped up on some kind of stimulant this evening, he distracted them for hours with anecdotes about worlds they otherwise only read about in Sunday supplements. Tea with Virginia Woolf. Dinner with André Gide. Tonight he went on about how theater architecture in London and Paris was a quarter century behind Berlin's. And then of course the Gropius Werkbund Exhibition at Le Salon des Artistes Décorateurs, German design light-years ahead of everyone else's.

"Personally, I think Germany's entering a sort of modern golden age of Greece." The count's face glittered in the candlelight. "Have you noticed, for example, how much more beautiful young people are than before the war? The whole national physique has toned up since people embraced nudism."

After a while Willi retreated to the kitchen for some water. Fritz trailed him and cornered him by the sink. "Hey, what's this I hear about a Shepherdess?" He was practically slurring his words. "Old blabbermouth Woerner let it slip over cocktails. Said the bitch was the most dangerous Köhler of all. That you were keeping it hush-hush so she wouldn't know you were on her trail. Shhh!" He put a finger to his lips. "I won't tell."

But he had.

Halfway through a tall glass of water Willi saw Vicki walk in. She'd overheard Fritz and lost all her color. In a look that tore at Willi's heart she seemed to wonder how he could betray her this way. Then before he could even finish swallowing, she strode back out crossing her arms and pretended to listen with fascination to Count Oldenburg.

By the time the election results were due in, the count had portrayed a dazzling odyssey of the nation's future—not only the Depression reversing in '31 but Germany soaring above all the other democracies, economically, scientifically, culturally.

If only the vote supported his prophetics.

All the experts, the straw polls, even Fritz, were completely wrong.

After hearing the numbers and listening to the breakdowns, nobody even moved.

"My God." Sylvie finally threw back the rest of her drink, then stumbled over and switched off the radio. "What a horrible day for Germany."

"For Europe." Fritz fingered his mustache.

The center had held, but only barely. Social Democrats, still the largest party, had been anemically weakened, while KPD, the German Communists, had bulked up with another 23 seats in parliament to 77. It was the NSDAP, though, the Nazi Party, formerly one of the smallest in the Reichstag, that had seized the body politic like a fever, swelling nearly 800 percent, from a mere 12 to 107 seats—to become the second-strongest party. Whole districts had swung to Hitler. Eighteen percent of the electorate; 6.5 million votes. Huge numbers of the unemployed, women, and, most tellingly, youth. The Nazis themselves had never imagined such a show of support. Overnight, shrieking, delusional Adolf Hitler—who didn't even have German citizenship—had gone from circus sideshow freak to one of the most powerful men in the nation.

"The impression abroad will be catastrophic," the count stammered, turning to them all as if to confirm he wasn't hallucinating. "I don't even want to imagine the repercussions on foreign and financial affairs."

"Not to mention here," Fritz added.

If governing Germany had been purgatory before, Willi understood, it would be real hell now. The cauldron, rather than simmering down, had only started boiling. One-third of the legislature's seats were in the hands of radicals—left and right—bent on dismantling the whole republic and replacing it with a dictatorship. The future, all of them with it, seemed thrust beneath a shadow.

"Here I've been sticking my head in the sand all this time." Fritz stared as if seeing those hysterical mobs at the Sportpalast all over again. "Even after witnessing it, I didn't want to acknowledge the spell this movement cast. Now it's impossible to ignore."

Sylvie fell back on the sofa with a whimper.

"What's bred in the bones will out in the flesh." She could barely pour straight. "Germans are addicted to tyranny. It's all because of the way we raise our children. With such brutality. And don't tell me I'm wrong, Fritz. If you had the least interest in the subject you'd agree. Ask Vicki. She's read all the latest literature." Sylvie raised her glass and smiled wanly, then hiccuped. "Dessert, anyone?"

"Liar! Stupid. Idiotic son of a bitch!"

Vicki started pounding him as soon as they climbed back in the Mercedes, punching his shoulder as hard as she could with both fists.

"How could you do this to me? To the boys? What if we'd let our guard down and something happened, huh?"

"I didn't let my guard down." He tried to block her.

"But I did!" She punched harder. "You don't want this psychopathic killer to know you're trailing her—so you keep it from me? What are you, a moron? You think I'd blab it in some bar?"

He felt like saying he simply forgot, but it seemed too absurd.

"I didn't want to upset you, Vic. You've worried so much. I was only trying to—" She tried to smack his face, but he grabbed her hand. "Cut that out, damn it!"

She sat there panting, glaring at him, waiting for an explanation. He had none. It just seemed easiest. That was all.

"How can I ever trust you again?" She was looking at him as if he were an addict, every idea warped by a single need. "Tell me, Willi. How?"

He swallowed, his entire consciousness striken as if by a sudden thunderbolt. Might she be right? he wondered, overwhelmed with a dizzying dismay. Had this terrible case with its kaleidoscope of horrors somehow transfixed him? Might he have actually put his family in harm's way? The possibility so mortified him he was almost unable to breathe, and he yearned to throw himself at Vicki's feet, begging forgiveness. Promising to quit his job. To join her father's company.

"If you want, I can take you and the boys to your parents' in the morning, Vic."

She jolted him with another round of punches. "I don't want to leave, goddamnit. I want you to tell me the truth!"

Collapsing in his arms, she cried harder than he'd ever seen.

"Oh, Willi, don't you see? I'm terrified. Not just the Köhlers. The Depression. Nazis. Everything."

"Shhh." He tried his best to soothe her. "It'll all work out one way or another. You'll see."

But the next morning it was hard to imagine how.

When he opened the apartment door to pick up the daily papers, Hitler's face filled the front pages.

Twenty-eight

At breakfast they were surprised by a sharp rap against the terrace window. Opening the back door, still chewing toast, Willi found Otto staring at him grim-faced, Irmgard and Heinz right behind.

"We'd like a word with you all, if you would, out here."

Willi shrugged—*I've no idea why*—as he and Vicki stepped out with the boys. When he saw the red, gold, and black *Hakenkreuz* pinned on Otto's lapel, though, he knew it couldn't be good.

The two families stood on the vine-covered terrace facing each other.

Willi remembered when the Winkelmanns had just moved in, a few months after he and Vicki. They'd sat with a bottle of cognac right here on a hot summer night, getting to know one another. Two young couples with boys the same age. Otto was saving to open his stationery shop, Irmgard supporting him by working as a seamstress. Vicki, home with Erich, volunteered to take Heinz in, five and a half days a week—for nearly two years.

"As you know"—Otto swallowed—"many things have changed in the past months." He wiped beads of moisture from his forehead, although it was cool outside. "We've all had to make adjustments." He coughed. "To survive. To secure even the most menial job, I had to join the National Socialists, as you can see. In doing so, much I'd not understood before was made abundantly clear. We've been neighbors, I daresay friends, a number of years now, but circumstance will no longer permit that. It's my duty to inform you, therefore, henceforth, that the Winklemanns are breaking relations with the Krauses."

Vicki and Willi'd looked at each other as if to decipher if this was a birthday joke or something. "Breaking relations?"

Irmgard's fingers, Willi'd noted, were digging into the vines along the terrace wall. Once, he recalled, she'd fallen off the stepladder out here fiddling with those vines and dislocated her shoulder. Having faced many injuries like it in the war, he'd quickly gotten it back into place, and she hadn't stopped thanking him since, especially as she'd never had to pay a doctor.

"If we've offended you in some way, Otto . . ." Vicki rasped.

"No, no." Otto shook his head. "It's nothing you've *done*. It's who you *are*. Not Germans. Blood-wise, I mean. People are throwing in now with the Nazis left and right, even in this building. We simply can't afford to associate with you any longer. It's how it's got to be."

Normally Willi would find it impossible to accept that a man such as Otto, who'd only last year rushed Erich in his arms to the hospital gushing blood, could bend so totally to political pressure. But having witnessed that spectacle at the Sportpalast, Willi understood the force at work. At least, he told himself, his neighbor was acting out of necessity, not conviction. A practical compromise might be possible.

"Well, then, Otto"—the pain, though, was no less intense—"what choice have we but to accept your wishes?" Willi, feeling his eyes burn, held his wife with one arm, embracing his children with the other. "Surely, though, you can't mean the boys?"

"Oh, yes." Otto nodded definitively, stifling a choke in his throat. "The boys especially. Heinz will be allowed no further contact whatsoever with Erich or Stefan."

Heinz, who'd grown up almost as much in their apartment as his own, tried to hide the fury raging in his chubby cheeks until he could no longer stand it.

"But I don't want to." He raised his head in a grief-stricken howl.

Irmgard turned and smacked him in the face, stunning the boy. "We've explained it all to you already, Heinz."

Erich let out an audible gasp. Stefan started to cry.

Vicki's chest heaved. "Irmgard"—she turned to her fellow mother—"you simply can't just—"

But their neighbor's face had hardened to steel. Whether Irmgard believed or not, wanted or not, thought it fair or not, no longer mattered. This was how it was. And she made her cut as swiftly as chopping off a chicken's head.

"It's nothing personal." She ripped a long strip of vines from the wall, creating a harsh demarcation where for years there'd been entwinement. "Purely a matter of health." She tossed the clump of leaves over the railing. "We wish to stay away from you"—she wiped her hands with grim necessity—"as we would any harmful bacteria."

Twenty-nine

Autumn mist draped Alexanderplatz. The afternoon hung thick and cold. Only a few hearty souls braved the open tops of the double-decker buses. As he stepped from the Police Presidium, Willi felt his very bones weighing him down, as if he were getting a flu. More than likely, he reflected, yanking on his hat and tilting the brim, given the sort of week it'd been, it was melancholia.

Almost everyone in Germany was down, except of course Herr Hitler and his masses. A week after the election, aftershocks still rattled, the national parliament reduced to a standstill, a sense of crisis looming, Nazi and Communist militias upping the ante from clubs and brass kuckles to knives and guns, business failures forever expanding the ranks of misery.

Crossing Dirksen Strasse, he was glad at least of one thing: no reporters on his butt anymore. It might have been a lonelier trek, but he preferred going about his business unobserved. It felt a hell of a lot safer. On the far side of the street he turned his collar up, taking a moment to peer into the abyss. Beyond the guardrail the future subway station was a pit of dark, wet slime. Massive pipes had been installed on the lowest levels, but the giant trench still seemed light-years away from its billboard depiction: silver escalators leading down to platforms tiled in beige or aquamarine, passageways lined with vendors. Eventually, he knew, he'd be able to ride from here almost directly home. Until then, though, he still had to hike the whole Alex to get to the S-Bahn.

It was 3:00 p.m. Saturday, the weekend officially under way, the sidewalks packed with the usual bedlam of hookers, pushers, hucksters—all overlooked, figuratively and literally, by the Police Presidium. In front of one of the larger beer halls, a contortionist was drawing a real crowd, his legs completely tucked behind his arms so that when he stood on his hands, his rear end practically jutted under his chin. It was bizarre and almost immediately pulled Willi back to a similar moment from childhood.

He couldn't have been more than five or six when, walking somewhere right around here with his mother, he'd seen a Gypsy in a headscarf pounding a drum and dragging behind him a huge dancing bear. What fascination and horror that towering, smelly creature had held: its snout muzzled, a thick iron chain around its neck, prods from a pole forcing it on hind legs. Every so often the Gypsy shouted at it, and the beast would swivel its furry hips or wave its paws. The fear, the pity, it evoked in Willi seemed to rise in his heart all over again, along with cruel mental images from this week's newspapers.

After the Nazi explosion at the polls, something not seen here for centuries had erupted with a vengeance: Jew baiting. Daily reports flooded from the provinces, and sometimes larger cities too, of Jews being pulled from bed, humiliated, beaten, homes ransacked, businesses torched. In town after town, rabbis and community leaders were forced to run gauntlets, pelted with excrement, not merely by neighbors but by local police, who gladly joined in. Berlin papers were filled with stories, and photos, sometimes close-ups of the victims' faces, their eyes like those of forlorn beasts. In Russia, Poland, Ukraine, these things had gone on for centuries. But here in the most civilized, most modern of all nations?

Nothing could have driven home the rising tide of anti-Semitism, though, more forcefully than the Winkelmanns. Even now, days later, on a crowded sidewalk filled with sausage vendors and organ-grinders and ladies beckoning with painted smiles, Willi could feel the sting. From years in the army and on the police force, his skin had at least had a chance to toughen. But Vicki'd never endured such treatment and hadn't taken it well. She'd lost her appetite, could hardly sleep. Erich and Stefan were merely sulking, but Willi feared in the long run it might be they who suffered most. People said children got over such things easily, but he wasn't so sure. To one degree or another it might haunt them the rest of their lives. And as long as he lived, he could never forgive the Winklemanns for inflicting such—

"Herr Inspektor!"

He turned, surprised to recognize a slim, mascaraed figure leaning against an advertising column. Kai looked older somehow, more mature than when he'd seen him just few weeks ago. But not happy. If only he'd quit with all that makeup. It made him look like a porcelain doll.

"How's it going, Kai?" Willi swallowed, knowing it always took a moment to get past the embarrassment of being seen with him. "Everything all right?"

"A little grouchy's all." The kid shrugged, his gold earring swinging. "Business wanting, if you know what I mean."

Willi knew precisely what he meant: the kid hadn't eaten today.

He glanced at his watch. Before leaving work he'd spoken to Vicki and everything was fine. He couldn't imagine she'd mind if he got home a little late.

"How about a nice fat lunch at Aschinger's, Kai—on me?" Willi asked, ashamed for hoping there'd be a table somewhere far in the back, with no light. "For all your help catching *Der Kinderfresser.*"

The kid's whole face lit.

An institution since the 1890s, with over a dozen locations, Aschinger's was Berlin's mecca of fine dining at cafeteria prices. Dishes were displayed in long cases numbered for easy reference and served by uniformed attendants who looked like servants for the rich. The selection was immense—case after case, shelf after shelf of schnitzels, cutlets, ragouts, fillets, purées, roasts, goulashes. Kai helped himself to a chicken fricassee with sides of creamed potato and corn, and a large glass of beer. Willi took a hearty bouillabaisse. Both got sugared plums for dessert. When they took a table, Willi didn't even mind that it had to be on the center aisle. Enough eccentrics were in the place—men who mumbled to themselves, women with crooked wigs—that Kai barely stuck out.

"Mmmm. Thanks, Inspektor. This is dandy." Kai dug in joyously.

Plus, Kai's spirits had risen so dramatically it was a pleasure to witness.

"The best fricassee I've had all week. Hey, I hear you got a promotion. Good for you. You deserve it! I may get one too, of sorts."

"Really. How's that, Kai?"

"Our chief went out and found himself some big tycoon to set him up, so he's abdicating—leaving us."

"Oh, I see." Willi figured this must have been Kai's "friend." He detected a shade of grief in the kid's eyes.

Kai threw his hands up, revealing his painted fingernails. "I don't think I can fill his shoes." He sighed, his mood plummeting. "It's too much responsibility." Beneath all the makeup, his adolescent face, Willi saw, had flushed with adult anxiety. "We've got ten boys in the gang. Chief is responsible for everything. Food. Clothing. Place to sleep. Plus, we keep an eye out for five or six Doll Boys, the little ones. The problems never stop. Uwe was a natural. Me?" Kai took a deep slug of beer.

Willi felt his throat tighten. It was hardly the sort of thing he was experienced at. But the kid, he saw, wasn't seeking approval. Just a word of encouragement. Willi thought about it a moment, then shared with Kai the only thing that came to mind.

"During the war, I was in a squad that penetrated enemy lines, Kai. We trained six months for our first operation, but hadn't made it halfway across no-man's-land when our sergeant and corporal both got killed by incoming mortar. The five left were all privates, none qualified to command—none wanting to. It was clear, though, that if someone didn't take charge, we were never going to make it. And I didn't want to die. So I stepped up. I hadn't a clue what I was doing, just acted like I did. Made the best decisions I was able. We accomplished our mission, and for the rest of the war I stayed squad leader. Eventually I wound up getting a medal for it—an Iron Cross, First Class."

The boy was silent a long while, then offered Willi a quick grateful look.

After they'd finished and were readying to leave, Kai's face painted an expression of curiosity mixed with caution.

"Inspektor, I certainly don't mean any disrespect. I know you accomplished so much. But you never caught *her*, did you? The Shepherdess, I mean."

A feverish chill ran through Willi's body. "We got her siblings, Kai. Their operation's all washed up. But she's a slippery one, it's true. We'll get her, though. You'll see."

The look of trust in the kid's eyes was frightening.

Parting from Kai and continuing past fields of new construction, Willi reflected on how the *Kinderfesser* case remained, in some ways, nearly as mysterious as the first day he'd seen that burlap sack. He'd learned where the victims came from. How they were abducted. How and where they ended up. But he still had no idea who'd administered fatal doses of carbon monoxide to their lungs—or how or where this atrocity even occurred. Two hundred and forty-four times. Plus, he still had no idea what the hell Tower Labs was, or what it had wanted with all those boys.

Passing a set of giant pneumatic hammers poised to resume pounding Monday, his head ached with frustration. A huge steam

shovel, though, at half gnaw in the earth, seemed to shout encouragement: *Just keep digging!*

From the moment they'd first found reference to it in Axel's ledger, he and Gunther had been trying to unearth Tower Labs. In all
883 square kilometers of greater Berline, however, only one company had that name—beneath a set of ten-story gas towers, a firm in
Treptow that manufactured everything from beakers and flasks to
agar plates. But there was nothing shifty about Tower Laboratory
Glassware. They'd searched high and low.

After that, they'd started in on records at every lab in the city, *A*
to *Z*—private labs, hospital labs, university labs, even the labs at the
Ministry of Public Health.

Two days ago he'd finally stumbled onto something. Housed in a
warehouse on the Landwehr Canal, Tower Toys popped up in the
files of one of Germany's largest electronics manufacturers. Siemens
lab records showed that six years earlier, in 1924, this alleged toy
company had custom-ordered a complex apparatus for chemical dis-
tillation that technicians knew could never be used for toy production. Siemens had put in a report with the Berlin police, but no
action had ever been taken. Willi'd soon found this same toy company listed in files of a major pharmaceutical firm, which made
yearly deliveries, also since 1924, to 146 Maybach Ufer, the address
of Tower Toys—substantial quantities of a substance called hydro-
chloride salt, definitely not for children's playthings. Then, just tonight, after surveying the address for two days, Gunther came back
and reported he'd seen two black vans pulling into the rear of the
warehouse, neither of which had license plates. Black vans with no
license plates?

Inside them—heavily armed men.

In another few days, Willi told himself, fixing on the long, arched
roof of the S-Bahn station ahead, he'd be able to make some kind of
move against Tower Toys. Right now he needed to rest. His whole
being was slipping into torpor. In another forty minutes he'd be
taking a nap, if he didn't fall asleep on the train and wind up in
Potsdam.

Vicki was the one taking a nap when he got home, under the blankets, sprawled diagonally across the bed. He didn't have the heart to wake her. The radio was on in the kids' room, and for a second he just stood in the hall deciding whether to pour some whiskey or take a nice hot bath. Then the doorbell rang. Answering it, he was more than surprised to find Irmgard Winkelmann hunched there, stone-faced.

"Is Heinz here?" she asked through white, pinched lips.

"Heinz? You know very well you forbade him."

"The boy can be stubborn. I can't find him. He's not in his room and he's not downstairs. I was wondering if you allowed him in."

"I hardly think so. Vicki's asleep. I just got home."

"Where are your boys? May I speak to them?"

Willi expected her to come in but she just stood there, outside the door.

"Could you get them for me, please?"

Only Stefan was in the kids' room, playing with the Red Baron's plane.

"Hey there, Stef, how's life? Where's Erich?"

Stefan blinked his large brown eyes. "I don't know."

Willi felt a little twinge, but figured Vicki knew. Maybe he'd gone to a friend's for dinner; he did that now and then. When Vicki was awakened, though, she turned paler than the sheet. "He should be here." She raced to the boys' room.

"Is there something wrong?" Irmgard shouted from the hall. "Where's my Heinz?"

"Stefan." Vicki clasped his little shoulders. "This isn't a joke. Where's your brother?"

Stefan started crying.

"Vicki, really," Willi said.

"What have you done with my son, you bastards?" Irmgard was yelling.

Willi took his son's hand. "Stefan, even if Erich made you swear on the holy Bible not to tell, you must, do you understand me?"

Stefan hid his face in Willi's arms. "Heinz came over after Mommy fell asleep," he bawled. "And then . . . and then . . . they ran away together."

"Oh, God," Vicki moaned.

Willi looked at his watch. "What time did you fall asleep, Vic?"

"Don't you dare blame me." She winced as if he'd punched her. "It's you who put us at—"

"Never mind now; they could be just downstairs for all we know. I'm only trying to figure out how far they might have gotten."

"What's going on in there?" Irmgard kept shouting. "Why won't you tell me?"

Vicki held her head, trying to think. "It must have been after I spoke to you."

Three o'clock. Nearly an hour and a half.

Willi turned and ran out the door.

"Where's my Heinz, you bastard?" Irmgard tried to grab his sleeve as he flew past. "I'm calling the po—"

Willi was already halfway out the door, downstairs.

Twilight darkened Beckmann Strasse, the little park across the street already lost in shadows. A man on a motorcycle sputtered by. A woman walked a dachshund on a leash. "Have you seen two boys?" he tried to keep as calm as possible. "One skinny, one not?"

She shook her head sadly. "I'm sorry, no."

"I seen 'em," a voice called from a second-story window. An old man stuck his head out, pointing stiffly. "Skinny and fatty. Right on that park bench."

It was empty now. Willi's heart raced. "Which way did they go?"

"Wasn't which way but how. One of those little white trucks selling ice cream. Man and lady practically yanked them off the street. I'd say an hour ago."

My God. Willi felt the earth sway beneath his feet. She'd been trailing him all this time. Waiting for her chance—

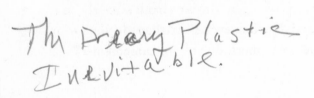

The Dreary Plastic
Inevitable.

Thirty

Fog hung shroudlike over the Landwehr Canal. The warehouse at 146 Maybach Ufer stood half-concealed in vapor. The rest of the block, apartments mostly, was a Monet-style blur of grays and blue-whites. The whole scene—empty streets, wet cobblestones, a briny, green canal—reminded Willi of the last tense moments before the March 1918 offensive. A cat tiptoeing down the sidewalk. Mourning doves under a cornice. He could almost hear the piercing whistle signaling the attack.

Only this time the stakes were far more personal.

Checking his wrist for the hundredth time, he saw he had just a few minutes left to launch his own offensive without endangering countless innocents. At *pünktlich* eight, this whole block would spring to life, all the windows open almost simultaneously, the maids and housewives begin setting out the bedding. All the metal security shutters cranking up at the shops of the butchers, bakers, and barbers. Streetcars would clatter down the tracks as sidewalks filled with men in suits, women out shopping, gangs of children in knee-high socks on their way to school. Even in troubled times such as these, *Ordnung*—punctuality, reliability—ruled in Germany. So where the hell was his last squadron?

The second hand ticked away.

Crouched behind a wall of wooden crates on a flat barge that had floated in before dawn, Willi took a deep breath and tried to slow his heart. Despite the morning chill, sweat was dripping from his forehead and neck, under his arms, all the way down his back. He'd ordered six rifled Schupo squadrons in place by seven, but the last had not arrived. He didn't want to go in shorthanded, but he couldn't hold off much longer. Next to him, Gunther smiled with saintly patience, as if waiting for nothing more than breakfast. He'd never been in combat before.

Never had his son kidnapped.

Willi swallowed painfully.

The men entering 146 Maybach Ufer last night had been armed, the kid reported, with Thompson submachine guns. Which may have been common in Chicago—but not here. Something huge was going on in that warehouse. Regardless of the obvious dangers in a residential neighborhood, assault by force was the only way to find out what. And get Eric and Heinz out. If that's where they even were.

The uncertainty made pain scorch at his eyes again, threatening to break out and devour him in a conflagration of grief. He'd lived through some long nights in his life, but nothing like last night. From the moment he'd heard the ice cream truck got them, an unbearable agony raged in his chest, searing him with every breath. Plus he had had to contend with Vicki's and the Winkelmanns' emotions—a conflagration of anguish and recrimination.

He looked again at his watch.

Fifteen hours and thirty minutes. What must Erich be thinking? Did he feel forsaken by his father? Had little Heinz soiled his pants, as he'd nearly done that day at Luna Park? What terror they must—

If they were even—

He couldn't bear to think it, or he would burn with insanity.

The second hand refused to slow. The big wooden barge bobbed gently up and down. On the far side of the canal a truck was already delivering morning editions to the news kiosk. Nearer, across from the warehouse, a baker in a long white apron was hurrying across the road with trays of *Brötchen*. Willi could almost smell the fresh dough. A girl with short, bobbed hair and a sailor jacket, flimsy white skirt blowing in the breeze, skipped from one of the buildings. It was three minutes to eight. His stomach clenched. There was just no more—

Gunther nudged him, pointing to the roof across the street. Three rapid flashes off a mirror indicated all the troops at last in place.

Not a minute too soon.

"Return signal," Willi whispered furiously.

With a gulp, Gunther flashed his mirror back.

Mirrors flashed up and down the block—and from a dozen directions crouching figures began inching forward, rifles ready. Willi broke out his binoculars and focused on 146. Okay, he chanted silently. Let's make this swift and clean.

Suddenly, a second-floor window flew open; a woman in a headscarf tossed a small, red carpet out and began beating it with a cane. For God's sake, hurry, Willi urged the troops mentally. A kid around Erich's age, in a blue serge suit with knickers, had joined the little girl in her sailor jacket, both with big leather briefcases on their backs. Her shiny shoes clacked against the pavement as she kicked up her heels.

Just as the first assault wave almost hit the warehouse, though, a loud *pop*, like the opening of a champagne bottle, ricocheted down the block, followed by half a dozen more. Across the street, windows began exploding one after the next. It was the worst that could have happened, Willi realized. The enemy had opened fire.

Turning his binoculars, he saw the girl in the sailor suit spin with her arms in the air as if doing a ballet exercise, then keel over and drop, the sidewalk reddening, her companion too stunned to move, the carpet woman screaming.

He dropped his binoculars and pulled out his Luger.

A hailstorm of bullets was pouring from the first two floors of the warehouse. Up and down the block, police were dropping, dogs howling, iron shutters hurtling back down. The barge captain, a beer-bellied man with a big mustache who'd been paid handsomely precisely because this might turn dangerous, stood up to see what was happening. A loud *sluck* sent a glutinous spray shooting from between his eyes.

Willi fell back to the trenches of the Western Front, operating mechanically on adrenaline, joining the terrific battle. He aimed his Luger, a semiautomatic handgun, getting off half a dozen rounds in as many seconds before he had to reload. The Schupo men had Mauser rifles with far superior range and penetration. But neither could outfire a Thompson submachine gun.

Bullets ricocheted off the walls and cobblestones, exploding the streetlights and clattering from metal pipes like hellfire brimstone. Each one felt as if it had penetrated Willi's heart. He kept picturing Erich and Heinz in there, cringing.

Damn it, he called to them. Live. Live! Reloading cartridge after cartridge, he pulled the trigger in a fit of resolve. If he could, he'd have dodged the whole rain of death to get to those boys.

But no firing was coming from his right, he realized, and turning, he discovered Gunther there, covered in blood. Not his own . . . the barge captain's. It had the kid paralyzed, his mouth hanging open, Adam's apple frozen midthroat, pants soaking wet. The proverbial slap across the face sometimes did the trick, Willi knew. But in this instance, he saw, it wouldn't make a difference. A line of splashes jumping down the canal was heading directly at them. He threw himself over Gunther and covered their heads, then the wooden deck shivered and sharded all around them. After a hard jerk to the left came the sound of gushing water. The barge was going down.

Gunther grabbed Willi by the collar. "I can't swim!"

"Never mind. We're right offshore. Just hold my—" Willi couldn't finish before they were dunked in ice-cold water.

Amid a clatter of tearing planks and floating debris, Gunther's grip grew implacable, his arms and legs, his whole torso, clenching like a gorilla on Willi's back. Blazing terror seized Willi when he realized he couldn't free his arms. The harder he tried, the harder Gunther clung to him. They were both going under.

Gunther, don't, Willi could only scream beneath the surface. We're so close to shore. But no matter how loudly he tried to convey this, his head remained pushed down. He couldn't breathe. His lungs were beginning to ache. He fought and raged, but Gunther was too terrified, and far too strong.

He thought about the boys waiting to be rescued.

And Vicki. What would she go through to lose both husband and son? He couldn't do that to her.

One more time. One more—an arm flailed underwater, free.

He started punching, hard, like a jackhammer, but it didn't stop the downward pressure. The exertion was depleting him. His lungs grew hotter, desperate to be filled. In another second, he knew, he'd have to gasp, suck in water, and die. One last frenzied effort, though, produced a sudden doubling over and the desired release of pressure. He'd located Gunther's testicles. In a moment he was bursting through the surface, inhaling in a frenzy of rebirth.

Gunther, though, was thrashing frantically only inches away. Unless he simply left him there to drown, Willi saw no choice but to knock him out with a hard blow to the nose. After dragging his big body cross-chest to the edge, and then by the arms up the embankment, he sat next to him in the weeds, dripping wet, shivering. Unable to fully catch his breath, as if in a dream, he dimly observed two red police boats race in from the west and spin themselves into position. Aiming at the warehouse with fixed machine guns, they opened fire. Simultaneously, a Reichswehr armored truck came rumbling down the street, mounted with artillery. When Willi saw the giant black vehicle halt and turn its cannon, his whole being shook from its torpor. They couldn't do that. He had to stop them! Before he so much as lifted a leg, though, there was a terrific burst and the very earth trembled. The first floor of 146 Maybach Ufer began crumbling to dust.

Along with Willi's last shred of hope.

He collapsed facedown, letting out a wail of agony.

When the firefighters had the flames out, he was the first to enter the building with them. Room by room, they found no survivors. Just six charred bodies on the first floor and two more on the second. No children among them. When he realized Erich and Heinz must still be alive, Willi nearly passed out.

An hour later, in the back of a Red Cross van with a blanket over his shoulders, he was alone, drinking coffee, Gunther already off to the hospital for observation. From all the equipment inside the warehouse, including a massive chemical-distillation apparatus, it had grown clear that they'd uncovered one of the largest illegal narcotics-manufacturing operations in Europe. Nothing to do with the *Kinderfresser* case, though. Wherever those two boys were, it hadn't been here.

"Inspektor." It was Ruta, sticking her head in the truck, panting, she was so out of breath. "I hurried as fast as I could. The queerest boy came up to the office, wearing lipstick and mascara! He insisted he had to see you. Said I should get you to meet him on the double at the foot of Berolina. To tell you that they'd seen her again—the Shepherdess."

Thirty-one

Willi's clothes were barely dry as he leaped between streetcars and in front of trucks, practically over a baby carriage, face unshaven, hair uncombed. Not that he gave a damn what he looked like. Only one thought pounded in his brain, raged in his bloodstream. Impelling his legs. Those boys. Needing him.

Far to the right, the clock on the Police Presidium sounded eleven fifteen, each chime, fingers on his throat. Straight ahead, towering over the rubble of the old Grand Hotel, big copper Berolina thrust her sword, readying for protective custody now in a halo of scaffolding. Since her arrival on the Alexanderplatz, she'd witnessed years of peace and war. Defeat. Revolution. Prosperity and depression. What pages of history might turn while she sat in a warehouse awaiting the New Alex? Willi could scarcely care.

Kai at least was where he'd said he'd be—beneath her giant toes, gold earring dangling as he looked around intently. When he spotted

Willi, he stamped out his cigarette and jerked a ring-laden finger in the direction of the streetcars.

"The kids that saw her are over at the Linden Passage."

Streetcar? Willi hailed a cab. Obviously Kai had no idea about his son.

He found out in the taxi.

An enclosed shopping arcade that had seen better days, the Passage, with its grimy glass ceiling and many layers of cracked paint, attracted a backwash of sordid types to its array of "rare book" emporiums, "postcard" shops, and exhibits of "curiosities." Its dingy corridors, warm at least in winter, were plying grounds for the youngest of Berlin's myriad male prostitutes, the Doll Boys. Willi's throat clenched when he saw them: nearly a dozen kids, ten, eleven, twelve years old, lined up outside the Anatomical Museum, all in some strange idea of a sailor's suit with a cap and floppy tie, eyeing passersby for "trade." How was it possible children were forced to survive this way? His chest hurt at the very sight of them. He wanted to rescue them all. But two boys needed him even more desperately.

The ones who'd supposedly seen the Shepherdess, Milo and Dolf, had gone off, though, to turn some lunchtime "tricks."

Kai was furious. "I told them to wait."

"We all gotta eat," a towheaded ten-year-old informed them.

"Inspektor"—Kai's blue eyes misted—"I'm so sorry for wasting your—"

"Forget it." Willi's stomach twisted as he dug into his pocket and handed the newly named chief of the Red Apaches a five-mark note. "Just promise me, Kai, the minute they're back—bring those kids to my office, okay? And don't take a streetcar."

At his desk, alone, leaning backward on his chair, the sensation of drowning overcame Willi. Of being dragged so far down he was going to explode. Down, down . . . he remembered how he'd nearly broken his neck this way, and as he pushed the chair back onto all fours, his body felt catapulted once more to the surface. Up, up . . . from his chest, through his throat, bursting from his mouth—a silent scream. Followed by a gush of anguish. *How can I live without Erich? I'll lose Vicki too. She'll never forgive me. What are the bastards doing to those kids? Oh, God, if they're hurting them . . .*

His teeth gritted as he clenched the chair. On the wall clock he saw it wasn't yet noon. They could still be fine. Just scared to death. Those boys in Madga's dungeon, he reminded himself, were making miraculous recoveries, though Lord knew the repercussions they'd suffer later on. He banged the desk, forcing himself to think. Think! He'd turned the city upside down looking for this fucking Tower.

A lanky figure filled his doorway, top to bottom, shoulders hunched, head hung. When the chin lifted, Gunther's eyes met Willi's. Then the big kid stumbled into the office and dropped to his knees, a felled giant.

"I faaaailed," he let out in a protracted bray, his bony shoulders heaving. "I cracked under fire."

Willi took a deep breath. Not two hours ago he'd been locked in this kid's death grip. Now he couldn't dwell on it. Neither could Gunther. There wasn't time.

"It's okay." Willi put an arm around the shivering torso. "Listen to me, Gunther. Under circumstances like that, if you don't crack, you're not human. Thing is, after it's over and you're all cleaned up, you pull yourself together."

Gunther couldn't manage. "I always thought I'd be so brave. But when that blood came spraying all over—I'd no idea it'd be that . . ."

Willi took an even deeper breath. "It's going to be okay, Gunther." But he had to get this kid on his feet. The clock was striking noon.

"And then in the water, all I knew was I had to keep my head out. Please, forgive me. Please."

Willi finally couldn't take another word. "For God's sake, Gunther," he said, loud enough for people outside the door to turn, "you're killing me all over again."

When the clock chime finished at the same moment he did, a

dead chasm of silence opened. Gunther looked at him, stunned. Willi'd never spoken to him like that, but his goodness had run dry. He was in too much pain himself, every minute a choking torture.

"My son and my neighbor's son are missing. Can you understand that? Are you going to help me find them? Because I don't have time to baby you right now."

The kid pulled himself to his feet, wiping his eyes, his clothes every bit a mess as Willi's.

"Make yourself useful at least." Willi winced at him. "Go have Ruta iron our jackets or something. Here, take mine." He frantically started unbuttoning it, then slowed, feeling sorry suddenly, softening. "We can't go around looking like we swam in a canal."

Gunther, sniffling, tried smiling.

Before Willi could even get off his jacket, a powerful odor of whiskey washed through the room, followed by Fritz, who flew in, ripped off his cape, and tossed it at Gunther as if the kid were a valet. Gunther just stood there looking at it.

"I'm such a moron." Fritz crashed in a chair, his blue eyes swimming in a flood of alcohol. "For getting you in trouble like that with Vicki. Really. How awful of me. And of course now, I can't even imagine what you must be going through. Poor Erich!" Clutching his heart, Fritz dug in his pocket and pulled out a cigarette case. "I'm just so grief-stricken I don't know what to say." He lit up.

"Please, Fritz."

"I know; I know. Now's not the time for my guilt." Fritz exhaled understandingly, pulling tobacco from his tongue. "But, listen, I'm gonna make it up to you. I'm gonna help you find those kids, okay? You saved my ass at Passchendaele and Cambrai and Soissons and at Rheims and—"

The name of each battle went off like a fuse in Willi's head until he just exploded.

"Would you shut the hell up?" He jumped to his feet and stared red-faced at his old war buddy. Fritz wasn't as sloshed as he could get, but halfway. "You think I want to hear about Passchendaele and

Cambrai? My son's been in the hands of a psychopath for twenty hours. I've got to save him."

Seeing the expressions on both Fritz's and Gunther's faces, Willi told himself to take his own advice and shut up, but he couldn't.

"From the moment Erich was born"—his chest heaved—"Vicki and I did everything we could to see that he was nurtured and loved to grow up healthy, secure. And then in a matter of days, out of nowhere." His voice cracked. "Such wounds. First the goddamn neighbors and now . . ." He swallowed. "Every second those boys are— Oh my God, *if* they're even—"

He fell to his desk, burying his head, seized by a fit of weeping, his whole body wracked with it, shoulders spasming, eyes and nose erupting. Every corpuscle trembling for his son.

Outwardly, he blamed everyone except himself. But deep in his core he had no illusions where the fault lay. He always thrust himself up—in his own mind—as such a loving parent, inwardly criticizing people such as Otto's brother-in-law for their warped expectations and soul-crushing cruelties. But if he really loved him so much, Erich would be safe now, wouldn't he?

A firm hand gripped his shoulder. Fritz hunched next to him.

"Willi, in my own stupid way I've been trying to tell you— there's this letter."

Fritz was pulling something from his jacket, waving it like a parent might a rattle.

"You know my friend, the baroness—of course you do, she was at the Admirals-Palast that night we saw Josephine Baker—anyway, her sister is married to the director of the Prussian Academy of Science on Unter den Linden, a Dr. Siegfried Sonnenfeldt. At least six months ago—as I heard the story—this Sonnenfeldt received a letter from Moscow, from a Dr. Vyrzhikovsky, or something like that, director of the Soviet Academy of Scientists. Fellow claimed a colleague in Leningrad had knowledge of a German scientist, in Berlin, committing monstrous crimes. I just came from Sonnenfeldt now and he told me it was true. He forwarded Vyrzhikovsky's cover letter in German along with the original Russian letter to a detective here at the Police Presidium months ago, but never heard back. Sonnenfeldt's secretary, though, had made a copy of the cover letter—and let me borrow it."

Fritz pulled it from the envelope and read:

Sehr geehrte Herr Dr. Sonnenfeldt—

As a fellow scientist, I am passing on an urgent missive from my colleague, the esteemed head of the Physiological Department at the Institute of Experimental Medicine in Leningrad, which it is imperative you get to an appropriate police detective as soon as possible. As I know there's no shortage of Russian émigrés there, I will not take the time to translate. Suffice it to say that, should the terrible claims made by this Doktor Spiegel at his tower in Berlin prove more than delusional, they would constitute a crime unprecedented in the annals of scientific history.

"I don't get it." Willi was by now sitting up, wiping his face. "What's this letter from Leningrad supposed to contain?"

"Sonnenfeldt had no idea. It's in Russian."

Willi sighed, ready to dismiss it all as another of Fritz's drunken rants, only—the Tower.

"Well, then, whom did Sonnenfeldt say he passed this letter on to here?"

"You won't believe it, Willi: Hans Freksa."

Willi threw his hands up. "Then God knows where it's buried by now. There're more records in this building than the National Archives."

"I'll find it." Gunther stepped up, flinging Fritz's cape back to him. "If it came by mail, it had to have gone through Central Records, and it so happens I'm on rather good terms with one of the girls down there."

Fritz threw the cape over his shoulders and began buttoning it. "And if it's in Russian, you'll need a top translator. Madame Grzenskya—I'm certain you've met her at some of our parties—was former lady-in-waiting to the czarina."

Willi simply sat there thinking: great, guys. Use your masculine charms. Screw them till they scream if you must. Just get me what I need. Fast.

He took a deep breath and watched them disappear.

A few minutes later when two kids appeared in the doorway, one thicker than the other, he practically flew from his desk, until he realized it wasn't Heinz and Erich but the Doll Boys, Milo and Dolf, being pushed along by Kai. Wild-haired, almost feral-looking, with round, sharp eyes, they clearly were not happy about being here.

"Satisfied you ruined our lunch?" The skinny one fearlessly sneered at Willi. "And me with a real millionaire on Motz Strasse until this one comes pounding at the door."

Willi couldn't help but admire the kid's spunk. And feeling sorry for him too, knowing no millionaires lived on Motz Strasse. He reached in his pocket anyway, getting the point. Kai stopped him.

"He gets compensated before he undoes a button." The chief smacked his subordinate's head. "The way he was taught. Now tell him what happened, Dolf. Unless you don't want the bitch to get caught."

Begrudgingly, Dolf seemed to acknowledge the point. "All right." He shifted from foot to foot. "Here's how it went, Inspektor. Me and Milo were coming back from our favorite bakery on Koch Strasse when all of a sudden this ice cream truck pulls up. We may be little, but we ain't ignorant. We know what happened, and sure enough it's the redhead behind the wheel, all right, with the bad skin, all dressed in white like we heard. Asks real sweet if we'd like some ice cream—free of charge—'cause she's got to get rid of what she's got left before she brings her truck back. 'Screw you, bitch,' Milo yells, then we both start screaming, 'Child-Eater! Child-Eater!'

"She speeds away, but there's a delivery truck coming—so we grab rides on the running boards, clinging real close so she don't spot us. After maybe ten blocks, though, the truck makes a left, so we gotta jump unless we want to lose her."

Willi by now couldn't help wondering if he was the one being taken for a ride, if a couple of hungry kids here weren't just on the make.

"Luckily there's a streetcar going the same direction, so we hop on her and ride between wagons—all the way to Landsberger Allee."

Willi straightened. Landsberger Allee. "And then?"

"And then we lose her."

Lose her? Willi's throat dried.

Little Milo, though, shook his head. "I didn't lose her. I saw where she went."

"Where, Milo? Where did she go?"

"That big place with the walls, where they kill all the animals."

"But this is from one of the most famous scientists in the world." Madame Grzenskya removed the old-fashioned glasses from her rouged face. "The head of the Physiological Department at the Institute of Experimental Medicine in Leningrad is none other than Ivan Petrovich Pavlov."

Pavlov, Willi thought. The guy who used dogs in experiments.

"Can you read it for us please, Madame . . ."

Squinting as she held the jeweled glasses, then widening her eyes and squinting more, Grzenskya began with what she obviously took to be an appropriate dramatic flourish.

"'A most disturbing letter'"—she modulated her voice importantly—"'arrived at my office earlier this week, which I quickly tossed in the fire.'" She reenacted. "'A fate that befalls all unwelcome correspondence I receive—especially from so-called animal lovers. As if I am not an animal lover! I am a lover of the highest of all animals, and what I do, I do in service of him.'"

Could no one, Willi thought, squirming in his chair—even a Nobel Prize winner—stick to the point?

"'Days after it went up in flame, however, this message continued to burn in my mind. I didn't want to believe such a man could really be a scientist, but his detailed knowledge of my work made his expertise indisputable. He called himself Dr. Spiegel, gave no first name; the return address merely Tower Labs, Water Street, Berlin.'"

Thunder clapped through Willi's brain. "Gunther, get out the directory and start hunting for every Water Street in this city— there've got to be half a dozen."

"So true." Grzenskya dropped the glasses. "The way they double name streets around here—"

"Could you please continue," Willi said, more forcefully than he'd intended.

Grzenskya twitched. To be addressed so! A member of the Romanov court. But she raised her chin and returned the jeweled glasses to her nose.

"'Dr. Spiegel's letter was in sophisticated Russian,'" she continued in a more businesslike tone. "'The man either knew our language proficiently or had an excellent translator—although anyone who'd read what he'd written would surely have gone to the police.

"'It began with a paean to me, not merely hyperbolic but grandiose to a pathological degree. He referred to me as one of the greatest scientists the human race had ever produced, having done more than anyone to destroy the Cartesian myth that body and soul were separate. Only gradually did he come to his point—that by climbing upon my shoulders or some such rubbish, he had reached *beyond* what I could ever have achieved.'

"The gall," Grzenskya blurted an involuntary cri de coeur, then pretended she was merely clearing her throat.

"'In intricate detail he explained how, in Berlin, he had re-created my famous Tower of Silence, so necessary for the type of experiments I do.'"

As if hit by lightning, Willi knew exactly where it was suddenly. Of course. Why hadn't he thought of it? Where else had Ilse just gone in her ice cream wagon? Where had all this emanated from?

The very first time he'd been there, he'd noticed it—that looming neo-Gothic hulk supposedly abandoned for years—the old Viehof water tower. Direktor Gruber himself described it as something out of a vampire movie.

" 'His experiments were proving beyond a doubt,' "—Grzenskya grew paler with each line she read—" 'that the cortex and its sub-structures were, as I'd postulated, the source of all higher nervous activity. That I had not been able to obtain definitive proof of this hypothesis because my experiments were limited to cats and dogs. But that without such constraints he had—' " Here her throat seemed to stop up entirely, her face, even through many layers of Pan-Cake makeup, flushing whiter than the letter. Slowly lowering the glasses, Grzenskya looked at Willi, then managed to utter, " 'By using hu-man beings, specifically children ages seven to fourteen, as subject material.' "

Spiegel, Willi was thinking. *Spiegel* meant "mirror." Dr. Mirror.

"You know who speaks perfect Russian?" Fritz's whole face had darkened.

" 'If we could see into the cranium,' " Willi was recalling the words, " 'we might view how a person—' "

Thirty-two

The six-sided tower rose like an abandoned castle, tall and bulging at the upper stories, masked with thick black soot. At its turret a long chain whipped in the afternoon wind, making a ghostly rattle. It was nearly three. Twenty-three hours since the boys had vanished. Every minute hell.

On the nearby streets, the *Viehof* pulsed with activity. Livestock agents held on to hats as they hurried down sidewalks or bartered on corners, smoking fat cigars. Trucks along Thaer Strasse groaned under heavy loads—some with piles of burlap sacks stamped SCHNIZTLER AND SON. Far down the block, a herd of pigs sang farewells as they marched toward the tunnel entrance. Willi watched it all from the shadows of an alley near the former pump house. A coiled predator biding time.

Everything was set for sundown. Gunther was requisitioning squads of armed security police, as he'd done for this morning's action, Fritz off digging up facts on Dr. Spiegel and planning to meet them here at dusk to assist in a two-pronged attack. Which would never take place, because Willi had no intention of risking another disaster such as 146 Maybach Ufer. All of it was a ruse to get them off his back. He was going in alone this time. Right now.

Stepping from the shadows, he calmly walked across the street, then ducked sideways, bolting toward a rear entrance of the old brick pump house, which according to maps was connected to a back staircase up the water tower. The door was completely enshrouded in spiderwebs, beneath which hung a rusted lock. The webs were as sticky as cotton candy as he swept them aside. Using the metal toothpick from his army knife, his fingers summoned years of experience both in wartime reconnaissance and as a Berlin detective, and in less than five seconds the lock popped.

Inside, pigeons flapped through the cavernous space, sending echoes ricocheting back, the old pumps and generators long vanished, dust on the ground thick as carpet. Padding across it guided by his flashlight, his heart only brightened when beams shone on a sign indicating WASSERTURM. Water tower. This time the security door was heavy steel and, from the looks of the rubber edges surrounding it, hermetically sealed. The lock was infinitely tougher than the first and caused him to break a minor sweat. But it gave way finally, and as he pulled it open, a strong gust blew over his shoulders. At once he saw that what looked like a derelict tower outside had been completely renovated within, strangely so.

Designed evidently for some specialized purpose, both the walls and the ceiling were swathed in some kind of quilted insulation, the windows triple-paned, the floor coated with rubberized pads—as if every possible measure had been taken to eliminate sound or vibration. Which was just as well for him, he told himself, wrapping fingers around the Luger and starting up the spiral stairs. All the better to keep his presence secret as long as possible.

On the first floor and then again on the second, and then the third too, the steel doors had no locks. They were completely sealed. No way in. A chilly fear ensnared him. Had he chosen incorrectly?

Ought he have waited and stormed in with plenty of support as planned? His heart pounded as he wound around the fourth and final flight, envisioning Erich and Heinz somewhere just on the other side, but facing another lockless steel door. Ready to pound in a fit of rage, he noticed suddenly there were also no hermetic seals this time, and yanking for the hell of it, his heart jumped when the door slid open.

Inside, total silence. Darkness. Until his eyes began adjusting. Then, along the walls, cases of equipment, bottles, jars filled with mysterious-looking tinctures, everything meticulously arranged, labeled. Long white tables bearing complex-looking gadgets with dials, switches, wires everywhere. Keeping the Luger warm in his fingers, he gingerly trod in until a muffled sound sent him jumping back against the wall. A fast glance told him some kind of passage opened to his right behind a bank of machinery. He ducked into it.

It wasn't long, just a few steps, until the view reopened and his throat jammed entirely. Ahead, his eyes were seared by what made Magda's dungeon seem almost humane. Or at least within the realms of recognizable cruelty.

In a room that took up the full tower floor, illuminated under bright spotlights, tall glass cages, such as might contain birds or lizards at the zoo, stood one per wall. Only here, in each, strapped next to one another in chairs, were sets of boys. At first glance they looked healthy enough, clean white hospital gowns neatly draped across their bodies, feet tucked into slippers. But as Willi focused on the tops of their heads, squinting to make certain he wasn't being tricked by shadows, he discerned something wrong with the crest of their skulls. They were missing. Completely sheared away—as one might do to a soft-boiled egg. It reminded him of a brutalist painting he'd seen some years back by the famous George Grosz, who caricatured the pillars of contemporary German society with similarly open skulls, and steaming piles of shit for brains.

What Willi beheld now was far more surreal.

And far more brutal.

It explained, at least, what had happened to those kids in the wheelbarrow down in Magda's dungeon; he'd never grasped why the tops of their skulls looked as if they'd been lifted off by a can opener. Now, leaning against the wall for support, having to concentrate on holding back a wave of nausea, he understood. All too graphically.

It was no can opener but a surgeon's knife that had lifted off their craniums—so they could be used as guinea pigs in some kind of sick experiment.

The kids in these cages, Willi saw, staring in horror, were definitely still alive, eyes glazed in a sort of narcotized trance, chests rising and falling, every so often a finger twitching. Wires ran from machinery outside the cages through the glass walls and directly into their skulls.

He stopped breathing.

A figure had appeared not a dozen feet away in a surgical suit and cotton mask, busy examining various levers and dials, jotting readings on a clipboard. Gradually, seeming to sense something, cold gray eyes looked up, scanning the darkness. A thin hand lowered the mask, revealing a long nose and spongy, red cheeks. Energy surged through Willi's muscles.

He clutched the Luger.

A lunge toward the tray of surgical equipment that included several long, sharp objects inspired him to step from the shadows.

"Freeze, Ilse!"

The youngest Köhler stopped. Her face slowly turned, the icy eyes fixing on Willi. Blinking several times, she recognized him, and from some hidden armoire deep within her psyche, she emerged suddenly garbed in womanly robes.

"Hello, Inspektor." A soft smile eased even the harshest aspects of her face. "It took you a while." Her eyelids flounced. "But you found me. Congratulations."

She'd never gotten a formal education, Willi knew. But if they gave a degree for survival instincts, she'd pass with honors. He could have used her behind enemy lines. A gifted blend of her brother's determination and her sister's guile.

She was parting her mouth now, moistening her lips.

"You're much handsomer than your—"

"Where's my son?"

He kept the Luger aimed at what was supposed to be her heart.

A single corner twisted on her lips. "Oh." She was grinning still, but with shifting undertones. "I see. You mean now that you know what it feels like to have loved ones taken."

A writhing rabbit dangled in his mind.

"Where is he?" Willi cocked the trigger. He'd finish the bitch with a single bullet even if he had to then turn the place upside down to find Erich. "I'll give you till—"

A sharp pain in his shoulder, though, followed by a loud gunshot, told him he was the one who'd gotten the ultimatum, his whole arm spasming, the Luger jumping to the floor.

"Stay where you are," a male voice commanded.

Willi grasped his shoulder, damning himself for his arrogance. He'd chastised Freksa for the very same stupidity, thinking he could go it alone behind enemy lines. And look what happened to Freksa. At least the wound was superficial. He clutched it tenderly. It burned like hell but wasn't bleeding; the assailant obviously had good aim.

"You okay, my dear?" he heard more distinctly.

"It'd take more than him to hurt me." Ilse ripped off her surgical cap and shook out a mane of greasy red hair, a smirk spreading across her pockmarked face. "A lot more."

From the far side of the room what seemed like a silver light approached, which quickly distinguished itself as a small oval mirror. A silver eye patch. A long smile underneath drawn across aristocratic lips.

"Well, Inspektor"—von Hessler was aiming a Mauser—"I suspected you might find your way here. I hope none of your friends follow suit. You're the first visitor we've had. What an honor."

Von Hessler's good eye danced with dark delight.

So it was him. The "top-hat" the Reverend Braunschweig had babbled about, who'd enthroned Helga as a priestess of her own cult. *You don't think she got her mansion banging a tambourine.*

And Magda in her prison cell, Willi recalled, lamenting how her little sister kept falling in love. First the doctor. Then the priestess. The doctor evidently had been there all along.

"You're going to let me have him, aren't you?" Gray eyes appraised ravenously, the sweet side of Ilse in tatters now.

Reflected off von Hessler's eye patch, Willi caught a glimpse of his Luger only feet away, beneath one of the lab desks.

"A little patience, dove." The doctor stepped into the light. "I know you don't get to practice enough, but it's a thrill for me to have someone to show off my achievements to. You know how badly I wish I could invite more people up, the whole world—if only it were ready. But do get his gun, before the Inspektor indulges in some foolish move that deprives us both of pleasure."

Willi considered a quick grab to make her a human shield, but with a shot such as von Hessler, he knew it'd be suicide. The man'd blow off Ilse's head anyway if it came to it. With a pang of despair Willi watched her shake her stringy red hair, crouch, and paw for his gun.

"Excellent." The doctor nodded as she placed the Luger on the table next to him. "Now fetch my four o'clock snack, *Liebchen*. You know how sensitive my stomach is."

Ilse lingered, her muscular figure taut.

"Ilse—"

She scowled, pink lips twitching, then obediently scurried off—a wolf in shepherdess's clothing.

"Such a sweet thing. And a great help in my work. I couldn't do it without her." Von Hessler kept the Mauser aimed with a surgeon's steadiness. "How do you like my place, Kraus?" He neared. "Took me years to construct. Not even that fat *Viehof* director knows I'm here. No one does. Except"—he smiled—"you." He pointed the muzzle around the six-sided room, the boys in their glass boxes seeming to follow him visually. "What you see is an absolutely unprecedented type of laboratory. All external stimuli brought under control, no accidental sounds, no fluctuations of light, no changing air drafts." He searched Willi's face for admiration. "Even the floors are supported on rubber-coated girders to eliminate vibrations. At my fingers, the most advanced measuring instruments on earth. This, Inspektor, is my Tower of Silence."

"Where's my boy, von Hessler?"

"Oh, yes." He laughed, rolling out a lab chair, keeping the gun fixed as he sat. "I forgot. Parental instincts." He kicked up his legs on a desk. "A purely unconditioned response. Sometimes as a scientist I put the horse before the cart. But relax, relax. Your son and his fat little friend are fine. You should have realized I knew where you lived, Kraus. Remember, I dropped you off? Rest assured—I've only given the best care to the darlings. I always do. They're perfectly tranquil in a state of suspended animation, as it were, sedated with carefully administered soporifics. And well nourished intravenously. Were you to awaken them, they'd remember nothing beyond the ice cream truck. *If* you were to awaken them." He laughed with the sudden volume of an artillery barrage.

Willi was scanning for some way out.

Von Hessler stopped laughing. "Don't think because I've only one eye that my vision's poor, Inspektor. I see that look on your face. I can tell exactly what you're thinking. You're wondering how such an intelligent, cultured man as myself could be so diabolical as to use children in scientific experiments. Now, there's an example of a conditioned response for you!"

He burst into more laughter, evidently his own best audience.

Ilse arrived with a shiny red apple and an exceedingly long, sharp knife, which glistened as she slashed it a few times in the air, indicating what fun she was going to have. Then she took up guard with Willi's Luger, sitting on a desk, aiming it at him.

"I notice you're perspiring, Inspektor," von Hessler said as he took the knife and began peeling the apple. "Another unconditioned response quite natural for someone in your predicament. Unless of course there's an impairment of some kind. I myself, for example." He was denuding the fruit in one long strip, around and around and around. "Happen to be a person who doesn't sweat. Not at least from fear. Oh, I did. But the shell that took my eye at Verdun, you see, damaged the part of my brain known as the frontal cortex, which is why that organ's so central now to my work. I don't sweat from fear. And"—he finished peeling in a single, unbroken coil—"I don't feel remorse." He smiled genially, shrugging as if puzzled. "Never."

He placed the apple on a plate.

"It doesn't mean I'm some kind of monster." He wiped his fingers with a napkin. "Or deranged. Or psychotic, as your cousin might name it. On the contrary. Because I'm unfettered by constraints of so-called compassion and bourgeois ideals of right and wrong, I'm able to explore where others would never dare, to lift a torch so to speak for future generations. They'll honor me someday, you'll see. Or perhaps you won't."

Another barrage of laughter.

"You're a national hero, Doktor," Ilse said, caressing Willi's Luger, then pretending to blow out Willi's brains. "A great servant of the German *Volk*."

"I employ children for very rational reasons." Von Hessler took the knife again. "The human cortex, you see, is completely developed by age seven, its cellular structures remaining malleable for another seven years or so, then growing fixed." Stabbing the apple, he carved out the core with a swift, hard twist. "The brains I chose are pefectly ripe for study." He deftly divvied the rest into slices. "Boys are preferable because they're hardier. Now don't look at me like I'm Attila the Hun." He speared a wedge and brought it to his mouth. "These children suffer nothing with me. Do they, Ilse?" His good eye fluttered as he chewed.

"They have it better than on the outside." She crinkled her nose, sniffing the gun barrel. "Dying to get in."

Von Hessler grinned at her patronizingly.

"My work, Inspektor"—he spit a remnant of pit on the plate—"requires extreme tranquillity. Distress is contrary to my needs. With fourteen billion neurons all subject to manifold influences, any irregularity can throw things off. Those boys feel no discomfort whatsoever. See for yourself." He picked over which apple slice to have next. "Electrodes can be placed on any part of the brain without the slightest pain."

Willi glanced at the nearest child. The face, it was true, showed no signs of pain, but also little of life, other than breathing and twitching. No apparent comprehension, either, of the insoluble predicament it was in—the top of its head no more.

"And the worlds unveiled beneath those skullcaps, Inspektor. Is there any more mysterious realm on earth?"

Ilse, unable to contain her excitement apparently, snatched the knife from von Hessler's plate and approached Willi with it.

"All that white and gray matter," she howled, circling him territorially. "And all the sensuous folds and clefts with all those . . . how do you call them again, Doktor?"

"Lobes." Von Hessler munched his apple, amused, keeping his gun aimed.

"Oh, yeah, right." Ilse touched the blade to Willi's scalp, sending a tingle to his heart. "There's a frontal lobe." She touched a different part of his head, a little harder this time. "And a back lobe. And another that gets messages from the eyes, right, Doc?"

The cold, sharp knife pressed against Willi's skin as if burning to penetrate.

"Very good, Ilse."

"He's training me to be a neurosurgeon." She leaned right up to Willi's face, practically touching noses. "But we can never find enough practice material."

Reflected in her gray eyes, Willi saw not only the infamous child abductor spreading terror across Berlin, but a tortured child herself. All the Köhler siblings—Magda, blood-drenched, a modern Medea, devouring children to protect them; Axel, a vengeful Minotaur, herding them to their deaths in an insane stampede of hatred.

"I think the Inspektor's had enough anatomy lessons for now." Von Hessler motioned Ilse to give back the knife. "He's far more interested in my work. An educated man can appreciate the world-shattering boldness of it. He knows that since time immemorial man's ached to understand the relationship between body and mind.

I don't claim to have discovered a simple formula. I'm not crazy, Inspektor. But with one eye I have seen where none dared previously look. Deep in the coils of the living brain ... the origins of thought itself. The pathways of learning. The basis of all conditioned responses. You don't believe me? Ilse."

She leaped, scenting meat.

"A demonstration."

At some kind of control panel, she rolled up her sleeves and began hitting switches, tilting her head as if she were hearing faraway music.

"Enfolded in the cortex"—von Hessler projected to some imaginary audience of peers—"I have unearthed the very front line of human behavior, a whole chain of command and control centers responsible for motor activity. Infiltrating them with electric pulses, I am now able to create actions normally undertaken only voluntarily. For example, Ilse—Box Two. M-one."

Licking her lips, Ilse flicked switches until the boys in the nearest glass cage began moving their mouths.

"Mastication!" she yelped.

Triumph flared across the doctor's face.

The more the boys appeared to enjoy a large, delicious meal, the funnier Ilse found it. She bayed insanely, cruelly, the way her father must have when he brutalized her. Could a child so tortured ever have turned out differently? Willi feared all the doctors on earth could never put her back together again.

"Forget Freud," von Hessler pronounced to the invisible world press gathered before him. "I have succeeded in discovering not only the origin of neurosis—"

Willi's eyes darted desperately around.

"—but actually creating and removing it again."

Willi couldn't just stand here. A band of electrical wires ran across the floor. To where?

"Brilliant, von Hessler!" Willi tried chucking the words like a diversionary grenade, letting real anger explode. "You've surpassed even the great Pavlov himself. The world should kiss your ass. But have you ever healed even one of these kids?"

"Healed?" Von Hessler burst out laughing.

Willi's eye quickly followed the wires to a large fuse box behind Ilse's desk.

"Don't be petty, Kraus. What do you think, I glue their skulls back on? Instead of human waste, these boys are ennobled by me to make the supreme sacrifice. Someday there'll be monuments to them. And their deaths, believe me, are more humane than their lives. Your pathologist no doubt deduced it was carbon monoxide that killed them, but you never figured out how, did you? All my subjects are alive when I finish with them. Until you messed things up, we simply shuttled them by van over to Magda's workshop on Bone Alley, the long way. Ran a hose from the exhaust pipe into the rear, made sure it was sealed airtight. By the time they arrived . . . quick, clean, inexpensive. Axel's idea. It was a beautiful relationship we had, those Köhlers and I, until—"

Willi dove, landing on his shoulder and rolling hard as von Hessler fired. Bullets hit left and right, then directly into the bank of wires. A surge of sparks flew across the floor, leaping to the fuse box, exploding it into smoke and flame.

Ilse let out a primitive shriek. She jumped from her chair. Willi tackled her and grabbed his gun back. Letting her go, he flung himself behind a desk and began firing at von Hessler, who'd taken cover too and returned the attack shot for shot. Ilse lay frozen, head lifted, eyes fixated on the curtain of fire spreading across the wall.

"Get the extinguisher, you syphilitic whore," von Hessler ordered her.

She seemed unable to hear, her pockmarked face stiff as a death mask. As the flames grew brighter, drawing across the doorway, she let loose a shriek of such primordial terror Willi felt it in his gut. Then she hurtled in a mad dash to save herself, and he could see her red hair flying, her wiry figure writhing in flame as she tumbled for the staircase.

"Bitch. Bitch!" Von Hessler fired after her.

The flames were rapidly intensifying, striking fear in Willi now too. An alarming stench of burning rubber stung his nose. Looking for a way out, he noticed von Hessler coughing convulsively, then smashing out a nearby window with a chair. Jumping onto the ledge and turning with his pistol aimed, he cursed wildly, "Damn you, Kraus!" then firing twice before taking a flying leap. A bullet sailed just centimeters from Willi's ear as von Hessler vanished out the window into a whirlwind of smoke.

Willi ran to where he'd leaped, coughing too, thrusting his head out, looking down. A crowd had gathered on the sidewalk, but there was no fallen body. Everyone was staring up—at him. The chain he'd seen earlier whipping in the wind ran directly into the open window below, von Hessler's obvious escape route. The rear staircase was still free, he saw, but there was no way inside again until the ground floor, and he wasn't leaving without those boys.

Vaulting onto the ledge, Willi indulged in a quick glance over his shoulder, instantly regretting it. Trapped in their glass chambers, all the little boys were thrashing madly as flames approached.

Thinking of Erich, he jammed the Luger in his jacket and jumped, clutching the chain and using the outside wall to rappel down. Relieved to gain distance from the flames, he was nonetheless alarmed by the intensity of pain in his shoulder, where von Hessler's bullet had clearly bruised him worse than he'd realized. Focusing on the distance to the window, he fought off the rapidly deepening agony until, just a foot or so above the aperture, it jabbed with such intensity the muscle just gave out, making him lose his footing. He found himself dangling there apelike by one arm, three stories over the pavement, the crowd below shrieking.

Trying to see through the sweat pouring down his forehead, he took a deep breath, telling himself to hold steady, that he'd been in tighter spots, although after a fast glance down he couldn't quite think of one. That night outside Soissons, he reminded himself as he tried to calibrate the exact angle he needed to reach the window. They'd been caught in the open between friendly and enemy artillery bombardments. Only dumb luck saved them. Here at least he had some say in the matter—he hoped. Swinging as hard as he could, he tried to clasp the brick ledge with his foot. But it was too far. And too exhausting, his left arm starting to cramp from strain. Worming back and forth he hoped to create enough momentum to propel himself through the opening. He managed one firm push off the wall, which got him out at a pretty good angle, then all too suddenly he was no longer holding the chain.

The next thing he knew he was shaken by a furious bang. Not the sidewalk, but the floor inside the window. He'd swung far enough, he realized, writhing in grateful agony.

Gradually his vision came back, and he saw what looked like a hospital ward—multiple beds filled with silent figures attached to tubes. Overhead the roar of flames was sending wisps of smoke down. With a loud explosion, a bullet hit the wall much too close.

"You're finished, Kraus," von Hessler declared from across the room. "You and all the other dinosaurs."

Willi fired at him, taking a fast glance at the nearest bed. It wasn't Erich or Heinz, just an innocent kid lying there, close-eyed. Narcotized. The skull intact. The tiniest hope flickered through Willi. Aother bullet came much too close, though, buzzing past his face. The smoke at the ceiling was thickening, dancing through the air. He fired one shot high, then flung himself beneath a row of beds, crawling on his stomach.

"There's a new age dawning." Von Hessler sounded drunk from lack of oxygen. He was lecturing again to nameless multitudes. "I don't know what form it will take. Hitler maybe. Maybe not. He's a genius—except for that racial crap. It's nonsense and I can prove it."

The scientist's legs appeared in Willi's vision now, past several more beds. The veil of smoke was faintly drawing downward, making his eyes start to tingle. His throat itched. Inch by inch he had to fight the urge to cough, bringing him back to the Western Front and the fields of chlorine gas they'd had to crawl through in masks. How he wished he had one now as he pulled himself ahead, wondering if Heinz or Erich were above, if they could breath.

"In terms of brain development, there's no more difference among races than between rich and poor. A child of savages raised by scholars is just as likely to turn out a—"

Willi fired, hitting von Hessler's hand, making the gun drop, but not stopping him from leaping backward with a yelp. Springing from below the bed, aiming, Willi cried, "Freeze!" But it was too late. Von Hessler, feet away, had grabbed one of the kids from a bed with his bleeding hand.

Erich.

"I'll snap his neck in a second unless you put your gun on that bed and step back," the one-eyed doctor swore with vengeance, dripping blood across Erich's chest. But the boy looked okay otherwise, Willi was thinking. Unconscious. But okay.

"Drop the gun, Inspektor. Or so help me."

Willi put down the gun.

Upstairs he could hear cracking wood and smashing glass.

"Step away." Von Hessler's eye patch reflected black smoke coming in from the windows. Willi thought he heard clanging bells. Was anxiety making his ears ring? It wouldn't be the first time.

Von Hessler let Erich drop into the bed and with his bleeding hand reached for Willi's Luger, all the intoxicated madness gone as he aimed at point-blank range.

Willi tried to reason with him. "Give yourself up. They're sure to be more lenient with you than you were with those kids. Anyway, your Tower's gone, von Hessler."

"You've no idea what you've done, Kraus. Set the development of the human race back a thousand—"

A shrill cry from behind spun von Hessler's head. From the gathering smoke Fritz landed like an incoming shell, knocking the doctor down with a blow to his jaw.

Willi, too anxious to be amazed, ran to Erich and scooped him up with an unbelievable rush of relief, especially once he felt the gentle breathing in his arms.

"Help with the kids," he gasped, suddenly swept into the most astonishing whirlwind of faces and motion. Kai. The Red Apaches. Gunther. Security cops. Everyone was swarming in. Von Hessler was being handcuffed and led away. Children lifted from beds.

On the winding staircase down, Willi burst into tears as he

clutched Erich to his chest, only half hearing Fritz proclaim Kai to be the hero of the rescue, that he'd noticed Willi's strange mood earlier and had his Red Apaches trail him, alerting Fritz when Willi had come up here alone. Willi could barely take it in. He only knew that his son was safe. And that upstairs many more boys remained in peril.

Once Erich was down, Willi raced back up again, shouting at everyone to hurry, desperately searching boy after boy as they were carried away. Where the hell was Heinz? The whole room was a pall of smoke now, flames rushing along the ceiling. Willi gulped down as much air as he could, then plunged back into the room.

It was almost impossible to see. The top of his head felt as if it were about to ignite. But in the last still-occupied bed he found the kid he'd practically raised as a third son and frantically unplugged the narcotizing tubes, then grabbed him up, limp as a doll. What joy as he ran down the stairs with him, picturing the gratitude in the Winkelmanns' faces when they saw their Heinzie safe. Wouldn't they be ashamed then of the way they'd treated Willi and his family.

Finally, there was no more going inside. Even the fire department was evacuating. On the street, ambulance crews were packing up kids from officers' arms and speeding off to hospitals, while crowds gathered behind barricades watching the fiery spectacle. As he raced off in one of the ambulances, wedged between Erich and Heinz, Willi looked out the window and saw the entire top of the water tower had exploded into a flaming torch, forever consuming the terrible legacy of Dr. von Hessler.

For the first time in a long time, he began to breathe easier.

Thirty-three

Terraced on a hillside in the city's oldest park, the Fountain of Fairy Tales was Berlin's grand monument to childhood. Four levels of cascading pools surrounded by neo-baroque arcades composed an enchanting world filled with travertine statues from the Brothers Grimm—Cinderella, Hansel and Gretel, Little Red Riding Hood—a civic shrine to youth and fantasy. It had opened with great fanfare not long before the war. Willi clearly remembered visting it for the first time with his sister, Greta. He was eighteen, already done with his university entrance exams, but not yet knowing the results—an unsettling void along life's path, although nothing compared to what was to come. He and Greta spent hours dawdling, examining statues, dipping fingers into pools, flooding with memories of their father reading to them, Mother's cakes, long walks in the Tiergarten.

Now, watching his children's faces, Willi was yanked not to the past but into the sun-filled present. No words could describe the happiness he felt seeing his sons side by side again, laughter bursting from their throats as they played with the squirting frog statues. Von Hessler had at least been right about one thing: Erich recollected nothing of his kidnapping. An ice cream truck pulling over. Some hands reaching out. Then waking up in bed exhausted. It remained to be seen what long-term effects might yet manifest. But after a month, to all appearances, he'd bounced back with remarkable alacrity. If only Willi could say the same for himself.

It was a warm October Sunday. Next to one another on a bench near the splashing fountain, he and Vicki were unconcerned, as they would not have been a month prior, whether they'd be a few minutes late to Grandpa's birthday party or if the boys might mess up their trousers playing. The ordeal they'd endured had left each with sharpened awareness of the fragility of life, and they sat next to each other breathing rhythmically in the autumn sunshine. Only Willi's celebrity interrupted.

"Inspector Kraus, aren't you? How marvelous! Won't you pose for a photo with my wife and me?"

With von Hessler behind bars and the rest of the case made public, Willi'd become the most famous detective in Germany. His face appeared in newsreels not only in Europe but America. The *Berliner Illustrierte* had done a cover story on him. More than one big-shot producer had contacted him about starring in a film, the very idea of which struck him as ludicrous; he'd probably put the audience to sleep. On the other hand, if they wanted Conrad Veidt to star . . .

After all, Willi gave himself credit, he'd done some good work on this case. Plus he'd come out with a promotion and a damned good assistant to boot, so it had a happy ending. The central gap of course was the Shepherdess. She had never been found. No confirmed sightings, no traces of her remains identified after the fire. But then neither had the remains of any of the boys on the top floor that night, trapped in their glass cages, been identified. The whole tower had collapsed in fiery hell. There'd been countless alleged sightings of the now-infamous redhead: in Frankfurt, in Leipzig, lunching on Potsdamer Platz. But with an old ID photo of hers in as many newspapers as

Willi's, even if she'd survived her descent down that smoke-filled staircase, Willi was confident the last of the Köhlers would never dare show her face in Germany again.

The case of *Der Kinderfresser* was over. Thank God.

Not that he deserved all the credit.

A day or two after his son returned, Willi'd wandered across Alexanderplatz to where the statue of Berolina had already been removed. Kai and his Red Apaches were still there, hanging around the empty pedestal, laughing and singing to a guitar one of them had somehow procured. Willi'd pulled the kid aside and thanked him from the bottom of his heart.

"Oh, come now, Inspektor." Kai was not only surprised but touched. "You helped me. I helped you." The corner of his pink lip trembled. "That's the way it should be, no?"

Since assuming "chiefdom," the boy appeared to have grown not only in confidence but in size, an inch or two at least, Willi thought, his shoulders broader, his face fuller. He still wore the makeup, but not as much as before. And for some reason it looked less like a mask now than a mark of distinction.

"What you did took courage, Kai. If it wasn't for you, I'd be dead. So would my son. And many other boys too."

"I know what it's like to be scared, is all." Kai made sure none of the other kids were listening. "I recognized it in your eyes. You don't think clear when you're too frightened. So I figured best keep an eye out on you, that's all."

"You're going to make a great leader." Willi reached in his pocket. "And I don't think your bravery should go unrecognized."

Digging out a small velvet box, he handed it to Kai. During the war he'd earned numerous decorations, not just an Iron Cross, but also a Golden Merit from the State of Prussia. Encircled with twenty-four-karat laurel leaves and embossed with the coat of arms of the House of Hohenzollern, it was quite a little work of art, something he'd always intended to pass on to his sons. Kai had earned it.

"You're giving this to me?" Ribbons of mascara fluttered from his eyes.

"As a badge of honor." Willi'd saluted with a quick click of the heels. "But if times ever warrant, Kai," he added from the side of his mouth as he pinned it onto the chief's chest, "it'd fetch quite a stack in some markets, if you catch my meaning."

Children's laughter mixed with the spashing of the Fairy Tale Fountain. On the sunny park bench, however, grateful as he was, Willi felt far from happy. A silent chasm still yawned between Vicki and him. And it hurt like hell.

Much as she said she didn't, he knew she couldn't quit blaming herself for what had happened, for having napped while Heinz and Erich ran off. Nor could she quit blaming the Winkelmanns for having put the boys in a situation they felt they had to escape. Most of all, though, she blamed Willi–for bringing it upon them. And he couldn't bear her distance much longer. He yearned for even a touch.

"Okay, let's go." She clapped, watching the boys jump from the fountain.

They were so excited to be leaving after lunch for a week's holiday with their aunt and grandparents, they practically ran the rest of the way. Willi hoped once they were gone, he and Vicki would reconcile.

At the Café am Teich overlooking the Swan Pond, it was warm enough that the Gottmans were having Max's fifty-fourth birthday on the Rose Terrace. Red flowers still opened here and there, despite autumn leaves tumbling from the sky. Everyone appeared in buoyant spirits. Max especially.

"They sing about Paris in springtime, boys." He threw an arm around his grandsons. "But wait till you see it in autumn!"

"Love your new suit, Vic," her sister, Ava, said, feeling it with her fingers.

Willi could see how happy Vicki was wrapped in the bosom of her family, and not for the first time he envied her a little. Just the other day he'd gone to visit his own parents' graves at the big Jewish cemetery in Weissensee. Wandering down the aisles of black marble mausoleums with their gold-leaf lettering and Jugendstil mosaics, he thought about what an accomplishment it must have felt like for them to purchase even the tiniest plots there, knowing they'd wind up in the same final resting place as philosphers and poets and department-store magnates.

"What'll we do the minute we get there?" Bette Gottman repeated Stefan's question. "Laugh aloud, child, as the Parisians do. Then we'll have a nice long visit with your great-aunt, my mother's sister, whom you met once but I'm sure don't remember."

"Mother." Ava put down her fork. "He was six months old."

"Afterwards we'll go to Galeries Lafayette and get you some new outfits. You can't go about Paris in German clothes; they always look out-of-date."

Vicki's mother could never get enough of Paris, Willi knew, but this time her excitement felt a little too urgent. She could barely conceal a desire to escape Berlin, even for a week, which one could hardly blame her for. The tension here refused to subside, even for an hour.

"Did you listen Monday night?" Ava, near the end of the meal, finally brought up. "Have you ever heard anything so grotesque?" She looked at them all.

She was referring of course to the live broadcast of the Reichstag opening session, when all the new Nazi delegates had showed up in jackboots and uniforms and disrupted everything with catcalls, giving credence to their declaration that they had not come to prop up what was collapsing, but to topple it. The legislative body now was at a total standstill, reduced to trench warfare.

"Must we, darling?" her mother begged, reaching to rearrange her daughter's scarf.

But Ava seemed unwilling to abandon current events. "I'm so proud of Thomas Mann, at least." She brushed away her mother's hand.

Before a meeting of the Prussian Academy, Germany's most prominent writer had cried out for democrats to lay aside their differences and unite against the Nazi threat. Even stormtroopers who'd infiltrated the hall hadn't been able stop him, although it did require police protection. Still, the reactionary tide was undoubtedly having an effect on Berlin's cultural life. When stink bombs caused hysteria at the premiere of *All Quiet on the Western Front,* the authorities, rather than standing firm, reversed an earlier decision and decreed the film "harmful to public morale," banning all futher showings.

"It's all because of the collapse." Max folded his napkin over and over. "People aren't thinking rationally."

"Even at the university," Ava concurred, "intelligent minds have deduced something 'mystical' about the Nazis."

The speed of their political ascendancy was indeed remarkable. The Social Democats had fought for decades for a first block of Reichstag seats. The Nazis had won a quarter of the floor in one election. People said such a triumph could not be explained by ordinary means. That it had the feel of the miraculous. Of destiny.

Willi's cousin Kurt called it a neurotic defense on a nationwide scale and was openly depressed about it. He diagnosed Germans as having an inferiority complex that caused them to overcompensate, deluding themselves with a sense of superiority and feeling outrage when reality didn't coincide with their inflated egos. Precisely the sort of neurosis, he said, that made shouldering responsibility for their own misfortunes impossible and required a scapegoat on which ills could be expiated.

There was no doubt who that would be.

True, in their second day in office the Nazi delegates quit catcalling and got down to business, introducing a series of anti-Semitic legislation that impressed even old-time anti-Semites. The goal: complete elimination of Jewish "influence" over Germany—in all professions, in all levels of government, education, civil service. Police included. As small a chance of a measure such as the Aryan Law had of passing, Kurt feared if the economic situation didn't stabilize, the position of Germany's six hundred thousand Jews might grow serious.

Willi'd faced a lot more anti-Semitism in his life than Kurt, a psychiatrist in a practically all-Jewish institute. But even if Kurt's analysis sounded extreme, Willi had a lot of respect for his psychological insight. He'd been dead-on with *Der Kinderfresser.* As sensitive as Willi was to issues of family security just now, he had to consider what might happen if they did ever have to leave the country. Where would they go? Join his sister in Palestine? The British had just curtailed Jewish immigration there. And last year, so many Jews had been hacked to death during the Arab riots.

Of course, the Nazi Party was far from running Germany. The larger their movement grew, the more cracks appeared within it. The other day stormtroopers had wrecked their own headquarters, furious at their meager sausage rations. Berlin police had to be called in before they killed each other. Anything could happen.

"For God's sake," Vicki's mother interjected, handing around helpings of Black Forest cake, "it's Papa's birthday. Must we really?"

"Mom's right," Vicki said, taking the knife from her. "Let's talk about the family. How're Tante Hedwig and Onkel Albrecht?" She cut a piece of cake for Willi.

"Perfectly fine." Vicki's mother adjusted her beads. Despite her vindication she still seemed uncomfortable. "But do you remember that nice young couple next door to them, the Liebmans? So terrible. The other morning, right at the breakfast table, he dropped dead."

Vicki put down the cake. "You mean the pharmacist? With the glasses?"

"Thirty-nine years old. Finished his toast and just keeled over."

Vicki flashed a look at Willi. "How awful."

The sun was already dipping westward when they hugged Erich and Stefan good-bye and closed the door on the Gottmans' Mercedes, wishing them a bon voyage. As the car sped off, Ava waved happily, thrilled whenever she got a chance to mother those kids.

Walking from the park amid lengthening shadows, Vicki inched nearer, then slowly, surely, slipped her fingers into Willi's, waves of relief spreading through his body as her head leaned against his shoulder. They stopped and embraced and stood there a long time.

"Oh, Willi. I'm so afraid of losing you."

"Shhh. I'm not going anywhere."

"But you never—"

"Shhhh."

A few minutes later, waiting for the streetcar, the sun had dropped behind the trees and a cool breeze picked up. Vicki put her hand in his jacket pocket while Willi kept it warm. Gazing across the busy avenue, he saw the many smokestacks rising from the *Central-Viehof*, and for a moment felt the world was as it ought to be.

Then something began pounding at his brain.

Drums.

And trumpets. Ringing glockenspiels.

Rounding the corner, a brown-and-black wall appeared down Landsberger Allee, backing up traffic, drawing crowds—uniforms four abreast, boots shaking the pavement, swastikas on bloodred banners. Clean, sharp, flawless, their precision reminded Willi of the Tiller Girls that night at the Admirals-Palast when Josephine Baker had appeared, the spectators equally dazzled now by the uniformity of movement.

Drawing directly in front of them finally, these ranks, they saw, were not composed of well-disciplined young men, but children. Willi'd witnessed them before—youthful legionnaires behind whom Germany was supposed to fall in line, tossing leaflets, marching in the Sportpalast—but never up so close. They barely had peach fuzz on their chins. Some looked no older than Erich, drums almost as big as they. But their faces were like steel traps slammed shut, eyes fiery furnaces, as if they knew nothing, saw nothing but the most bitter enemy ahead.

Not unlike the look Irmgard and Otto had the morning Heinzie died.

Poor, sweet kid next door. Willi'd rescued him from the flames that night, but unlike Erich and the others, he'd never come to. The narcotics von Hessler'd pumped through his body had sent him into a coma from which he never emerged. When he was finally gone, the explosion of anger from their neighbors' mouths made their prior confrontation seem cordial. The severing of relations, they'd repeatedly stressed, had been nothing but a matter of self-preservation. With their only son's death, though, some ancient hatred burst to the surface as if from the bottom of a deep, dark well.

"It's true what they say, then—you *are* only out for yourselves. You manage to save Erich, but our boy is dead. Chosen ones!"

"Madness," Vicki said now of the neat-combed hair and grimacing faces storming by. "I don't understand, Willi, what is it they want? Another war?"

"They're not even old enough to remember the last one," Willi said, pulling her closer. Holding her tightly, he began to see not merely the mechanized rows of defiant youth but all the homeless, hungry children of Berlin. The nine- and ten-year-olds lined up in the Linden Passage. The miserable faces at the peddlers' market, behind their barrels of slop. The wretched butchered prisoners in the Köhlers' chambers of horror. Even little, round-cheeked Heinzie Winkelmann, cracked across the face. All the punishments, the canes and whips, the sticks and spankings. The brutal insistence on submission. *I'd rather have a dead son than a disobedient one.*

"Willi, please, can't we go?" Vicki clenched his hand.

He took her arm, ready to walk, but the streetcar finally clanged around the corner and they jumped on board. Grabbing seats, they could see them outside, these furious children, and hear them shaking earth and sky with their song:

We are the joyous Hitler youth!
Our leader is our savior
The Pope and Rabbi shall be gone
We want to be pagans again!

Epilogue

WINTER 1947
BRITISH MANDATE, PALESTINE

Sun beat down on Dizengoff Circle, the modern heart of Tel Aviv. In the planted oasis at its center, well-dressed couples pushed baby carriages or relaxed on benches in the shade of palms, watching the fountain dance. Beyond the greenery, long avenues lined with angular white buildings rolled up the turquoise coast—a glistening new metropolis.

Willi took a deep breath. The top of his head was burning. Yet again he'd forgotten a hat, he realized. In the eight years since he'd been in the Middle East, he still couldn't remember half of what he was supposed to: the sun, the heatstroke, that Dizengoff wasn't Kurfürstendamm. That January here was like August in northern Europe. As much of a fish out of water as he sometimes felt, though, how much lighter and freer Tel Aviv was than Berlin.

Whatever was left of his old hometown anyway, he mused.

Not that trouble hadn't followed him here. He inched into the shade as he waited to cross Ben Ami Street. If it ever came to all-out conflict, he knew there'd be no escaping this time. For one thing, both the boys would be in it.

Erich and Stefan had joined the Haganah, the underground army of Jewish Palestine. Erich, twenty-five, named Eitan now, was with the intelligence services, a chip off the old block, training for work, Willi was sure, behind enemy lines. Stefan, who'd changed his name to Zvi, was twenty-three and in the Palmach, the most elite "strike force" unit. Willi was hurrying to meet him now, on one of the rare weekend leaves Zvi got from Beit Keshet, a secret training camp in the Galilee.

But passing a news kiosk just a block from their meeting place, Willi's feet froze to the pavement. My God. His throat parched painfully. Plastered across the morning papers: that face.

Grabbing a copy, he sank onto a bench, reading. The caption called her Ilse Koch, but there was no mistaking that pockmarked skin. Those dead gray eyes. She *had* made it down the smoky staircase all those years ago.

Now her infamy was worldwide.

Quickly, he ascertained from *Ha'aretz* that after fleeing the burning tower in the *Viehof* that night in 1930, the youngest Köhler had slipped across the frontier into Poland and cocooned herself in German-speaking Danzig until the spring of '33, when her kind seized power in Germany. Then she flew back on butterfly wings. Married a handsome SS colonel. Became a Kommandant's wife at one of the premier concentration camps. Now she and her husband were both facing war-crimes charges. Ilse Koch was said to have been so insatiably cruel that those she tormented had dubbed her the Bitch of Buchenwald. Some of the acts she'd been accused of included, Willi read with a mounting vertigo, having inmates skinned alive for tattoos and using their flesh for making . . .

He let the paper slip to his lap.

My God, he thought.

Handbags and lampshades.

Under twirling electric fans, Café Esther was crowded with Tel Avivians from around the world. Egyptian Jews with wide lips. Polish Jews with bright blue eyes. Loud, laughing Romanian Jews, decked out in jewelry. And *Yekkes* such as himself, Willi thought— German Jews, fussy and fastidious, sipping tea not from glasses but regular china cups, thank you.

Quickly surmising his son had not yet arrived, he sat at a corner table and tried to relax, but couldn't suppress ugly memories of the Köhler siblings. Just last month, the Tel Aviv press had published pretrial testimony for the tribunals being prepared against Nazi physicians in Nuremberg. In them, he'd been shocked to discover the ghastly destiny of Ilse's older sister, Magda. A fate shared most ironically with her twisted business partner, the mad Dr. von Hessler.

Both had wound up at the Berlin-Buch Psychiatric Hospital, Ward 6, for the criminally insane, where von Hessler had not surprisingly managed to talk his way out of custody in the mid-1930s, and nearly succeeded in getting his Tower of Silence rebuilt. Some in the regime very much supported his work, wanting it resumed on a far grander scale. But the one-eyed doctor apparently hadn't been able to keep his mouth shut about the fallacy of Nazi racial theories and wound up, once the war began, reinstitutionalized.

In the winter of 1940, all inmates in Ward 6, Berlin-Buch, were among the early participants in something called Aktion T4, for the mentally ill. Patients deemed "unworthy of life" were led into rooms disguised as showers and gassed with carbon monoxide. The cheap, clean death von Hessler himself had so enthusiastically embraced for his boy guinea pigs came back to return the favor—and went on to be a prototype for the extermination of millions.

Willi looked at his watch, impatient but not concerned by Zvi's tardiness. He'd learned by now the Middle East did not run on German clocks. Taking a slow sip of tea he remembered how long each second had felt during those twenty-three hours von Hessler'd had his son.

The genius scientist with his damaged frontal lobe had at least correctly forecast the memory loss: to this day Erich remembered nothing of his kidnapping. He never forgot what happened that morning on the terrace with the Winkelmanns, though. It marked the beginning of the end for them in Germany. For all of them.

Beneath the slowly turning fans, the kind, bright eyes of Dr. Weiss wafted through Willi's mind. In those last years before the Nazi takeover, the deputy president of the Berlin police had sued Joseph Goebbels twenty-eight times for slander, and won each case. To no avail. Goebbels became one of the most powerful men in the Third Reich, and Weiss—a truly great figure in the history of German law enforcement—was forced to run for his life, a disenfranchised exile, destined for obscurity.

"*Slicha.* Inspector Kraus, I expect?"

A slender woman in her mid-thirties, dark hair swept under a yellow scarf, eyes like shiny olives, was standing over him suddenly, clutching a handbag.

"The maître d' asked me to let you know you got a call from Zvi." She frowned sympathetically. "I'm sorry. He can't make it today after all." She lowered her eyes, embarrassed, it seemed, to have to bear such sad news.

"Thanks very much. I appreciate your telling me." Willi nodded, knowing very well that in Zvi's line of work, plans changed like the wind. The woman didn't leave, though. In fact, she pulled up a chair and sat rather near.

"It's not why I came, Inspector. I'm just passing it along from that guy."

Moishe the maître d', whom Willi knew well, nodded from the front of the café.

"I see," Willi acknowledged, noticing she was beautiful, her taut frame and tan complexion reminding him of some desert gazelle that could keep its footing even on the rockiest precipice. "Then how can I help you, Mrs. . . . ?"

"I'm a social worker with the Jewish agency. My name's Leah." He caught the faintest hint of lavender on her neck. "Something happened I need to speak to you about." The olive eyes cast a quick glance behind her shoulder. "A week ago." They fixed back on Willi. "Just like that"—she snapped her fingers—"one of my clients lost her memory. She went to sleep with it, but the next morning woke up and recognized no one, not even herself."

"How awful. Did she have a stroke? You've taken her to a doctor?"

"Don't patronize me, please" came a prickly response.

This Leah, Willi'd already discerned, was what they called a sabra—a Jew born in the Holy Land, named for the cactus that sprang ubiquitously from the driest soil here, prickly on the outside, sweet, supposedly, within.

"She's seen top specialists. More than one. Everyone agrees it wasn't a stroke. And everyone agrees there's no other explanation for it."

"So, why come to me?"

She smiled vaguely, her dark eyes softening. "Because I heard you specialized in such things. Medical mysteries. At least take a drive to Beersheva with me and see."

Something in the glistening look she gave him pulled a chord in Willi's heart and threw him back in time. He could practically still feel that crisp autumn day in the Berlin park. Grandpa Max's birthday lunch. That frightening Hitler Youth parade. When they'd gotten back to Wilmersdorf, he'd taken Vicki out to dinner, then spent the rest of the evening at home, making love for the first time in weeks. How tender it was. How passionate and playful. And in retrospect, how grateful he was to have no idea it would also be the last time.

Next morning Vicki met a friend at a café on Joachimstaler Platz. She was sitting near a window when a truck jumped the curb. A piece of glass slashed her carotid artery, and she was gone in under a minute.

"Beersheva isn't my jurisdiction, Leah. Sorry." He averted his eyes.

Her hand reached across the table, gently touching his arm. "It won't take long. Please. It's important. She lives in the middle of the desert in a settlement surrounded by enemies, with very little protection. It would have been easy for someone to sneak through the fence and—well, I don't know what they could have done."

"You're saying you think someone *did* this *to* her?"

Leah shrugged and nodded simultaneously. "It's why I came to you. There's no better criminal inspector in Palestine and everyone knows it. Such a terrible fate when you think about it, isn't it, Inspector? I mean, what are we without memories?"

Willi didn't want to think about it. Amnesia didn't sound so bad. There were plenty of things he sometimes wished he didn't have to remember.

He wanted Leah to go away. He was tired, suddenly. He'd seen too much in this world. He'd no room left in his heart, in his mind, for more sad stories. He made the mistake of looking into her eyes, though, and shivered at the tug of the same dark whirlpool Fate kept casting him into.

Note on Historical Accuracy

The real Ilse Köhler Koch is a historical figure, wife of a Buchenwald concentration camp commandant whose cruelty earned her the moniker the Bitch of Buchenwald. After the war she was tried by both the Americans and the West Germans and spent the rest of her life in prison. This book presents an entirely fictionalized account of her youth. The account given of Berlin Police Force Deputy Chief Bernhard Weiss, also a historical figure, is essentially accurate.

ACKNOWLEDGMENTS

I'd like to thank everyone at St. Martin's Press for encouraging me to write this book, especially my editor Michael Homler. Also, Jon Sternfeld, my great agent. And most of all, Colin for his brilliant insights and endless support.